# IRON BUTTERFLY

# IRON BUTTERFLY

## THE
## MEZZOGIORNO TRILOGY

### BOOK ONE

LEVEL
BEST BOOKS

AUTHOR PHOTO: Erin Usawicz Photography

First edition

ISBN: 978-1-953789-02-0

Cover art by Level Best Designs

This book was professionally typeset on Reedsy.
Find out more at reedsy.com

*To my mother, who in her struggle to navigate her personal computer, uses "family" as her password.*

Butterfly
colors bright
always flutterin', firin'

Oh, the mystery to behold
that her wings are made of
iron

# Contents

Part Two

# Praise for IRON BUTTERFLY

"Pulsing with feeling, haunted by the past, Anselmi's novel—the second in a trilogy charting one Italian-American family's journey in the 1980s U.S.—finds a young man confronting the mysteries of his immigrant mother's youth.… The crisp, often lyric prose…tells the story with swiftness and power while always suggesting deeper meanings. Here's rich, resonant fiction written with a welcome sense of play."
—*BookLife Reviews*

"Iron Butterfly is an affecting drama about love and family. The family dynamics are well written and relatable as personified by the Bennett Clan. Anselmi writes with a keen grasp of his character's emotions.… An emotionally satisfying and overall enjoyable read."
—*San Francisco Book Review* (4.5 out of 5 Star Rating)

"Searching for the past, even though it might lead to discovering unexpected events and emotions, is something all families can relate to on some level.… [Anselmi] create[s] lively dialogues between family members in this tale. It sometimes felt like I was sitting at a kitchen table with people I knew.… I enjoyed the Bennett family's journey into the past, and this book did more than enough to make me interested in the books that are to follow in this trilogy."
—*Manhattan Book Review* (4 out of 5 Star Rating)

# Part One

*CONQUEST*

# I.

## Summer Passion,

## A Dark Goodbye

I t was night, but the heat of a long summer day was still smoldering. Edward Bennett, midway through his college days, drove up an unlit mountain road with his high school sweetheart Celeste Del Nero beside him. Though his Oldsmobile Cutlass Supreme was a homely two-tone of burgundy and white given to him by his father, Edward believed that he and his date, tanned and taut, made it look sleek. Determined to exude ease while he focused on the tricky course ahead, he had just three fingers on the steering wheel.

"Where are you taking me, Edge?" Celeste asked as she chewed a piece of gum.

Edward loved when Celeste used her nickname for him, coined to describe the daring spirit she was able to draw out of his straight-laced ways. Indeed, in seventh grade, it was Celeste who coaxed him to peel away from a party she was having in her parents' basement, into a closet, so the two could share their first kiss. Now enjoying the rumble of the driver's seat, Edward's body tingled. "You'll see." He smiled toward the windshield.

"Cool. A little mystery," responded Celeste, curling her black hair around her finger.

Edward had long awaited his time with Celeste. Since that first kiss, she

3

had been his only desire. With chocolate-brown eyes and a body cut with dangerous curves, she was a beauty he had always craved but never allowed himself to consume. When he headed off for the ivy-covered halls of New England for college, leaving Celeste to remain local, he promised to save himself for her while he concentrated on his studies. He had been true to his vow even though he was not always confident that Celeste had done the same.

"So are all of your buddies at school going to miss you during your junior year abroad?" Celeste asked, chewing her gum louder. "One less guy to throw their arms around, singing songs about how great you all are for being part of some silly tradition."

"The one weekend you came to see me at school was freshman year..." Edward paused to make the point that it was her only visit.

"Yeah?"

Celeste's boldness initially pushed Edward back. He took only a small step forward. "I'm just saying that the guys really liked you," he continued, recalling how his fair-skinned friends crammed around the cafeteria table where he and Celeste sat that Friday night for dinner—all of them angling to add a little spice to their dull white plates of haddock and green beans. Her Mediterranean look, New York accent, and sharp wit had fascinated the boys, even as she poked at their crusty environs. "It's too bad you didn't stay for the big game the next day," he went on. "Everybody was asking for you."

"I told you that my allergies were killing me. I had to leave."

"It was just kind of abrupt."

Celeste yanked a folded newspaper from between the seats of the Cutlass Supreme. "Since when do you read the newspaper?"

"I don't know," Edward answered nervously. "Matt said that since we're gonna be studying at the London School of Economics this year, it would be a good idea to know what's going on in the world."

"You and Matthew Coyne. First you went to high school together, then college. Now the two of you are doing a year abroad in London. Should I be concerned?"

"Very funny." Edward raised his shoulders as he drove. "Why are you always taking shots at Matt?"

"He's too serious. It's 1982. There are so many other things to get excited about. He's the only guy I know who thinks Donald Trump is an American hero—and will gladly talk about it at a party! All the man has ever done is build a tower in New York and plaster his name on it. I'm not impressed."

"Check this out." Edward could not help but join in. "Last semester, Matt actually wrote a paper in our philosophy class about Trump, describing him as a Nietzschean *Übermensch*."

"What is a *Nachomensch?*"

Not wanting to embarrass her, Edward tried to keep his response simple. "Nietzsche was a German Philosopher. *Übermensch* means 'Superhuman'—a kind of master of an otherwise slavish life. It's a really cool idea." Seeing that Celeste was more interested in checking herself out in the mirror of the overhead visor, Edward exited the discussion he regretted starting. "Matt can get a little extreme sometimes."

"No kidding!" Celeste answered, pushing up the visor forcefully.

"Yeah, he can stand to take a chill pill."

Feeling affirmed, Celeste opened the newspaper. "So let's see what Matt thinks is important for us to know." She lowered her voice and chin to read from the first article she saw. "Circle yesterday's date—August 25, 1982. The day United States Marines landed in Beirut. It will forever change the face of politics in the Middle East." Celeste threw the paper down on her lap. "I don't care what some reporter says. I'm not circling any date. What does the Middle East matter to us?"

"It matters," Edward replied, cutting himself off before he said more. He wanted to scold Celeste for her lack of intellectual curiosity, but did not want to lose the momentum of his drive. He tempered his words. "I don't know exactly what happened in Beirut yesterday, but my guess is that we are doing a big favor for the country of Lebanon and the entire Middle East."

"War is stupid," Celeste said. "We would all be better off if we just minded our own business. I wonder how the people in Beirut feel about having another country's soldiers in their city. I'd be scared. I bet those boys in uniform are not always angels."

Edward was struck by the insightfulness of Celeste's plain speech. He dropped the subject.

She refolded the paper, and slid it back in its place. She reached into her handbag and pulled out a cassette tape. She jammed it into the car console, and turned up the volume. A male voice began singing.

"What's that?" Edward raised his eyebrows.

"It's called 'Maneater,'" Celeste replied, bobbing as she snapped her fingers. "It's a new song by Hall & Oates. It's not out yet. My cousin gave it to me. He works in the recording industry. He's got connections."

Edward hit the *eject* button.

"If you don't mind." He popped open his glove compartment to swap Celeste's cassette with one of his own. He slid the tape into the player gently, shooting a downward glance Celeste's way. He lowered the volume, but only slightly. The song began with a guitar riff.

"Aw! 'Jack and Diane' by John Cougar," Celeste said, pinching Edward's cheeks. "Edge, you're so corny."

"It's not corny," Edward said, lifting his chin. "It'll be a classic. But that's something you wouldn't understand."

Celeste grew quiet. Although she enjoyed playful banter and even a good argument with Edward, she did not appreciate it when she thought he was belittling her. As a grade schooler, she had the same potential he did, competing with him for honor roll and in track, where she bested him in hurdles. She got particular glee out of making fun of the way Edward ran, with his arms down at his side. She mocked him that he looked like a robot.

In high school, however, her mother and father grew estranged. She was pulled away from homework and extracurricular activities so that she could help parent her younger siblings. She became more cynical and rebellious. She never told Edward how she felt—that if she had enjoyed the same home life and opportunities he did, she too might be going off for a year abroad—probably in Paris, which had always fascinated her because of its style. But she refrained from expressing any overt resentment for

Edward, because beneath her increasingly racy exterior remained the little girl—the one who loved to share her lunchbox cookies with him in Sister Joan's fifth-grade homeroom.

"Whatever," she said. "Your music is superior. You always have the better answer. I guess that's why you're going to that fancy school in London."

"I'm not leaving until tomorrow," Edward said. His spirit lifted, he made a sharp left turn off the unlit road onto an even darker path. "We still have a lot of ground to cover."

"Edward, where are we going?" Celeste asked again, lowering the visor. She clicked on the light beside the mirror, and began to apply lipstick. "Don't we have to get home?"

"We're okay." Edward braced as the path's wood debris cracked beneath his wheels.

"Wow, Edge," Celeste said, leaning over to whisper into his ear. "I'm liking the dangerous side of you."

Edward forged on, eventually arriving at a large clearing. He pulled to the center slowly, before easing down on the brakes. As "Jack and Diane" concluded, he stopped the car and reached under the seat for the recline lever. Lying back, he looked through the windshield, and saw that the stars were clustered like a silver-sequined dress—the kind that rich married women wear when they want to be saucy. He always enjoyed staring at these restless wives, to get their attention so that he might feel their desire to be wanted by someone—something—virile. But his Catholic upbringing had conditioned him to never get too close, lest he violate the commandments. He had convinced himself that being with Celeste was different, as nothing had been written in stone to proscribe it.

"We're here," he said, taking a deep breath. "In our own special place. You can't imagine how long it took me to figure out…"

Celeste cut him off, stepping over his seat to straddle him, supplanting his starry view with that of her gray crop-top shirt. She grabbed his deltoids, finishing his sentence. "You're right. I can't *imagine* how long it took you to figure out," she said. She bit his neck before ending with a twist of her head. "You know how to get me to where I want you." She blew on her mark. "Circle the date—August 26, 1982."

A paralysis came over him. He had anticipated this moment for so long—indeed, he had prepared for it like a Boy Scout. Yet something was holding him back. Feeling short of air, he pushed the button to lower his window. In the distance, he could hear a river. But its sound was only a trickle, its waters low from a long drought.

Celeste took off her shirt. Her breasts swelled, as did Edward's eyes upon them. To prompt him into action, she ran her finger over the alligator logo on his *Izod* polo. She pinched the gator.

His body inflamed and his hand quivering, Edward grabbed the sides of his seat.

Back pressed against the steering wheel, Celeste drove her spandex-covered pelvis into him.

Edward thrust back.

She panted into the swelter. "Hmm. That feels good."

Edward swallowed for composure.

Celeste pulled Edward's hand off the fake leather to which it was stuck, and trapped it against her bosom. Her cool moist skin filled his palm with vigor. He squeezed gently. Her sigh of satisfaction compelled him to pull at the prize.

Celeste freed Edward's hand. She reached down to the fly of his denim jeans. As she lowered his zipper, it crackled. She clasped his surge; her hold was commanding. She licked the inside of his ear, the swipe of her tongue wetting it. She whispered, "Come on, Edge, this is what you've always wanted."

Edward's feet were numb, and his stomach began to drain itself of long-suppressed desires. He tried to stem the loss by lowering his window further, and letting more air in. But the air was humid, making it difficult to breathe. The burble of the nearby river amplified in Edward's ears, as if the body of water was somehow transforming into rapids.

Just then, a butterfly flew in, flapping its wings between him and his would-be lover. Its colors were a blur.

"What the hell?" Edward yelled.

"Shh," Celeste said, swatting the insect away. She placed her finger over his upper lip, drawing him closer. She lost her smile and gritted. "C'mon, Eddy. Give it to me."

Edward's eyes were drawn to the dashboard, above which the butterfly stood sentinel; its design remained unrevealed from his angle. Below it, the digits of the clock read *1:01 a.m.* His mother's curfew had passed. His nape grew cold.

"Damn it." Edward banged on the dash to jolt the butterfly off it. As the insect escaped, he closed the window hurriedly, muting the river's calling.

Feeling Edward getting away from her, Celeste implored him. "Let's go, Eddy."

Looking back at Celeste's bare chest, Edward noticed, for the first time, a small brown birthmark on one of her breasts. While others might have found the oddity tantalizing, to him it was a stain—a sign of something burnt or dead. Edward's desire turned to revulsion, Celeste's perfection to grotesquerie. He suppressed a dry heave.

"What?" the girl gasped.

He pushed her back. "You know I hate to be called Eddy."

"What are you talking about?" she asked, raising her voice.

"Get back in your seat. This was supposed to be special. Then you turn around and call me Eddy. Twice! You know I hate that name."

"I was only kidding, Edge," Celeste responded. "I thought it would excite you." She returned to her seat and looked through the windshield. "You know, this being your first time."

"It is not my first time." Edward shoved the gearshift to a make K-turn back onto the path that he had labored to create. "Let's just go home." He paused before speaking again. "It's late anyway."

Celeste twirled one of her long strands of hair around her finger. "Ohhhh." She smiled mischievously. "So that's what this is really about. You don't want to break your mommy's curfew." She paused, and then perked her ear. "Quiet. Listen. I can hear Mommy calling now." She threw her voice into falsetto. "Edward! Where are you, baby?"

Edward reached the road, and made a right toward home. "I was just making an observation. It's late. Leave my mother out of this." He concentrated on the pavement.

Celeste leaned over and grabbed his groin. "What's the matter, Eddy? Did Mommy say she doesn't like me? Too fast for you?"

Edward did not respond; instead, he drove for a while in silence. He approached a traffic light that was turning from amber to red. He slammed on the brakes, stopping short to obey the prohibition. He swatted Celeste's hand off his lap. "Leave my mother alone." The silence thickened as the couple waited, staring at the red. When the signal turned green and Edward drove through the intersection, he added, "What did my mother ever do to you?"

"What did she do to me? The question is what did I do to her?"

Celeste looked away from Edward to the empty sidewalks rolling by. "I think she's afraid I'm going to take away her little boy."

"That's not true," muttered Edward as he negotiated a turn into Celeste's unfinished driveway. He noticed that there was no curb to keep the gravel from spilling onto the unkempt lawn. "You know nothing about my mother." Stopping the car, he gazed at the windows of Celeste's home, their panes dark. "You just don't understand." Waiting for a flicker of light from the upstairs or foyer, but seeing none, Edward continued, "You *can't* understand."

Celeste fiddled with the door lock. "And I guess I never will." She opened the glove compartment to take back her cassette. "I thought this was going to be our night," she said casually while exiting. "The same way I did when I came to visit you at school." After getting out, she tapped the window for Edward to lower it.

He hit the button, not knowing what to expect.

She leaned in. "Have a good time in London, Eddy. I will think of you on Guy Fawkes Day."

Edward said nothing.

Celeste relished the void, and stepped boldly into it. "You know—the day the Brits celebrate how they stopped Guy Fawkes and his gang from blowing up the king." She withdrew from the window and paused, before she turned on him and walked away.

Regret setting in, Edward watched as Celeste navigated the entrance to her house, the uncut grass growing over the path. He was thrown off by her knowledge of the English holiday that he himself had learned of only in the materials that the London School of Economics had sent him. *How did she know?* he asked himself. *Why did she know?*

Celeste reached the front door, and rather than ring the bell, crouched down to lift the mat for the key. After opening the door, she made a movement as if she was going to turn to say goodbye—but instead proceeded in. In an instant, the door was shut.

As he looked over his shoulder to put the car into reverse, Edward wondered why he felt compelled to let his mother guard him. But first, he had to speed home to calm her.

# II.

## His Mother's Wailing,

## Sharing a Sandwich with His Father

Edward skidded around neighborhood street corners, his heart beating more violently than when Celeste wrapped around him like a sea serpent. No matter how hard he pushed the accelerator, time was moving more quickly than his wheels could turn. It was already 1:35 a.m., and his lateness could not be explained by a traffic jam or gas station stop. Edward knew that his mother would eviscerate any such tale.

Finally, he was home—a sprawling Tudor with a façade adorned by exposed timbers. The roof was steeply pitched with side gables, punctuated by dormers. There was not one, but a collection of chimneys, each featuring an octagonal pot on the top. The door was thick oak, boasting hinges that looked medieval. The tall and narrow windows were framed by stone mullions. Though it was night and the openings were stingy, a blue ray of light flashed from one of the rooms. Edward could see his father watching television in the den. He peered into the other lit rooms. His mother was nowhere to be found.

Edward reached to his visor, and pushed the button to open the family's three-car garage. The door rose like a curtain over his mother. At five feet tall, Marie Bennett was waiting center stage—barefoot and solemn on the cold concrete floor, draped in an old nightgown untied at the top. She could have been dressed in the finest silk, but that was not her way; she always wanted to keep things simple, lessening the risk of loss. She glared at Edward. Without cracking her trembling lips, she turned to go inside.

Edward braced himself for the inevitable reprimand. Although he had achieved great successes—star athlete, championship debater, and pioneer of charitable causes—his mother insisted he be home when most of his friends were only beginning their youthful revelry.

Others his age might have shriveled with embarrassment. But for Edward, obedience was not just borne of love, but also of admiration for the compassion his mother showed to others. Since she was ever-sensitive to the needs of those around her, he felt that he must be especially attentive to hers—even if he believed they made no sense. And one of the few things she asked of him was to be home by curfew.

Walking through the garage, he navigated past his father's garden hoe and wine press, as well as his mother's extra refrigerator, where she kept replenishments of Italian meats and cheeses. As he stepped into the kitchen, a melodic cry drifted in the air. From the wall speaker, a soprano was singing in Italian. The music from the spaghetti western that his father was watching in the adjoining room was trying, but failing, to overrun the soprano's voice. Edward's mother sat at the kitchen table, with her face in her hands. Her back bounced as she wept.

Edward went to his mother, placing his hand on her shoulder. "Mom, is everything all right?" When she did not look up from her tears, he grew nervous. He yelled to his father, hoping to be heard over the gallop of the movie's cavalry. "Dad? Is everything okay?" He walked to the living room door. "Dad, what happened?"

Edward's father, Guy Bennett, lowered the television's volume. Without letting go of the remote, he stood. His large frame was clad in nothing more than a tank-top tee shirt and boxer shorts. His eyes still on the movie, he rasped, "You're late." Then he stomped on the floor and hollered at the television. "Get that sonofabitch!"

Edward tried again. "Dad, what happened?"

Guy tilted his head toward where Marie was still crying. "You better talk to your mother. She was worried about you." He stomped again, fist pumping the remote. "Got 'em!"

As Edward stepped measuredly back to the kitchen, Marie darted down the hallway and into her bedroom. She slammed the door and locked it.

A jolted Edward followed her, rapping on the door. "Mom, what's going on? Why are you so upset? I'm okay."

Marie would not respond.

Edward could hear her sniffling, struggling to catch her breath. Edward knocked again, this time harder. "Mom, there is nothing to worry about. I'm fine."

Still sobbing, Marie began to sing to herself in a whisper.

"Mom, please come out. I'm sorry. But I wasn't that late." As he listened more closely, he heard that his mother was singing in Italian.

"*Piangi? Perché?*" she sang. Her voice quivered.

"*Piangi? Perché?*" Edward asked, processing from his rudimentary understanding of the Italian language. "That's exactly what I would love to know. Mom—why are you crying?"

When his mother still would not answer him, Edward stormed back to the kitchen. Instinctively, he opened the refrigerator door. He stared at the compartments and shelves, overflowing with the bounty that Marie stocked daily: two gallons of milk, orange juice, grapefruit juice, two kinds of butter—salted and unsalted—mozzarella, tomatoes, onions, peppers, zucchini, a block of provolone, two loaves of bread, and a tray of leftover lasagna. The fruit and cold cut drawers were packed. Without taking anything, he threw the door shut and went to sit at the kitchen table.

Guy entered the kitchen, his bare feet slapping against the floor. "I'm hungry," he muttered, making a beeline to the refrigerator.

"What's going on, Dad?"

"Your mother was worried about you," Guy answered as he yanked open the cold cut drawer. Not finding what he was looking for, he stormed out to the garage fridge.

"This is more than just worrying," Edward yelled after his father. "What is it?"

14

"How the hell do I know?" Guy reemerged, slab of meat in hand. *"Prosciutto di Parma,"* he said with an exaggerated Italian accent, raising the delicacy overhead. "She hid it so that it wouldn't go too fast. She thinks it's too expensive. You gotta love that woman." He went to his meat cutter, turned on the switch, and started slicing. Edward watched as Guy mounted his pile. In a minute, Guy was done, turning off the switch. He opened the door to the refrigerator again, collecting a ball of mozzarella and a plate of long hot green peppers. He sighed. "Perfect." His hands nearly full, Guy shut the refrigerator with his broad shoulder, finessing a bag of oven-baked Italian bread into his cradled arms, while struggling to the counter to prepare his mini-meal.

"Dad, I'm serious. What's going on?"

"I don't know, son. You kids are your mother's life. She went to all your games when you were little, chaperoned all your class trips, had dinner ready for you every night. You are her world. My world is business, and making enough money so that you and your kids don't have to worry about money, or think that the elite, from their perch, are going to spit on your head. Those goddamn WASPs act like they just stepped off the Mayflower. They forget that the Pilgrims were savages. Ask the Indians." He began sawing off a piece of bread. "I started working when I was sixteen. The only thing my father gave me—"

"—was a pick, a shovel, and a wheelbarrow. I know. You've mentioned that only a few hundred times over the years. What you usually say next is that you're also a first-generation Italian-American who didn't know how to spell; that you got your start by building driveways; that you went into roads, bridges, and real estate; and that you now own the type of skyscraper in New York that you had to pay to get to the top of when you were a kid. It's all very impressive. You're the poster boy for the American Dream."

"I think so," replied Guy, as he began to assemble his sandwich. He nodded toward a bottle of virgin olive oil. "As a token of your gratitude, how about passing me that oil? Or do I have to do that myself, too?"

"Sure." Edward smiled and brought the olive oil to his father's side. His jitters from his initial encounter with his mother began to calm. He always felt that if all was right with his father, all was right.

"Go ahead, pour a little on top," Guy instructed his son.

"Are you sure?" Edward grinned. "It looks like there are only two inches of prosciutto on the bread so far. Don't you want two more?"

"Very funny, wise guy." Guy offered his son a slice. "Go ahead, taste that *Prosciutto di Parma* from Louie's in the Bronx. You would never find it in this cultural wasteland."

Edward took his father's offer. "That *is* good," he said as he chewed.

"You bet your ass it's good, my boy. It's the best." Guy layered the mozzarella and topped it with the long hot pepper. He closed the sandwich and cut it, giving half to Edward. "C'mon, let's eat."

As they sat, Edward gestured toward the stereo console. The soprano seemed to be screaming from the speakers. "Dad, what are we listening to, anyway?"

Guy salivated as he readied for his first bite. "It's Puccini." He laid his final red wet pepper. "I think it's the love scene from *La bohème*."

Edward took a bite. "Hmm. This is really good." He looked at the speaker. "That woman sounds awfully sad, for someone who's in love."

"She's falling in love," he shot back. "What do you want me to tell you?"

Edward then heard two words from the music, seizing upon them. "That's it! *Piangi? Perché?* I just heard mom singing those words in her bedroom. My Italian is not great, but I think that means 'Are you crying? Why?'" He sniffed contentedly. "Hardly a love song."

"That's pretty good for an American kid." Guy pinched his son's chin.

"It would be better if I did not have to wait until college to take a class in Italian. You should have taught us as kids."

"Blame your mother. I wanted you to learn Italian. She was ashamed. I don't know why. Italy just happens to be the greatest civilization man has ever known."

Edward rolled his eyes at his father's overlooking other great civilizations like the Greek, the Chinese, and the Egyptian. But he did not argue, knowing that just like the WASPs his father disdained, Guy was trapped in his own version of history. He got the point Guy was trying to make—that for some

16

reason, Marie did not want her children to grow up knowing the language of her youth.

"Your mother wanted you kids to be American." Guy took another bite. "Besides, I worked so that you could learn proper Italian in school, not some dialect."

Marie entered the kitchen, startling Edward. "You are an American," she rasped. "You don't need to speak Italian."

Her swollen eyes made Edward uneasy again. He tried to keep the conversation light. "Dad and I were just talking about this opera, *La bohème.*"

"It's not *La bohème,*" Marie said, calmly yet sternly. "It's *Madame Butterfly.*"

"Your mother is better on opera." Guy gulped another mouthful. "I just make the money to buy the season tickets. She drags me there eight times a year. I usually get a good nap in the first act."

Happy that his mother was speaking to him again, Edward went to the music console to find the case for the cassette that was playing. He studied it. "What a tender picture of a Japanese woman with a baby in her arms," he said.

"You better enjoy it while you can," Guy said. "I've heard that Japan is going to make tapes obsolete with a disc made of plastic that will be read with light. I think it's called a compact disc. It'll never scratch."

Edward could see that his mother was growing annoyed. He pointed to the air. "What is this song? It's beautiful."

"It's called 'Un bel dì vedremo,'" responded Marie. She translated, "One beautiful day, we'll see."

Edward leaned back against the refrigerator. "If it is such a beautiful day, why does the woman sound like she is crying?"

Marie snapped back, "Edward. I'm not done with you. You were late again. Where were you?" The fire in her eyes began to dry her tears. "You were with *her* again, weren't you?"

Edward was defensive. "Who do you think 'her' is?"

"I wouldn't try to duel with your mother," Guy said, retreating to the refrigerator. "She may have only finished fifth grade, but she can out-argue the best of 'em."

Marie waved off Guy, and pointed toward Edward. "Don't play games with me. You know who I'm talking about. Your little friend, Celeste. With all that makeup." She glanced at the statuette of the Madonna on her windowsill. "I don't even want to say what or who she looks like." She yanked a chair from the table, and sat upon it.

"Vixen," Guy chimed in, as he returned to his place with a bottle of wine and a glass.

Edward turned to him with a questioning look. "What?"

Guy laughed to himself, pouring a cup of the red. "Vixen. That's what your mother calls her."

"Mom, how can you say that?" Edward said as he took a seat.

"Never mind. You were supposed to be home almost an hour ago. Now go to bed." Marie pushed back her chair, keeping her eyes fixed on Edward, and shaming him into studying the grains of the wooden tabletop.

Finally, when Marie turned to walk to her room, Edward began making his case. "But Mom, all the other guys..."

Marie stopped, turned, and was silent for a moment. She spoke slowly, with a resolute softness. "The other guys are not my sons. You are." Her voice rose slightly, and she lowered her left brow. "And that girl is going to ruin you." She placed her hand over her face, as if to push back a headache. She turned slowly, like a door on a weary hinge. "I'm going to sleep." She moved her small feet toward her room.

Body coursing with guilt and frustration, Edward was focused on the table again. The debris from Guy's feeding frenzy was scattered. Edward picked up a piece of fallen bread crust. "I hope you at least enjoyed your sandwich," he cracked.

"The bread is the best," Guy replied. "Brick-oven baked, made just like in my mother's home town in Italy. Not like that barbaric food I had to give the bankers tonight. Your mother and I had a big party, with a lot of important people. You should have been here." He frowned. "I told your mother we needed to serve those guys celery and cream cheese. Goddamn English animals. I have to try to impress them with rabbit food. We should've served the prosciutto and hot peppers. Maybe even eggplant *rollatini*—your

18

mother's is the best."

Irritated, Edward shot back. "Dad, if you have such an objection to the WASPs, why do you grovel to them instead of being yourself? You build bridges and skyscrapers. These idiots couldn't put together a mailbox. You even bought a Tudor-style house. You're always complaining about how thin the windows are—about how they restrict the sun. You once said, 'We are noble peasants from the mountains. We are people of the light!'" He pounded his chest.

"Did I say that?" Guy beamed. "Someday, you and your brother and sister are going to write a book about me. How I struggled to pick up where my father left off. To make a better life for all of you. To make you into leaders."

Edward interjected. "Those are the glorious parts, and are only about your side of the family. I would write about Mom's side as well. I bet she has a great story that needs to be discovered and told."

"Not like the Bennetts."

"How do you know?"

"Because if there was something interesting in her past, we all would know about it. Anyway, if you're going to include your mother's side, the book is going to be a little long and the part about them isn't going to be too exciting."

"Maybe I'll have to write two books."

"When your books become movies, make sure that you get someone handsome to play me."

"If only Clark Gable were still alive."

"I'd take Gregory Peck—Lou Gehrig in *Pride of the Yankees* and Father Chisholm in *The Keys of the Kingdom*."

"And now he'll play Guy Bennett in..." Edward slapped the table. "I got it." He pointed at Guy. "We'll call the movie *The Pride of the Kingdom*."

Having enjoyed the joust, Guy sipped his wine. "Ah, the WASPs are okay. I'm only kidding about them. Anyway, I'm doing it all for you guys. To take you to the next level. You can stack your money only so high. Then, you need *social* wealth. Bankers have social wealth. Their names are carved in stone on the wall when we go to the opera. I may be able to build something great, but only after they decide I can build it." He took another sip. "When you write the book, remember that this house was once owned by a Rockefeller."

Edward squinted. "Okay, so what's up with Mom? What I was going to say, before she walked out, is that the rest of my friends don't even *have* a curfew. Most of the time they have to drop me off before going to the next party. I'm old enough to be drafted into war, yet my mother has me on a curfew."

Guy went to the cabinet to get a glass for Edward. He came back to the table and poured him some wine. "Last year's homemade wine is like velvet. It's out of this world."

Edward took a sip and raised his glass. "Indeed, another great autumn crush for the Bennett family. I love that term for making wine. It's so wholesome. That's what we should call that movie about you—*The Autumn Crush*."

"I still can't get over how you and your brother got in the vat and stamped the grapes with your bare feet. You guys laughed your asses off. We'll miss you at this year's crush. Your brother and sister will be here. You'll probably be sipping tea in London."

"That's because Albert and Lisa Marie are done with school. Who knows, maybe I'll surprise you and fly home for the weekend." He took another sip. "So why the curfew? What is it? Why do I have to get home early? And why the hell does she cry? It's not as if I got caught with drugs. I've never even tried drugs." He held his glass of wine to the light, to assess its clarity. "Mom is so strong and is such a great mother, but on nights like tonight I feel like I don't really know her. I don't recognize her."

"Son, I don't know what to tell you. She bounces around like she's always running out of time. She has us going out every night." He began counting off on his fingers. "On Tuesdays we go to the opera. On Thursdays we go to dinner with her friends—and God knows she has a million of them. She is practically the goddamn mayor." He took a deep breath. "And on the weekends, she is...she was all about you kids. Now that you're gone, she takes me on field trips. Last week, we went to the Berkshires, just to hear a one-hour lecture about music. I tell you, son, that woman is on fire. Always running."

"Yeah, but why does she cry when I come home late?"

"That's what I'm trying to say. I don't know. She lived in Italy and didn't meet her father until she came over here after World War II, when she was fifteen. Her father was busy trying to make a new home. He even fought for the Americans in World War I. Back and forth, back and forth. Go figure." He took a gulp of wine. "Damn, that's good. We should sell it."

Edward got up from his seat to lower the volume of the music. When he sat back down, he drew from his glass. "Go ahead. Tell me more about Mom."

Guy held the glass by its stem, placing it on the table and staring at it. "Years after she got here, the American government sent her mother back to Italy because she was sick. Some wild law that I think is still on the books. The old man spent a few bucks trying to fight it legally, but eventually let her go back to Italy. Your mother never saw her mother again."

"Wait a minute. How was Grandpa able to stay in America?"

"After he fought in World War I for the Americans, he became an American citizen."

Edward pushed away his glass of wine, wanting not to be distracted. "And he sent his wife away alone?"

"It was a different time, son. People did desperate things not only to make it to America, but also to be seen as American. You said it yourself before—the history books you read don't tell it all. I think that is why your mother went from Maria to Marie. That's why she wouldn't speak Italian to you. Once she sailed to America, she left Italy behind. It's as if she has had two different lives."

"Mom's name was Maria, not Marie?"

"You knew that," Guy reprimanded.

"Yeah, I guess I forgot," said Edward, sobered by the realization of his self-absorption.

Guy craned his neck slowly. "Hers was one of many journeys," he said. He reached over for Edward's glass of wine and finished it for him. "I should tell you one day about my dad's coming to America in the steerage of a boat.

21

He was only seventeen years old. He ran away from his family, snuck on the boat, and jumped into the water when he saw the Statue of Liberty…"

"With all due respect, Dad, I doubt Grandpa jumped off the boat, but if that's what makes you happy, go with it. I'm trying to figure out Mom's issue. And you are telling me that it has something to do with her not meeting her dad until she was fifteen, and how once she did, her mother was deported to Italy."

Guy shook his head. "No, I think there is something else. But she won't tell me. There is something else in that little town where she was born. We have been to Italy a dozen times, forty miles from that place, in Salerno. I always say, 'Marie, let's go see your family.' She won't even acknowledge me. It's as if I'm asking her to pet a scorpion." He sucked out the last speck of wine and refilled his glass. "She is a hard little woman. Maybe something happened in that town, and she won't talk about it. I don't know what the hell to tell you."

"What's the name of the town?"

"Lavenna."

Edward went to the drawer, and pulled out a pencil and piece of paper. "How do you spell it? Because I am going to find it during spring break in my year abroad at LSE."

"What does LSE stand for?"

Edward shook his head in disbelief.

"I know that I am paying for it. I just don't know what it means. London something or other."

"London School of Economics. My year abroad!"

"And what spring break are you talking about?" Guy fired back.

"I get six weeks in March."

"Another boondoggle I'm paying for."

"Let me refresh your memory. We made a deal based on my grades—if I got As, I could boondoggle through Europe with my friends." He paused. "Now, I need the spelling of mom's town. C'mon, Molly, give it your best shot."

"Who's Molly?"

22

"Molly Dieveney—this year's national spelling bee champion," Edward laughed.

"Get the hell out of here," Guy laughed back. "I can't spell because I have bad eyes. I couldn't see what the teacher was writing on the chalkboard." Guy went on the offensive. "Meanwhile, you don't know the difference between a nut and a bolt." He grabbed the piece of paper and a pencil, and wrote "L-A-V-E-N-N-A." He folded and pushed the scribbled leaf across the table. "There. Give that a try during that six-week spring break from that fancy London School."

Edward read the piece of paper out loud. "Lavenna." He stuffed it in his pocket. "I'll find it."

"Be careful. I don't know why she has not gone back there. There was some story about her grandfather getting killed in a fight."

"*Murdered?*"

"Yeah." Guy took a sniff. "There are some hot tempers on your mother's side."

Edward retorted, patronizingly. "Don't worry. I can take care of myself." He reached over for his father's glass of wine and downed it. "You just keep our little secret."

Guy gestured as if locking his mouth shut.

The soprano's tempered volume was crisp in the silence. Edward pointed to the speaker. "Now, Ms. Butterfly's words seem a little sweeter, even if I don't understand them."

Guy turned off the tape player and removed the cassette. "Opera is pure beauty."

"How would you know? You sleep through it."

"I may not know all the names and follow all the verses the way your mother does, but I am always awake for the high notes. I feel their power." He slid the cassette back into its casing. "It takes you to another place," he mused as he laid the music back on the special shelf he created for it. "Someday, you'll appreciate it." He dimmed the kitchen light. "But for now, go to bed. You have a big trip ahead of you."

# III.

## Admiring the Triumphal Arch,

## What it Takes to Peel an Onion

E dward and his American classmates flexed and shot their way through the first six months at the London School of Economics. They were the first to raise their hands in class, and they had to have the last word whenever there was a question of America's place in the world. Although they were often loud, and sometimes brash, they always attracted a crowd, with Edward taking his usual place in the center. For spring break, he pushed off for continental Europe with his high school pal, Matthew Coyne, who was also his roommate in college. They bragged to one another how, in their travels, they were conquering the continent at a faster pace than Napoleon.

On a sunny afternoon halfway through the break, Edward and Coyne strolled through Rome's ancient Forum. Edward was a few steps ahead of Coyne, who was preoccupied with a map.

"You and me, Matt," Edward said, beaming. "Together at one of the most important places in history—where Romans and gods fought to the death and marched in triumph, dragging their prisoners of war. I can see it now. The victorious general, processing through the Forum with his face painted red—the immortal man—with Cleopatra in chains."

The April sun had been unseasonably harsh. Coyne's pasty skin had already turned pink. "Edward, I think that you're a little off on that. If I remember from our class at Benedictine, Cleopatra herself was not in chains. They had to use an effigy. And I think there was something about a slave whispering in the general's ear. I don't remember what the slave said."

Edward stared off, smiling—ignoring Coyne's correction.

"You want to take a break?" Coyne asked with a parched mouth. "It's hot as balls."

"C'mon, Matt—it's practically dusk," Edward exhorted. "This is nothing compared to our cross-country practices at Benedictine. I'll never forget the day that Brother Sebastian outran you wearing his brown robe."

Coyne panted, "You wouldn't even be here if it wasn't for me. I convinced you to go to LSE. You wanted to go to Hong Kong."

"Hong Kong would've been interesting—a remnant of another great empire. I could've also learned more about China. God knows what goes on there."

"Your spring break would have been a day trip to the Great Wall. Big deal. You walk up one side, take a picture and get on the bus. Backward country with no economy."

"There are over one billion people in China," Edward said, pulling further ahead.

"With no real jobs and nothing to eat. They ride around on bicycles." Coyne closed some of the distance. "Besides, LSE looks better on your resume. Wall Street and law firms love it."

"Ever the pragmatist, you are."

"Ever the dreamer, you are."

"Touché." Edward gestured for Coyne to catch up. "Let's go. We'll be done in a few minutes."

Coyne folded his map and shoved it in his back pocket. "I'm with you."

Edward could hardly control his excitement. "We read about these great temples, but now we're seeing them firsthand, touching them." His words gave fuel to their gait. "This is awesome. Maybe someday, our grandchildren will be visiting Bennett-Coyne Stadium." His mind clicked back to the crack Celeste had made about Donald Trump and his tower. He proceeded nonetheless. "We'll have a flame burning on top for everyone to see, and it will never die."

"Roger that. We just have to make sure that we don't pay for it ourselves. Maybe we'll issue a fat bond. It shouldn't cost us a penny."

"Always counting the beans—aren't you, Matt?"

"Someone has to figure out how to pay for greatness."

"I guess," replied Edward. "I'm just glad that you're good at math, because I haven't got a clue."

"That's why we're a team," said Coyne, taking a large stride forward and finally catching up with Edward. When Edward did not answer, Coyne followed up. "Right?"

"Right," responded Edward, offering his pal a high five. The clap of the boys' hands echoed in the Forum.

Edward and Coyne passed the Temple of Venus and Rome, coming to rest on a large bold rock with a view of the Arch of Constantine. They were at the spot where they had agreed to meet their classmate and fellow traveler, Karl Prigler, whom Edward had befriended at their Ivy League convocation, and cajoled into joining him at LSE as the intellectual in his collection of his friends. Perched atop the sun-heated boulder, Edward strategized about the trip he planned to take the next day to his mother's hometown of Lavenna. He imagined himself like the virtuous generals who had once stood in his place.

Suddenly he felt a sharp cramp in his side. Instead of passing, the pain pierced deeper. Edward tried to rub it away.

"You all right?" Coyne asked.

"I'm fine," responded Edward as he continued to massage himself.

Prigler's approach from the distance relieved him. Edward elbowed Coyne. "Look, here comes Prigler." He shook his head in disapproval. "As always, head buried in a book." Edward cupped his hands and yelled, "Hey Prigler, what are you doing, looking at a *Playboy* centerfold?"

Prigler was startled by Edward's booming voice. He recovered and looked up with a smile. "Bennett, you're so loud," he called.

"I just wanted to make sure that you heard me," Edward bellowed.

Prigler reached Edward and Coyne on their boulder. He looked around for a place to sit, finding three smaller rocks next to one another. The product of a New England boarding school, Prigler was fair-haired and slight of build, with thin legs. His eyes were always squinted. He held up his book. "For your information, asshole," he said, "this is what I was reading." The title, written in thin black cursive without an accompanying cover image, was *Rome's Jews*.

"Is it required for one of your courses?" Edward asked.

"I don't read only what's required, Bennett. It's called leisure reading. My uncle lent it to me. Said he read it in a weekend."

Coyne stepped in. *"Rome's Jews?"* He looked at Edward quizzically. "That's like me reading an Irish cookbook. It's a fucking oxymoron. Are you sure *Rome's Jews* is not a new slapstick comedy?" He laughed out loud nervously, looking for Edward to join.

Edward looked down, suppressing a giggle.

Coyne persisted, his howl growing more aggressive. "I know, even better—it's a story about the emperor's accountants." He gripped Edward's shoulder. "That's it. *Rome's Jews* is about the accounting department for the Roman Empire."

Edward sensed that Coyne was close to the line, if not already across it. "Back off," he mouthed silently. He tried to diffuse the situation by extending his open hand until Prigler placed his book in it. *"Rome's Jews,"* he exclaimed. "I bet it's interesting." He turned a page, pretending to read. "Must be a pretty smart uncle if he read it in a weekend. None of my relatives ever lent me a book. Are you Jewish, Prigler?"

Prigler loosened the straps on his backpack, but kept his eyes on Edward, as if not certain where he was headed. "Yes, I am. Are you Roman?"

"Well, sort of. I'm Italian. I guess that's as close as you can get."

Prigler swiped his hair off his forehead. "Not really. If your family emigrated from Southern Italy, as is the case with most Italian-Americans, I don't think the Romans would be happy with the affiliation. I know your father is in construction, but I suspect that the Romans would not consider being a soldier for *Cosa Nostra* quite the same as being in the emperor's army."

Despite the dig, Edward stayed cool atop his boulder. He bent the ear of another page of *Rome's Jews*, trying to be engaging without affronting Prigler. "I would imagine that there were not many Jews at your boarding school," he said. With the implication of his statement hanging, he followed quickly, placing the book at his side. "I always thought boarding schools were filled with WASPs—guys whose first names sounded like last names."

Prigler's jaw relaxed. He dried his sweating brow with a thin bicep. He nodded, grinning. "Funny you say that. One of the first guys I met at school was named P. Brinkerhoff Ruckleshaus. A little guy with horn-rimmed glasses. The only thing he could ever talk about was flying with his father. For a while, we all thought his dad was an airline pilot. Until one day, a guy with a black cap came to school and told Brink—that was his nickname—he told Brink that the family jet had arrived to take him home for Christmas." Prigler's smile was mixed with resentment and envy. "Meanwhile, my parents would show up in a station wagon with the wood panels on the side. It was the only thing they could afford after paying the exorbitant tuition for that dungeon." He spat. "I hated that damn place."

A cool breeze swept through, and Edward sensed in that moment that he had forged a bond with Prigler. He tried to exit the thorny act about Judaism. "I tell you one thing I miss since we have been in England—a good bagel with lox."

"Bagels and lox," Prigler suddenly bristled. "Is that the first thing you think of when you are with a Jew? Next, why don't you ask whether I am related to the fiddler on the roof?" He shifted his seat among his islands of rocks, beneath Edward and his boulder.

"Or maybe you're wondering whether my dad sits around the table eating spaghetti with Vito Corleone."

Prigler bit his lip.

Before Prigler could attack again—and surely he would—Edward mused peripherally from his rock-on-high. "But isn't Rome incredible?" He pointed. "Guys, we are sitting next to the Arch of Constantine."

Edward shifted his attention back to Coyne. "You remember, right?

Constantine was victorious because he had a vision of Christ in a dream. Hence, the triumphal arch." Edward dangled his feet off the edge of the large rock, like a contented child admiring the crystalline lake from his family's dock. "What a magnificent work—all a tribute to one great man, at the divergence of the *Via Triumphalis* and the *Via Sacra.*"

Coyne raised an imaginary glass. "Very impressive, Master Edward," he toasted with an English accent.

"Cheers, Master Matthew." Edward reciprocated with his own invisible glass and dash of affect. "We studied it in Father Cornelius's world history class."

Mouth agape, Prigler could not hold back any longer. "Listen to you guys. What did the monks teach you at Benedictine? Constantine did not even convert until his deathbed, and did so only because he was a mamma's boy just like you, Bennett. And do you think that this was all part of some glorious urban beautification campaign? Bennett, if you had studied for real your so-called 'Triumphal Arch,' instead of being infatuated with it, you would know that most of its medallions and reliefs are not even original. They were scavenged from earlier works dedicated to Trajan, Hadrian, and Marcus Aurelius. Sure, it's monumental—a monumental fraud, just like the conquest it memorializes."

Edward didn't budge on his comfortable surface. "Prigler, don't you think you are going a bit too far?" He smiled at Coyne. "That just tells me that the Romans were conservationists—forerunners of recycling." He pointed back at the arch. "But look at it—regardless of whether you think it's made of scraps or in ruin, it will make people say Constantine's name forever."

"I know you're good on your feet, particularly when you're passionate about something," Prigler answered with a hint of a patronizing tone. "I saw that during our debates in poli sci. That's what makes you dangerous. You argue with bravado, and when you get into unfamiliar territory, you pull the debate back to where you want the fight to be had. You get into these shifting sands. You have no idea what you're talking about on this one. Did you ever study the reliefs on the arch?"

Edward thought quickly, and pointed. "How could I? There's a fence around it."

"I'm talking about in your class with Father Cornhole."

"Sounds to me like you're the only one getting cornholed," Coyne interjected. "How did it feel taking it Greek-style at boarding school?"

Prigler lit into Edward. "Had your beloved Father taught you well, you would know that many of the old reliefs, referred to as *spolia*, were placed next to newly created ones, which were much simpler with disproportionate figures—probably the work of the inferior artists of Constantine's time. Far from being an arch of triumph, it was probably more reflective of Rome's decline. Constantine thought he would become immortal through his conquest, his disciples thinking this would give him some sort of afterlife. But look—two thousand years later, tourists with fanny packs are looking down on a pile of rubble, laughing at his vanity." Prigler whispered caustically, "Remember, you are mortal."

Coyne snapped his fingers. "That's what the slave whispered in the general's ear!"

"Are you finished with your lecture?" Edward asked Prigler without flinching.

"Only if you've learned your lesson," replied a contented Prigler.

"Well, I think that you might've missed the point of whatever you read, wherever you read it." Edward cracked his knuckles. "Regardless of what you consider Constantine's vainglory, *I* think that the old reliefs next to the new ones could represent respect for the past and transition."

Coyne bobbed with enthusiasm, encouraging Edward to keep on with the fight.

"And the simpler figures might pack more symbolism, more for the viewer to interpret for himself." Edward pointed again to the arch. "None of us will really know until we get up close to the arch, on the other side of that fence. Where we would not just see the reliefs closely, but also interact with them—touch them."

"So right, enlightened one," Coyne said, extending his arm, palm down toward Edward. He snickered at Coyne. "That's a Roman salute. I saw it on one of the sculptures on the arch."

## III

The skin on the bridge of Prigler's nose bunched. He moved among his rocks again, to a higher one, so he could look Edward straight in the eye. "You guys just don't get it," he said. "You think it's all a big play. Nobles wearing laurels, eating grapes and making grand speeches." He took a breath. "Fellas, there are lots of layers to it. Lots more layers. Truth is like an onion. You have to keep peeling it, no matter how strong the odor."

Coyne countered, "Yeah, the next layers were the orgies and the vomitoriums." He snorted. "Edward's right. Those guys were ahead of their time." He raised his arms over his head and cheered "Toga, toga, toga!"

Prigler gripped his book, and aimed it at a point behind the boulder upon which Edward and Coyne had enthroned themselves. "Let me peel away some more layers for you. You two altar boys believe that Constantine's so-called conversion to Christianity was the result of a dream."

Edward and Coyne looked at each other and shrugged their shoulders. "Yeah," Edward answered.

"That's the abridged version." Prigler lifted his chin. "The longer one is that while he was marching before the epic Battle of Milvian Bridge, at midday, he saw a cross, superimposed over the sun, carrying the message *In Hoc Signo Vinces*—'In this sign, you will conquer.'"

"Interesting," Edward said, having no choice but to go along.

"The next night, Constantine supposedly had the little dream of your mythology, where Christ supposedly told him to use the sign as standard for his army. Hence, the Chi Rho of Constantine's forces at Milvian Bridge."

Prigler bit his upper lip, hoping Edward would chase his bait. When Edward didn't, Prigler pretended to save his friendly adversary from a parochial gaffe. "Before you embarrass yourself, Bennett, Chi Rho was not some tribute to Egypt—that city of golden pyramids that you breezed through in one page of your history books. It was the first two letters of the Greek word *Christos*: Chi and Rho. Apparently, there wasn't enough time for the monks to teach you that while you sipped frothy coffee topped with cinnamon."

Edward stroked his eyebrow slowly in order to project poise. "The coffee to which you are referring is called *cappuccino*. There is some myth that it was invented by the Capuchin monks." He smirked, smugly. "Our monks were the Benedictines, the true inventors of *Bénédictine*, that most excellent after-dinner drink."

"Yes, most excellent," repeated Coyne, reverting again to an English accent.

Prigler moved to yet another rock in his archipelago, from which he continued his gladiatorial attack upon Edward and Coyne. "Whatever. Capuchin or Benedictine, they all were naked under those ludicrous robes, hiding in the mountains, babbling to themselves." He glided his right foot through the roasted dirt. "We don't even know if Constantine ever really converted—whether his Christian campaign was genuine or a reaction to the political times—or if the whole vision and dream were concocted by his propagandists."

Edward and Coyne sat stunned.

Prigler feigned peeling an onion, speaking slowly and patronizingly. "Truth is in the layers. It's like an onion. You have to keep peeling, going deeper. Endless layers that you have to keep removing, even if it makes me want to cry."

Coyne cut in. "Listening to your self-righteous bullshit is the only thing that makes me want to cry."

Prigler reached into his backpack, and pulled out a pad and pen. He opened the pad, and wrote slowly. He presented his drawing to Edward and Coyne.

"It's an X over a P," Coyne stated matter-of-factly.

"It's the Chi Rho," Prigler boasted.

"It looks like a butterfly," Edward observed. Having seen that image and said that word—*butterfly*—Edward recalled his mother's aria and realized how little he knew. Perhaps there were more layers of truth that he had never addressed. His belief in Catholic rectitude, in the unblemished mettle of his family's immigrant journey, in the virtue of power and living on—could it all be more complicated? He wondered whether he needed to thank Prigler for prodding him to ask these questions.

Coyne grabbed Prigler's drawing. "I'm not sure that I see a butterfly." He closed one eye. "It looks to me like the crossed sabers that the good guys wore on their hats in that other great conquest¾the North over the South in the Civil War."

Edward ignored Coyne. He focused on Prigler, respectful of his intellect and deliberate ways. Noticing the many compartments on Prigler's backpack, Edward thought about the Lavenna trip he had planned for the next day. *Am I prepared? Where was the town? Why had Mom never returned? How would I be received? Maybe my campaign toward truth had been ambushed before my first step. Maybe I shouldn't go.*

Coyne looked at Edward, tilting his head toward Prigler so that Edward would resume the offensive.

But the heat had made Edward dizzy. He leaned back, hoping to clear his head.

# IV.

## Whether to Fear the Bite of an Iguana

"Argument getting to be a little too much for you?" jeered Prigler. "You'll always live in your shallow world. It's an inch deep and a mile long."

Edward slid from the high point of his and Coyne's rock, easing into a crevice. He reset himself by planting his feet so that he would not slip further down the boulder. He looked ahead without blinking, still thinking about the place to which his mother wished he would never return.

Prigler waited patiently, ready to strike as soon as Edward opened his mouth.

Edward then felt something cold and leathery crawl across his feet. In reflexive terror, he jumped up. "Ahhhhh!" He turned. "What the hell is that?"

A large lizard with a serrated crest stood defiant in Edward's place.

Coyne and Prigler remained seated, smiling at Edward's reaction.

Edward shuffled backwards. "What the fuck is that, a Komodo dragon?"

Prigler chuckled. "A Komodo dragon! That's a good one. You must've picked it up when you were watching television late one night in your silk pajamas, waiting for your mamma to bring you warm milk."

"Very funny, Prigler."

With his book in hand, Prigler assumed Edward's initial place atop the boulder, next to where the creature stood. He reached out to pet the

34

intruder.

"What the hell are you doing?"

"It's not a Komodo dragon. If it were, it would be about four times this size. It's an iguana. But don't worry. It won't bite you—it's an herbivore." Still stroking the iguana, and without looking back at Edward, Prigler continued. "That means he is not attracted to meat." He glanced at Edward's crotch. "Not even a small piece of Italian salami."

Edward gathered his courage and approached the iguana slowly. The iguana glared back.

Prigler coached the iguana. "Go get 'em, boy."

The iguana scurried off the rock, past Edward and into the shadows of the ruins, causing Edward to jump again. "Goddamnit, Prigler, you're crazy."

Prigler remained on Edward's spot next to Coyne on the boulder, forcing Edward to sit among the smaller, more uncomfortable rocks. "And you, Bennett," he retorted, "are irrational."

Edward moved from rock to jagged rock, trying to find one that was comfortable. "Irrational?"

Prigler cracked his knuckles, as if readying his sinewy fist for a good punch. "I just finished explaining that your little beast was an iguana, and that an iguana is not interested in your flesh—unless you jump like a little girl, in which case you may scare it and cause it to lash out defensively and bite. All the more reason why your leaping away was irrational—if you knew that it was an iguana, and knew that iguanas are herbivores, you had nothing to fear except what might happen if you expressed fear."

Feeling as though Prigler had launched one too many attacks on his being, Edward rose from the small rocks and firmed his legs. "Irrational?" he said again. "A four-legged thing walks across my feet, and in that moment, I jump. *That's* irrational? I thought it was something that could hurt me—maybe even a Komodo dragon."

Prigler clicked his tongue against his roof of mouth like a scolding parent. "You're playing a little fast and loose with the facts," he said. "You jumped without even seeing what crawled across your feet. You went on nothing more than a feel or touch. You acted irrationally—plain and simple."

Edward glared at Prigler. "Let me get this straight. There's a creature crawling across me. And I jump because I believe it could possibly bite me before I figure out exactly what the hell it is. You're saying that I have acted irrationally?"

"Precisely. You responded without a true understanding that the iguana on this boulder would not have bitten you unless you scared it, which you nearly did by screaming hysterically, therefore acting irrationally." Knowing that he had stunned Edward, Prigler hit harder. "The same irrationality that has you believing in that God of yours—the idea of that magic man in the sky that consoles you with the same notion of immortality that led your Roman ancestors to their ruin."

Edward could not believe his ears. He pointed at Prigler's book. "My God is no more a 'magic man' than yours."

"I don't have a god."

"What?" Edward asked, incredulously. "You're Jewish."

Prigler responded quickly, well-versed for a moment like this. "Judaism is both a religion and a culture. Jewish culture informs my morality, but I do not believe in God. It's irrational, just like your fear of the iguana. There are no facts to support it. No evidence."

"No evidence of God? How about the miracles?"

"There are no reliable first-hand accounts."

Edward turned to Coyne for reinforcement.

Coyne's head stayed bowed.

Edward took up the fight himself. "No first-hand accounts? How about the Gospels?"

"Second- or third-hand hearsay, written years after Jesus's life."

Edward looked back at Coyne, who lifted his head slowly. He nodded and raised his eyebrows, confirming for Edward that Prigler was right.

Edward scrambled. "How about the building of St. Peter's? You don't believe that was divinely inspired?"

"I think that your revered basilica was created by talented architects and artists who were being paid by the pope. I take it that you believe the magic man created the world in seven days?"

36

Not wanting to embarrass himself again, Edward turned the question back on Prigler. "How do you think it was created?"

"I subscribe to the Big Bang theory—that everything started with a small mass called a singularity, which had infinite density and intense heat. About thirteen billion years ago, it expanded to form the universe."

Edward bit the inside of his lower lip. "So what came before the singularity?"

"There was nothing before the singularity." Prigler stopped abruptly, and looked at his watch. "I would love to continue this discussion, but it's getting late. I need to get back."

Years of arguing with relatives around the kitchen table had taught Edward how to recognize when an advocate felt vulnerable. Edward sensed that Prigler was at his wall. "Wait a minute," he said. "If there was nothing before the singularity, who or what created it?"

Prigler laid his book on the ground. "Well, there are many theories, none of them yet confirmed."

The timbre in Edward's voice strengthened. "Name me one."

"I'd rather not until they are confirmed. I have faith that science will answer the question definitively."

"Faith—interesting choice of words." Edward glanced at Coyne, and back at Prigler. "So your faith in science and the so-called Big Bang is no more rational than my faith in God. In fact, you have no basis to deny that God, be it mine or someone else's, created your singularity." He picked up *Rome's Jews* from the dirt and threw it back into Prigler's lap, where it gave off a cloud of dust.

Prigler rubbed his eyes of the grime. He spoke, but only softly. "Going back to what started all of this—there was nothing to jump up about. It was an iguana. Iguanas don't bite humans."

Sensing Edward's victory, Coyne jestingly raised his thumb up like a Roman emperor, demanding that the gladiator deal the fatal blow.

Wanting to stay above both Prigler and Coyne, Edward allowed Prigler to have the last word.

Prigler responded in kind by retreating to his original archipelago and book.

Edward reassumed his place next to Coyne on the boulder. Sitting motionless in their original stations, they each gazed amid the sea of ruins. As the heat dissipated, they began to tinker with their backpacks.

Edward fastened his pack to his shoulder and picked up a stone. He launched it with all his might toward the Arch of Constantine. He smirked at Prigler. "I'm going back to the hotel. I have to get up early tomorrow to find my mother's hometown."

While Prigler fiddled with his pack, another book fell out.

"What's that one?" Edward asked politely.

"*Christ Stopped at Eboli.* Just another book about how even your Almighty Lord was afraid to go deeply into southern Italy."

"Good one," Edward said as he began to walk away.

Coyne cried out, "Don't be silly, Edward. Come drinking with us and sleep late. Forget about Lavenna. You don't even know where the place is. It's not on the map."

Edward kept his stride, without missing a step. "Don't worry. I'll get there—somehow." He stopped and turned. "Prigler, please don't make too much noise when you come in tonight. Irrational people get jumpy when they are startled. Who knows how I might react?"

Edward could hear Prigler gasp to Coyne. "He's nuts. If Lavenna is not on the map, he'll never find it."

Leaving the Forum as the sun lowered toward the horizon, Edward focused again on the arch, relishing its hues of conquest and faith.

# V.

## Second Thoughts

That evening, Edward lay in bed in the *pensione* in Prati, which was one of Rome's less glamorous neighborhoods, but also one of the most economical, making it attractive to Prigler and his limited budget. He persuaded Coyne and Edward of the choice of lodging by convincing them how cool it would be to brag that they had slept blocks away from the Vatican. On his side and staring at the wall, Edward could feel the bedspring pressing up against his rib.

Prigler and Coyne burst through the door, bringing with them the smell of beer. "*Bueno ser,*" Prigler slurred, loudly.

Edward laughed to himself at Prigler's drunken and botched pronunciation of *Buona sera.*

"Quiet, you slob," Coyne said, slapping Prigler on the shoulder. "Edward's trying to sleep."

"That's okay," Edward said, popping up and onto his feet. "I'm wide awake."

Coyne helped Prigler into bed. "He must have said *bueno ser* to every girl in Rome after his third liter of Peroni." He turned to see that Edward was putting on his jeans. "Where are you going?"

"I have to call home. Do me a favor, Matt. Set your alarm for 4:30 a.m. That's what time I have to wake up for the train."

"So you found a train to your mom's town?"

"No. But I figure if I'm going to get back here tomorrow night, I better get to the train station early and figure it out as soon as possible. There is a 5:15 to Salerno. There must be a connection from Salerno to her town."

"Are you sure this is a good idea?" Coyne asked as he began to remove Prigler's sneakers. "Why don't you stay the extra day with us and see the Borghese Gallery? It has art from Bernini and Caravaggio."

"Awfully nice of you to put Prigler to bed like that," Edward said. "I would've thought you would leave him to sleep in the streets."

Matt pulled the heel hard to relieve Prigler's beer-swollen feet. "He can be a prick sometimes, but he's all right. I actually had a good time with him tonight. You should have seen him try to hit on an Italian girl. He asked me how to say 'You have beautiful breasts' in Italian." He threw Prigler's sneakers to the ground. "Seriously, Edward. Stay the extra day and screw that little town. God knows if you'll even find it. We should take in as much of this stuff as we can—it's great to write about on grad school applications."

"I've had my fill of art. You'll set the clock for me, Matt?"

Coyne got the message. "Sure thing."

"You're a fuckin' idiot, Bennett," snorted Prigler. He closed his eyes and smiled. *"Bueno ser."*

Edward searched the Via Germanico for a phone booth. Although his mother insisted he keep in contact whenever he was traveling, he could just as easily have checked in after his trip to Lavenna. But guilt was getting the better of him, as was a growing reluctance to proceed. Deep inside, he thought the call might give him an excuse to bow out. He found a phone, and pumped a pocketful of 500 lira coins into it. An extended *beep* filled his ear, indicating that his long-distance call was ringing.

"Hello?" Edward's father answered.

"Dad. It's me, Edward. I'm in Rome."

Guy's response overlapped Edward's words, which were delayed slightly by the transmission. "Edward, is that you?"

Before Guy could continue, Marie yanked the phone out of his ear. "Give me that," she said. She spoke directly. "You listen to me, Edward. Don't you dare go back to that town."

Jolted, Edward feigned ignorance. "Mom, what are you talking about?"

From the background, Guy yelped his defense. "She made me tell her you were going to Lavenna."

Marie would not entertain a quarrel between her husband and her son. "Never mind that. You know what I'm talking about. Don't you dare go back there. And don't even think about bringing Matt with you. The South is an ugly place, filled with terrible people. I'm telling you—don't go!"

Chilled by his mother's harsh words, Edward did not protest. "Mom, I have no intention of going to Lavenna. The guys convinced me not to go. I just called to tell you we're in Rome."

"Edward, are you sure? Don't lie to me on this one. I mean it. The South is an awful place. There's nothing there."

"I'm positive, Mom. Tomorrow, Coyne wants us to see the Borghese Gallery. Says we need to take in as much of this art as possible. It will be good for our grad school applications."

"So you are staying another day in Rome?" Marie began to de-escalate.

"Yes, Mom. The gallery has Carpaccio. Matt wants to see it."

"*Caravaggio*," Marie corrected him. "You should know that. You've always been so bad with art."

"What can I say? I like history better. It's more real. But I'm going to give art a try. The day after tomorrow we go to Florence. I'm telling you, Coyne has a detailed itinerary all set for us."

"Hmm," Marie exhaled. "Listen to Matt. He's got his head on straight."

"Yeah," said Edward as his mother cooled.

"Are you going to see the statue of David in Florence?" asked Marie.

"Of course," Edward tapped the outside of the phone's handset nervously.

"That's good. You'll like that."

"But tell Dad I appreciate him keeping my secret."

Marie's voice spiked again. "Never mind your father and your secret. You stick with Matt. He's smart. Think about your future, not my past."

Guy yelled out again from behind his wife. "She made me do it, Edward. She near tortured me. She knew something was up, and forced it out of me. She should have been a damn prosecutor."

Edward closed out the conversation. "I have to run, or else this little phone call will cost a fortune. Don't worry, Mom, I would never go against your wishes. I'll call you from Florence—after *David*."

"Okay. Be careful."

Walking the Via Germanico back to his hotel, Edward pondered his mother's admonition to focus on his future, and her plea to be careful. He knew that her concerns were very real—her memories so bad that she did not want to talk about them.

A young man sped by on his Vespa with a woman wrapped around him. The couple drove without helmets, their hair blown by the night wind as they weaved through the traffic. Cars honked their horns as the duo passed and cut. "*Vaffanculo!*" shouted one motorist from his window.

Edward concluded that not going to Lavenna was definitely the more prudent and safer course. And it was what his mother wanted.

Upon Edward's return to the room, Coyne opened the door for him. "That was quick."

"Yeah. About tomorrow—I was thinking." He took his wallet out of his pocket, flipped it in the air, and caught it without looking. He placed it on the night table, smiling.

"I knew it. You decided not to go. The whole idea was crazy."

"Yeah, it's crazy." Edward unbuttoned his pants and climbed back into bed. "It would make more sense if I had more time for the trip."

"Yeah," Coyne agreed, happy that Edward would be spending the last day in Rome with him and Prigler.

Edward pulled the chain on the lamp to turn off the light. "So instead of meeting you back here at nine tomorrow night, let's make it midnight. That'll give me plenty of time to get back from Lavenna."

# VI.

## Making the Train

When Coyne's clock alarm rang at 4:30 a.m., Edward silenced it immediately so as not to wake the others. He dressed in the dark, and stuffed his camera, pad, and map into his backpack. Walking on his tiptoes, he did a pirouette, returning to his bedside to scoop up the sweater he had left behind—the one his mother had knitted for him before he went to college. Back at the door, he looked over his shoulder to see that Coyne and Prigler were still sleeping. He turned the knob slowly.

"Hey, Edward," whispered Prigler.

"What is it, Karl?" Edward whispered back. When Prigler did not speak, Edward called out again. "Karl, are you awake?"

"Good luck today," Prigler groaned. "I hope you find your mom's town."

Edward smiled to himself in the darkness.

Prigler added, "And I hope that there are no iguanas."

Edward thought about making a wisecrack of his own, but instead chose to show his appreciation for what was a rare act of tenderness by Prigler. "Thanks, buddy. Enjoy the Borghese."

Still lightheaded from his lack of sleep, Edward walked slowly out of the elevator and through the small lobby. He went to the front desk, touching it delicately with his fingertips, to ask about how to get to the train. The clerk advised him that the station was at the other end of town. He said that Edward's best bet was to take the subway from the Ottaviano station, near

43

the Sistine Chapel. Looking at his watch, he told Edward that he might get there just in time for the 5:15 a.m. train to Salerno.

As soon as Edward was back on the Via Germanico, he was greeted by a full view of St. Peter's. The exterior lighting of the basilica melded with the moonlight, giving the dome a corona. A divine work indeed, Edward mused. But perhaps it was wrapped with Prigler's layers of truth after all—most of them glorious, others perhaps not.

Despite the desk clerk's warning about the time crunch he was facing, Edward stopped. Though not falling to his knees, he genuflected before the most glorious house that had ever been built for God. From his wallet, he took out a black-and-white photo of his mother's father, with miniature Edward on his knee. His grandfather's face was barely visible, tilted to admire his grandson. He prayed to the old man, whom he had known only for a few years as a boy, asking for his protection. Somehow, Edward knew that his grandpa would want him to go to Lavenna. He kissed the photo and placed it carefully into his wallet, as if it were a frail icon or treasure map. The cobwebs were starting to clear from his head.

Walking faster to compensate for lost time, he reached the subway entrance, only to find its overhead doors rolled shut. After waiting respectfully while a newsstand owner babbled with a delivery driver, Edward asked him, "What time does the subway open?"

The man picked up a newspaper. *"Mille lire."*

Edward knew that buying the paper was the price for the information. It was worth the sixty-some-odd cents. He dug into his pocket, and pulled out the money. "Here."

The man handed Edward the paper, and spoke in near-perfect English. "It opens at 5:30."

Edward grabbed his schedule. After the 5:15 a.m. train, the next was not until 8 a.m., making a same-day return to Rome impossible. With only minutes left to make something happen, Edward threw the newspaper on the stand, as if to reject what the man had sold him. He began running back toward the *pensione*, aimlessly. He pounded his sneakers upon the cobblestone, which absorbed them without so much as a patter.

As he began to sweat, he reached a man sweeping the sidewalk slowly. The broom's bristles were long and crisp. Edward yelled excitedly, "Excuse me."

The man remained fixated on his broom.

Edward tried again in his primitive Italian. *"Scusi, signore."* In his panicked state, his adrenaline rushing, he identified the man only as what struck him most—his broom.

Broom looked up. His eyes were like the murky windows of a neglected home.

*So sallow*, Edward could not help but think to himself. They must have been a reflection of the bristles and garbage at which he stared—for hours, days, and years on end. Edward huffed. "A cab. A taxi. Where can I find a taxi?"

Broom clamped his toothless gums without a response.

Edward could not afford to wait any longer. He bolted. The journey to Lavenna was slipping away. His mother's wish was being respected. Looking at his watch and realizing that he could not make it, he stopped in his tracks. Dejected, he tried to catch his breath.

*"Piazza Risorgimento,"* Broom rasped without looking up.

Edward turned.

Broom pointed, signaling for Edward to make a right at the intersection he had reached.

*"Piazza Risorgimento,"* Broom repeated.

In the distance to the right, Edward could see the flicker of a cab's rooftop light. He yelled back to Broom. *"Grazie, signore."* Broom remained hunched, fixed on the garbage that he was sweeping away. Edward then looked to a sky that was beginning to brighten. "Thanks, Grandpa." Smiling like a boy at school recess, he ran to the cab, leaving Broom to his solitary strokes. When Edward asked the cabby if there was enough time to get to the train station by 5:15, the driver patted the passenger side seat, inviting Edward to enter.

Edward arrived at the train station and went directly to the ticket window marked "Naples-Salerno." He leaned into the opening in the glass, and made one last attempt for someone to make his trip to Lavenna direct. *"Un biglietto per Lavenna."*

The clerk folded his ear forward, and replied from behind the clear divide. *"Cosa? Il vino?"* his words echoed, making them difficult to follow while they ricocheted against the narrow walls. The reverberations were particularly disconcerting at such an early hour, after Edward had hurried through the streets of Rome on little sleep.

Echo looked to the clerk next to him—a lanky fellow with a long nose, marked prominently with a bulge along its ridge.

*"Il vino,"* Echo snickered to Nose. For a split second, Edward thought that Nose was going to offer an answer. Instead, he giggled.

Edward knew the clerks were starting their morning with a laugh on him. "Lavenna," he said. He tightened his voice and spoke only in English. "Lavenna. I need a roundtrip ticket to Lavenna. It is very important."

Echo looked to Nose again. The two spoke for what seemed to Edward a deliberately long period of time. Finally, Nose shifted his beak and lifted it toward a drawer beneath the counter, careful not to move an inch with the rest of his body.

Echo opened the drawer, a gold bracelet hanging from his wrist. He retrieved a one-foot-thick directory, plopped it on the counter, and began leafing through.

Nose shifted his seat closer to the directory, appearing to assist his colleague, but hardly able to do so with his eyes glazed over.

As Echo glided his finger down each page, Edward blurted, "I think it's near Salerno."

Echo went through several pages more, and turned to Nose. The two spoke rapidly among themselves. Edward hoped that despite the inauspicious start, they might have something to offer him.

Echo issued a simple reply. "We can no find Lavenna on the *mappa.* You like a ticket to Salerno, roundtrip? It will be seventy thousand lira."

An exasperated Edward laid his money on the counter. As he reorganized himself, Echo and Nose mumbled in Italian. When Edward left, Echo called out, "Sorry we can no help you, *Americano."*

Echo's resonance having been thinned by the distance, Edward detected a mocking tone.

# VII.

## Getting Past Naples

Edward knew that the train would not arrive in Salerno until 8:30 a.m., after a stop in Naples. In his seat, he wanted desperately to sleep, but his unease would not allow it. As passengers exited at the first few stops, the smooth elegance of Rome slipped away and was displaced by a hard edge. At one station, a young woman, primping, brushed by an elderly woman, chin jutted, who hobbled down the aisle in search of a seat. The odors of perfume and mothballs clashed, upsetting Edward's stomach. With the train running again, he saw a constrained beauty in a dormant plow amid an overgrown field. The sun struggled to rise above the clouds, like an infant wanting to escape its crib.

Two and a half hours into the trip, the train window framed for Edward a bleak portrait of Naples. Houses were abandoned—some partially collapsed and shorn of walls, leaving their entrails exposed. In the back yard of one decimated home, a dog sniffed at a discarded and burnt mattress, its sharp springs exposed. Nearby, there was a stagnant puddle of water; seeing a red plastic container with a yellow nozzle, however, Edward realized that the "water" was gasoline. In the yard of another fallen and flayed home, the innards of pipes and furniture were piled high in the open air, topped by a toilet lying on its side. The lid was flipped open, flaunting a streak of human feces upon the white porcelain leading to the hole; flies swarmed in front of it. *Mom is right*, he thought. *Naples is ugly.* This was a place where evil lived, or at least spent its leisure time.

Once in the Naples train station, Edward had to walk across it in order to get his ticket stamped and make the transfer to Salerno. En route, the racket from outside compelled him to look through the door and onto a busy square. He observed all the Neapolitan stereotypes—a group of middle-aged men, the self-proclaimed lords of the square, shouting as they played cards and sipped espresso; women in black shawls, trying to make their sales out of wooden carts; a boy playing an accordion, as his sister extended a tin cup; and a vagrant man, a winter overcoat hanging from his body as he paced and yelled to himself and the entire square, no doubt foretelling the downfall of his beloved *Napoli* like the prophet Amos.

Looking closer at their faces, Edward realized that there was nothing relaxed or easy about these Neapolitans. The skin around their eyes was pinched and leathery—so dry that they could not shed another tear even if they had wanted to. From what he could discern of their banter, it was more rant than rave. People barked past one another, and no one was listening. They spoke not conversation, but noise, and the clamor made a muddle. In the distance, a castle rose above the bedlam.

Edward stepped into the next leg of his trip—the train ride from Naples to Salerno. The skies remained gray and misty, as the rails cut a swath through modest-sized backyards, where women tended to their vegetable plots, indifferent to the rumble of the locomotive.

*Sow and reap—reap and sow—backs like sickles, bent by woe.*

Edward still craved sleep, but was too agitated to shut down. The rotation of the wheels became a piercing rhythm, keeping him awake. His head began to spin; motion sickness set in.

Just as his thoughts were getting away from him, the train slowed for a stop. When the signpost came into focus, he saw that it read *Pompeii*—the famous city frozen by volcanic fire. Edward got excited when a group of children ran by a spouting fountain. They plunged their faces into the water and shouted with elation.

Through his window, Edward saw that when the parade ended, a lone teen straggled by in torn blue jeans. He glared at the same upwelling of water. Instead of immersing himself in it, he slapped it scornfully. After a pause, he slapped it again, this time harder, appearing to be frustrated that he had not discontinued the spring. He prepared for a third swipe, but stopped when the train's whistle blew. His feet resumed their slow shuffle, and his head dropped.

As Edward's train pulled away, he tried to moisten his cottony mouth to stave off a bitter thirst.

The train wheels turning again, Edward's misgivings raced through his mind. Perhaps he should abort in Salerno and return to Rome to rejoin Coyne and Prigler. There was still enough time to get back for pasta and wine at a trattoria, over which he could share his mini-adventure. Before Edward could think through the logistics, the train darted into a mountain tunnel.

*Turning and blackness, blackness and turning—fear, hope, and pride, violently churning.*

Edward felt as though the ride was shrieking at him in an unknown language, like one of the Neapolitans in the square. He closed his eyes to get away from it all, only to see the tortured face of the vagrant. He wanted Edward to listen, but Edward could not comprehend him.

When the train shot out the other side, the shrill cry subsided into the calm and spaced clicking of the wheels upon the track. The beauty of the Sorrentine Peninsula popped, the flowers blooming under the sun and blue skies of the high-cliffed coast. Even the overgrown brush appeared to waltz in the breeze. For the moment, Edward felt at ease, recognizing that he was in Amalfi, a place he had visited with his family just years earlier. He opened the window and bathed in the fresh air. He rested his eyes, choosing to see the landscape through its scent and sound.

# VIII.

## Walking a Familiar Promenade

Edward was awakened by the absence of movement. The only sound was a chorus of birds chirping. A conductor made his way through the aisle, inspecting the empty seats. The sign outside his window read *Salerno*.

He hurried off the train in search of a bus that would take him to Lavenna. Despite not knowing if such a route existed, he felt he was almost there. He found a ticket window, and stood in line. A young man roughly his age filed in behind, wearing a deep purple shirt. Purple Shirt's pearl-white buttons had been stitched on sturdily. Famished for conversation after his long and lonely ride, Edward placed his hand on Purple Shirt's shoulder. *"Mi scusi. Non parlo bene l' italiano."*

Purple Shirt smiled charitably, placing his hand over Edward's. "Your Italian is okay, my friend, but me speak English. Where you want to—"

"Lavenna," Edward replied before Purple Shirt could finish.

Purple Shirt perused the chalk-scribbled board overhead, which listed the schedule of buses. "It look like there is no..."

Edward's heart thumped into his throat.

Purple Shirt continued. "Ah! Bus for Lavenna." He turned square to Edward. "Only one bus for Lavenna today." He looked at his watch. "It leave at two." Purple Shirt squinted to find the right slot on the board again. He made a full clockwise loop with his hand. "It come back here again from

Lavenna at six."

Edward squeezed his new friend's arm, with all of the gusto of his *Americanismo*. "*Grazie*. Thank you. Thank you, *molto*."

Purple Shirt tipped his head and pursed his lips humbly. He returned to his place in line, and retrieved the rolled newspaper from beneath his armpit to read while waiting. Edward felt a sense of irony when he saw that Purple Shirt was skimming the same paper that Edward had bought hours earlier in Rome, when he was scrambling to get to the train station.

After Edward purchased his bus ticket, it was only 8:45 a.m. He needed something to do for the next few hours. Ambling out of the station, he was drawn by the sparkling of the sun upon the bay, and the promenade beside it. Rather than being a treadmill for morning joggers or a raceway for hurried businessmen, as it would be in New York, the walkway was less ambitious, the travelers upon it moving at a leisurely pace. A lone woman stepped slowly, her hands clasped behind her back as she looked out at the water's horizon. A young boy was being pulled by his dog at the end of a leash. A trio of men, dressed smartly in business attire, strolled arm-in-arm; the tall one in the middle wore a brimmed hat, doing most of the talking—probably brokering some kind of business deal. It was all so different to Edward, so relaxed and movie-like, that he had to be part of it. He spilled out into the street, without even checking for oncoming cars. A driver pulled up short, barely missing him. Instead of honking his horn, the man smiled, extending his hand for Edward to cross in front of him.

On the promenade, Edward recognized the mosaic of brown cobblestones that he stood upon, framed elegantly with beige concrete. He realized that he had walked this way before, with his mother, father, and siblings, during a previous family trip to Italy—years ago. Slowing his natural pace to that of those around him, he saw that the cobblestones were not laid in linear fashion, but instead appeared to be in a scallop-shell design. Not distracted by a debate with his brother, nor a rush to get to the next place, he enjoyed the smell of the sea's salt from one side, and the stand of fuzzy trees on the other. Mountains rose in the distance, protecting the shore like the Praetorian Guard. He stopped to read a sign, and learned for the first time that this slice of tranquility was named *Lungomare Trieste*.

No sooner had Edward immersed himself in the peaceful interlude, than he felt a stir in his stomach. He and his family had been so close to Lavenna, yet returning to the small town was a subject never broached. He and his brother and sister did not even know the name "Lavenna," as any questions about their mother's past were dismissed summarily. As his father had told him back in the family kitchen, asking her about her childhood in Italy was like asking her to pet a scorpion. If only he could go back and read her mind when the family had walked this same way without a care in the world. Edward looked to the sea. Boys wearing oversized rubber boots boarded wooden boats, loading their nets and poles. At home, out in the Hamptons or on Cape Cod, they would be splashing around, their tanned chests bare and glistening.

In the hope of making the unease in his belly go away, Edward stopped at an open-air storefront. Although it was still morning—a time which he was trained to eat only eggs, pancakes, or cereal—he bought a *panino* of prosciutto and mozzarella. As he gripped the sandwich to sink his teeth into it, he laughed to himself, thinking how much smaller and less garnished it was than his father's supposedly proper Italian creations. Edward wondered whether there was more of America in his dad's appetite for the homeland than his dad realized.

Before Edward could take a bite, a woman in her fifties offered him a newspaper titled *Le Notizie Cattoliche*. She did not utter a word. She was not attractive, except for her olive-oiled skin. Though the woman was only inches away, Edward began to speak loudly and slowly, as if that would help her understand him. "I do not live here. I am an American visiting."

"*Va bene*," the woman whispered. Her sweet breath overcame the fish-and-salt-scented air. Sweet Breath stroked her hand along Edward's cheek, flush with pride. "But you are *italiano*," she said. "You start here, I know. *Come si chiama?*"

Edward was stunned by her insight; he replied reflexively, without translating her question in his head. "My name is Edoardo." He rested his sandwich on the counter. "And I am a Catholic." He clenched his fist, as if to test his own vigor for the words. *"Un cattolico."* Church bells rang across the promenade. Edward pointed with fervor to the church bells, and clenched his fist again, thinking of the image of Prigler making fun of the Benedictine monks. "Catholics. We are the best!"

Sweet Breath did not turn—instead, she kept to Edward with the evenness of a mother. She smiled, caressing his face again. *"Che bello che sei,"* she said, and then paused. "But God is not best, or in a bell. God is only and everywhere." She laid her palm flat on his chest. *"Dio sta qua."*

Entranced, Edward noticed that the straps on one of the woman's leather sandals were frayed, about to snap. He reached for his pocket, only to have Sweet Breath intercept his hand. She guided it back to his breast. "God," she said, waiting for Edward to feel the beat of his own heart, "is right here." Before departing, Sweet Breath shared one last thought. *"La cosa più importante è non dimenticarti mai le tue origini."* She caught herself and translated. "Most importante, Edoardo. No forget your beginning."

"I will not forget," he replied. *"Le origini."*

As Edward parted from the woman and the promenade, he pulled his wallet from his back pocket, and retrieved the picture of himself on his grandfather's knee. *"Le origini,"* he whispered.

# IX.

## Riding a School Bus to His Mother's Home,

## Swishing the Ball through an Imaginary Net

When Edward reached the bus for Lavenna, he found himself among children playing. The boys' loosened collars and ties suggested that they had just finished school. Through a gap in the hubbub, Edward saw a young girl standing alone against the rail. Taken aback by the way she resembled his mother when she was a child, he fumbled through his backpack for a picture of Marie in her youth. The resemblance was uncanny, as if the photo had come to life: the girl was petite, with hazel-green eyes, ivory-white skin, and a perfectly straight nose. She was at once angelic and strong. Even the hair looked the same.

The roar of a bus interrupted Edward's reverie; its sign read *Lavenna*. The boys continued their pursuit of one another up the bus steps, and Edward followed. On the bus, he waited for the girl to board. He studied every face that entered. Hers was not one of them. Still he waited, certain that she would become part of the plot and lead him back to Lavenna. When the doors slammed shut without her, Edward listened intently in the hope that she would knock to reopen them.

But the bus pulled away, its engine idling while the driver cranked it into the next gear.

On the highway, Edward felt as though the children's energy was enough to propel the bus the remainder of the way. The girls jammed in the first few rows, heads bobbing with chatter, legs dangling giddily. The boys buzzed around the rest of the bus, competing for the attention of the one they called Gianni. Taller than the others, with a combination of blond hair and blue eyes that Edward had not seen since he left Rome, Gianni was the leader of the pack. With his back to the driver, Gianni stood in the center of the aisle. He rolled a ball from a newspaper, nodding at the heaviest of the boys to go to the rear. *"Dai, Ubaldo."*

*"Si certo, Gianni,"* answered Ubaldo, as if taking an order. He chugged his portly frame to the rear, turned toward Gianni and the rest of the crowd, and made a hoop with his extended arms.

Gianni completed his paper ball, and reached in his back pocket for tape to fasten it. It was apparent to Edward that Gianni and his minions were taking part in a daily ritual. Gianni cut the tape with his teeth and applied it to the ball. *"Finito,"* he gasped. He winked at Ubaldo, who braced his legs and hooped his arms. Ubaldo replied with a jowly smirk, just happy to be a part of Gianni's court.

Edward sat amused, thinking of his own elementary school days on the bus, and the bravado, insecurity, and excitement that filled the seats.

*"Ho scelto,"* Gianni called out. He headed toward Ubaldo to pick his team. Gianni dominated the aisle with his swagger, and cries of his name filled the air as each of the boys pleaded for his favor. Gianni surveyed the anxious crowd, stroking his lips with his forefinger.

"Pippo." Gianni tapped the head of a tiny boy with buck teeth and slicked back hair. Pippo jumped up and down in place, elated that he had been selected.

Gianni continued his paces down the aisle. "Paolo," he said, squeezing the shoulder of a tall bespectacled boy, his shirt buttoned all the way to the top and tucked neatly into his Sunday pants. Paolo went into his pregame warmup, extending his arms horizontally, and moving them in circles.

As Gianni reached the end of the aisle, he gave Ubaldo a playful jab in the belly. Ubaldo remained unflinching, his arms extended as the hoop. Gianni turned to the other side of the aisle.

"Crispino," Gianni said, announcing his next choice—a boy with black locks and a devilish smile. Crispino winked back at Gianni, as if they were equals. Gianni patted him on the head to remind him that they were not.

Gianni returned to his spot at the point. He looked next to him, at a boy whose attention was elsewhere, gazing out the window. "Severino," he said, emphasizing the last two syllables. Shaken from his trance, the boy turned toward Gianni. Pale, and wearing a crucifix outside his white-collared shirt, Severino accepted the nomination with a tender smile. Gianni slapped him on the chest and repeated his name—this time louder. "Severino!"

Before the game could go any further, a man with a moustache and cap approached Edward. The cap had a shiny black visor. *"Biglietto?"*

Edward gave Visor his ticket. "Lavenna." He asked a favor in the best Italian he could muster. *"Per favore, dimmi quando arriviamo a Lavenna?"*

Without looking up, Visor nodded—he understood Edward wanted to be told when the bus arrived in Lavenna. Returning to the front, he patted Gianni on the head.

Gianni swiped his hand through his hair, returning it to its original place. *"Andiamo,"* squeaked Pippo.

*"Aspetta,"* responded Gianni. He turned toward Edward, and extended him the ball. *"Americano,* do you want to play?"

"How do you know I'm an American?" asked Edward, certain that Gianni would comment on his struggle with the Italian language.

Instead, Gianni pointed to Edward's backpack, stitched with a JanSport label. "We use if we are in army."

A few laughs flitted from the crowd.

Gianni grasped an imaginary backpack on his shoulder, and lifted his knees high in the air. "Or if we climb *una montagna.*"

The students bellowed with glee.

Edward enjoyed the image of his more youthful but similarly charismatic and confident self. He did not want to upstage the king in his miniature court. "No," he said. "*Grazie.*"

"That's okay," Gianni said, passing the ball to Pippo. "You are afraid to lose because we are better."

Edward felt an inner roil, but suppressed it by reminding himself he was among children.

Standing atop his seat, Pippo caught the ball with his small hands. "But I think *Americano's* food is better. Hamburger, cheese hamburger, hot dog." His buck teeth biting hard on his lower lip, he pretended to dribble the ball.

"You no need hamburger or hot dog," Gianni scolded, "when we have pasta, pizza *napolitana*, and *gelato*." He pointed to Paolo, indicating to Pippo that he should stop dribbling and pass the ball.

In possession, Paolo extended his long arm slowly, arched it and bent his wrist without releasing the ball. "But America send a man to the moon."

"And Italy discover America—Columbo, Verrazzano, Vespucci." Gianni's brow furrowed. He thrust his forefinger mightily toward Paolo. "America is named after Vespucci." He waved the back of his hand toward Crispino.

Paolo stopped shooting and distributed. He tucked back into his pants the inch of his shirt that had been loosened.

Crispino moved the ball through his legs. "You guys make Gianni mad. He think Italy better than Ameriga."

Gianni nodded.

Crispino went behind his back with the ball. "Mad like King Kong in New York—on top of the Building Empire State!"

"Made into a great movie by *un italiano*!" Gianni peered at Edward for confirmation.

"Yes. Dino De Laurentiis," Edward replied, admiring the boy's mental agility.

"Dino!" Gianni shouted, thrusting his arm in the air.

"Dino!" his fans joined in.

Gianni clapped, commanding them to resume the game. He pointed his thumb toward Severino beside him.

Crispino raised his thick eyebrows and dished.

Severino's reflexes were too slow. The ball hit him on the chest, on the spot where his crucifix hung.

Edward swooped in to pick up the ball for Severino.

"*Grazie*," Severino said as he reached up to accept the ball from Edward, who stood a good eight inches taller. He turned. "America is very kind, Gianni."

"But all the saints," Gianni whispered. "They are Italian." He pulled the ball delicately from Severino's clasped hands. "San Francesco, Sant'Antonio."

Edward was surprised that the clever boy had not pointed out that America had emulated the saints' names in two of its cities.

"*Sì*," Severino smiled. "San Francesco, Sant'Antonio, San Gerardo."

"San Gerardo," echoed the others, in honor of the patron saint of expectant mothers, who had lived in the nearby town of Caposele.

Satisfied by how he had closed out the round, Gianni exclaimed, "And I am like Giulio Cesare, strongest man of all times." Gianni took his shot at the hoop.

Ubaldo widened his eyes to track the ball's trajectory. Nervous the shot might miss, he lunged forward. As the ball drew close to his rim, the bus took a turn. Ubaldo stumbled and fell in the aisle. The shot went over him.

The crowd erupted at the spectacle.

"*Un'altra volta!*" Gianni shouted, silencing them so that he could try again.

Ubaldo stood up and dusted his stomach.

"*Vesuvio!*" Gianni yelled out, jesting that Ubaldo's rumbling belly had caused the bus to shake.

Ubaldo scrambled to the ball, picked it up, and threw it back to Gianni before re-forming the hoop.

"This time, no move," Gianni instructed. "I need no help. *Sono Giulio Cesare.*"

The shot floated toward the hoop. It banked off Ubaldo's chest, hit the rim, and fell off. Ubaldo bent down immediately to pick it up. "*Un'altra volta,*" he puffed.

Edward could no longer resist. His competitive juices overcame him. When Ubaldo threw the ball back to Gianni, Edward intercepted it. As Gianni stood stunned, Edward gestured for Ubaldo to make the hoop.

After checking with Gianni, Ubaldo did so.

Edward's shot sailed through, a dead center score. "Swish!" Edward exclaimed.

"Sweesh," the admiring girls said, in harmony.

"And I am Julius Irving," Edward said, sticking his finger into Gianni's chest, grinding it as he spoke. "The greatest player ever in a game made by America."

Gianni winced. He rubbed his chest where Edward had poked him.

Edward looked up to see that everyone was staring at him. Their eyes, just seconds ago fixed on him in admiration, were now beginning to bore a hole through him.

A little girl stepped up to Gianni. Edward saw that it was the one at the station who resembled his mother as a child. She had in fact boarded the bus without Edward noticing. "*Stai bene?*" she asked Gianni, maternally.

"*Sto bene,*" he replied, confirming that he was all right. To prove that he could take care of himself, he rubbed his chest clean of Edward's jabbing.

The little girl paused to look at Edward, and then turned her back on him.

Embarrassed by his ugly show of zeal with a boy half his size, Edward sat down.

# X.

## A False Start

As Edward sulked in his less-than-glorious performance, a classic stone-built village appeared in the window, with a church standing in the center. The scene was just as Edward had imagined. He had finally arrived in Lavenna. The boys filed out quietly, shoulders dropped. Gianni leaned into his mother's aproned embrace. Edward brought up the rear. As he descended the steps, he enjoyed the evergreen smell of the mountain air.

But before Edward set foot on the walkway that led to the church, he was halted by Visor, who had already exited and was planted outside the door. "This is no Lavenna. Lavenna next."

Edward looked back at the bus driver, desperate for a different answer. The reply was the same. "Lavenna next stop."

"How long?" Edward asked. "How many minutes?"

The driver looked at his watch. "Thirty *minuti*."

Dejected, Edward dragged himself back on the bus, taking a seat behind the driver. As it wended its way through barren mountain slopes, Edward was the only passenger; he felt more alone than he had ever been. Nausea set in again. As the bus climbed the undulating mountains, he felt lost at sea. The passage was precarious—one hasty turn would send them off the cliff into a deadly gorge. Edward concentrated on the only thing that seemed steady and reassuring—the driver's thick-veined forearm shifting the engine's gears. Forearm was in control of the stick, whistling tunes through the grade changes. Forearm would deliver him—or so Edward convinced himself.

His tour of *il Bel Paese* was again getting ugly. At one pass, a sickly goat staggered by the roadside, its flesh hanging from the bone as an equally famished and despondent herder prodded the animal from behind. Around the next curve, which was bordered by scattered gray rock, an old man rode a bicycle in the opposite direction. He had an expression of relief, Edward thought—as if he was happy to escape the yet-undiscovered misery of Lavenna. The rims of the bike's wheels were bent, making his exodus wobbly. In the distance, trees were robbed of all their leaves, left only with dying branches pointed upward to the sky as they wailed like the biblical Job, despairing in undeserved plight. Under the branches, an exhausted laborer sought refuge from the pummeling sun, his eyes rolled up into his head. Beneath a bridge, an arid riverbed gasped.

Edward mused as to what could possibly await him in a town that was a destination for no one or nothing.

Finally, Forearm let go of the stick to point ahead. "Lavenna," he said. He retook the stick and resumed his whistle.

Edward could not discern a skyline, but he assumed it would arise from around a corner. In the meantime, he moved to confirm that the bus would return at 6:00 p.m., as Purple Shirt had told him at the bus station in Salerno. *"Torni alle sei?"*

Forearm shifted into low to take the hill. *"Sì."*

Edward reclined in his seat, and looked at his watch, which read 3:30. *"Fra due e mezzo ore, sì?"*

"No." Forearm pushed hard to stabilize the bus on the rugged incline, causing the engine's innards to bray. *"Alle sei di mattina—tra quattordici ore e mezza."*

Edward's face went ashen. *Six in the morning!* He cursed himself for not picking up that Purple Shirt's clockwise gesture, in the bus station under the chalkboard, meant the next day. His pores opened wide, and sweat began to stream.

62

Forearm, still struggling with the rough terrain, was no longer whistling.

The bus climbed to its end and kicked up dirt all around. When the dust settled, the medieval town Edward had envisioned was nowhere to be found. There were no fountains, stone facades, or narrow streets. All that he could see were brown-stained wooden cabins cowering in an encampment. Edward looked into Forearm's eyes, desperate to change the reality of what he was hearing and seeing. *"Non è Lavenna. Non è possibile."*

Forearm reached through his side window with a rag, to wipe the dirt off his windshield. *"Sì, è Lavenna,"* he replied evenly, as he scratched a stubborn speck with his fingernail.

With his backpack over his shoulder, Edward moved timidly down the bus steps.

Forearm halted his cleaning, and called after Edward, *"Amico mio, non c'è niente qua. Torna con me ora a Salerno—gratis."*

Edward understood that Forearm was telling him that there was nothing in Lavenna, and was offering to take him back to Salerno, free of charge. He declined. Having come this far, he knew that even if there was nothing for him to learn or discover in the town, it was his filial obligation to understand every inch of the nothingness.

*"In bocca al lupo."* Forearm wished Edward good luck.

Thinking of the prospect of a cold night, Edward checked his backpack—not for his map or the picture of him with his grandfather, but for the never-worn sweater his mother had knitted for him.

# XI.

## The Taste of Dirt

Edward dragged his feet across the dirt and broken asphalt, his legs cramped from the long ride. The wind swept the dust into his nostrils, making him uneasy. Though he had learned the touch and smell of dirt as a summer laborer for his father's construction company, in those days he filled his shovel to improve or fortify something—a sidewalk, a roadway, or a lamppost. That dirt was soil, moist and rich, almost like coffee; this dirt was something worse—disparate and faded, incapable of being gathered or compacted.

As he continued his slow shuffle, he gazed at rows of brown wooden boxes with no sign of inhabitants. The doorways of the brown boxes were empty; strands of beads hung from aluminum-lined lintels, lending an illusion of separation from the dirt outside. Each brown wooden box was the same; only the beads were different. Anyone could enter them from the crudely cut road that was just inches away; the beads were indifferent. The dirt was everywhere—on the road, in the air, sticking to the brown boxes and their beads.

*Wood and dirt, dirt on wood—a gale to cleanse the town, if only one could.*

Edward looked back to call out to Forearm, but the bus was too far gone; only its exhaust remained. Edward was abandoned and scared in the place where his mother had been born. He clutched the sweater she had made for him.

Without a sound or face to track, Edward crept to the town's makeshift church, which was constructed of the same brown wood, and enveloped in an iron fence with a gate at the front. Beyond the church's iron gates were the front doors, made of thin plywood; unlocked, they flailed in the wind. He shook the gate to get to the doors, but it would not open. Pressing up against the gate's irons like a prisoner, Edward searched for any glimpse of the church that the shuddering doors might give. A dust-filled breeze opened the left door. The sanctuary was dark, and Edward was unable to discern anything.

A sudden gust pinned the right door open against the wall. There was still not enough light to see much, but the interior of the door had a poster nailed to it, featuring four images of Mary. Edward waited for his eyes to adjust so that he could read the subscripts beneath each picture. The blur of the letters clarified: *Semplicità, Purità, Ubbedienza, Mortificazione.* He understood why simplicity, purity, and obedience were associated with the Virgin Mother. But why the inclusion of mortification? Why were shame, humiliation, or degradation being extolled? To Edward, mortification was not a virtue, but an undesirable state of defeat and decline, to be fought against rather than embraced—a sacrilegious way of saying "no" to God's gift of life. He grew uneasy at the possibility that he did not really understand the word. Another draft blew, and the right-hand door slammed shut.

Amid the lashing of the doors, Edward heard a matronly voice from across the square, leading a lesson for a group of little girls. The nun's honey-dipped tones eased the tension he felt at the threshold of the church. On their instructor's cue, the girls repeated in high-pitched tones the great cities of Italy: "*Roma, Milano, Firenze, e Venezia.*" They paused for their teacher's prompting.

Edward rushed for the brown box in which the class was being held, leaving behind the church's forbidding gates and doors.

The girls began again: "*Napoli, Salerno, e Laven—*"

Edward's knock on the door interrupted the recitation.

The girls cried out, "*Avanti, avanti,*" each in their own note.

Edward opened the door easily and stepped through.

The girls fell silent, their mouths agape.

Edward beheld a young nun at the head of the class, wearing a brown wooden cross around her neck. Unlike the town, her brown wood was clean, its grains deep. The nun greeted Edward with a smile that flooded the room with light. *"Buon giorno."*

Edward walked to Young Nun. He took a gulp to wet his dry throat, and spoke in his best Italian, trying to explain that he was from the United States—that his mother had been born in Lavenna, and left around 1946. *"Io sono degli Stati Uniti. Mia mamma era nata in questo paese, è partita circa mille novencento quarantasei."* With Young Nun listening graciously, Edward stuttered to ask her for help in finding his mother's birth records. *"Sto guardando,"* he said, remembering the right word for "looking for" and correcting himself. *"Cerco il suo certificato di nascita."* Remembering to pay respect, he asked for aid, *"Mi potrebbe aiutare?"*

Young Nun turned to the little girls, instructing them to remain in the classroom. *"State qui."* As she led Edward out the door, the girls disobeyed, jumping from their desks to the rally cry of *"Andiamo!"*

They all reached an unshaven man, slight of build, standing in the shadow of what appeared to be the town hall. He was smoking a half-lit cigarette. The municipal center was a small brown box, just like the others. Only its entrance was different—a solid door, with a sign above it.

With deference to Half-Lit and on Edward's behalf, Young Nun requested that Edward be permitted to search for his mother's birth records. *"Lui sa leggere un certificato?"* When Half-Lit appeared unmoved, Young Nun continued, emphasizing that Edward's mother was born here, perhaps at the same time as Half-Lit. *"Sua madre è nata qui, forse allo stesso tempo come Lei."*

Half-Lit did not bother to remove his cigarette from his mouth. *"No. È chiuso. Apre lunedi."*

Edward was shaken, knowing that Half-Lit had said that the hall was closed and would not reopen until Monday. He pleaded his case directly, stepping up with his American size, hoping to impress the man. "I have come all the way from the United States. Monday is three days away, and I have to leave tonight. I need to see the records."

Half-Lit pulled his cigarette from his mouth and stared back.

Edward could sense that something was registering.

Half-Lit peered hard.

Edward smiled.

Half-Lit looked over at Young Nun, and then askance. He tapped his ash and drew, puffing a ring of smoke. "*No. È chiuso.*"

Edward turned to Young Nun for support, but she did not speak.

One of the little girls, cheeks rosy, volunteered "Don Raimondo." She ran off to the church, shouting "Don Raimondo," while the other girls giggled. After darting into the church's side and disappearing momentarily, the girl ran back, gasping for air. "Don Raimondo. He will help. He say wait fifteen minute."

Young Nun stroked the girl's cheek. She raised her hand to wish Edward luck and God's protection, "*Buona fortuna e Dio ti protegga.*" She walked back to her place in the school.

Half-Lit spat out his cigarette without bothering to stamp out its dwindled flame. He stepped with purpose up a path that was dead-ended by a mound of garbage. As he made a right to pass through his bead-draped lintel, a rodent scurried from the refuse.

Edward stood in the middle of the square, surrounded by the girls—the smallest ones gawking, their older classmates trying to make conversation. The girl who summoned Don Raimondo started in. "My uncle go to New York City," she said. She looked around at the town's brown boxes and shot her hand up as high as she could, standing on her tiptoes. "Buildings are big in New York."

Edward opened his backpack, and placed his sweater back inside. "Yes," he said. In his mind, he made the comparison between Lavenna's squat brown boxes and the sleek towering glass of New York City—*mindboggling.* "Yes—they are called skyscrapers. They nearly touch the clouds." He took a deep breath. "Like the Twin Towers in New York. They are tall and strong—nothing can destroy them."

Another girl stepped up, her face narrow, her eyelashes rising. "Woman can have skyscraper, yes?" She shook her head anxiously. "Yes?" she said again, already knowing the answer.

Edward expounded. "Women…" He stopped himself and pointed at the girl. "You can build a skyscraper and keep it all for yourself."

The girl turned toward her classmates, extended her arms as high as she could, and clapped.

The other girls responded by giving themselves a standing ovation.

From a different brown box, a pack of young boys emerged. The capo of the visiting troop was a miniature man whose strut led the rest. He stopped before Edward, his soldiers huddled around him. His brow was laden with flecks of cement, a trowel protruding from his side pocket.

Edward was shocked that a boy so young was already a mason, and that his demeanor was so mature beyond his years. Edward could not help but to focus on the cement on the boy's brow—so heavy, Edward thought, that it must be obstructing the boy's vision.

The girls raced to explain Edward's situation to Cement Brow. Processing the barrage of excited chatter, he remained steady. His voice cracked, revealing that beneath his weathered exterior, he was still a boy going through puberty. "What is the name of you mamma?" he said.

"Maria Del Cielo," Edward responded, with his best Italian accent.

Cement Brow nodded like a businessman, careful not to show emotion. He waded through the rows of other boys, and pulled out a paunchy one. His skin was smooth, Edward thought to himself, yet untouched by the rigors of labor. Cement Brow kept cool. "He is Nicola Del Cielo."

Edward grabbed Nicola's hand, and knelt on one knee so that he could look him in the eye. "Do you have family in the United States? Do you have Del Cielo family in America?"

Nicola paused, looking back at Edward without a blink.

Edward repeated himself. "Do you have cousins, aunts, or uncles in the United States?"

"*Boh*," responded Nicola, turning to Cement Brow for help.

Cement Brow translated in a subdued voice.

Nicola's body seemed to burn with the desire to say "*sì*"—instead, he whispered *"no."*

Edward picked up a pebble, and pelted it back into the town's dirt. "Damn it," he said. After taking a deep breath, Edward cleaned his hand against his back pocket, and squeezed Nicola's narrow chin affectionately, though he was clearly disappointed. *"Grazie, Nicola."*

Cement Brow interceded. "Del Cielo is name *molto commune*. There are many. Your *famiglia* maybe *sono tutti morti*, except in America." Cement Brow tried to push Nicola back to the spot from which he had been plucked, but Nicola would not budge.

Pretending to be amused by Nicola's resistance, Cement Brow changed the subject by continuing his interrogation of Edward. "Where did you mamma live in Lavenna?"

"I don't know."

"Did you mamma have cousins in Lavenna? Aunts or uncles?"

"I don't know."

"Who were you mamma's friends in Lavenna?"

Edward bit his lip and raised his eyebrows, embarrassed by his ignorance. Cement Brow laughed. "Do you know you mamma?"

Saddened by the profundity of Cement Brow's question, Edward did not respond. He did not really know his mother; that was why he had set off for this desolate place. The wind kicked more of the town's dirt into his nostrils, causing them to sting. Edward wanted his journey to be over. His simple questions would be left unanswered, their layers unexplored. There was nothing but vile dirt, and Edward was being forced to eat it. Disgusted, he spat on the ground.

# XII.

## Creating a Record

A door creaked opened from behind the church. "Don Raimondo!" the children yelled.

Realizing that he would not find any relatives, Edward still relished the possible appearance of a white-collared town elder, someone who may have been a young priest when his mother was running around as a little girl—or at least one of her contemporaries. He got neither. A man emerged; his gait and hair suggested that he was no more than thirty-five, and he was dressed in layman's clothing. The priest grinned, speaking in perfect English. "My name is Father Raimondo," he said. "Raymond if you like. May I help you?"

Edward moved two steps closer to rattle off his facts. "Yes, Father. My name is Edward Bennett. I am from the United States. My mother lived here as a little girl. Her name was Maria Del Cielo. She left in 1946, after the war." He took the black-and-white photo of his mother out of his backpack, and thrust it in Don Raimondo's face. "This is what she looked like as a girl." He also removed from his wallet the photo of his grandfather. "And this was her father, with me on his knee."

Don Raimondo examined the first photo. His dimples grew. "She was a beautiful young lady." He shifted his gaze to the second. "And your grandfather was very proud of you."

Edward's hopes grew.

Don Raimondo returned the pictures to Edward. "But I am sorry. I do not know her or her family. I am new to this church. I was raised in Acquaviva delle Fonti, near Bari on the Adriatic Coast." He gazed above. "I'm still getting to know these mountains. They are beautiful, yet strange, and made of many mysteries. They used to fill the rivers with water, but now the rivers run dry." His dimples reappeared as he looked at Nicola, standing at Edward's side. "He is a Del Cielo. His name is Nicola Del Cielo."

Edward folded his arms. "I already asked him if he knew of any family in the United States. He didn't."

Don Raimondo pushed his thick, black-framed glasses up the bridge of his nose. "Let me try and ask him. Perhaps he did not understand you." After a back-and-forth with Nicola, Don Raimondo remained silent and chagrined.

Edward relieved him. "I know." He glanced at Cement Brow. "This guy told me there are a lot of Del Cielos in the town. It's a common name."

"He's right, but still." Don Raimondo held his finger in the air. He seemed eager to help. Edward wondered whether it was just because he did not want to end the excitement for the children, who must have been in need of a break from the valley grunge. He invited Edward into the church sacristy. "Let's go to the church and check the baptismal records. Maybe we will find something there." He turned to the short but bubbling crowd, and gave them the same instruction to remain. "*Restate qua.*" He pivoted toward Cement Brow. "*Assicurati che loro restino qui. Sai quanto è piccola la sagrestia. La settimana scorsa, mentre facevi il chierichetto, mi hai spinto, rovesciando tutto il vino.*"

The rest of the children giggled, covering their mouths so as to not laugh more at the blushing Cement Brow.

"What did you say, Father?" Edward asked with a smile.

"I told him to make sure that they stay behind. He knows how small the sacristy is. Last week, when he served as altar boy, he bumped into me and spilled the wine."

Cement Brow clapped loudly and repeated the priest's instruction to the children. "*Restate qua.*"

Inside the well-appointed room, rich with mahogany and scarce of light, Don Raimondo's white sparkling garments hung on a peg, above a table of chalices inlaid with gems. The priest opened the door to a glass cabinet, filled with leather-bound ledgers labeled by decade. "What year was your mother born, Edward?"

"1935. November 16, 1935."

Don Raimondo pulled down the volume titled 1930–1940 and carried it to the table. He reached for a handkerchief to clear the dust from the cover. Folding the handkerchief and putting it back in its place, he dabbed his forefinger into a moist circular sponge, making it easier to turn the tome's thinning pages. "Very well, let's see if we can find your mother, Signora Maria Del Cielo."

He turned page after page. It was a marvel that the aged parchment had not disintegrated, Edward thought. He glazed over the litany of entries that meant nothing to him. As the priest turned faster, the yellowed leaves were beginning to merge into one another, a jumbled mess that Edward could not keep up with, much less grasp.

Don Raimondo stopped on a particular page and studied it. He moved his finger among the names so that Edward could follow. The blue ink popped, and the cursive lines were crisp, as if they were still wet, penned just before Edward entered the sacristy. Edward followed Don Raimondo's finger with his own, sliding it over each inscription, hoping to touch his mother. Edward looked ahead to see that the priest was about to finish the page. They were running out of space. Don Raimondo lifted the bottom corner of the page to peek at the next without interrupting Edward's search. The holy man grimaced, and pounded on the table. "I thought it would be on this page!" He looked at Edward sadly. "I'm sorry. There is nothing."

"How do you know?" Edward asked.

"Because the next page begins with children born in 1936."

The two sat silently, in a pall of disappointment.

"Are you sure that your mother was born in 1935?"

"Positive," Edward responded, impressed that the priest had become so emotionally invested in Edward's search. "But I really appreciate that you tried. I don't even know you and…." Edward fumbled. "It's very kind of you."

"Don't flatter me," Don Raimondo replied. "Or yourself for that matter. This is as much a puzzle as anything else, and I am frustrated that I cannot piece it together."

Edward was touched by the priest's modesty, knowing that despite his deflection, he was genuinely interested in helping Edward. At the same time, Edward was stirred by the holy man's competitiveness, which he felt was real and similar to his own. "You remind me of the priests who taught me at home."

"Oh, yeah? Who were they?"

Edward noticed that the top corner of the page they both had scanned was splitting. "Benedictine monks," Edward answered as he reached for the frayed corners. He began to pull them from one another. "Is it possible, Father, that we have two pages stuck together?"

"It's possible," Don Raimondo replied with a widening smile.

Edward checked to see if the priest minded if Edward proceeded. "May I?"

"Please."

Edward peeled the pages slowly, careful not to rip them. The separation completed, he laid the left leaf down, and smoothed it with his palm. He glanced at Don Raimondo, then back at the page. He moved his head back and forth, line to line. He looked at Don Raimondo again, as the priest was reclining in his seat. "Aren't you going to help me?"

"You don't need my help, *amico mio.*"

"Thanks for nothing." Edward smiled at his new friend.

Edward read the names out loud. "DeMarco, Palladini, Bezzone…" His eyes shot from their sockets, and he planted his finger on the page. "There it is, goddamnit," he shouted. He looked up immediately. "I'm sorry, Father, I got excited."

"Don't be silly." Don Raimondo drew closer to look. "What did you find?"

Edward bit his lip. "November 16, 1935—Maria Del Cielo. My mother. We found her, Don Raimondo. That's her." Edward scrutinized the names on the birth certificate, but could recognize only his grandmother and grandfather, Nedda and Maurizio. He pointed. "Father, I know that Nedda and Maurizio were my mother's parents. So who are these other people?"

Don Raimondo opened the sacristy's lone transom to allow more light. He squinted. "Well, written here is an Antonio Del Cielo. This space is for godparents, but he's too young." After a studied pause, he elaborated: "Then again, some families have a young relative serve as a godparent."

Edward cut in. "Oh my God—there are the names of my brother, my sister, and me, and the years we were born. How the hell?" Edward halted. "I'm sorry, Father. I did it again..."

Don Raimondo gripped Edward's shoulder. "Don't worry. Hell is not a bad word. It's what our church leaders teach us to fear."

Edward was surprised at the ease, almost disdain, with which the priest referred to the fiery depths that had been seared into his consciousness as a youth.

The priest continued. "What's your question?"

Edward spoke more deliberately, trying to control himself. "Father, how did my name get recorded in here?"

"Your grandparents must have somehow reported it to the church."

"And all these other names, like Vincenzo Del Cielo and Angelina Scocoziella. Who are they?"

"I'm afraid that I cannot give you answers to all your questions. You would have to look in the town hall."

Edward rolled his eyes. "I already tried that. The friendly man smoking the cigarette said the town hall, which I think he believed was his hall, was closed for the weekend. When I told him I was from America and I had to leave tonight, he was not very moved. I can guarantee you that he was no relative of mine."

Don Raimondo smiled. "At least you have a sense of humor about it, having come such a long way." He picked up the ledger and walked over to his typewriter. "What if I type you a copy of your mother's birth certificate?"

Edward looked around the sacristy. He asked meekly, "You wouldn't happen to have a photocopier, would you? So that we can duplicate the original records?"

Don Raimondo shook his head in amusement. He cranked the paper into the typewriter. "No, we do not have a photocopier, my friend. You Americans—a beefsteak on every plate and a photocopier in every office. *Che abbondanza!*"

Through the arched window and the fence that surrounded the church, Edward saw a young woman standing in front of her home, drying a sheet by holding it at each corner and flapping it in the wind. As she continued to beat her outstretched arms, the light-green cotton undulated in the dry air, seeming to be immune from the town's ever-swirling dust. She looked toward the sacristy opening, as if she knew she was being watched. With one last flutter, she threw the sheet over her shoulder like a Greek goddess's sash, before receding through her door.

"The houses are so close together," mused Edward.

"Yes they are," responded Don Raimondo. "Which is why we have the fence."

Finding the idea of a fence around a church objectionable, Edward stayed quiet, directing his attention back to the record that the priest was creating for him.

As Don Raimondo alternated between squinting at the ledger and pecking the keyboard, a patter sounded through the doorway. It was the kind of step that neither overextends nor seeks attention, but begs pardon to be of service. Edward turned to see a full-bodied young woman carrying pressed laundry—the one who had been flapping her sheet in front of her home, on the other side of the church fence. The outline of her body was aglow from the sun that beamed through the arched window.

Don Raimondo jumped up nervously and wrested the cleaned linens away from her. He explained to Edward, "Ah, my laundry. She does a fine job." He went to place the bundle next to his gemmed chalices, and under his white sparkled habit, which hung from a peg.

With her arms relieved, the maidservant locked eyes briefly with Edward, and then looked down shyly.

But Edward's jaw remained dropped, as he admired her flowing dark hair and sharp facial features, untouched by makeup. Her bountiful chest fought the straight stitches of her home-sewn bodice, tied together at her clavicle by a thin bowed lace. As the sun continued to pour like molten gold through the arched window, Edward pondered how warm her breasts must be, strapped as they were beneath the bowed lace. He fantasized about undoing the strings, and admiring her glaze of sweat.

After placing his cottons on the table, and rearranging his chalices, Don Raimondo rushed back to Bowed Lace. He reached for her shoulders as if by reflex, but just as quickly pulled back, looking over to Edward. "*Grazie.*" He gestured toward the door.

Bowed Lace curtsied and departed, with Don Raimondo ushering her from behind. She looked back at Edward with a wistful batting of her eyelashes. Though her body was now wrapped in the darkness of the sacristy's shadows, her face shone through, as if it had absorbed the sun's light.

Don Raimondo returned to the desk. "Okay, back to where we were before the interruption." He unrolled the certificate from the typewriter. Laying the parchment flat, he opened a drawer, retrieving from it a long silver box that he placed alongside the record, perfectly even with it. He flipped open the lid, pulled out a stamp, and directed it squarely into the blotter with practiced aim. He pressed the church's chop to make an indelible record of the birth and lineage of Edward's mother. He held the paper at its edges, taking stock in his work. He handed it to Edward. "There," he said. "Your mother will enjoy that."

Edward's excitement lifted him. "This is great," he said. "Thank you, Father, thank you."

Perusing the document, he was taken aback at the sight of his own name, thinking of how long it had been written, and perhaps read, in a place that was unknown to him. Where had he been when the entry was first made? Perhaps resting in his mahogany sleigh crib, beneath a glistening chandelier; or maybe he was strapped in the back of his family's station wagon, for one of his father's famous upstate drives that was longer than the distance between Lavenna and Rome; he may have been sitting in his high chair in the kitchen, opera music rumbling while his mother cut him small pieces of sirloin. Edward glanced back at the sacristy and its close walls. "I feel like I have something to show my mother, and so much to share with her."

Don Raimondo cleared his desk, moving everything back to the appropriate location. "I wish there was something more I could do to help."

After depositing the certificate in his backpack, Edward looked at his watch. "I'll tell you what you can do. Is there a cab back to Salerno?"

"Yes."

"Can you get me one to Salerno, so that I can catch an evening train to Rome? I have to meet my friends there."

"Of course," Don Raimondo said, gesturing to the door for Edward, with more ease than he had exhibited with Bowed Lace.

Edward stopped under the door's frame. "There is something else you can help me with," he added. He whispered, so as not to impose. "This town. Brown wooden boxes everywhere. It's not what I had in mind. I thought it would be all stone with fountains." He extended his open palm outside the sacristy door. "And a church tower that…"

Don Raimondo brought Edward forward, into the full daylight. He put his arm around the American's shoulders. "This I can tell you about your mother, even without knowing her personally." He pointed to ruins that pocked a distant plateau. "That's where she was born and lived. The old town." He peered at the brown boxes with disdain. "Not in this wooden squalor."

Edward stared at the plateau. "But I don't understand. Why?"

As the crowd of children trickled in behind, Don Raimondo explained, "The earthquake of 1980 destroyed everything." He looked up. "Those mountains saw it all and have shed no tears ever since. It is as if they are either angry or in shock." He turned to the little faces. "It was devastating. Many of them lost parents." He stroked the hair of young Nicola, who now stood just inches from Edward. "This little guy lost his baby sister."

Nicola smiled back, not knowing what Don Raimondo was saying.

Don Raimondo shifted to the brown boxes. "This," he said, choking on the dust swirling in the wind. "This was built by the Italian government after the earthquake." He cleared his throat. "It is only temporary, until the original town can be rebuilt." He picked up a soccer ball that rolled into the crowd, and threw it back to its kicker. "And these children will eventually return to where they were born."

Edward took his camera out of his backpack for the first time, and began clicking feverishly, trying to memorialize every sight and sound of what Don Raimondo was explaining. When he finished, he noticed Nicola's fascination with the camera. He stooped next to the boy, inviting him to give it a try. "Here, Nicola, do you want to take a picture?"

Edward and Nicola simultaneously squeezed an eye into the viewfinder, and surveyed the landscape together—the plateau of ruins, the desolate valley, and the brown boxes; how different this shot would be from the postcards exported abroad. Edward halted the sweep when Bowed Lace entered the viewfinder; she was walking across a square, with more tied laundry in hand. Her noble peasantry captivated Edward. He zoomed the lens.

Before he could take a picture, Nicola moved the camera to focus on the devastated plateau. Sensing this was what the boy wanted to capture, Edward placed Nicola's finger under his, on top of the camera's button, and clicked.

Edward hurried back to snap a shot of Bowed Lace, but she was gone. Keeping his eye in the viewfinder, he moved the camera in search of her. For a moment, his obsession with her tantalizing form made him forget about his disappointment in not discovering any of his mother's relatives.

But even that obsession lapsed when he noticed Nicola jumping with joy. How proud the young boy must be, Edward thought, that his first photo had captured for posterity his family's fallen town.

# XIII.

## The Better Horseshoe,

## A Cap on a Jug of Wine

D on Raimondo instructed Nicola to have his mother call for a cab for Edward. He spanked Nicola from behind. *"Vai, Vai!"*

Nicola scampered away, his feet barely touching the ground.

Edward, Don Raimondo, and their audience waited, talking about everything—from how big and strong things would be in the new old town to how much bigger and stronger things already were in America.

The exchange was interrupted when an elder appeared—a man in a hat, approaching with the aid of a cane. When he joined the conversation, he raised his cane—suggesting that perhaps he did not need it at all, but used it for effect. He aimed it inquisitively at Edward, the obvious visitor. *"Chi è lui?"*

Looking up the other end of the barrel of the cane, Edward was struck by the stubble on the man's face, a brittle gray. He was curious why the man was not cleanly shaven, and whether it was indicative of a certain meanness. His stare was in a perpetual squint.

Don Raimondo started explaining. *"Lui è un americano. Sua madre—"*

Stubble cut in. The words he babbled, which Edward could not decipher, ignited a spontaneous belly laugh from the group. Throughout, he kept his cane raised, moving it with his every word.

Edward wanted to get in on the fun. He tapped Don Raimondo on the chest. "What did he say? Why is everyone laughing?"

"He said, 'Why is this American here? Did he fall off one of their rockets shooting into space?'" Don Raimondo gathered himself, snickering. "He said that he will whack you with his cane to send you back to your rocket."

Through the continued laughter, Edward asked Don Raimondo to see if Stubble knew Edward's mother. He gave the priest the black-and-white photo of her as a girl, as well as the snapshot of his grandfather with him on his knee.

Stubble's response elicited more giggles. Don Raimondo translated. "He says, 'Do you think I had time to play with little girls as a boy? I was a blacksmith since the day I could walk, surrounded by men and horses. If your mother was a horse, I might know her.'"

As Stubble continued to speak, Edward felt as if the old man's contorting face was rubbing against his own, his grains cutting like shards of glass. Edward gripped his cheeks in his right hand and squeezed, indicating his displeasure. He moved his hand down, sliding it over his throat, pinching his Adam's apple.

"Don't mind him," explained Don Raimondo. "He's always like this. It's just his way. Maybe he was behind too many horses, and the smell got to him."

But Edward wanted to take his own swipe at Stubble. He interrupted by grabbing back the photo of his grandfather, and thrust it in Stubble's face. He nodded toward Don Raimondo, signaling for him to interpret, and then leaned into Stubble's grains. "Tell him that my grandfather, Maurizio, was also a blacksmith. He was the best blacksmith that ever lived in this town—so good that his shoes made the horses dance." Edward began dancing the *Tarantella*, mouthing the instrumental accompaniment. "De-run-de-run-de-run-de-run-de-run-de-run-de-ruuuuun..."

The audience cackled applause—all except Stubble, who had fixed his feet into the ground, his eyes more squinted than usual. He gestured for Edward to give him back the photo of his grandfather. He studied the aged image, tilting it as if he was trying to insert himself between Edward's grandfather and his grandson. He shot his hand into the air to indicate a certain height. "Maurizio?" he asked dramatically, holding the picture firmly, at a height of a little over five feet.

"Sure," Edward answered, looking at Don Raimondo. "No offense, but there were thousands of men in this area who were that height."

Stubble hulked his body to project strength. "Maurizio?"

Remembering how his grandfather's short body was uniquely stout, Edward's interest grew. "Yeah," he replied, suspending his gasp long enough to invite another description.

Stubble rose, confident of his finish. He angled his polished wood at Edward's lips. *"Si chiama Nedda la moglie!"*

Edward was once again looking up the barrel of Stubble's cane; it was now shining, and the elder's uncut stalks of sharp facial grays looked like grains of salt. He could see a glint in the red veins of the old man's eyes. Edward spoke slowly. "Yes. Yes. My grandfather's name was Maurizio, and his wife was Nedda."

Stubble erupted, dropping his stick. He snatched the black-and-white photo of Edward's mother. Holding the picture over his head, he danced, singing "Maria, Maria, Maria." He kissed her gelatin image, exclaiming, "Maria Del Cielo!" The children emulated the song and dance. Stubble, his cane cast aside, now raised nothing but revelry. Flashing the separate images of Edward's mother and grandfather, the old man regaled the little ones with memories that Edward could not understand. The pitch and tone, however, indicated to Edward that the reminiscences were real and tender.

Returning from having told his mother to summon a cab, Nicola came running back to Edward, anxious to join the merrymaking.

Stubble limped toward the little boy. He grabbed Nicola by the shoulders, shouted an exuberant command, and sent the mini-courier on his way.

Previously able to sift some of the thick southern Italian dialect he was hearing, speculation flash-flooded from Edward's mind into his ears and eyes, disabling his senses.

Stubble, his baton back in position, was yelling to explain what was happening.

Edward heard nothing. The raging waters of possibility were overcoming him, tumbling him. Struggling for focus, he heard Stubble say his mother's name. He started to gain a footing. As he looked through the calming and crystalline waters, Stubble's face was a blur, his words an echo.

Stubble pointed behind and beyond Edward to a man standing across the square. Though the man was bald and short, his solemnity and straightness of posture made him appear tall. His shirt and trousers were pressed, his moustache so fine that it had to have been groomed daily. At the sight of him, Edward's little friends stilled.

Off to the side, the taxi arrived. Don Raimondo gave a hand signal for the driver to yield. The taxi crawled to a stop. The driver cut the ignition and lowered his window. With a smile, he crossed his arms over the steering wheel and leaned forward to observe. Idle but engaged, the cab sat.

Stubble spoke directly to Don Raimondo, repeating himself for emphasis.

"*Capisco*," Don Raimondo responded, asking Stubble for silence. What the priest said next filled the windless air, unimpeded by the swirl of Lavenna's dirt and dust. "He says that is Vito, your mother's first cousin. He was like a brother to her. Go to him."

Edward traversed the makeshift square that separated him from his cousin. Each step seemed to take a year—the sum of which represented the decades since his mother's departure. Edward felt compelled to run and hug the man, but something held him back. Perhaps it was the force of time, or maybe it was just the way he stood—straight and blank. A sudden wind blew between the generations, throwing Lavenna's dirt into Edward's eye. Wiping his socket with his sleeve, he looked back into Vito's unblinking gaze.

Vito was focused, ready and waiting—just like Edward's mother when he returned home after curfew.

Three steps more, and Edward arrived. "*Io sono Edoardo Bennett*," he said. "*Il figlio di Maria Del Cielo*."

Vito said nothing. A smile began to crack on his face, but did not extend all the way. It looked to Edward like joy, but just the same, it could have been sadness.

XIII.

Edward retrieved his camera from his backpack. He spoke in a hurry, checking on the cab driver, who sat mesmerized with his chin atop the wheel. "Photo?" he said, pointing back and forth between Vito and himself, and keeping an eye on the cabby. "Photo of you and me? Then I go. I go in taxi to Salerno."

Vito ignored the request for a photo, pulling Edward out of the square. When Edward did not follow immediately, Vito turned and waved for the cab to leave.

Edward looked back at the cab. "But I have to meet..."

Vito let go of Edward's hand and kept walking, leaving Edward to choose.

Edward looked at the man as he moved further away. He called out, "But... " He looked back at the cab. It was reckless to stay, for he had no way to return to Rome. But if he left, the layers of his mother's past would remain untouched, unpeeled. Stay he would. Edward nodded to the cab driver, indicating that he would not need the ride after all. He scurried to catch up to Vito.

Vito strode with quiet deliberation, looking only at his shoes as he traveled the dusty ground. Edward kept to his side, trying not to disturb his cousin's thoughts, kicking through the dirt, and peeking over only sparingly, in the hope that he might elicit a response without being disrespectful. There was none—only the taste of Lavenna's dirt sticking to his nostrils, and the sound of Vito's pant legs rubbing against one another.

*Dirt and rustle, rustle and dirt—a chafing so regular, it no longer hurt.*

Little Nicola caught up to them. It was not clear to Edward why he was joining. Once the little boy's shoulder made its way under the wedding-banded grip of Vito, however, it was apparent that there was some kind of special relationship between the two, familial or otherwise. From the rear, Stubble pushed his pace lest he be left behind.

Vito led Nicola, Edward, and Stubble into one of the brown wooden boxes, entering through the family's hanging wooden beads. His first step was into the kitchen, which was tended by a matron who was fighting the hot oil that was jumping from her pan of veal cutlets. She wore a homemade dress with a pattern of faded flowers, and her ponytailed hair was pulled back to reveal her creased face. Her feet were swollen in her buckled shoes.

The matron abandoned her pans. *"Edoardo, caro Edoardo. Io sono Luisa."* She squeezed Vito's gold-ringed finger as he passed to assume his seat at the head of the kitchen table. She wobbled toward Edward. *"La moglie di Vito,"* she chirped as she embraced him, her cutlets sizzling with the aroma of oregano.

With sound and smell seeping into the box's walls, Stubble waded through the hanging beads to compete for Edward's attention. *"L'ho fattoio."* He took a deep breath. *"L'ho trovato io."*

Edward understood clearly that Stubble was taking credit for having done it all—for having found Edward. *"Grazie,"* he said as he pointed at the old man.

Vito sat earnestly in his chair at the head of the table. It appeared to Edward that he was bracing. He rested his hand on a nearly empty jug of wine. Through the green glass, Edward could see the sediment on the bottom. Vito kept gazing forward, with his hand on the drained jug.

Nicola parked himself next to Vito, nibbling on almonds.

Luisa sat Edward down beside Vito, and heaped a mound of her cutlets onto a plate in front of him. Stubble also pulled up a seat, on the corner next to Nicola. The legs of his chair were rickety.

Luisa wiped her hands on her apron and shuffled into a room off the kitchen. She reemerged with a blue volume trimmed with gold leaf—this one not as tall and imposing as the birth ledgers in the church. She put it in front of Edward, and from over his shoulder, began turning the pages.

*"Cos' è questo?"* he asked.

*"La tua famiglia,"* Luisa responded.

It was indeed a photo album of Edward and his family, beginning with his parents' wedding day and continuing through his and his siblings' adolescence. The book ended abruptly with his older brother's high school graduation, leaving several pages thereafter unfilled.

With Luisa and Stubble bantering, Edward could not help but be distracted by Vito's cool meditation. While Edward was delighted that he had been part of this world without realizing it, he was eager to get inside Vito's head.

Another man entered through the beads—this one with a studied beard and brow. He introduced himself immediately, and in English. "Hello, Edward," he said. "My name is Giovanni. I am Vito's and Luisa's son." He glowed as he pointed to Nicola. "And he is my son, Nicola." He turned to identify Stubble. "This guy is…"

But Stubble was gone, having exited the house while Giovanni spoke.

"Oh well," Giovanni said, shrugging his shoulders. "He's not one of our relatives, anyway."

Edward felt a tickle inside. He realized that Nicola, his ardent sidekick since they first met, was in fact his cousin. Energized by having an English-speaker in the house, Edward skipped the niceties and did not bother to ask for Stubble's name. "Giovanni," he said. "How do you all know so much about my family?" He reached over to touch the album. "And where did you get the photos?"

Giovanni sat across from his father. He spoke slowly, glancing at his parents, as if he was being extra careful to get it right. "Well, of course, we know about you, your brother Albert, and your sister Lisa Marie." He planted his elbow on the table, with his palm open wide, as if he was holding a giant plum. "And of course, your father, Gaetano. The great one in America."

Luisa perked up. "*Sì, Gaetano è ricco.*" She strained to translate. "You fadder ees very rich. Ees big builder." She shot her thumb, index, and middle fingers in the air. "He has-a three couch in heez TV room-a."

Edward wanted to laugh, but caught himself. In the confines of Luisa's makeshift house, there wasn't even a place for one couch.

Giovanni paused, seeming uncertain whether to proceed. He looked at his father, who had yet to utter a word to Edward. "Did your mother ever talk about her life in Lavenna?"

"Not really," replied Edward as he thrust his fork into another one of Luisa's cutlets. "Only that her mother and grandmother raised her while her father was in America."

Vito finally addressed Edward; his voice was low and scratchy. "*Tua mamma,*" he said. He took a deep breath. "*Perché lei non torna mai?*"

Edward was thrown off by being asked the very question for which he sought an answer. *Why did Mom never return?* He tried to maintain his poise, and to use the house tongue so as not to betray his ignorance on the subject. *"Perché, perché..."* He searched his mind for the probable explanation and the right words to express it. *"Perché sua mamma, Nedda. Dopo la guerra, è stata rimandata qui dagli Stati Uniti."* He turned to Giovanni. "I said it correctly, didn't I? My mother never returned because of her mother, Nedda. After the war, she was sent back here from the United States."

Giovanni stroked his chin. "If that is what you wanted to say, you did so."

A tear welled in the corner of Vito's eye, and he nodded. *"Lo so,"* he said, pouring from what little remained of his wine from the green glass jug. *"Lo so."* He served a glass to Edward. Grape skins floated near the top.

Edward turned to Giovanni. "Are you sure that your father understood what I said? I think, but I cannot be one hundred percent certain, that the reason my mother never came back was because after she, my grandmother, and my grandfather were finally together in the United States following the war, my grandmother was deported. She was sick, you know. My grandmother died here without ever seeing my mother again. So I think coming back would just be too painful for Mom." He looked to Vito, wondering whether he had a better answer. "Please, make sure he heard me right. Whether that makes sense."

Giovanni responded without asking his father. "Don't worry, he knows. That is what he told you. He knows about your grandmother, Nedda. My mother took care of her when she returned to Italy. She was at your grandmother's side every day. Your grandma talked about all of you, when she could." He sighed, and then lifted himself with a smile. "My mother knows you very well." He gave the glass of wine to Edward, and instructed him, "Here, take a quick sip of father's wine so that I can get you some of mine—a nice new white."

Edward raised his glass to the master of the house, and drank until the grape skins reached his lips. He swallowed hard. *"Grazie."*

Giovanni took the glass from Edward, and emptied it subtly in the sink, en route to the cabinet that held his homemade wine. "You will like my wine, Edward," he said. "It's sweet—different from the traditional wine from this town, which I find to be too bitter."

Edward bit into the tender veal. "Giovanni, I never really knew what sickness Grandma had." He paused to look at his glass. "You are right—that is good stuff." He returned to the subject of his grandmother. "What was wrong with her? Like I said, all that I know is that one minute she was with my mother and grandfather in America, and the next, she was back here."

"Yes, she was sent back, without your mother and grandfather," Giovanni said slowly, as if trying to comprehend his own words.

Giovanni put Edward's question to his parents, and got an excited flurry of responses through their long faces. He held up his hand for silence. "I am a teacher. Sometimes, my parents are like my children at school. I have to tell them when to stop."

Luisa raised her eyebrows and returned to the stove to tend her frying pan, even though it was empty.

Vito tightened the cap on his green glass jug, so no air could enter or escape.

Giovanni spoke haltingly. "Your grandmother, she was..." He reached across his chest to itch his left shoulder. "She had some kind of nervous breakdown and never was the same."

Luisa muttered from the stove.

Giovanni repeated her words in English. "My mother said that your grandmother had a voice like an angel. She would sing all the time. Her favorite was opera, the music of Giacomo Puccini—before she became ill. Even then, she would..."

Edward chewed on, more interested in his grandmother's ailment than her arias. "She became sick while she was with my mother and my grandfather in the United States?"

Giovanni peered at Vito, who again screwed the cap on his green glass jug until it screeched. "Yes. Nedda had a nervous condition that deteriorated while she was in America." He paused. "With your mother and grandfather."

Giovanni rotated to Luisa, who kept her back to the conversation and her eyes on the empty black pan. She sang quietly to herself.

87

The teacher continued his lesson. "Yes, Nedda deteriorated while your mother and grandfather were with her in America." He sped to the finish. "Some law of your United States said that if you were ill before you immigrated, you could be deported. So inhumane. It would never happen in America today. Anyway, when Nedda came back because of her nervous condition, my mother was at her side always. She took good care of your grandmother."

Luisa remained frozen at the frying pan, her song dissipating.

Giovanni stood, trying to lighten the mood of the room. "Now, we should take you to the old town, to see where your mother was born."

Wanting to lift the trio from the somber mood that he felt he had created with his questions, Edward gulped down the last of his veal and chased it with Giovanni's wine. "Sounds good to me."

Giovanni reached over to collect the album and give it to his mother. From the album's carefully assembled pages fell a cracked black-and-white photo of a handsome young man, sitting glumly in a suit.

Edward picked it up. The subject had a pure white face, shrouded on one side by a shadow. His tie was knotted perfectly, his collar curved. His brow was thin, and his eyes sagged beneath it.

"Who is this guy, Giovanni?" Edward asked.

Giovanni retrieved the picture and flapped it in the air, aggravating its rift. "This is just someone else—another guy, who is not related to you. The son of a family friend. It must have been mixed in by accident." He yanked open the first cabinet he could find, and threw the photo inside. He gave the album to his mother to return to her room. Then he went to the sink to wash his hands. "Let's get to the town. There's a lot to see."

# XIV.

## Homes Reduced to Silhouettes,

## A Window that Remained

Vito, Edward, and Nicola crammed into Giovanni's Lancia. Since space was limited, Luisa stayed behind. Giovanni was in the driver's seat, with his father on the passenger side. Nicola was next to Edward in the back, leaning into his cousin's shoulder.

As Giovanni and Vito bickered, pointing in different directions through the windshield, Stubble shuffled to the car and tapped on Edward's window. When Edward lowered the glass, Stubble handed Edward the pictures of his mother and grandfather, which Edward had forgotten to take back in the excitement. *"Dai un bacio a Maria per me."* He then gripped the door with his frail hand, and gave Edward a kiss on each of his cheeks.

Wanting to know Stubble's name, but too embarrassed to ask after all the time they had already spent together, Edward instead placed his hand over that of the old man. *"Va bene."*

Stubble lifted his hand off the door, and squeezed Edward's cheek between his thumb and forefinger. Without saying another word, he turned and walked away. Rather than use his cane, he carried it over his shoulder.

The car began rolling up the hill to the old town. As Giovanni navigated the rock-littered road, he shouted over the prattle of the shattered landscape. "The earthquake was terrible when it hit the town. It showed little mercy."

He turned to Edward and then directly to Nicola, whose smile was not shaken by the bumpy ride. "Many people died—even little children, younger than him."

Processing how nature's cruelty had touched his family—a phenomenon that, to Edward, had previously been a mere news item about other people—he snapped his gaze away from Nicola and stared out the window. He pondered the absence of life everywhere: no traffic to contend with; bees buzzing in search of nectar; no flowers to be found. Everything was past; there was no sign of present or future.

Edward's melancholy was disrupted by Bowed Lace. She was walking down the hill toward the car, without the benefit of a sidewalk or path; she carried herself and her laundry well, perhaps returning from a secret spring in which she cleansed her load. She and Edward locked glances, and the Lancia rolled on.

"Are there any plans to rebuild the town?" asked Edward, distracting himself.

Giovanni turned a narrow corner unbound by a rail, as Vito studied the hillside drop. Giovanni did not miss a beat. "Yes, of course. But the Italian government moves slowly. We do not have the money that you have in America, so we cannot rebuild quickly, like you. But we rebuild all the same."

With the sheer drop behind them, Edward thought of how his father's construction company alone could resurrect the old town in mere months. He felt the impulse to share the sentiment, with only the best intentions—but on second thought decided to keep it to himself. He did not want to offend or further sadden his newfound family.

The Lancia reached the hill's crest. Giovanni stopped the cart to enable a view of the old town below. There were broken homes everywhere, without a continuous line of road to navigate them. From the heights, the remaining foundations were haunting silhouettes of what had once been. "Wow!" exclaimed Edward. "Devastating." In the midst of the silhouettes was a lone and twisted tree. It stood conspicuously among the levelled.

"The *terremoto* took everything," replied Giovanni, looking out the front window without blinking. "Everything." Everyone remained silent.

Reverence for the dead, Edward thought.

"Let's see how close we can get," sighed Giovanni. He struggled with the stick shift to put the Lancia into drive, and glided the car down the crest. Moments later, they approached the remains of a foundation. A piece of one wall remained standing.

Vito tapped Giovanni on the shoulder, cueing his son to stop the car. The halt threw everyone. After taking a deep breath, Giovanni exited first. Nicola and Edward followed. The slamming of the car doors echoed against the half-standing wall.

Edward waited for someone to speak, but neither Giovanni nor Nicola would do so until Vito had joined them. As the older man pushed himself out of the car and onto his feet, Edward could hear water dripping from the wall fragment. *Drip-drop, drip-drop, drop-drip.* Edward asked himself how long these shattered walls had been crying, while the nearby twisted tree looked on without a handkerchief to offer.

Vito joined the group, mumbling. "Where you are standing," Giovanni translated, grimacing at the outline of a home, "was where your mother lived before she left."

Feeling a momentary chill that he had been lured into his mother's home without knowing it, Edward surveyed the floor. Perhaps it held a clue to her secret. Or maybe it would satisfy him that there was no secret at all. He stepped tentatively within the foundation, as if walking across a minefield. The once-living space was tiny, by American standards. He leaned over and parted the weeds, hoping to find a relic, or some trace of his mother—a ribbon, a page of writing, or even a thread.

Nothing.

He crouched and lifted a rock with both hands, uncovering only slithering worms among twitching slugs.

A revolted Edward dropped the rock to look around for something else—anything else—he noticed a piece of paper on the other side of the foundation. He dashed over to it in the hope of finding a message; instead, it bore the mark of a recent cola vintage.

Ready to give up, he spotted something made from black leather, protruding from beneath a piece of concrete. He got excited. He walked slowly to where it was, bracing himself for a revelation. He raised the slab, and pulled out the leather. It was a weathered casing in the shape of a pistol. He unbuttoned the holster's strap hurriedly, pulling so hard that he snapped the rusted buckle. It was empty. The inside of the flap was inscribed with German writing. "Why the heck?" Edward asked himself. He looked over at his cousins.

Giovanni and Nicola were also walking through Marie's shattered household, looking down at what lay at their feet. But Vito stood still, staring at Edward, as if he had been watching; his expression was steely. When Giovanni pulled Nicola back from reaching into the ruins to grab a piece of metal, Edward surmised that Vito's stare was an agitated one, not wanting Edward to disturb or disrespect the dead. Edward got nervous. He felt that he had to stop digging. He pretended to inspect the leather casing, concluding that the owner must have bought it because he believed it was better than any Italian brand; to Edward's thinking, German goods were always more durable than their stylish Italian counterparts. So as not to disturb Vito, Edward tossed the holster back into the ruins. He looked at Vito and shrugged with an embarrassed smile.

Vito smiled back.

Giovanni interrupted, "I'm sure it is difficult for you to imagine what your mother's house looked like. Let me help." He pointed to the middle of the outlined area. "There was the kitchen where your grandmother cooked for your mother." He walked through the kitchen and planted his feet. "This was the room of your grandparents, Maurizio and Nedda." He pretended to sit. "This would have been their bed, where your mother would have also slept while your grandfather was away. Your great grandmother would have slept in the kitchen."

Edward felt a sudden adrenaline rush of nostalgia, as if he were watching an old-time movie that glorified the simplicity of poverty.

"But we have no time to waste if you are going to get back to Salerno tonight," Giovanni said, smiling wryly.

Edward did not take the bait. "How do you know so much about the house?"

Giovanni blushed. "After Nedda died, the house was deserted and fell into disrepair. I rebuilt it with my father, making it a little bigger—without disturbing the original foundation, of course. After I got married, my wife and I lived here." He rubbed the head of Nicola, who had wrapped himself around his father's leg. "Nicola slept here with his little sister, Donatella." Giovanni looked up. "Until the night the earthquake came and the roof fell in. She was only three years old." He choked up. "We always kept your mother's house happy and full of love."

"I'm sorry about the loss of your daughter," Edward offered. He wanted to ask about Donatella, but was wary of deepening Giovanni's pain. "I know that you kept my mother's house—your house—full of love."

Vito came over and put his arm around his son; he led Giovanni over his eviscerated threshold. "*Va bene*," he whispered. He glanced at Edward, and strained to smile. "*Andiamo alla casa.*"

Giovanni cleared his throat. "Yes, to papà's house. That's a good idea."

The cousins walked in procession, until they came upon another silhouette. One wall remained standing, with a glass window that did not suffer so much as a crack. Its side lock was undone, giving way to the howling wind that swept across the town's ruins. Vito went directly to the window to secure its latch.

Giovanni switched back from consoled to consoler. "This will always be his house, no matter where he lives. I cannot tell you how many times he has come up here just to fix the lock on that little window," he said as his back straightened. "The wind keeps blowing it open."

"That's okay," Edward replied. "I'm sure that his new house will be stronger."

"If the Lord wants to tear it down again, nothing can prevent it," Giovanni reflected as his father continued to struggle with the latch. "But I guess we all have a need to do something to show that we are in control."

Vito finally caught the latch. He took back his handkerchief politely from Giovanni, and used it to clean the window.

"Tell your father that this looks like it was quite a place. I would have loved to have been a guest."

Giovanni smiled and translated to his father, who answered immediately in monotone, while putting the finishing touches on his window. "He says you could have never been a guest." He paused while his father continued, then began again. "Because you are family. And this was your house, too. He said you might have been out playing with your friends on a big American field when it all came down, but you also lost something that dreadful day. You just didn't know it."

Edward could say nothing more about the fallen house before him. He felt as though layers of truth were being peeled back, exposing a wound. He wanted the cut healed right away. "What about the church, Giovanni? Where is the old church where my mother was baptized?" He looked around. "Can we drive to it?

"Yes," Giovanni said slowly, clinging to the *s*.

As Giovanni stared off to one side, Edward thought that his request had upset him even more. Edward remained in abeyance.

Giovanni shook his head and raised his voice. "Very well. We do not need the Lancia. *Santa Maria D'Assunta* is right here. You just couldn't see it on the other side of the tree." Giovanni called back to his father, who was still studying his small window, on his lone remaining wall. "*Papà. Andiamo alla chiesa.*"

Vito checked the window again to see if it was secure. When he had taken just a few steps away to follow his son, the latch blew open again, and the wind whistled through.

# XV.

## A Displaced Olive Tree,

## A Dry Baptismal Font

T he cousins continued on foot. Edward was surprised that none of them were affected by the dust that Edward found so dreadful, and that made him feel so dirty. Without breaking stride, Edward tried to swipe his shoes clean. When he looked up, he was inches away from the tree. He stopped short so as not to be scratched in the eye by one of the branches.

Giovanni laughed. "That old olive tree. Legend has it that Christ planted it here." He paused. "Some in town believe that when he comes back, he will be crucified on it again."

Edward gawked—wanting to believe the story of the tree's origin, but perplexed by the dark view of the Second Coming.

"The problem is that before World War II, the people moved the tree so that a statue dedicated to Mussolini could be in the center of the square."

"So we are not in the center of the old square?" Edward asked.

"Oh, we are," Giovanni answered. "After the earthquake, the tree was replanted in its original spot. Some people believe that moving it in the first place is what caused the earthquake. In any event, it is the first step in rebuilding the old town." Without an expression to indicate conviction or doubt in what he was about to say, Giovanni elaborated, "My grandfather used to tell us that the first time that Christ died, he saved everyone else. When he returns, he will save all of us—he will save Lavenna."

Edward touched the flowerless branch. "But it seems dead."

"It will come back." From afar, he traced its curves from bottom to top. "Give it time."

Edward paused, so that he might commit to memory what Giovanni had said.

Vito caught up and shuffled ahead, making the sign of the cross as he passed the olive tree. The others followed.

On the other side of the tree stood a tall façade, its walls and ceiling missing. To the left, a bell tower was reduced to a heap, topped by the bell itself. The bell's clapper was unattached; to Edward, it appeared like a tongue cut from the mouth, left behind like a killer's warning. Frightened by the thought, he walked through the façade's entrance with trepidation. "This must be the church," he whispered reverently. Once inside, he looked to the right, at the remnants of two confessional booths. "Seems like there was a lot of penance going on in this place."

"There were seven confessionals altogether. Father Masseo said that there was one for each day of the week."

"Sounds like Father Masseo was pretty strict."

Giovanni kicked at one of the rocks that had rolled away from the pile. "Yes, he was—until the earthquake."

Edward bit his lip. "I'm sorry. Was he killed?"

"No. Shortly after that day, the good Father disappeared with the organist." Giovanni made the sign of the cross and looked up, and then laughed. "Even Jesus was human, right?" He used his foot to push another rock back to the pile. "I guess it was too much for him. We all have our weak moments. The problem was that his time of weakness came when we needed him most." He took a breath. "But Don Raimondo has been a fine replacement. He really cares for this place."

"Do you mind if I just scout around for a couple of minutes, Giovanni?"

"Go ahead. See where your mother was baptized." He pointed to the front of the church. "The baptismal font is still standing."

Edward went immediately to the concrete saucer that rested on a thick column. The surrounding debris made the font nearly unapproachable. When Edward arrived, there was no water in the oversized dish. He placed his fingers in it anyway. The surface was cool and smooth. He imagined his infant mother smiling rather than crying as she bathed in the Holy Spirit, enjoying the same refreshing sensation that he was feeling now.

He rushed back to share the moment. "Guys…"

Edward halted when he noticed his cousins, side-by-side, fixed on the collapsed altar. He saw three generations mesmerized in disbelief, and not one of them, despite their apparent deep faith, having a clear understanding of why God had allowed the earth to shake with such ferocity. Edward scrambled inside his backpack for his camera. He aimed and pushed the shutter release, but the button was jammed. Edward pressed harder as his cousins remained stoic, but the release stayed stubborn, the shutter stuck. Edward exhaled a frustrated gasp.

Giovanni broke out of his trance. "So now you have seen your mother's house, my father's house, and the church where your mother was baptized." He looked at his watch. "All in less than an hour. Not bad for so many years of history." He undid his watch's strap, and tightened it one hole. "But we should get back. Mamma will be waiting with dinner."

"Dinner? Didn't we just eat before we came up here?"

Giovanni waved Edward on. "You call that dinner? That was just a snack. Now come, or else you will insult my mother, and then you will have to deal with her *and* me."

"But what about getting me on a train back to Rome?"

"I was just talking to my father about that. We would love for you to stay a week, or even a month, if you want. We would put you to work rebuilding some of these houses with those American muscles of yours." When Edward did not bite, Giovanni turned away and began to walk. "But if you insist on going back tonight, there is a train from Salerno to Rome that leaves Salerno at 12:30 a.m. It is 5:00 p.m. now. That should give us plenty of time to eat."

Relieved that Giovanni had backed off on the extended stay, Edward rubbed his stomach. "I'm ready. *Mangiamo!*"

# XVI.

## Eating a Native Dish,

## Admiring Stars from a Different Mountaintop

It was a feast indeed. Luisa unleashed an array of foods that Edward could not resist: an escarole and white bean soup; a tomato, basil, and cucumber salad drenched in oil; baked ziti in a light red sauce, flavored with small meatballs and chunks of pepperoni. In the background, a transistor radio reported the day's news, but it was barely audible above the excitement of the reunion.

After two dishes of pasta—which would have been the main course at home—Edward loosened his belt. "Well, that was an incredible meal," he said. "I don't think the Prodigal Son was served this much when he returned home."

Giovanni, who was headed for the stove, stopped in his tracks. "*Bravo,*" he said in a voice just above a whisper. He waved his finger at Edward. "Yes, the Prodigal Son." He went to his mother, who was holding another pan from the stove. The stove's thick black iron, without a trace of steel, suggested to Edward that it predated the quake and endured it. Somehow, the stove must have been hauled from their shattered home and placed in their provisional brown box. Giovanni relieved his mother of the pan and walked back to Edward.

"You have not even had the main course yet," Giovanni said. He served

Edward a piece of white meat with a light-brown sauce on it. "Here, try this. It is my own recipe. Tell me if you have ever had anything like it."

Edward took a bite. "Hmm," he said. "It tastes like it has parsley with onions, eggs, and cheese." Seeing in Giovanni's nods that he had identified the ingredients correctly, Edward speared a heftier portion, so large he had to bend it to fit in his mouth. He chased it with Giovanni's homemade wine. "What do you call this—*lamb à la Giovanni?*"

Giovanni giggled boyishly—a sharp departure from his otherwise thoughtful demeanor. He looked over to his father, who smiled slightly.

"No, I call it *Capra Del Cielo*," explained Giovanni. "It's a family thing."

"*Capra?*" Edward kept chewing. "Is that the word for lamb?"

"*Agnello* is the word for lamb, but you are not eating lamb."

"What is it then, pork?" Edward took another swig of Giovanni's wine.

"No." He waited for Edward to take another bite and swallow. "*Capra Del Cielo* is one of our favorites, but something I do not think you get very often in America." He struggled to keep a straight face.

"Well, the only *Capra* I know is the film director, Frank Capra. He's one of my favorites. Every Christmas, I watch his film *It's a Wonderful Life*, starring Jimmy Stewart." Edward pointed with his fork. "Frank Capra is a great Italian-American."

Giovanni spread his arms in front of himself, as if swimming the breaststroke in slow motion. "You Americans and your movies. Everything is on a big screen, and you are free to leave your gigantic theater any time. I don't know anything about your *Wonderful Life*." He took a sip of wine, and savored it with a husky inhale, followed by a gradual exhale. "Il Signore Capra might create great American movies, but I bet *il regista* does not know how to make *Capra Del Cielo*."

Edward became anxious. "So, what is *capra?*"

Giovanni's eyes grew wide. "I think you call it goat."

Edward spoke slowly, "You think we call it *goat?*"

"Yes, goat," Giovanni continued, enjoying himself. He pinch-stroked his beard where it covered his chin. "The animal that, like me, could use a shave." He imitated the pre-cooked version of the four-legged animal, holding his index fingers behind his head to make horns. *"B-e-e-e-h. B-e-e-e-e-e-e-e-h."*

Keeping a poker face, Edward swallowed hard and asked for more—even though the thought of eating goat repulsed him. "If you don't mind, Giovanni, please pass some more *Capra Del Cielo.*"

Giovanni became serious, taking on an apologetic tone. "Sure, Edward. But really, you do not have to."

"No, I love it," Edward said with the beginnings of a smirk. "And when you come to America, I will make my specialty for you. I call it 'Alligator Edward'—straight from the Florida Everglades." Having difficulty restraining himself from laughing at his own joke, Edward nearly spit his wine. "I will serve it in a nice light sauce so it tastes like lamb."

*"Bravo!"* Giovanni responded with a belly roar of his own, and raised a glass. "To eating Alligator Edoardo in America."

Vito treated himself to the sediment from his jug, and joined the toast. "To Edoardo in Ameriga. *E la mamma, Maria.*"

The new cousins' merriment continued for hours—over provolone, nuts, fruit, and grappa—relieving the angst of the family's reunion after so long a time apart.

When the meal was finally over, Vito asked Edward if they could surprise his mother Maria with a telephone call. "I don't think so," replied Edward, apologetically. "She did not want me to come back…" He stopped himself. "Let me tell her about this visit first. I promise that she will call."

*"Capisco,"* said Vito, holding up his hand to acknowledge that he understood, and that nothing more needed to be said. He shuffled to his room, retrieved a pen and piece of paper, and brought them back to the kitchen table to draft a letter to his estranged cousin.

Edward was warmed by the fact that in his own house, replete with studies and lounge chairs, the kitchen table was the place for serious writing. He pointed to the door. "I'll go outside." Edward stepped through the beads, where he found Giovanni smoking a pipe. "Boy, the stars are bright tonight," exclaimed Edward.

"This is probably one of the few things we have that you do not," Giovanni said, gesturing to the sky, "because you live so close to the city, with your bright lights and smog. We get views like this all the time up here in the mountains. There is very little between us and the stars. They say that for every tear from one of our infants, God compensates us with a new star. God has stolen the earth from us, but repaid us with the constellations."

"We all have the same constellations."

"But they are not revealed to everyone with the same clarity. Your richness in America is in the fleeting present. Ours is in the hope of being delivered from the past."

Looking at the night's infinite light, Edward was only beginning to understand the pain and suffering these people, his family, had gone through. His mind raced to the star-filled view that he had during his last night at home with Celeste, from the mountaintop clearing, before shoving off for his junior year. This vista was every bit as dazzling as that silver sequined dress, and held the same allure. He checked his watch. "Giovanni, I really need to get back to Salerno—but do I have time to go back to the old city one last time?"

Giovanni blew a puff of smoke that obscured the stars. "Yes, but be careful. Those rocks are loose and sharp, and can be dangerous. Make sure you are back here by 11:00 p.m., so we have enough time to drive to Salerno."

# XVII.

## A Walk Alone

Edward threw on his mother's sweater for the first time. It fit perfectly. He started off to the old town, ebullient with the prospect of a quiet moment alone in his mother's house. As a shortcut, he detoured along the backside of the brown boxes. He walked so fast that he was nearly running, clicking past one brown box after another, nervous he might be detected. Each box gave off the sound of life—a pot being scrubbed, slow footsteps on the wooden floor, a baby crying. As Edward sped up, the boxes' whispers whirled in his ears. He stumbled once, but did not fall—instead resuming his pursuit of the old town.

He was brought to a standstill when a shutter from one of the brown boxes flew open and nearly hit him; his reflexes kicked in and he jumped back in fright. When he uprighted himself, he he leaned forward to peek inside to see what had tried to smack him. It was a kitchen of identical size and layout as that of Vito and Luisa's. But there was something strikingly different at its center. Bowed Lace was kneeling at the feet of an elderly woman, who was sitting in a chair. The elder's face was frozen, her stare over and beyond Bowed Lace.

"*Sei pronta, mamma?*" Bowed Lace murmured.

"*Sì,*" her mother said simply, feeling for her daughter's head. It was clear to Edward that she was blind.

Pouring steaming water from one pitcher, and milk from another, Bowed

Lace bathed the woman's scaly limbs in a tin basin. As she leaned over to give more milk to her mother's chafed skin, her exertion loosened the knot of her bow.

*Water and milk—milk and water—a mother in need, nourished by her daughter.*

Edward shifted his footing and lost his balance, bumping up against the thin brown wall that separated him from temptation.

Bowed Lace looked up. She continued bathing her mother, boring into Edward's eyes with her own. As she applied another round of hot water to her mother's legs, she untied her bow with her free hand.

Edward bit hard into his lower lip.

She then opened her collar, pushing each side of it to the edges of her shoulders. She stroked her throat with her fingers, slowly and repeatedly.

Edward felt as though someone was watching him from behind, ready to scold him for his voyeurism. He turned to see the arched window of the makeshift church surrounded by the fence, through which he first admired Bowed Lace flapping her sheets. After just a few seconds, he could not help himself. He had to turn back to Bowed Lace's window. The afterimage of the fence and arch remained between him and the native beauty.

Using nothing more than the force of a fingertip, she moved the sleeves off her shoulders, exposing her breasts. To Edward's eyes, they were a perfect form—smoother than the rest of her skin, and abundant. There were no blemishes. She grabbed the pitcher of milk and began pouring it across her chest. She placed the pitcher on the floor, and then looked back at Edward. She spread the milk evenly over each bosom with her hand, applying the excess to her neck and sternum. She removed her hand from her body, pointed it toward Edward, and flicked the residue at him, like a sorceress casting a spell.

Edward writhed with guilt and desire. To resist hurtling through the window to have some of what Bowed Lace was offering, he turned back to the church's arched window. He grabbed the fence to suppress his internal chaos. He resumed his run to the old town.

After only a few steps, however, he wanted to see more of Bowed Lace. He rotated to return to her window. The shriek of a cat startled him. He reconsidered, and directed himself to his mother's home before it was too late. His heart pounding as he sprinted, he took the incline with ease.

Back at the remains of her house, Edward was overcome with a feeling of serenity. He was on time, with nothing to explain. He walked the grounds again—not in search of an artifact, but instead to gather his own thoughts on how this place, rather than the Bennett family mansion, could be the cradle for them all. A night breeze blew gently, calming him more, before he was startled by a rabbit crossing his path. He flinched and the rabbit was gone, back into the darkness.

While walking his mother's floors, he spotted a patch of grass between the house and the olive tree. He stepped outside the foundation to lie down on nature's bed. He took off his mother's sweater. Rather than use the pullover as a pillow, he folded it and placed it by his side.

His hands clasped behind his head, Edward sighted a cultivated plane higher than the one that he was on. *What could it possibly be? How did anyone get there?* Rather than ponder the plane any more, Edward gazed beyond the elevation at the silver sequins of the night sky, proud that he had broached the layers of truth as Prigler had implored him to do in the Roman ruins. He had found all that he needed to know about his mother's secret—that it was the profound pain of her mother being taken away from her, and so something more than the grief that comes from the mere passing of a loved one. He saw the difficulty his cousins had in coming to terms with the earthquake and the destruction that it wrought—but at least they found comfort in attributing it to God's will. His grandmother's deportation was cruel, separating two ends of a natural and nurturing bond while mother and child both were still alive. And the sorrow was neither limited nor local. Edward heard it in Luisa's voice—the unmistakable mourning for Nedda, her ward. He saw it in Vito's face, in the wrinkles that time had carved.

Edward folded his hands on his chest and closed his eyes. He envisioned the tide rolling in upon the shores of both Italy and America—the abyss that separated past and present, mother and daughter.

As Edward lay slipping deeper into a dream, a scent of lavender rolled in, tantalizing him. When the fragrance grew stronger, it compelled him to open his eyes. It was Bowed Lace, walking barefoot over the quake-cut rocks. The collar of her bodice was untied and spread open, just as it was when Edward had seen her lathering in milk. She strode easily, her gaze fixed on Edward.

When Edward tried to prop himself up with his elbows and forearms, she put her foot upon his chest. Her toes were dirty from the walk. After a brief pause, she pushed with her foot, easing Edward back to the ground. She stepped between his legs. She pulled her lace from the eyelets and grasped it in her hand. She then shed her dress until it dropped to her feet. With her left foot, she cast the dress behind her.

The sharp edges of the rocks beneath Edward's back only added to the pleasure that he was feeling.

She looked at the lace in her palm, for so long a time that it seemed as though she was considering what to do with it. She closed her hand and reached back to throw, but stopped herself. Instead, she proceeded to tie the white strand around her neck, looking down at her fingers as she worked them. Finished, she stood upright. She took a deep breath of the evening air, looking over and past Edward, toward the town. When she exhaled, the cloud passed and the silver-sequined sky reemerged. Her voluptuous naked body glowed. In the night, her skin was a rich olive, as if she was channeling from a reservoir within the sacred tree. The white lace was bowed around her neck, accenting all that it wrapped.

As she lowered herself onto Edward, he tried to speak. "What are—"

Bowed Lace pressed her finger to Edward's upper lip to quiet him.

"But wait, who are you?" Edward gasped nervously.

Unrelenting, she began unbuttoning his shirt and loosening his belt. As she undressed him, Edward could see that her fingernails were neither grown long nor polished. Rather than feeling put off, Edward was attracted by the grit of her naked majesty.

After Bowed Lace pulled off his pants, Edward's arousal was apparent and irrepressible. She looked briefly and smiled. Had she been one of the girls back home, wearing lipstick and caked rouge, Edward might have thought she was mocking him. With her unpainted face, however, he sensed the tender appreciation of her soul, natural and mature. Having stripped Edward fully, she kissed his washboard abs. He tingled. She mounted the awakening she had stirred, enveloping it.

It was Edward's first, and he felt a perfect fit.

Bowed Lace rode Edward, joining in his joyful cries. Her movements accelerated, and she breathed heavily. She began to sweat.

Suspecting that it was also her first, Edward scrambled for a foothold that might enable him to withstand the test of passion. He knew that the mere sight of her chest, broad and luscious, would rob him of his virginity. Wanting to continue pleasing her, he turned to the right, toward the desiccated tree. Its curved trunk was writhing.

The wondrous and unleashed beauty threw back her head and shouted to the stars.

Edward understood nothing.

She shouted again, digging her modest nails into Edward's chest. The pain diverted Edward from his surge, allowing her to enjoy more.

Bowed Lace stroked back her hair with both hands as she began the descent from her peak. Her lips wet, she kissed Edward on his forehead.

With what little control he could muster, Edward rested his lover to her side, so that they were facing one another, their bodies still joined. Over her shoulder, Edward could see his sweater. He tried to speak, but was silenced by another kiss, this one on the lips.

Bowed Lace reached behind Edward and pulled him deeper inside her. She retreated from her kiss to look into his eyes. Their bodies one, she waited, clamping his buttocks in her firm hand.

He reached for her bow and held it, making the moment last.

With an unanticipated display of her dimples, however, Edward began to weaken. His core thrashed. Losing his grip on her bow, he let go. He felt a rush, an emptying that drew from his every limb. He was at once defenseless and omnipotent. As his lover had, he shouted into the night.

A shooting star cut the sky, leaving in its wake a luminescent tail.

Bowed Lace stroked Edward's face, and reached aside to give him back his sweater. She then kissed him on his exhausted midriff.

Edward turned to dress himself, so that the couple might lie together beneath the stars in his mother's house. He reached for his mother's sweater and smiled; he pulled it over his head and adjusted it. When he turned back, Bowed Lace was already dressed and walking away. "Wait!" he called out.

The distance between them grew as she journeyed off. Wending her lace through her eyelets, she never looked back.

"But…" In an instant, he could no longer see her.

They would forever be each other's first. And he did not even know her name.

# XVIII.

## The End of the Train's Platform

E dward practically hopped back to Vito's house. He took in the night air of the hilltop town as if it were cotton candy. He desired more—so much more—of the entire town and Bowed Lace.

His wish was granted. When he walked through the beads of Vito's brown box, a crowd awaited him.

Giovanni stepped forward. "Edoardo, these are your cousins," he announced, proud of the assembly he had gathered. "We were worried. We still don't trust those rocks. The earthquake cut the stone very sharp, you know."

"I'm fine," said Edward, throwing his arm around Giovanni like a boyhood pal. "I'm pretty sharp myself. Show me who we have here."

Giovanni went around the packed room, introducing Edward to each family member. Edward felt that they were marveling at him like an emperor returning from a victorious campaign. The eldest from each clan gave him something to bring home—a picture, a religious article, or a simple kiss and smile. As Edward accepted, he looked into the eyes of the presenters, wondering about their relationship with his mother while she had been among them, and how they might have said goodbye.

Giovanni pushed Edward along, until he reached the last in line—a woman holding what looked to be a bag of large cookies, shaped like donuts, covered with icing and sprinkles. Since the woman was standing beside

Nicola, Edward assumed that she was Giovanni's wife, but questioned his supposition based on what appeared to be a frail and aged frame.

"*Mia moglie*, Marietta," Giovanni confirmed. "She is giving you her *Taralli Dolci di Pasqua* Easter Cookies."

"But Easter is over."

"For my wife, Easter is all year round."

As Edward drew closer, he was entranced by Marietta's cleft chin and white teeth, but could not reconcile them with her deteriorating body.

Giovanni seemed to know what Edward was thinking. "She has just overcome a battle with cancer," he said. He kissed his wife on the forehead. "It's a miracle."

Marietta gave Edward the *taralli*. "Here, Edoardo, this I make for you family." She kissed him on both cheeks.

"*Grazie*," Edward replied, wondering whether Marietta had baked the cookies since his arrival, perhaps during the time that he was with Bowed Lace. He thought that the bag felt warm.

"Please come back," Marietta replied.

Marietta's understated elegance and erstwhile beauty charmed Edward. He wanted to talk more with her. "I'm so sorry about the loss of your daughter."

Marietta smiled gratefully. Giovanni pulled Edward away. "*Andiamo*. We must go now if you are going to catch the train from Salerno." Giovanni turned to his father, who was putting on his hat. "*Andiamo*."

The crowd shouted its farewells as Edward exited the brown box. Through the tumult, Nicola clung to his side, wearing a jacket.

When Giovanni saw that his son wanted to join the long ride, he knelt before him. "*Nicola, no. È troppo tardi*." He turned to Edward. "I see that he wants to come. I told him that it is too late."

Nicola ran to his grandfather, throwing his arms around him, pleading for intervention.

"*Va bene*," Vito said, looking to Giovanni.

"*Lui deve svegliarsi al mattino presto per la scuola*," retorted Giovanni. He explained his case to Edward. "He has to wake up early for school."

Edward could see that Giovanni was rankled that his father was trying to overrule him.

Giovanni turned to Marietta, giving her the last word.

"*Va bene*," she whispered.

"The Queen has spoken," Giovanni said before kissing his wife on her gaunt cheek. "And I cannot disobey her."

The four packed into the Giovanni's Lancia. Knowing that Nicola wanted to be next to him, and in deference to Vito, Edward insisted that Vito take the front passenger seat, next to Giovanni. Edward sat behind. As they rolled out of the town, the night hid the dirt that the car's wheels kicked up. Edward ventured a peek into Bowed Lace's brown box, hoping to catch a last glimpse of her. The house was dark.

Giovanni drove on.

Edward mused regretfully about how the one who had taken him to an otherworldly place would stay behind, in her brown box with her blind mother.

As Giovanni descended the mountain, the conversation became less provincial and more general. Rather than talk about family and the earthquake, Edward and Giovanni spoke of the Italian divide between north and south, and the American line between Black and White. They debated with zeal, and laughed with gusto. In the excitement, Giovanni took his eyes off the road to look back at Edward. "Your mother's family were good people. Maurizio, Nedda—"

"*Attenzione!*" yelled Vito, pointing to the curve in the road ahead.

Reflexively, Giovanni started to turn the steering wheel hard to the left, but stopped when he saw that he had more time. "We're okay," he said, as if there was no reason to be alarmed.

Vito pointed his finger in Giovanni's face. "*Smettila di raccontare storie mentre stai guidando*," he scolded.

"He wants me to stop telling stories while I'm driving." Giovanni gritted his teeth as he stared through the window.

Seeing that Giovanni was bristling from the reprimand, Edward stayed quiet. In the meantime, Nicola had fallen asleep on his shoulder. The Lancia

111

soon hit the straight and paved highway. From then on, Giovanni and Vito's exchanges were limited to the miles that remained, and which exit would be best to take.

The platform at the station was lit like a stage; Edward felt that he was under the spotlight. With a few minutes left before the train's departure, Giovanni excused himself. He returned with a cup of espresso for Edward. "Here, Edward, you'll need this to stay awake." Giovanni widened his eyes for emphasis. "Stopping in Napoli can be very dangerous. They will slice your pockets to steal your wallet. You won't even know it."

Edward thought to himself how Giovanni and his family had given so much to him in so short a time. Besides the food and hospitality, they had unlocked for him his mother's past, by bringing to life the desolation of his deported grandmother, and the pain it must have caused her daughter. They walked with him in the ruins of his mother's crumbled home—a place she must have thought of on so many occasions, without ever telling anyone. They brought him to his mother's baptismal font, the wellspring of his being. They had connected him with the extended family. Marietta's resilience in the wake of loss and illness had inspired him.

Edward felt it was time to reciprocate. After downing his espresso, he noticed that Nicola was curiously touching the camera that hung from his shoulder, and recalled the fascination the boy had displayed for it all day. Edward tinkered with the shutter until he got it to work again. He wound the film until it reached the end of the spool, then popped it out and pocketed it. He knelt down and offered the camera to Nicola. "Here, this is for you. You keep it until I come back."

Nicola did not even look to his father and grandfather. He merely pushed the camera back politely. His was not to take, Edward reflected, but only to give.

The guards blew their whistles, indicating that the train was ready to leave. Edward made his goodbyes, bear-hugging each of his elder cousins. Vito stuck a double-taped envelope in Edward's backpack. *"Per Maria,"* he said. *"Carissima Maria."* Whatever it was—a letter, enclosures, or both—Vito must have prepared it while Edward was with Bowed Lace.

"I will make her read it," Edward said. "And I promise you, I will get her to come back." He hugged Vito and Giovanni and rubbed Nicola's head fondly. He hopped over the train's first step onto the second.

"One at a time!" Giovanni shouted.

Atop the steps, Edward turned and gave a thumbs up. He found his couchette and hurried to the window to bid his cousins a final farewell. Giovanni instructed him, "Make sure that when you leave the train in Naples, you walk to the other side of the platform and stay there. Don't move." He grinned. "In Naples, they steal everything—even your smile."

"Thanks," Edward glowed. "But that would be impossible. You gave me too much to smile about today." He pointed to the corner of his mouth, still lit. "It would be too big to fit in their little sacks."

"My American cousin—whose smile is so big it cannot be stolen," laughed Giovanni, his hand raised affectionately.

"Don't worry. I'll be careful." All else that needed to be said had been spoken, or sealed in the envelope. As the train began to depart, Edward felt a tremendous sense of who he was and what he had found.

Nicola chased his cousin and the locomotive. As Edward admired Nicola's push to keep up, he noticed that his little friend ran the same peculiar way that he did, with his arms down at his side, in the robotic manner that Celeste loved to kid him about. A more introspective mood took over Edward: he realized that but for his grandfather striking out for America, Nicola's life was what his could have been, regardless of talent or virtue. As Nicola puffed for air, Edward assumed that his cousin hoped that if he ran hard and fast enough, his own life might someday be like Edward's. When Nicola reached the end of the platform, he climbed the railing that kept him from falling, and bid his American cousin goodbye. His arms swung rapidly from his sides to over his head, like an innocent creature trying to fly but kept back by the irons.

Behind the boy, Edward could see that Giovanni and Vito were arguing, with Giovanni pounding on his own chest as he barked. He surmised that Giovanni was probably telling his father that he was angry about how Vito had interfered with his parenting, or was embarrassed by the reprimand on the road. No different than the spats he had had with his own father, Edward thought to himself—particularly after an emotional day. Everyone would be fine by morning; the tiff would get lost in the savoring of the reunion.

# Part Two

*REMEMBRANCE*

# XIX.

## Mamma's Boys

It was a Saturday morning at the Bennett home, the summer following Edward's junior year abroad. The day dawned where it always did, through the east-facing picture window and into the kitchen—the place the Bennetts gathered for their meals, debates, and music. The light cascaded over an outside bush and through the glass, falling onto the pane's inside sill, which Guy and Marie lined with statuettes of saints. To keep their parents off balance, the children had contributed a miniature of a monk surfing to the plastic procession. After steering through the idols, the sun's rays splashed across the tabletop.

Above the table was a lamp. Crystal slats hung from the fixture, embracing three bulbs and creating a sparkle. Marie's meticulous housekeeping had always left them sparkling. On the side wall was the cuckoo clock; Guy had purchased it in Switzerland and carried it home so that he might have precise time.

Marie was making breakfast for Edward, who was still sleeping off the night. She chopped pepperoni for her son's omelet, listening to her cassette of *Madame Butterfly*, and singing to herself.

Upstairs, Edward's light snoring bounced off the trophies lining his bedroom—a permanent shrine that Marie kept while he was away at college. Edward had earned the awards while he lived at home, his mother said—so she insisted that they remain in his room.

Guy was in his expansive backyard, directing the laborers who worked for his construction company during the week, but whom he also used on the weekends to do odd jobs around his house. He was steadfast in preening his lawn every Saturday, obsessed with keeping it verdant. Guy pulled open the kitchen's sliding door, allowing the clatter of the mower to spill in. "Is Edward up yet?"

"Not yet," Marie replied as she tended to the pepperoni and eggs.

"It's nine o'clock, for chrissakes. I never slept that late when I was his age. I would've been up over four hours already. I would drive my grandmother to get vegetables for my mother's store. I was on the road at 4:30 in the morning, and I didn't even have a driver's license." Guy stepped into the kitchen. "I'm going to wake his ass up."

"Guy, let him sleep, he's tired," Marie called out.

But Guy was already stomping toward Edward's room, his shoes leaving behind a trail of green clippings.

Marie swept the excess grass into a dustpan and emptied it in the yard. She closed the sliding door to protect her territory from further intrusion.

Guy knelt at the foot of Edward's bed, and began squeezing his son's toes lightly—one by one—starting with the smallest. "Edward," he whispered in a matronly voice, "wake up."

From the first toe, Edward knew it was his father's famous morning torture. The idea was to provoke the body, slowly and incrementally, until the sleeper becomes so angry that he can rest no more. In futile desperation, Edward turned over in bed, hoping his father would leave him alone, but knowing he would not. He clamped a pillow over the back of his head to muffle the inevitable chiding.

Guy resumed with the next toe. "Edward, my son," he said, before reverting back to his own grandmother's voice with a smile. "*Figlio mio*, it's time to work. We have to get the vegetables for the store."

Edward shot up violently, as if from a nightmare. "What goddamn vegetables? There are no vegetables to buy, and there has not been a fucking store for over thirty years."

Foul but playful language was a unique breach for the otherwise devout

Bennett men. Edward got out of bed and yanked a pair of blue jeans off the floor. As he kicked his legs through the denim, he upbraided his father. "You have some kind of Oedipal complex with your grandmother that skipped a generation." He went to his closet, ripped a sweatshirt off a hanger, and punched through it.

"Don't hurt yourself," said Guy, his smile widening.

Edward stormed downstairs to the kitchen, controlling his laughter while continuing to lash out at Guy. "You're a goddamn lunatic. You should go see a shrink. Lie on a couch for an hour and get it all out of your system."

Guy quick-stepped playfully after Edward. "My grandmother was the best," he protested with a boyish grin. When they reached the kitchen table, Guy took the knife that Marie had set for her son, and went to the stove; he pushed Marie and her pan aside. He heated the knife.

"Guy, what are you doing?"

Guy kept his grin. "You'll see." He removed the knife from the flame, and threw the pan back on top. He returned to the table and sliced through the untouched bar of butter that Marie had unwrapped for Edward. "My grandmother's mind cut like a hot knife through butter. She made me into a man. She taught me how to think for myself and stand on my own two feet."

Edward rubbed the sand out of his eyes. "The butter was soft before your hot knife touched it." He looked at one of the grains he had plucked from his lower lid. "You really need professional help."

"And you really need to brush your teeth." Guy looked at a flowerpot in the middle of the table. "Your breath is wilting your mother's orchid."

Edward laughed, knowing that he was defeated by his father's crude wit. He marched back upstairs, to his bathroom.

"That wasn't very nice," Marie chided her husband.

"He loves it," Guy answered. "Makes him tougher for the real world."

When Edward returned, Marie served him the omelet. Without missing a beat, she wrested the butter knife from Guy, cleaned it with a napkin, and placed it back next to Edward's plate. "Here, Edward," she said. "You must be hungry. If you want some more, I will leave it on the stove, where it will stay warm."

Edward pushed back. "Mom, that's too much. I can't eat it all."

Guy sported a devilish gleam. "I wish I had a mommy who took care of me, making me eggs in the morning. My father was crippled. I had to work so my mother could open her store. If I didn't work, we couldn't afford any eggs."

Singing the bars of *Madame Butterfly* that were playing from the kitchen console, Marie went to the refrigerator to get Edward the orange juice she knew he would want. She interrupted her aria only momentarily to humor her husband. "Oh, be quiet. You did just fine."

"Your ass, I did," Guy replied with his salty brand of first-generation affection.

Marie returned to the table and poured the juice for Edward. "Are you kidding?" She craned her neck to look only at Edward, putting her back to her husband. She pointed to the corner of her mouth and spoke softly into Edward's ear. "Do you know how many times he has come home for dinner with gravy stains all over him because he already ate at his mother's?"

Guy sat quietly, content to let Marie complain about his devotion to his mother.

"Why do you think he keeps his office right next to where he lived with his mother and grandmother?" she continued. "He's a mamma's boy. Wrapped around her finger." Marie put her hands together, as if to pray. "His father, God rest his soul, had a stroke when he was young. I can't say anything about him." She became somber. "The poor thing couldn't move."

Edward filled the melancholy void. "So, Dad, tell me about your grandmother. What was her name?"

"Her name was Vincenzella," Guy said, his spirit lifting. "But we called her Nannone, which is Italian for grandmother."

"The Italian word for grandmother is *nonna*," Marie corrected as she cleaned her stove.

Guy waved her off. "Nannone was five feet tall and dynamite." He jerked his head at Marie. "Just like her. Dynamite." He got up to increase the volume on the stereo.

"Don't pay any attention to him, Edward," Marie shouted through the music. "He lives in a fantasy world." She turned to bark at her husband. "Do you want the rest of Edward's eggs?"

"Sure, dear—I would love my son's leftovers." Guy went back to his favorite subject. "When I was just paving driveways, it was Nannone who told me I should be building bridges. She even taught me how to do it."

Edward took a bite of his mother's pepperoni and eggs. "Oh, yeah? How? What was she, an engineer?"

"I'll show you how, you little shit." Guy went to the pantry, returning with two squat boxes of rigatoni and a long, thin package of spaghetti. He put the two boxes of rigatoni on the table side by side, like pillars, and laid the spaghetti across the top. "'Just like this,' she said. 'This is how you make a bridge.'"

"That's it?" he asked Guy. He looked at his mother, who was giving her husband scraps from Edward's plate.

Marie rolled her eyes.

"That's it." Guy glanced at his plate. "Marie, can you give me some crushed red pepper? My grandmother always put red pepper on our eggs when we were kids—she said it would keep us more alert." He turned back to Edward. "Nannone's simplicity was genius."

Edward swallowed. "If you say so."

# XX.

## Firstborn,

## A Seared Hand

The doorbell rang like church chimes. Marie dropped her pan and went to the foyer. "It must be Albert," she muttered to herself. "He said he would come by to see us this morning before work."

"What work?" Guy cried out, incredulous. "These damn law firms push these young guys to the bone." He looked down at his model bridge. "But the only thing attorneys make is *agita* for everyone and billable hours for themselves. Nannone and I created bridges that will defy time."

"You were the one who told Albert and me that we have to be professionals," Edward reminded him. "Wear a tie to work, keep your hands clean, and be part of the social elite. Do you remember that speech? You must've given it a thousand times."

"Yeah, yeah," grumbled Guy, still marveling at the pasta box bridge. "They don't make them like Nannone anymore—she was a great one."

Marie and Guy's eldest son, Albert, came striding in. The firstborn child in the first real American generation of Bennetts, Albert felt the pressure early on to acquire for the family the social wealth that Guy did not have enough time to attain for himself. Albert was expected to be a lawyer, fluent in the language and political system that Guy and his parents found so unwieldy. All was going according to Guy's plan. Albert had shot without interruption through law school, always at the top of his class. He landed a job at the most venerable law firm in the New York City area, Goddstone & Brock. But Albert's smoothness always had the wrinkle of a misgiving. His true desire was to be at his father's side in business. His father forbade such a venture. He wanted Albert to reach further—to engrave the family name on placards in country clubs, to etch *Bennett* in stone in universities and music halls.

"Oh geez, he's at it again," Albert complained, gripping the suspenders that were strapped over his starched white Oxford collar shirt. "I've heard this so many times. He's talking about how his grandmother used pasta boxes to teach him how to build bridges. Or maybe he's describing how Einstein's theory of relativity was really Nannone's idea."

"No, just how she and Roebling collaborated on the Brooklyn Bridge," Edward joined in.

"Everyone knows that the real key to Dad's early success in construction was Zi' Peppino," Albert said, sitting down across from Edward. He reached over to pick from the pepperoni and eggs on Edward's plate. "That man had a vision."

Edward used his fork to push back his brother's hand. "Have Mom make you your own eggs. These are mine." He pulled the plate closer, out of Albert's reach. He looked down at Albert's belly, which was beginning to spill over his belt. "It appears that you've already had enough." Edward pointed to his brother's hair. "And I think I see some grays. You're only twenty-seven years old, but at this rate you're going to look forty before you're thirty."

"Hmm," Albert said, smiling and sucking in his stomach. "But just remember. At seven years younger than me, you will always be my baby brother." He straightened his back and lifted his chin. "And an inch shorter than me."

"Stop it, you two," Marie interceded as she sat down with her boys. "For a while there, people were saying that you looked like twins. It's just that now that Albert is working, he doesn't have as much time to exercise."

Out of respect for his mother, Edward refrained from pushing his brother further. "Tell me, who was Zi' Peppino?" Edward asked.

"So now you want to know about Uncle Joe?" Albert replied smugly. "He was Nannone's brother," he explained as he grabbed Edward's glass and took a swig. "Mmm. That juice is good." He glanced over at his mother. "Hey Mom, how come you never make breakfast for me?"

"You and me both," Guy joined in.

"Never mind," Marie said defensively. "You two are grown men." As she looked at Edward's unshaven face, she caught herself. "What I mean is that you both have wives to take care of you. Edward doesn't have anyone." She paused. "Albert, do you want eggs? I have the pepperoni. Or if you want ham, I have ham. Try the ham."

"No, thanks. I already ate. And no, my wife did not make me breakfast. I had it at the diner, alone."

"How's Elizabeth?" asked Marie.

"You mean my dear Queen Elizabeth?" Albert pushed back from the table. "I wouldn't know. When I woke up this morning she was already gone. Off to her tennis game at Pine Ridge."

"I hear that's one of the most exclusive country clubs around," Edward said. "I'm surprised that they let you in."

"She has been going since she was a little girl," Albert said, dusting off his pants.

"Her father is a very wealthy man," offered Guy.

"I know," Albert shot back. "That's why you told me to marry her. 'A power couple,' you said. We would bring the family to the next level—social wealth."

Guy responded, "I said no such thing. It was your decision—"

"So you see, Edward, Uncle Joe..." Albert interrupted, leaving his words hanging. He was content to have zinged his father without bringing the volatile issue of his marriage to a head. He gathered his thoughts to gain distance from the subject of Elizabeth. "Uncle Joe," he repeated, "knew that although the driveway and sidewalk business was lucrative at the time, the company needed to diversify or it would go bankrupt, just like Dad's early competitors—Boliggi Brothers, San Pietro, Sanzini. All of them were once giants—and all of them eventually went belly-up, taking their sons with them."

Guy looked down at his hands folded on the table, as if accepting an award for his vision. "Albert's right, they're all gone. Families turning on each other as they fought over their last nickels. That's why I didn't want you guys in my business. Too wild—not a place for my family. You belong in suits with briefcases, above the fray." He pointed at Albert. "But the person with the vision was Nannone, not Uncle Joe. He had a problem keeping his *thing* in his pants—a different woman every night. He finally got caught when he had a child out of wedlock. He named him Oscar so that no one would ever know."

"No," Albert said, jumping in. "Wrong again. Uncle Joe's son was Oliver."

"Was it Oliver?" Guy asked.

"Yup," Albert said. "He wound up moving to Oklahoma and working on a farm." Albert burst with pride. "I know more about your family than you do. Zi' Peppino, Zi' Jimmy, Zia Lucia."

"You're like an old lady," quipped Edward. "All you do is dwell on the past. You might as well be knitting in your rocking chair."

"No, punk," Albert snapped. "The difference between you and me is that I take pride in Bennett family history." He looked to Guy for approval. "I used to sit with Grandma before you were even born. She would tell me all about the Bennett journey to America." He looked over to Guy. "I guess it's always up to the firstborn to keep the history and traditions. Right, Dad?"

"What about the Del Cielos?" Edward countered, at a lower volume.

"What about them?" Albert laughed, peering at his father.

Edward pushed away his plate. "Mom has a fascinating family, too. There's a lot there."

"Yeah, a lot of nothing." Albert got out of his seat and walked to his mother, still at the stove. He put his arm around her and tried to be diplomatic. "Don't get me wrong. I love my mother. There's just not much to her story. Born poor, but with food and a home. Her father fought for the United States in World War I, and she came over after World War II. She married Dad and is now queen of her suburban castle. Nothing real exciting in between marrying Dad and ruling this place—except for her brilliant eldest son."

Marie squirmed out of her son's clutches. "Never mind. Albert, did you get your season tickets to the opera yet? Your father will pay you back for them."

"I don't know if Elizabeth and I are going to do it this year. We just can't get into it. She loves the whole scene when we show up in the grand atrium, with all the beautiful people on the red carpet. Once the opera starts, she's asleep within twenty minutes." Albert laughed nervously from his throat. "We might as well be home in bed—the other place where she falls asleep within minutes."

"Shush," Marie said, slapping her son on the arm. "You remind her how hard it was for your father and I to get those seats for you. The waiting list is ten years." As she wiped the table of the crumbs left by her husband and sons, she added, "Music is good for your soul. You and your wife need it."

Albert raised his eyebrows. "Is that right, Anna Freud?"

"Good call on Sigmund's wife," applauded Edward.

"I was referring to his daughter, you meathead," Albert replied. "She was also a psychoanalyst, following in her father's footsteps." He looked at Guy.

"I wouldn't know about psychoanalysts," Edward shot back. "I've never thought about consulting one."

"Look at my boys go at it," Guy said proudly. "Arguing at the next level." He sniffed. "Except for the meathead part."

Albert stayed trained on Marie. "I thought the opera tickets were part of the package for my becoming a lawyer instead of joining my father in business and making ten times the amount of money that a lawyer could ever bill."

"Whoa," Guy interceded. "Didn't you just finish telling your brother about how all of the family-run construction businesses self-destructed?"

"That was them," Albert said defiantly. "We would have been different. We're smarter and closer as a family. Edward and I would have worked fine together, building a bigger and better company than you could ever imagine."

"Is that right?" Guy said. "And what about your sister Lisa Marie? I guess you think she would've been happy staying out of the business. Or maybe she would've been content just being your secretary." Guy covered his eyes with his hand. "I thought about it a lot. That your lives might be easier. But you would've cut each other up," he added softly.

Satisfied that he had made his father feel guilty, Albert returned his fire to his mother. "I'll tell you why I haven't bought opera tickets. Elizabeth and I have seen all the major operas already—*La bohème, Turandot, Tosca…*" He counted them on his fingers. "Puccini found two or three catchy bars and incorporated them into every opera. If you've heard one, you've heard them all. Then there's Verdi—*La traviata, Rigoletto, Aida.* The guy needed a hundred-person chorus to sing every time he wanted to make a point. I can see it now: nineteenth-century village peasants dropping everything in the middle of the day to belt out a few notes while their kids are starving. And let's not forget Rossini." He paused to laugh out loud. "I would rather take poison than sit through another *Barber of Seville.*"

"What about *Madame Butterfly?*" asked Marie, as the soundtrack continued playing behind her.

"I know it's your favorite, Mom, but it's no big deal. A Japanese woman waiting for her ex-beau—an American soldier with whom she sired a son—to return to Japan. When he does finally come back with an American wife, Butterfly kills herself. A story of hopeless love and suicide—not exactly uplifting."

"It's the music and the passion that make it, my dear son," Marie replied. "It allows you to escape the everyday for a little bit. It lets you forget about the parts of your life that—"

"The parts of your life that what, Mom?" Albert asked.

"Never mind. When you feel it, you'll understand."

Albert turned back to his father. "Personally, I'd rather be watching football. Dad, did your company get the luxury box for the Giants yet?"

"Fifty-yard line," Guy exclaimed, proudly. "Why don't you see if Elizabeth's father can get the governor to join us for a game? I can see it now: the Bennett boys watching a game with the governor!"

Edward tried to steer the conversation back to his mother and her music. "Mom, how did you first come to enjoy opera?"

"My mother," she said wistfully. "When we were in Italy, she used to love to sing. She had such a beautiful voice. While my father was away in America, she would always sing 'Un bel dì' from *Madame Butterfly*." As if on cue, the opera's signature aria began, Cho-Cho-San's voice rising and gliding. "My mother knew these words by heart," Marie explained, gesturing to the kitchen speakers.

"It sounds pretty, Mom," Edward said, "but what does it mean?"

"She's saying 'One fine day, we'll notice a thread of smoke arising on the sea. In the far horizon, and then the ship appears.'"

"I never hear you speak like that, to wax so poetically. That's amazing."

"It's pretty obvious," Albert jumped in. "It touches a nerve with Mom. How Grandma was sad at the long separation from Grandpa while he was in America—he a former American soldier no less. The parallels are as big as your ego—or your nose."

"I thought you had to go to work." Edward felt the bridge of his beak.

"He doesn't have to be at the office," Guy said. "It's all for show." He looked at Albert. "Stay here with us."

Edward looked cross at his brother. "I just wanted to make sure that he with the bigger nose, my brother Pinocchio, doesn't get in trouble at work."

Guy, his voice becoming somber, took control of telling his wife's story. "Once they finally were reunited in America," he said, "your grandmother became very ill. The pressure was too much."

"I know—that's when she was deported back to Lavenna," Edward added, resolved to contribute his newfound knowledge. "I got the whole story straight from the horses' mouth when I went to Lavenna. Neither of you two buffoons had the guts to go back there. I was the first."

"Do you know how many times I tried to get your mother to go back?" shouted Guy.

"I knew there was nothing there," said Albert.

"There was something there," Edward cried. "You have to hear it told by Mom's cousin Vito, and his son Giovanni—about how they took care of Grandma in Lavenna after she was deported because of her nervous breakdown."

"I'm still mad at you. I told you not to go back there," Marie scolded her son. "You lied to me."

Edward could sense in the tone of his mother's voice that despite her words, she had pardoned his defiance and fib, or ultimately would do so. "I'm glad I went," Edward said proudly. "They were a beautiful family. They took care of your mother."

"That's not what I'm talking about," Marie replied. "And it was my cousin Luisa who took care of my mother." She turned down the volume on the cassette console.

"I am just telling you what I heard when I was there."

"Luisa always loved my mother's music and did her best to surround Mom with it for the rest of her life. She would write to me about how my mother would always light up when she turned on the little transistor radio. Luisa made Vito buy the radio for my mother." Marie bit her lower lip. "Albert, you need to get those opera tickets."

Albert started back in on Edward. "If you found out so much about Grandma on your little trip," he lectured, "how come you don't know that her 'nervous breakdown' precipitated her schizophrenia, which was the real reason she was deported?"

Edward sat numb, embarrassed that he had missed this important fact during his journey.

Marie nodded that Albert was correct. Her voice quaked as she raised it. "Get those opera tickets, Albert." She went back to the console to turn up the volume.

As if calling from the grave, the soprano climbed her final notes. *"Tutto questo avvera, te lo prometto. Tieniti la tua paura. Io con sicura, fede l'aspetto!"*

Edward translated the verse as best he could inside his head. It was something along the lines of *This will all come to pass. Drive away your fears. He will return.*

Oblivious to the lyrics, Albert continued smugly, "So you see, Edward, I didn't need to go to Lavenna to know more than you."

"You obviously don't know what specifically caused our grandmother's nervous breakdown. Otherwise, you would've said it."

"You boys do not know my mother's story, her song, or much of anything for that matter," Marie said. "You're too busy trying to beat one another. You're always thinking about what you are going to argue about next, instead of listening. Argue less, listen more." She turned to Guy. "That includes you."

"Me? What did I do?" Guy's jaw dropped.

"All you and your mother ever want to talk about is your family. Nannone making a bridge with boxes of macaroni—please. Whenever someone talks about someone else, like my family, you don't want to hear it."

Guy sat up in his chair like a schoolboy. "What exactly is it that I haven't heard? I knew about your mother. I sent the money to Vito to take care of her."

"I told you before, it was Luisa who took care of my mother," Marie snapped. "No man could take care of my mother in that condition—especially after the war."

"What war?" shot Guy.

"*The* war," screamed Marie. "World War II!"

"There was no World War II in those hills," scoffed Guy.

"World War II," sighed Edward. "Maybe Prigler was right when he tried to take a wrecking ball to the Arch of Constantine. It's all about layers of truth."

"Why are you talking about the Arch of Constantine? And who the hell is Prigler?" Albert asked.

"Edward's friend from school," explained Guy. "Jewish kid. Real bright. Edward told me the story about the arch. I don't get it."

"So what does the Jew mean by 'layers of truth'?" sneered Albert.

"Nothing. It's just that oftentimes we think we know the truth, when there is a better truth that we never find or want to avoid. They're all truths, just different layers." Edward raised his eyebrows. "Prigler says it is like peeling an onion—so much so that it might make you cry."

"Well, like I said. Prigler is a bright kid," Guy said with his eyes cast down

130

toward the table. "But the better truth here is that your mom's mother was deported because of her schizophrenia, and she died alone." He looked at Marie, and jumped to correct himself. "With Luisa taking care of her, of course."

Marie nodded as she shuffled among her counters.

Guy cleared his throat. "You said 'No man could ever take care of her—especially after the war.' I still don't know what you're talking about. There were no soldiers in those hills." He laughed. "Except maybe for marching band practice."

Forgetting herself for a moment, Marie reached for a serving spoon she had left on the stove. The hot metal seared her hand. "Ow!" She bit her lip to suppress the stinging pain.

"What happened?" Guy jumped. "Let me put some ice on it."

"I'll be fine," Marie said, waving him off. She grabbed the butter from the table and applied it to her burn. "I can take care of myself." She tied a rag around her hand.

"That's your problem," Guy said. "You never need anybody's help. You're like a goddamn stone wall. You never let anyone in."

"You don't want to be in," she shot back.

"I think I can handle it, my dear. I have seen quite a bit in my day."

"The reason you do not know what I am talking about with my mother is that you've never seen war," Marie said, squinting in pain as she squeezed her seared hand with the rag.

"What war have you seen?" repeated Guy, his voice cracking.

"The Second World War. It was a horror. I don't want to talk about it."

"What about it?" asked Albert. "We firebombed the Nazis, A-bombed the Japs, and raised the flag. End of story." He plucked a plum from the fruit bowl in the middle of the table, and bit in as if to swallow it whole, spurting its juices.

Marie removed the rag from her seared hand to wipe Albert's mess. "Everything is a neat little story, isn't it? The good guys beat the bad guys, and everyone lives happily ever after. Life is more complicated, my dear son. Your history books are fairytales. I was there. I know what it was like."

"I guess that's why you never read us nursery rhymes as kids," replied Albert, still not willing to give. "Since they are just a bunch of fairytales." Seeing that no one was amused, Albert refrained from saying more. He took another bite of the plum, slobbering more of its juice.

Marie was jarred. Her seared hand throbbed. Instead of wiping Albert's new puddle, she reapplied the rag to her hand. She stared without blinking. "You'll never know. You never saw war. You didn't know the Nazis." She shook her head. "Oh, God. What am I saying? Someone get me some ice."

Guy went to the freezer, punched loose some ice, and brought it back to his wife. His voice leapt. "What are you talking about? When did you ever see war or know the Nazis?"

"Never mind," answered a straightened Marie as she grabbed the ice from Guy and applied it to her swelling burn. "I was confused. Leave me alone."

"Wait a minute," Edward said, lighting up. "When I was in Lavenna, I found a holster that had German writing on it. I didn't think anything of it at the time."

Easing himself back into his seat, Guy waved off the notion. "And you shouldn't think anything of it now. There were no Nazis in that little town." He took a shot from his coffee cup, even though it was empty. "Like I said—maybe the German marching band practiced there. But there was no fighting in those hills."

"Your father is right," Marie said as she pinched the temple of her head. "I'm just tired this morning. Albert, don't you have to go to work?"

Albert shrugged. "It's Saturday. The courts are closed. What can a judge possibly do to me? Besides, Dad says he wants me to stay."

Marie cleaned the table nervously. "C'mon, then—both of you help your father with the lawn. It is a good day to get work done."

"Easy, Mom," Edward joked. "We're having a nice family conversation."

"Nice for you. Not for me." She went to the sink, where she wrestled with the knobs for the cold and hot water.

# XXI.

## The Cook's Helper

A tiny knock came from the front door. "Somebody is here," said Marie. "I'll go see."

"What is she talking about?" Albert asked, his mouth agape. "I didn't hear a doorbell. I think she's hallucinating."

"I'm telling you," Guy said, cracking a smile. "That woman doesn't miss a thing. I think she has dog ears."

Edward opened his mouth wide and pretended to shout without a sound. He held a mute note for a few seconds. "Hey, Mom. Did you hear that?"

"Never mind," Marie quick-stepped through her palatial foyer, still clutching the rag to nurse her hand. She struggled with the oversized lock, and pulled open the thick oak door. A small girl spilled inside.

"Sunny, what are you doing?" asked Marie, as she scooped up the child into her arms.

It was Sonali Bruckenhouse, the seven-year-old who lived next door. She had become a grandchild of sorts for Marie, whose kitchen aromas of pasta and cookies tantalized the little girl like carnival lights from afar. With a father who was a hard-driven executive, and a mother preoccupied with being gracious, the only child was first drawn to Marie's kitchen during one of the many afternoons she spent with her nanny on her swing set. When the scent of Marie's homemade meatballs sneaked across the property divide, Sunny gave up her idle swinging and went pounding on Marie's back door.

She volunteered to be Marie's helper in the kitchen—a room rich with pots, melodies, and chatty visits from Marie's friends. Marie accepted Sunny's offer that day and every day thereafter.

Marie knelt to wipe Sunny's face with the rag she had wrapped around her burnt hand. "Sunny, you're crying. What's the matter, honey?"

"My…my…my," the girl stuttered, her breath heaving and tears gushing. "My daddy."

"Who's there?" Guy called from the kitchen.

"I'm coming," Marie shouted back, before redirecting her attention to the little girl. "Sunny, what about your daddy? Is he all right?"

Sunny bit her lower lip. "I don't know."

"What happened to him?" Marie asked softly, gripping Sunny's shoulders to calm her obvious inner turmoil. "Take your time, sweetie. Then tell me what happened."

Her head still shaking, Sunny caught her breath. "When I woke, my daddy wasn't there. Mommy said he went away during the night. She said that he doesn't love us anymore and that he's never coming back."

Sunny's momentary strength gave way. Her tears began to pour again and her little body shrank with fear. She threw her short arms around Marie's neck, and squeezed her eyes closed over her protector's shoulder. "Mrs. Bennett, am I going to see my daddy again?"

"Of course," Marie assured her. Still on her knees, Marie pulled back to look at Sunny. She dabbed the little girl's eyes to open them. Marie was startled at the sight of her own reflection in Sunny's tears. In that mirror, Marie's wrinkles smoothened and her hair was longer, transforming her into a little girl again. Sunny's wails became those of little Maria—weeping as she yearned for her father to come back to Lavenna from his new house in that New World, so that the family might share a home. Home was not a building for Marie, but a feeling of love, hope, and sanctuary—a place that she never found until she married Guy, and created one of her own.

Marie stood up, lifting Sunny with one arm. "Grownups do these things sometimes. But in the end, everything works out. Don't worry." With her free hand, Marie closed the door and locked it. She pulled on the door to confirm that it was in fact bolted. "Everything will be fine." Marie puckered her lips playfully. "C'mon. Let's go eat some of the fudge you and I made the other day."

Marie carried Sunny into the kitchen, where the men were waiting.

"Are you sure you locked the door like you always do, Mom?" asked Albert. "We all know what a crime-ridden area this is."

"Yeah," Edward followed. "Don't you remember that violent break-in—when the Armisteads found a deer in their foyer? The deviant doe walked right through their open front door."

Albert raised his open palm to give his brother a high five. "That was good."

"Locking the doors is a habit from when I was a little girl," Marie smiled. "What can I tell you?" She turned to Sunny. "Boys," she said, "this is Sunny from next door. Say hello." Marie lowered Sunny and the volume of her music.

Sunny's red face and racing breath made apparent to everyone that she had been crying.

"Hello, Shelly," said Guy to the timid little girl, as he pulled up a seat for her. "I'm glad to meet you. You must be one of Mrs. Bennett's friends who she keeps secret from me."

"I've mentioned her to you," Marie countered. "You just weren't listening."

"And Dad, it's 'Sunny,' not 'Shelly,'" Edward explained. "You're terrible with names." He turned to Sunny. "Sunny, my dad is so bad with names. I remember one time, I wished my dad a happy birthday, and he called me by our dog's name—Caesar."

Sunny smiled.

Edward continued. "I said, 'Happy birthday, Dad,' and he said, 'Thank you, Caesar.' I was waiting for him to throw me a bone."

Sunny put her hand over her mouth and started to giggle.

Guy joined in the fun at his own expense, seeing that it would cheer the little girl. "Maybe the reason I called you 'Caesar' is because some of the girlfriends you bring home look like dogs. Woof, woof!"

"Can we stop with the dog jokes?" groused Albert, upset that he was not part of the joust. "First it's Mom's hearing, then Edward's girlfriends. Enough, already."

Marie came back to the table with a plate of fudge, and set it in front of Sunny. "Don't mind them, Sunny. They're silly. Here is the fudge we made on Wednesday, sweetheart."

Sunny took a bite of the fudge, rubbing her remaining tears with the back of her hand. "I wish I had silly brothers and a father."

Marie wrapped her seared hand, still bound in the dishcloth, around Sunny's. "Sunny is upset because her daddy went away for a little bit," Marie explained, widening her eyes to indicate that she was telling a cover story for Sunny's father having left home.

"Shelly," said Guy, unable to correct his chronic name problem, "a lot of times daddies need to go away to take a rest. It's because they work so hard."

"Have you ever gone away to rest?" asked Sunny, staring at him with her big brown eyes.

"Sure, sure," Guy said, swiveling in his chair. He pointed to Edward. "I used to go away all the time with this guy when he was a Boy Scout."

"I became an Eagle, the highest rank," boasted Edward. "Most guys quit at Webelos." He looked at his brother. "In case you didn't stick around long enough to learn it, Webelos stands for 'We'll Be Loyal Scouts.'"

"But my daddy did not take us with him," squeaked Sunny. "Not me or Mommy. He just went." She stopped chewing the fudge. "He didn't even kiss me goodbye."

Marie fiddled with the rag on her hand, rewrapping it.

Albert gave a try at consoling Sunny. He spoke with a serious tone. "Life is hard to figure out. Sometimes there's no answer."

Sunny frowned, fearing what Albert might say next. Marie and Edward glared at him, to stop him from saying something that might make her feel worse.

"Relax," Albert said to his mother and brother as he stroked Sunny's long black hair. "But I promise you one thing, Sunny. Nobody in the world loves you more than your mommy and daddy."

"Really?" the little girl looked up.

"Really," Albert leaned back.

The doorbell rang.

"That's probably her nanny," Marie mouthed from behind Sunny. "I'll go get her. You keep talking with Sunny," she said as she pointed to her men.

Feeling he had made a connection, Albert continued. "Sunny is such a pretty name. Is that a nickname?"

"Yes," the little girl responded, licking the fudge from her fingers. "My real name is Sonali. That's my mommy's name."

"How did you get the nickname?"

"My daddy."

"You see that?" Albert said. "Your father loves you so much that he nicknamed you after the sun. You're his sunshine."

Guy bowed his head and raised his eyebrows at Edward.

Marie brought Sunny's nanny into the kitchen, pretending that it was like any other day. "Boys, this is Sunny's nanny, Rosa."

"*Hola*, Rosa," waved Edward. "*Cómo está usted?*"

"Rosa does not speak Spanish, Edward," his mother chided.

"Nice try, little brother," laughed Albert. "Or should I say *Eduardo?*" The others joined in Albert's glee.

Marie clapped her hands and stayed upbeat. "Rosa is going to take Sunny to her aunt's house for a sleepover, where she can play with her cousins."

Sunny's mood grew heavy. "But I want to stay here with you," she said, pulling on Marie's apron.

Marie knelt. She again saw her reflection in Sunny's eyes—this one true to her age. She gazed without speaking.

"Mom, are you trying to have a staring contest with Sunny?" asked Edward.

Marie snapped out of her momentary trance, and turned to him.

"Made you look!" he said, pointing. "Sunny wins the staring contest."

Marie turned back to Sunny. "Don't worry, honey," she said. "Everything will be fine. You're going to have a great time with your cousins. And when you get back, we'll cook some new recipes." She handed Sunny a plate of fudge. "Share some of this with your cousins. Tell them you made it all by yourself."

"Okay," said Sunny with a long face.

"Go ahead," said Marie, suppressing her own sadness for Sunny. With the rag from her seared hand, she wiped some fudge from the corner of Sunny's mouth. "You'll be fine."

"Thank you, Mrs. Bennett," Rosa called out as she escorted Sunny slowly to the front door, her plate of fudge in hand.

"You're welcome," Marie whispered, still kneeling.

# XXII.

## Sorting through the Hype

O nce everyone heard Rosa and Sunny close the front door, Edward joked, "Mom, aren't you going to lock the door?"

Marie did not move.

Guy congratulated Albert. "That was very sensitive of you, Albert. The way you handled that little girl was very impressive. Maybe you and Elizabeth should have a little girl."

Albert was at the counter, pouring himself a cup of steaming black coffee. "What are you talking about?" he asked with uncharacteristic humility. "I was just trying to make her feel better."

"You were very tender. That's all I am saying."

As Albert sipped his coffee, he hardened, leaning back against the counter. "From what I know, 'Sonali' is an Indian name. And we all know that the guy next door—Taylor Bruckenhouse—is the head of his family's hardware empire."

Edward looked puzzled.

"You know, the Bruckenhouse screw," explained Albert. "The guy is worth millions. He's practically an English knight. What was he thinking marrying an Indian?"

"Probably the same thing that your Queen Elizabeth thought when she married a greasy guinea-wop like you," jibed Edward.

Marie remained aside the table, kneeling in the wake of the emptiness and despair that Sunny had left behind.

"No seriously, Edward," continued Albert. "Those are major cultural differences that are hard to overcome in a marriage. The mother is probably a Muslim, and the father is a WASP."

"What makes you think that the mother is probably a Muslim, when the majority religion in India—the vast majority—is Hinduism?"

"Same thing," Albert responded without hesitation.

Guy also ignored Edward's inconvenient fact, which would stand in the way of the generalization he was about to make. "Well, it depends whether her mother is a Sunni Muslim or a Shiite Muslim. My financial guy at the office, Arvind, is Sunni. He and his wife are beautiful people. It's the Shiites that you can't trust. So it really depends."

"Judging by her nickname," said Edward, "I'm betting that you guys think she is one of the good ones—a Sunni."

The men continued to fill the air over the still-genuflected Marie.

"All I know is that they are all killing each other—Sunnis, Shiites, Jews," said Albert. Overhearing the twenty-four-hour cable television news from the adjacent living room, Albert went to the couch to retrieve the remote control. He turned up the sound.

"A bomb went off in a market in Jerusalem today," reported the newscaster. The screen flashed an image of a little boy crying.

"This is what I'm talking about," explained Albert. "Centuries-old hatred. No one can stop it."

Guy turned reluctantly from his chair, toward the television. "It's not as bad as people on the news make it out to be. The press needs a story. They'll show the same picture of a little kid crying ten different times, just to fill the airtime. Used to be that the news was on between 4:30 and 6:00, and that was it. Now, on cable TV they are starting to blast away twenty-four hours. It's all hype." Guy folded a twenty-dollar bill, and used it as a toothpick to clean a gap between his teeth.

"Hype?" Marie rose to her feet. She went to Albert and grabbed the remote. She tried to push the buttons with her seared hand, to click off the little boy crying. Her numbness made her fumble.

"Yeah. It's all exaggerated hype," said Guy, continuing to floss with his money.

"How do you know? Have you been there?" Marie continued, still trying to find the right button. "These remote controls are so complicated. *Mannaggia!*"

Edward went to his mother's aid. "Mom, what are you trying to do?"

The little boy's face continued to fill the television screen, crying. "This boy is looking for his parents," the reporter continued. "Rescue workers are still making their way through the carnage."

She handed the remote to Edward. "Here, turn it off." She went back to the kitchen, her seared hand trembling.

Guy finished cleaning his teeth with his folded bill. He reclined in his seat, his hands clasped over his head. "As a matter of fact, you and I were both in Israel. We had a fabulous trip. I felt safer there than when I am in New York."

"We might have been in Israel, but you were never *there*—never in war," Marie countered, standing over her sitting husband. "Those pictures of kids crying wouldn't be exaggerated if they showed them a thousand times." She scurried back to her sink.

"And you know that because of the Nazis that were supposedly in your town during World War II?" asked Guy—half-joking, but half-serious.

"Lavenna is in the hills, Mom," Albert said, laughing. "Why on God's earth would there have been Nazis in Lavenna?"

"Whatever you say. You two know it all," Marie replied, back at her sink, her eyes glazing and voice trailing. "I think you and your father are the ones filled with hype."

The air in the kitchen grew tenser than Edward could ever remember. He could never recall his mother being so distant, so persistently defiant. It was not that she was some obedient servant; it was just that ordinarily, she remained above the fray, immune from the rantings of her testosterone-driven husband and sons. For the first time, she was part of the mess, and appeared unable to clean it up. Edward thought he saw his mother beginning to shake.

"Mom, are you all right?" asked Edward. He went to the sink to join her.

"I'm just a little cold." She paused. "Seeing Sunny so upset really bothered me. It reminded me..." Marie looked down at her hand. "I can't believe I burned myself."

"I'll get you the ice again," Guy said. "It'll make you feel better."

"I'll be fine," Marie said, raising her voice. "Leave me alone."

Edward went to the refrigerator and made a wrap of ice. He led his mother from the sink back to the table. "Here, Mom—sit and relax. You have been going all morning."

"I hope Sunny's father comes home," Marie sighed. "That little girl needs a father. And that boy on television..." Her pent-up emotions became too much, and she began to bawl. She buried her head in her arms on the kitchen table. Her seared hand lay outstretched, vulnerable and unattended. The tears kept coming. Guy pulled his chair closer to Marie, to hold her hand.

The boys went quiet. *Madame Butterfly* had ended. The only sound was the ticking of the cuckoo clock on the wall, which Edward began counting to himself. His mother's weeping would not subside until the clock ticked forty times, he thought—one for each year since she was last in Lavenna.

When Marie raised her head, her eyes were red. She tried to say something, but no words came.

"Mom, it's all right," Edward said softly. Heeding Prigler's warning about truth and its volatile layers, he looked at his mother, determined only to listen, hoping his brother and father would do the same.

It was not all right. Marie pushed her chair back. She looked at her husband and sons, and then around the room, as if she was searching for something. She began pacing her kitchen, from wall to wall, squeezing her temples.

The men sat tight. Edward gripped the arm of his chair to keep himself from intervening.

When Marie stepped quickly toward the doorway, Edward was not sure whether she was exiting or about to fall. He sprang up to help.

As she staggered toward the door, Marie grabbed the frame and leaned against it. Her forehead upon her hand, bent over and breathing heavily, she looked like a runner after a grueling race.

Edward approached and held her elbow gently.

Marie straightened up. "I'm okay," she said unsteadily. She appeared lightheaded.

"C'mon, Mom, let's go back to the table," Edward told her.

Marie accepted Edward's escort. Once she sat back down, Albert spoke. "Like you always say to us, Mom—if you have something inside of you, let it out. We're here for you."

After a long and turbulent pause, Marie Del Cielo broke her vow of silence.

# XXIII.

## Imprisoned Without Bars

I t was the late summer of 1943. The winds of World War II were
blowing from the battle-plagued coast of Sicily toward the sleepy
gulf of Salerno. In contrast to Naples, whose personality drew from
its brewing volcano Vesuvius, Salerno had long held the role of the quiet
second city, its boat-filled harbor content with a modest catch. At this
coincidence of place and time, however, the notch of land on sea had the eye
of Allied leaders, who were intent on stamping out the German forces on
continental Europe. With the fall of Mussolini in July, the plans for invasion
were finalized. The Allied heads, deliberating safely away from the lines of
combat, decided that they would use Salerno's favorable offshore gradient
to touch down and move north, so that they might hasten the end of a war
that had already gone on too long. Anticipating a landing, the Germans
were moving defensively and aggressively, like an animal being tracked in
the wild.

This was the climate one Friday as eight-year-old Maria Del Cielo
returned from the beach in Salerno to her hilltop town of Lavenna. Though
the thunder of war could be heard approaching, with the sounds of artillery
shots and low-flying planes advancing from the south, Maria and her mother
Nedda persisted with the annual stay at their lido, determined to keep one
of the few family luxuries that had survived the Great Depression. Her
father, Maurizio, was a native-born foreigner. He had left Lavenna early,

144

earning his new citizenship as an American soldier in World War I. For much of his marriage, Maurizio was absent, busy establishing a new life in the new land, which he promised his family would benefit all of them. The money he made in America as a blacksmith and tanner—currency he sent home to Nedda—justified his passage.

Their skin still rich with the sea's salt and the sun's butter, Maria and her mother stepped off the bus to walk the rest of the way to their house. Maria stopped to scoop up some fresh water from a roadside stream. As she drank, Nedda broke off a yellow flowered shoot from a juniper bush, its berries not yet bloomed. A car with whitewall tires honked as it passed, causing the two to jump. Once grounded, they looked at one another and laughed. Nedda slid the juniper shoot into her daughter's hair, between her ear and head. As they entered the town gaily, Maria enjoyed the smell of olives growing from the tree in the corner of the square. A man swept around the monument in the center as two children chased one another around its pedestal. Mother and daughter stepped through the narrow doorway into their home.

Maria's grandmother, Angelina, waited inside, sewing in her chair. "How was the beach?" she asked flatly, raising her strained eyes only briefly, without missing a stitch.

"It was beautiful, Grandma," glowed the diminutive Maria as she ran to her grandmother's lap. "We swam all day and ate seafood for dinner. One night we ate peppered mussels that were almost as good as the ones you make. And then we watched the sun set. You need to come with us to the apartment next summer."

"I'm not a swimmer anymore," replied Angelina. "I'm getting too old."

"Don't let Grandma fool you," Nedda said, pinching her daughter's chin. "She's still strong as an ox. We'll go in the ocean together next summer. I promise."

"We'll see," Angelina replied with a glint of hope. Her fingertips numbed by the misses of her needle, she kept to her sewing. "What a beautiful flower in your hair," she said, without looking up.

"Mamma gave it to me!"

145

Nedda was delighted by the pleasure she had given her daughter, and shared with her mother. Only in her thirties, her early-graying hair and hazel-green eyes had been an irregularity in the town since the day in 1926 when she had arrived for her arranged marriage to Maurizio; she was just eighteen at the time of their union, he ten years older. She had been born and raised on a neighboring hill that might as well have been a distant country. Her father and Maurizio's, both successful blacksmiths, thought the union a healthy one: she the beautiful and dutiful wife and mother, he the provider. But her look, at once elegant and haunting, did not quite fit into Lavenna's squares. Given their age difference, she was never Maurizio's contemporary. The locals always stared at her and whispered, as locals are wont to do when faced with an unknown quality. Long deprived of her husband, Nedda was nourished by Maria's smiles.

"Mamma, did Maurizio write?" asked Nedda.

Angelina tossed her head toward the kitchen table. "Over there," she replied, noticing the flutter in her daughter's eyes.

Nedda dropped her bag and raced to the table. Her veined ivory hands quivering, she tore open the thick envelope. Wrapped in a piece of paper was a wad of freshly minted Italian lira, which Maurizio had exchanged for the American dollars that he had earned. Nedda cast the money aside and rummaged through the paper for a message from her husband, something she could cling to and muse about in her marital solitude. The sheet was blank. Though she had never enjoyed a deep connection with her distant husband, her heart still sank.

"What did he say, mamma?" Maria said, bouncing. "What did papà say?"

As Nedda stood still with the paper, her mother shuffled to her aid. Looking over Maria's shoulder with her threaded needle and material in hand, Angelina fabricated a message for her granddaughter. "The summer has been hot, and I have been working hard. I'm sorry I have not been able to write more, but I find it too painful in these difficult times." Angelina squinted, feigning to see Maurizio's message. "I miss you, Nedda, and my little Maria. Give her a kiss for me. We will all be together in America soon." She looked to her daughter's pout. "Love always, your husband Maurizio."

146

Nedda smiled as if the words spoken by her mother were actually written by her husband. She recast the paper around the money, and went to an armoire in the kitchen to make the deposit. In Nedda's simple kitchen, with its wood-burning stove and a square table on a stone floor, the armoire was her art and treasure. Maurizio had it custom made for her, and had attended to its every detail, from the curves of its drawers to the leather on its top. Maurizio himself crafted the iron knobs in his blacksmith shop. To anyone who asked, Nedda said that the armoire was in the kitchen because it was too large for her bedroom; the real reason was that she wanted to show it off, as a sign of her husband's devotion. From the top drawer, she pulled a golden tin box.

Nedda opened the golden tin and put the money in its place. Before sealing it again, she lifted the bills to look at the black-and-white wedding picture of her and Maurizio that lay loosely on the bottom. The fading photo was the only image that remained of that day. His face was determined, hers youthful and abiding. She drew a slow breath. She stuffed the money back in the golden box, over the snapshot, burying it. She struggled to cap the tin with its lid. The lid's grooves were resistant, but ultimately relented.

"*Achtung! Achtung!*" blared a loudspeaker from down the street.

Nedda dropped the tin box. The lid flew off on impact; the money and wedding picture scattered across the floor.

"*Achtung! Achtung!*" came the blaring voice again—this time closer, and accompanied by the buzz of an engine and the grinding of slow-turning wheels.

*Wheel and engine, engine and wheel—the rhythm of a raid, ripping the town seal.*

"Mamma, what's that noise?" Maria cried.

Nedda and Angelina looked at one another, and took measured steps to huddle with Maria. They knew that war had arrived uninvited. "Some men with guns from another country have come to visit," explained Angelina. "But they are not here to hurt us. They are looking for Americans."

"But papà is American," Maria squeaked.

"No, he's not!" replied Angelina, in a hard whisper. "If anyone asks you, your papà was Italian, and is dead. *Dead*—do you understand?"

"I understand," Maria whispered.

Angelina tightened her grip on her daughter's shoulder, and Nedda tightened her grip on Maria's. The door rattled from the clatter of armored procession. The wheels and engines stopped. Six steps more came from the boots, heavier and closer. War was at their front door.

Maria started to speak, but Angelina covered her mouth.

The doorknob turned—once clockwise, then slowly the other way, followed by a series of impatient jiggles.

A shout came from further up the German line.

The doorknob snapped back to its natural position. After the sound of six steps running from the house, the military march resumed and passed.

"Everything will be closed today," said another voice amplified from the engine and wheel, this one Italian. "The courts, town hall, and all of the stores."

Nedda looked at her mother. "That is—"

"This is *Pretore* Clementino," continued the loudspeaker. "Everyone is to remain in their home. The Germans mean no harm. They are our friends. Stay inside for your own safety."

Nedda rushed to peek through her front window, still in shock from the intruder at the front door, and what she had heard. In the receding distance, she saw the back of a military truck and its driver in foreign helmet, topped with a spear aimed at the sky. The truck was flanked by a platoon of twenty soldiers, goose-stepping in unison, with their rifles over their shoulders; their high kicks intimidated Nedda. Lavenna's judge, Massimo Clementino, was standing in the passenger's seat, facing opposite to address the captive town while pulling away. He used the title of *Pretore* that Italy had given its judges since Roman times. The turning of the war truck's wheels threw dirt on his glasses, and on the black robe that he was still wearing. Pretore Clementino attempted to clear his spectacles while he spoke—but finding it futile, he dropped his free arm to his side and pinched his garment. He would struggle to see through the dirt. A string of army tanks followed.

"They have Pretore Clementino," gasped Nedda to her mother and daughter behind her. "And he looks completely different—not himself. I think he is—"

"Going to be just fine," interrupted Angelina, with her arms draped over her granddaughter. "Pretore Clementino is going to be just fine—isn't that right, Nedda?" She held Maria close.

Nedda followed. "That's right. That's exactly what I was going to say. Pretore Clementino is going to be fine. Like he said, so long as we stay inside, the Germans mean no harm."

"Are you sure?" Maria asked.

"Positive," Nedda replied, glancing above Maria at her own mother, in search of the same affirmation.

"Mamma, who is Pretore Clementino?" Maria peeped.

"He is a wise man," said Angelina, looking down at the girl. "Why don't you tell her about him?" she added, nodding to Nedda. "I'll cut some *soppressata*," she added.

"Sit down," replied Nedda as her smile widened, anticipating the spicy taste of the hard salami. "I will tell you a story about Pretore Clementino."

Her girls secure, Angelina bent her brittle frame to gather Nedda's strewn money and wedding picture. She deposited the valuables back in her daughter's tin, and returned the gold box to the top drawer of the armoire. She sliced the *soppressata* judiciously, and placed it on the table.

Nedda started describing Pretore Clementino with animated detail. "Every town has its justice…"

Angelina shuffled to her station on the far end of the kitchen table and resumed her sewing. She reached into her dress pocket to pull out her wooden spools of colored thread. She chose black, wet the end of it on her tongue, and placed it through her needle.

# XXIV.

## The Judge's Hat

Nedda began her story by describing a trial call in Lavenna's town hall, which doubled as the courthouse on the third Friday of each month. Packed inside were the townspeople, with their causes and claims, shifting to find balance on their uneven folding chairs. At the head, where the pretore was to sit, a table stood precariously, with its legs ready to buckle. Next to that was a chair with a gray coat of paint that set it apart from the rest, occupied by a snoozing elder with pants pulled above the navel of his pasta-filled belly. Mouth open wide and head lurching back, his mid-afternoon snore was drowned out by the pre-call clamor. He was the pretore's clerk, and his job was to keep the order. In his sleep, he kept a tenuous grasp of the court ledger on his lap.

Nedda and Angelina stood in the back, waiting for Nedda's case.

Without ceremony, Pretore Clementino entered through the side door, silencing the crowd. He wore an unzipped black robe over his suit. His neck was draped with a white band that had a white bow-tie stitched upon it; his large cranium was squeezed by his judicial toque. Nedda was struck by the handsome and studied lines of the pretore's face. His spectacles were perfectly round, rimmed by subtle gold frames. His large blue eyes and cleft chin were strong, but not aggressive. As he sat down behind his judicial table, he removed his stiff round hat and placed it at his side. Its weight made the meager table wobble.

"Good afternoon everyone," he said with a smile. "If the clerk will give me my ledger, we will get started."

The clerk's snores continued, becoming audible.

The crowd snickered.

The pretore reached with his foot to step gently on the clerk's toe, so as to wake him without further embarrassment.

"Silence!" the clerk shouted, jumping up from his slumber. He caught the ledger of cases before they slipped from his lap. "Here is the list of cases for the day, Pretore Clementino," he said as he stood to present the ledger. Still a bit dazed from his nap, the clerk gave the judge a military salute. He turned. "Silence," he repeated for the crowd, pulling up his pants, which were already secured by both belt and suspenders.

"If he hikes his pants up any higher," Angelina told her daughter, "they will cover his mouth. Maybe then, we won't hear him snoring."

"Thank you," Pretore Clementino said to the clerk after accepting the ledger. "As always, your services are much appreciated."

"Thank you, *illustrissimo Signor Pretore*," the clerk said, bowing in full.

A man burst in through the main entrance, pulling a goat on a leash, dragging a youth by his ear. The crowd gasped, surprised by the intrusion. "Pretore," called out the burly plaintiff, "I just caught this scoundrel stealing my goat. I give him work, and this is how he thanks me. He is a no-good thief, and I want him punished. Now!"

"You will not raise your voice in my courtroom," replied Pretore Clementino evenly. "And you will let go of your employee's ear, for there is only one animal among you." He looked to the employee, whose ear was clearly throbbing in pain. "Your name, sir?"

"Corrado Piccolo," the accused boy replied meekly.

"Clerk, please escort Mr. Piccolo to the defendant's chair," continued the judge, with his eyes on the imposing one. "Although your case is not listed, I will hear you first, as I assume that this is an emergency and that you are prepared."

The man caught his breath. "Yes, it is an emergency," he replied. "And I am prepared."

"Very well. Your name, sir?" the pretore asked.

"Arrigo D'Abruzzi," answered the man with his goat.

"If you and the goat will please sit to my left."

Once everyone was in place, including the goat, the pretore started his questioning. "Mr. D'Abruzzi—explain to me what happened."

"This little piece of shit," D'Abruzzi said, pointing with his thick fingers, "is supposed to take care of the animals on my farm. He's lucky I even gave him a job. He's my sister's son, and has been lazy since the day he was born. I always told her that she was too easy on him, but she wouldn't listen."

"I am not interested in your family history," said the pretore, holding up his hand. "As you can see, I have many cases to hear. Just tell me what happened."

"This little disgrace asks me this morning if he can take a break. Twenty minutes later, somebody tells me he sees the boy freeing my goat in the valley, telling the animal to leave and never return—as if the animal understands his stupid words." D'Abruzzi reached over to the goat and peeled back its ear, displaying the brand. "AD—Arrigo D'Abruzzi. The little bastard was throwing my property away." To underscore his point, he pulled on the goat's ear. "*My* property. He was stealing *my* property."

With the tug from D'Abruzzi, the goat went into a frenzy, bucking and freeing himself from his owner's hold, running wildly through the courtroom.

Women screamed and men yelled. "Don't let him bite me," one woman shrilled, cowering in the corner.

"Slay the beast!" cried a man hiding behind the pretore.

For his part, the pretore stood atop his chair, studying the situation with a fixed and empty gaze, content to let it play out.

"Mr. D'Abruzzi, restrain your goat," exhorted Pretore Clementino, bending down to slam his gavel. He straightened his glasses.

D'Abruzzi chased the goat through the aisles, his girth tussling skirts and hats along the way.

Eventually, the goat went to Corrado Piccolo, submitting to the boy's gentle strokes of his hair. "Good boy," young Corrado whispered to his hollow-horned friend. "Good boy."

The crowd, too busy with its hysteria, did not take notice. One man ran out the door, yelling, "I'm going to get my gun!"

"Order, order!" Pretore Clementino demanded. "There is no need to shout, and no need for guns in my courtroom. Mr. Piccolo has the situation under control, and will keep it that way. Won't you, Mr. Piccolo?"

D'Abruzzi stood over his nephew's shoulders, obviously wanting to reclaim his goat, but knowing that it now would be impossible, in light of the pretore's request that the boy keep the animal restrained.

"Mr. D'Abruzzi, you can return to your chair. Leave the goat with Mr. Piccolo until we are finished."

"Yes, sir," answered a diminished D'Abruzzi as he lumbered back to his place.

The pretore took in the tenderness between the boy and the goat, as the rest of the crowd whispered. "Is there anything else you would like to say, Mr. D'Abruzzi?"

"No, sir," D'Abruzzi said, still catching his breath.

The pretore continued to look at the boy and the goat. "I have heard enough. Mr. D'Abruzzi, you have failed to make your case."

"But Pretore," D'Abruzzi growled, "it is clear that he stole my property. What more proof do you need?"

"The problem, Mr. D'Abruzzi, is that you have no proof at all."

"What do you mean?" asked D'Abruzzi, his thick eyebrows crunching.

"The only so-called evidence that you have is the allegation of some stranger who says he saw the boy in the valley with the goat, telling the goat to go away. That witness is not even here, so I have no testimony to rely upon."

"But I can get him here," D'Abruzzi offered. "It will take only a few minutes."

"Too late, Mr. D'Abruzzi. You stormed in here, telling me that you had an emergency and that you were prepared. I heard your case, complete with testimony from the goat," opined the pretore, with a trace of a smirk. "Besides, by your own admission, there was no theft, because the boy was not keeping the goat for himself or giving it to another. He was asking it to leave to return to the wild—perhaps so that you would not put more hot irons on it to inscribe your initials." He paused. "And you yourself said that no animal can understand the words of a boy, much less a stupid one."

The crowd laughed out loud as D'Abruzzi boiled.

"As for you, young man," the pretore said, turning to Corrado Piccolo. "Mr. D'Abruzzi is your uncle, who has been kind enough to give you a job. You must be grateful and respect him. The next time you are in my courtroom, the result might be different."

"This pretore is so intelligent," Angelina whispered to Nedda. "He did nothing, but achieved everything." She exhaled a sigh of relief. "We will be fine."

"The next case," Pretore Clementino read from his ledger, "is Nedda Del Cielo."

Nedda looked at her mother, her fear welling. Angelina stood, but paused, not sure if she was entitled to accompany her daughter. The pretore signaled with his hand, inviting Angelina to join her daughter at the defense table.

For the prosecution was Giacomo Andratti, a young advocate whose hands clung to the white band around his neck. "Pretore Clementino," he said with a lift, "I am Giacomo Andratti, *Il Procuratore Del Re.*"

"Mr. Andratti, what is the charge against Mrs. Del Cielo?"

"Adultery," answered the procuratore, stroking his ascot. "Mrs. Del Cielo is accused of committing adultery with Marcello Di Bello, while her husband is abroad."

The crowd took a deep breath of indignation. "She was trying to steal the tenor's voice!" yelled a man.

"Mrs. Del Cielo," the pretore said, pursing his lips, "do you understand the charge?"

Nedda stared at her mother, who nodded. "Yes I do, Pretore."

"I am sorry, madam, but I can barely hear you. You will have to speak louder. Do you understand the charge?"

"Yes," said Nedda, as her mother put her hand on her back. "I am not guilty," she continued, with more volume. She looked over to the clerk and back at the pretore. "Not guilty, *illustrissimo Signor Pretore.*"

The pretore leaned forward toward the procuratore. "Mr. Andratti, I assume you have witnesses."

"Yes, signore," said the procuratore, clearing his throat. "Three upstanding women of Lavenna saw the whole thing with their own eyes. I will let them speak for themselves." He turned to the three women in the crowd to join him at the table.

The women filed forward. The first to speak had her right arm elevated and her index finger frozen, pointing and crooked. "Pretore Clementino," she said, "we all saw it as clear as we see you. It was last Saturday night in the Piazza Barrini, after the concert by Lavenna's Marcello Di Bello. God bless his voice."

The women in the crowd swooned at the mere mention of Di Bello's name.

Despite her bravado, Crooked Finger passed the story on to her second. "She can tell you the rest. It makes me too upset."

Filling in was a frumpy woman, still wearing an apron stained with her cooking. "They were singing together," Frump explained, bracing her legs to approach the pretore. Her fingers flittered in the air. "Singing like two lovebirds, long after everyone else had left the piazza—and when she should have been at home, watching her daughter." With the crowd buzzing, Frump glared over at Nedda. "She thinks she is different from us. Above it all—prettier than the other women." The crowd's murmurs sharpened, emboldening the accuser. "She has never been one of us since the day she came!" Others from the assembled chorus called out to agree.

"Order, order!" commanded the pretore. "I thought we had already captured the goat." The pretore himself filled with a bit of indignation. "If you please, madam, stick to the facts and leave the judging to me."

The third woman, who had a limp, stepped forward. She pushed Frump aside. Limp corroborated the charge. "I saw it, plain and simple. When they finished their singing, she gave the tenor a kiss on the cheek. That little whore. Her husband Maurizio is such a good man. If only he knew about this over in America."

"A kiss on the cheek?" Pretore Clementino asked softly.

"Yes," Limp responded, with conviction. "A long and romantic kiss on the cheek. It was clear she wanted more, but the tenor would not sin so gravely."

"Not the great tenor!" a man shouted.

The pretore reprimanded the man with a stare. "Of course not the great tenor," he said, placing his toque back atop his head. He looked to the procuratore. "Because as we know, Mr. Andratti, a man cannot commit adultery. But this woman only gave this man a kiss—no more than a mother would to a son."

The procuratore closed his eyes and shrugged.

"And what are the names of your witnesses, Mr. Andratti?" the pretore asked. "Start with the woman who spoke first." The clerk offered the pretore a pen, but the pretore declined. He leaned forward, with his hands folded.

The procuratore stood silent.

"The name of your first witness?" the pretore asked again.

Andratti remained mute, his head down.

Crooked Finger batted the procuratore on the back of the head. "Tell him, son!"

The pretore leaned back in his chair. "I thought so," he said, looking over Andratti's beet-red face, and out into the crowd. "Signor Procuratore, Mrs. Del Cielo, if you could come to the corner with me, to speak privately." The pretore looked at his clerk. "The clerk will keep the order."

The clerk shot up and saluted. "Yes, *illustrissimo Signor Pretore.*" He panned to the crowd. "The court will stay in order."

In the corner with his back to the gallery, Pretore Clementino addressed the procuratore and Nedda in whispers. "Giacomo, what are you doing with your mother as a witness?"

"I am enforcing the law?" answered Andratti with a question, without looking up.

"Well, I'm not about to convict this woman for a kiss on the cheek, based on the word of your mother and her friends. I don't want that, and I don't think you do either."

"Correct, Signor Pretore."

Sensing shadows and breathing from behind, the pretore turned. Led by the clerk, the crowd was just a few feet away, shuffling closer with perked ears. "Can I not trust you to keep the order?" the pretore asked.

The clerk saluted, clicked his heels, and pivoted. "You heard the pretore," he said. "Now everyone—return to your seats or I'll have the *carabinieri* arrest you!"

Pretore Clementino resumed with the procuratore and Nedda. He took off his toque and held it low, along his hip. "Now, Giacomo, I don't want this thing going any further. So I am going to go back and tell everyone that you agree that this case cannot be brought properly until Mr. Del Cielo returns from abroad and can be present. It will be up to him. Until then, we are adjourned, and there is no charge against Mrs. Del Cielo. And before you say anything to Mr. Del Cielo, I want to speak to him. Do you understand?"

"I understand."

"Mrs. Del Cielo," the pretore said, with a sigh. "I do not know you, and dare not judge what is in your heart. I do know that you are a beautiful woman." He stopped himself.

Andratti looked away.

The pretore continued. "I know that you are a woman whose husband is far away, and that other women might confuse their own envy with suspicion—particularly when it comes to someone whom they already regard as an outsider. I just ask that you keep that in mind."

"I will, Pretore," Nedda said, with her characteristic terseness. "But is it true that a man cannot be guilty of adultery?"

"That is the law," the pretore responded. He held up his toque and studied it. "And I must respect it."

"I understand," nodded Nedda.

The pretore placed his toque back atop his head, and stepped toward his judicial desk. "Next case."

Nedda Del Cielo walked out of the court that day with her head held high, proud that she had survived the horde's insatiable appetite. It was one of the few victories life had given her—for that, and a glimpse of justice, she was grateful.

# XXV.

## Brushing Her Mother's Hair

Back in the kitchen bunker, Maria chomped happily on her *soppressata* salami and slice of bread from the round *pagnotta* loaf that her mother had given her while telling the story of Pretore Clementino. As she chewed through the crispy brown crust of the *pagnotta*, the juniper shoot bobbed in her hair.

"Mamma," she said. "Why doesn't Pretore Clementino just take care of everything with the German soldiers, the same way he did with the man with the goat and those three mean women?"

In the distance, Pretore Clementino's voice echoed atop the German war machines, repeating his plea to the townspeople to remain calm.

Nedda looked towards the sound, and back to Maria. She drew so close to Maria that her nose was touching her daughter's. "I'm sure that Pretore Clementino has it all figured out. Everything will be fine."

Angelina was in her chair, stitching with her black thread. "Just be patient, and we will be all right. The German soldiers are men, and all men are the same. They love to give orders and act strong. The worst thing you can do is feed their fire by defying them. Just stay quiet and let them think they are in control." Angelina bit her lower lip and nodded, as if to convince herself. "That's the key. Let them think they're in control."

"But Pretore Clementino isn't that way. He's nice. Mamma, is papà like the German soldiers? Does he love to give orders and act strong?"

Nedda paused, embarrassed by her inability to answer questions about the husband she hardly knew. "No, sweet baby," she said. "Papà is not like the German soldiers. In the last war, he fought as an American." Realizing that she was describing more of a similarity between Maurizio and the dreaded Germans—that is, that they both took up arms against Italy—Nedda pursued another course. "Which is why he went to America." Her voice grew wistful. "So that one day," she said, "*someday* we can all be together where no man or soldier gives orders—where everyone does what they want, when they want."

"I can't wait until we go to America to be with papà," Maria said, bouncing in her seat. "I heard that the sun in America is bigger than ours. Is that true, mamma?"

"Yes, it is," Nedda said. "And the fields and mountains are much bigger, too. Everything in America is bigger, so that people like the man with the goat and the three mean women don't bother one another. Americans have space—lots of space—to keep their own gardens, however they want." Hearing Pretore Clementino's voice again, Nedda pressed her finger against her daughter's lips. "But that's enough for today. That little head of yours is doing too much thinking. Let's go brush your hair."

Nedda took her daughter to the bed they shared in Maurizio's absence. "Go ahead and sit on top. I will get the brush." She went to her armoire in the kitchen, and picked up the plush bristled brush with its engraved silver handle—the one she used on her daughter's hair every night. She removed the juniper shoot from Maria's head and placed it on the night table. "Let's see if we can straighten those knots," Nedda said as she pushed through her daughter's dark locks. Then she handed Maria a silver compact, patterned with a raised cherubim.

"What is this, mamma?" Maria asked, pointing to the cherubim.

"It is an angel, just like you."

"So what am I supposed to do with it?"

Nedda reached over and clicked its button. The lid popped up, revealing a mirror.

"Oh, to make sure I look pretty?" Maria said, beaming as she looked at her reflection.

"Well, yes," Nedda replied, slowly. "But also, to always remind you that whenever you are wondering where to go for strength, look in the mirror—it is inside of you." Nedda tilted her head as she continued her brush strokes. "Do you like it?"

"I love it," Maria said, caressing the cherubim and admiring her mother's reflection in the mirror.

"It's yours, sweetheart. Keep it always. If you have a daughter someday, you can give it to her."

"Mamma, how come you never brush your hair?" Maria said, shifting the mirror to better frame her mother's face.

Nedda kept silent, scrambling for an answer. She looked at her image in the compact. "Because women do not need to comb their hair as much as little girls. It's very important to get the knots out while you're young."

"Women don't get knots in their hair?"

"Of course we do," Nedda said as she felt for her own premature grays, finding them dry and split. "It's just that it is harder to get the knots out when you're older, so we don't try as much."

"I can get the knots out of your hair," Maria said, as she turned toward her mother's tender strokes. "Let me try."

Fighting through a reluctance that she did not comprehend, Nedda handed her daughter the brush. "Be gentle."

"First, let me put my new mirror away," said Maria. She scampered to her side of the bed, and slid the silver compact under her mattress. Then she went back and stood behind Nedda, smiling from ear to ear. As she began her strokes, she imitated her mother's nighttime questioning. "So, how was your day?"

"Very nice," Nedda replied, suppressing a girlish giggle. "I came home from the beach and..." Nedda had leapt into her response before remembering the German invaders; her tone reverted from daughter to mother. "We came home from the beach and Pretore Clementino said that we should stay inside the house for a little while. And then I told you a nice story about Pretore Clementino."

"Mamma, are they going to leave us alone?" Maria asked as she pushed through her mother's tangled gray hairs. "Are the German soldiers mean?"

Nedda reached over her shoulder to grab her daughter's hand. "Some of them are mean. Some of them are good, but we have no choice. Pretore Clementino and Grandma are right. If we stay quiet, we'll be fine." She turned and pouted at her daughter playfully. "Now finish brushing my hair. You promised. There are a lot more knots to take out before I can look beautiful like you."

Maria resumed her strokes, contented by the notion that her mother would protect her.

Before that evening's brief sleep, Nedda lay for hours, with eyes peeled, watching for the unknown. All the while, she stayed calm by caressing her hair, which her daughter had smoothed and straightened.

# XXVI.

## Morning Darkness,

## Muting the Music

T he morning after the German troops arrived in Lavenna—the second day of the siege—was a Saturday. The sun began to rise over the mountains as it always had, but the town's locked doors and shuttered windows denied entry to the light. Nothing and no one stirred, except for a few birds in the fountain at Piazza Barrini. The cobblestone roads, usually busy with the feet of farmers and cattle going to pasture or market, remained untouched. The only footprints were left by the implacable tracks of the German war machines.

Nedda woke before Maria, and went to the kitchen. Her mother was already sewing. "Anything?" Nedda asked.

"Nothing," Angelina said.

Ordinarily, one of them would have gone to the family's vegetable plot outside the town, or joined Lavenna's other matrons at the common market to buy their daily fill. Lorenzo Spezzano was the food merchant of choice, for he was able to garner the best variety of fish and dry goods from Salerno, and compliment them with dairy, vegetables, and meat from the surrounding farms. The occupation, however, had jolted Lavenna from its routine.

As Nedda placed some wood in the stove, she heard someone sprinting outside, his breathing heavy. She went to the door.

"Don't open the door!" Angelina commanded.

"I'm not. I'm just going to see what's happening." Nedda slid open the shutter latch. She saw the broad backs of two German soldiers, beating a man violently with the handles of their guns.

"I'm just trying to get food for my family—food from my store!" the man pleaded as he was being bludgeoned.

Without responding to their victim's cries, the soldiers kept up and then accelerated their bashing. Finally, the man stilled; his voice could be heard no more. The soldiers shot him for good measure, leaving his body in the street as a warning to the next who dared to defy the curfew. A soldier kicked the corpse over, so that Spezzano lay with his cheek against the curb, staring sideways; his eyes were stuck in terror, fixed on Nedda. Blood dripped from the head and into the street.

Nedda jumped back, threw the shutter's latch, and retreated. "They killed Mr. Spezzano," she said, in shock. "They killed Mr. Spezzano, when all he was trying to do was get food for his family. This is terrible, mamma." She sat crying next to her mother, who kept to her sewing.

"What's the matter, mamma?" squeaked Maria from the bedroom doorway, rubbing sleep from her eyes. "Why are you crying?"

"Your mother just had a bad dream," said Angelina. "A nightmare." She looked toward the door. "She has a lot of nightmares lately," Angelina muttered to herself. "Where is the pretty flower that was in your hair?"

"I don't know. I'm hungry."

"Come," replied Angelina as she rested her sewing needle on the table and braced to rise. "Let's have some breakfast."

"I want *spaghettini alla zucchini*," demanded Maria, gaining back some playfulness.

"You look like *spaghettini alla zucchini*," her grandmother returned, smiling as she shuffled to the sill above the stove, tickling Maria along the way.

Nedda went back to the front window. Slowly, she slid the shutter's latch and opened it. She peered through the crack at the body once livened by Spezzano's soul. His blood still dripped from curb to street, like water from a leaking faucet. Nedda's eyes locked with those of the corpse. She hoped that the carcass would somehow roll away, impossible as that would be. Unable to take her eyes off Spezzano's, she began to lose her breath. She became lightheaded. Her mind began to play tricks.

Nedda started blaming Spezzano for the horror that befell him. She asked herself why he would leave his house when he probably had the best-stocked kitchen in town. He must have panicked. But he did not need to, because the Germans would probably be gone by sundown. His recklessness served only to anger the soldiers, putting everyone in danger.

Her eyebrows feeling like they were clawing into her forehead, Nedda thought that she saw Spezzano's face transforming into a fiendish grin. He stood up, armed with a German rifle. He raised the rifle over his head. He walked toward Nedda—the bloody butt of the rifle, rather than the barrel, aimed at her.

Nedda slammed the shutter and threw the latch. In her rush back to the kitchen table, she knocked over the chair.

The crash startled Angelina and Maria at the sill above the stove. Maria ran to clutch her mother. "Mamma, mamma, mamma," she yelled.

Angelina remained at the sill. "It's all right, Maria. Mamma is fine—just a little clumsy. She always has been." She laid a plate of *pagnotta* on the table, and walked to the front shutter through which Nedda had gaped at the dead Spezzano; in Nedda's scared hurry, the latch had not caught. Angelina pushed the bar firmly into its clasp. "There, now we can see. The glare from outside was too much," she said, confidently. She returned to Nedda's armoire to pull a candle from the bottom drawer. She lit the candle and placed it in the middle of the table. "This is better. Let's eat."

With Nedda still puffing from the sight of Spezzano, the three sat in what was still early morning, to have a breakfast of leftover *soppressata* and cheese. Outside their confinement, the sun was not yet fully overhead.

The morning's darkness passed. While the sun outside was reaching its highest point above them, beating down at full strength, the three generations sat around their candle with nowhere to go, fixating on the remaining precious scraps of food. Angelina rocked in time with her stitching. With Spezzano dead and the soldiers indulging themselves with his inventory, Nedda readied the house for hunger. In order to ration, she cut into smaller pieces the bread and *soppressata* that had been a snack the night before. The bread was beginning to harden. The water supply—a few pails' worth fetched from the pump at Piazza Barrini the previous day—was dwindling. By mid-afternoon, little Maria's stomach began to ache.

"Mamma, my stomach hurts."

"I know, sweetheart," Nedda said, "but we can't go outside to buy any food. We need to save what we have for as long as we can, because we don't know how long we'll have to stay inside." Nedda looked at Angelina, who raised her eyebrows, unable to offer any answer or encouragement. She remained focused on her sewing.

"Try to not think about food," Nedda told her daughter. Seeing that her explanation did not erase Maria's famished frown, Nedda offered an enticement. "If you hold out, I'll boil an egg for dinner." Nedda placed her hand upon her daughter's shoulder. "You and Grandma will share the egg, because I'm not hungry." She gave her daughter a peck on the forehead. "But in the meantime, go rest on our bed, and have sweet dreams—dream about eating chocolate and ice cream when we are with papà in America."

Maria did as her mother asked, and went to lie on their bed. She could not help fantasizing about the desserts she craved so desperately—chocolate and ice cream—and eating them with her father. As her pangs deepened, she thought how happy she would be just to be with her father. She might not waste time on the ice cream; she would have so much to tell him. The ice cream could wait. Her longing began to abate, and she fell asleep.

"*Achtung! Achtung!*" The engine and wheels again came rumbling through Lavenna, robbing Maria of her rest.

*Wheel and engine, engine and wheel—the sweetest of dreams, trampled by steel.*

"Mamma," Maria called out as she popped up in bed. "Where are you?" she shouted. Climbing out of her sheets and onto the floor, she bumped into the night table, throwing the juniper shoot to the edge. She ran to the kitchen.

"This is Marcello Di Bello," called out the voice next to the driver of the lead truck through a hand-held amplifier. Performing at the direction of a soldier's rifle rather than a maestro's baton, the tenor's voice cracked, his divine sound debased to that of a mortal. "Everyone must remain calm and in your houses. There will be no music in Piazza Barrini tonight," he explained.

Nedda went to the window, and pulled the shutter's small bar. Di Bello's firm stature appeared diminished atop the war truck. Normally singing from the tips of his toes for maximum timbre, he stood flat on his heels. "The Germans mean no harm. They are our friends." He paused as he spotted Nedda. "Stay inside, for your own safety," he continued mechanically, as if hypnotized.

Di Bello and the tanks passed by Spezzano's stuck stare. Flies lingered over the dried blood on the dead man's head. Nedda closed the shutters slowly.

"Mamma, who is that?" asked Maria, back on her small bare feet on the concrete floor.

Nedda closed the shutter hastily. She leaned against it to catch her breath in the cool darkness.

"That was Marcello Di Bello," explained Maria's grandmother from her stitching chair. "He is Lavenna's best singer. Probably the greatest singer in all of Southern Italy."

"That's the man the three mean ladies said they saw you singing with—right, mamma? Like two birds." Maria flicked her fingers in the air, imitating Frump's colorful courtroom testimony.

The heaving of Nedda's chest eased. "Yes, that's the man. He has a beautiful voice, from a beautiful heart."

"Tell me about him, mamma. Tell me, tell me, tell me." She turned to her grandmother. "And don't forget my egg! You promised!"

Both mothers laughed at their little girl's spunk, which for Nedda served as a distraction from her own fears. Angelina rose to prepare a boiled egg for her granddaughter. She threw wood in the stove before emptying water from a reserve pail into an iron pot—pouring carefully so as not to lose a drop. She struck a match to start the fire, and centered her pot atop the flame with egg and water inside.

Nedda took a deep breath and blushed, trying to find the right words to begin a story about Marcello Di Bello. "Marcello was…" she began, before stopping herself. She looked at her mother, who was back to her sewing.

Without turning from her work at the stove, Angelina raised her hand and rolled it in the air, signaling to Nedda that she should proceed.

Nedda caressed her daughter's cheek. "Music is the passion of life…"

As Nedda waxed on about the power of music, Angelina returned to her chair. She used her teeth to cut the black thread that she had been using for her stitching. She reached for the red, and guided it through the eye of her needle.

# XXVII.

## Concert in the Square

Nedda told her daughter about a Saturday the previous spring. Lavenna's mountain breezes were fragrant with the scent of blooming flowers. Though Italy was at war, the bullets and bombs were far away. The town had been moving *adagio*, to the pace and tone set by a young woman who sat on her stool daily in a corner of Piazza Barrini, beneath the displaced olive tree, playing her cello. As dusk approached on this late afternoon, however, other instruments filed into the piazza. The tempo picked up in anticipation of the concert by the town's much-adored hero, Marcello Di Bello.

At the front door of her house, Nedda was bidding goodnight to her daughter, who was standing at Angelina's side. Nedda gave Maria a peck on the forehead, and looked at Angelina. "Are you sure you'll be all right?"

"Absolutely," replied Angelina. "Go and listen to the music. You have waited a long time for this. We'll be fine." She looked down at Maria. "We're going to cook some *spaghettini alla zucchini*, and sew you a new dress."

Heartened by her mother, Nedda walked to the concert, bouncing as she went.

When she arrived at Piazza Barrini, the square was brimming with people and pre-event entertainment. It was a festival atmosphere. On the stage, a group of flag throwers, dressed in medieval costumes, tossed and caught in synchronicity. They did so to the accompaniment of a man playing the trumpet. A clown on stilts walked through the crowd, throwing candy to the children.

Nedda was drawn to a puppet show featuring Pulcinella, the famous Neopolitan marionette whom she had always enjoyed. With a black mask and hooked nose, Pulcinella wore his baggy white blouse, oversized trousers, and sugar-loaf hat. He crouched—his way of showing how he had been beaten down by those of higher social standing.

The strings above Pulcinella pulled him to stand straight, and throw back his head. "I am thinking of shaving my hair," he said in his signature high-pitched peep, "to be like the great one: *Il Duce*, Benito Mussolini."

The audience's lips tightened.

"To be strong like him," said Pulcinella.

The spectators looked to one another for agreement.

"To be smart like him," Pulcinella continued.

The onlookers shook their heads more readily.

"To be courageous like him."

"*Sì*," voices murmured.

Pulcinella panned the crowd, and pointed to his crotch. "I just hope that when I look inside my big pants, I am not small like him."

The audience roared.

Nedda chuckled to herself.

As she set off further into the square, Nedda saw a teenage boy combing back his hair. He was looking at a young girl, a yard away, who had her back to him. "I hope she says 'yes,'" Nedda whispered to herself.

The evening turned less amusing, however, as Nedda struggled to cut through the gathered mob. The husband and wife couples of the Barbarossas and the Caggiatos, childhood friends of Maurizio, were reluctant to let her pass. The wives stood in her path, staring her down.

"Excuse me," Nedda said, firmly, standing her ground.

The women gave way, Signora Barbarossa gasping. "She dresses so inappropriately."

"Her house must be a mess," replied Signora Caggiato.

Indignation flared from the Altezzanas, the town's wealthiest family, when

Nedda stepped inadvertently on the signora's toes. "That was my foot," scowled Signora Altezzana. She took a deep breath, enlisting her husband's umbrage. Signor Altezzana followed with, "You really should watch where you are walking."

"I'm sorry," responded Nedda, bending down to dust her misstep from the signora's leather shoe. The signora kicked back with a laugh, causing Nedda to stumble into the clutches of another woman.

"What's the matter?" asked Crooked Finger as she caught Nedda and stood her up. She thrust her malformed pointer inches from Nedda's eye. "Are you looking for your daughter?"

"We never see you together," added Frump, her pleasure with Nedda's misfortune apparent.

"You should give your mother a break," joined Limp. "She is too old to be raising your child."

Tangled in a net of recrimination, Nedda tried to escape, to get away from Crooked Finger, Frump, and Limp. But every turn found her further enmeshed in stares and innuendo. She regretted having left her house. Preoccupied with what people were saying and thinking about her, she nearly tripped when a rubber ball rolled up against her feet.

"I'm sorry," chirped a golden-haired little girl. "It was an accident. We were just playing."

"It's all right," Nedda said with pause, wondering whether she was dealing with a friend or foe.

"Are you okay?" asked the little girl, her eyes wide.

"Yes, I'm fine," replied Nedda, feeling as though she had washed up on a small island in a sea of scorn.

"You're a very pretty lady," the girl continued. "I don't know why my mother says such bad things about you."

Nedda caressed the girl's face. "Thank you," she said. "And you're a pretty girl."

The girl's mother swooped in and pulled her child away. She rubbed her daughter's cheek clean of Nedda's touch. "What did I tell you about talking to strangers?" scolded the mother, shooting a glare at Nedda. "They're dangerous."

"But mamma, she was so pretty."

The little girl's tenderness warmed Nedda.

The thundering of drums turned all eyes to the stage, bringing all gossip to a close. Nedda looked for a seat upon the piazza's circular marble pedestal, which supported an obelisk; supplanting the sacred olive tree that was moved to the corner, the monument was meant to imitate, on a smaller scale, Benito Mussolini's tribute to himself at *Foro Mussolini*, the imperial-style sports complex that he had built on the outskirts of Rome. The work was never completed, however, as the artist who conceived and sculpted it abandoned Lavenna without inscribing "Mussolini Dux" from top to bottom. The unfinished monument at its seating capacity, a spot became available when one young boy got up. Nedda snuck in. As Marcello Di Bello ascended the platform from its rear stairs, it appeared to Nedda that he was emerging from the twilight.

Standing tall in high boots, the tenor's barrel chest projected from his open white shirt. His brown leather vest had a shine. He looked to the Maestro below him for his cue.

Silence.

A violin sounded prematurely, earning a grimace from the Maestro.

"That's okay," Di Bello said, extending his arms to his audience. "We are all a little bit excited tonight."

The square laughed and applauded. The tenor had the crowd already, before singing his first note.

The Maestro waved his baton, and the orchestra began its prelude. With impeccable pitch, the tenor belted out his opening line about how a woman is fickle, like a feather in the wind: *"La donna è mobile, qual piùma al vento."* The townspeople were engrossed. After he finished his first aria, the throng's yells for more became the tenor's oxygen. The ten songs that followed flowed effortlessly, the tenor showing no more strain or exertion than would someone in mere conversation.

There was a heightened buzz and call when the orchestra began the prelude to Puccini's "Nessun dorma"—it being gospel that only those in rarefied air could deliver the song's last note. The tenor sang the initial verses slowly and sweetly, drawing the crowd into the hero's quest for the love of an icy princess. In the middle, his voice thickened with courage. With an elongated recitation of the words *"all' alba,"* he had arrived, now having to vow that with the rising of the sun, he would win the princess's heart. He raised his arms and stepped forward. The audience braced, grabbing each other's sleeves. *"V-i-i-ncero! Vincero!"* Di Bello belted out with measure, before throwing his head back for his High C crescendo. *"V-i-n-n-n-n-c-e-e-e-e-eero!"*

His face was turning so red that Nedda was concerned he might pass out.

When the singer was done, he closed his eyes and smiled, knowing that he had been victorious.

*"Stupendo!"* a man bellowed, timing his accolade perfectly so that it was heard just before the applause began.

The crowd erupted into a raucous call for an encore. *"Bis!"* they shouted.

Di Bello gave them what they wanted—two more encores. After that, the tenor could offer nothing other than kisses to his still-ravenous mob. He held his hand over his heart and smiled. As the calls of *"bis!"* continued, he thanked the orchestra, and walked off the back of the stage.

The spectators exited the square contented that they had been a part of something special. There was no glowering or boasting. Couples who had forgotten what it was to hold one another's hands left arm-in-arm. Children sang, trying to imitate Di Bello—all while the tenor sipped a glass of red wine at a nearby bar, the bartender eager to pour another for the phenom. Piazza Barrini, which had been bursting with energy just moments before, was quiet again, like lovers after consummation.

Nedda remained, sitting on the unfinished monument in the middle of the deserted square. She sang solo, as she had so many times in her bedroom. In the open air and with no one watching, she reached within, for a fuller voice. She hit notes she had previously not dared to attempt.

A little boy rode his bicycle through the square, ringing his bell. Time to return home, Nedda told herself. Her night was over—and what a grand night it had been.

As she got up to leave the square, however, Nedda was startled by a series of claps from behind. She jumped nervously and turned. It was applause from the hands of Marcello Di Bello.

"That is some voice you have, my dear lady," he said. "So when will you give your concert in this square?"

Nedda was so taken aback with shyness that she could not even look at the man with the colossal lungs. "Oh, I just like to sing to myself," she said. "It's really nothing."

"Nothing?" he asked. "Nothing? I recognize what you are singing—'Un bel dì, vedremo,' from *Madame Butterfly*. I have sung that opera more times than I can remember, but never with a woman who could sing like you just did. Do you know how many sopranos would give all of their jewels to be able to sing like that?"

"Oh, stop. You're just being nice."

"I'm telling you, those divas could not stand to go on after hearing you." He slid his finger across his neck. "They would take their own lives."

Nedda blushed.

"No, I'm serious," he said as he gestured for her to sit back on the monument. He held up his hand. "Wait here, I will be right back." He ran across the square to the bar. He jogged back to Nedda, his glass of red in hand, without a spill. He sat below her, cross-legged on the square. For the moment, the great tenor wanted to watch rather than be watched. As he sipped his wine, he looked up at Nedda's sweet face. "You love to sing. I can see by the twinkle in your eye."

Nedda did not answer, because she knew that her gleam was for Di Bello.

"Where did you train?" he asked. "At the San Carlo opera house in Naples?"

Nedda wrung her dress in her hands to contain her embarrassment.

The tenor offered her his glass of red wine, and she accepted with both hands, taking a humble sip.

"I'm sorry if I insulted you," said Di Bello. "You could not have trained at

San Carlo. Your look is much too northern." He rose courteously to stroke her nose with his forefinger. "Your profile is too noble. You must have trained at La Fenice in Venice, under the instruction of some old guy with a white wig."

Nedda's voice, which minutes before had been soaring, was now nowhere to be found. She buried herself in the glass that the tenor had given her. She stared at the wine, keeping her lips away from the scarlet.

In grand operatic style, Di Bello knelt below Nedda. He touched her hand. "Do you know 'Che gelida manina' from Puccini's *La bohème?*"

"Of course. It is so beautiful."

"But do you really *know* it?" Di Bello prodded Nedda. "Tell me about it."

"How the young woman from another apartment knocks on her neighbor's door, looking for someone to light her candle." Nedda stopped.

"Go on."

"Once inside, the woman gets faint." Nedda bit her lip. "You know the rest."

"No, tell me," the tenor implored Nedda. "You speak as melodically as you sing."

"Well," Nedda said slowly. "When she gets up to leave, she realizes that she lost her key. The neighbor found it, but would not tell her because he wants her to stay longer. With both of their candles out, he drops the key so that he might touch her." Nedda covered her mouth with her fingers, and then removed them. "When he feels her hand, he sings to her about how cold and small it is—*Che gelida manina*—how he would like to warm it in his own."

"*Bellisima!* I could not have described it any better myself." The tenor looked to the ground before gazing up again and grabbing Nedda's hand:

> *Che gelida manina*
> *se la lasci riscaldar*

Nedda squeezed her knee with her free hand. The singer rushed to the last lines of the aria:

> *Or che mi conoscete parlate voi. Deh parlate chi siete?*
> *Vi piaccia dir!*

Nedda wanted to resist the tenor's operatic plea to tell him more about herself, but could not. She proceeded with the heroine's response, singing about how she had earned the nickname of Mimi for reasons that she did not know, and lived a solitary life. Her tone was luscious.

"*Brava!*" applauded Di Bello with a slow clap. "*Bra-va!*" He waved his finger in the air. "But we both know that you are being very tricky."

"How?" Nedda asked, knowing that the tenor had caught her.

"Mimi was only her nickname, not her real one. If you sang the first verse instead of the second, you would have told me your name, the way Mimi in *La bohème* explained that her real name was Lucia."

Nedda would not look up. She was ashamed that she had gone too far.

"And I don't believe the verse that you sang—that you live and eat alone in your little white room like Mimi. The part about not going to mass often but praying frequently..." Di Bello extended his hand, with his palm facing the square, and rocked it. "Same with me." The tenor tickled her under the chin. "C'mon. Tell me more. Who are you? What is your name?"

"You were the one who chose *La bohème*. I was singing *Butterfly*—a solo," she pushed back.

"But you sang both arias so beautifully. Come on. Who are you?"

Nedda sat with sad eyes, wanting to tell, but knowing her mouth would not open. She grabbed the silver cross that hung from her neck and clung to it.

The entertainer would not give up. "Shall I sing 'Nessun dorma'—a private rendition just for you?"

Nedda knew she had to leave. She rose to brush the wrinkles out of her skirt. Before walking away, she took a long and final sip of the tenor's wine, and gave the empty glass back to him. She started to bow her head to say goodbye, but instead found herself flexing to stand on the tips of her toes, getting as close to the tenor's face as possible. Unable to resist, she gave him a peck on the cheek. After the kiss, Nedda kept her eyes shut.

"Goodbye, Mimi," whispered the crestfallen tenor.

Nedda pulled back, and turned to traverse the piazza. She was galvanized by the music she had made—proud of how it had wooed the town's great tenor. She left him wanting more. His wine, and her lips upon his cheek, had made her feel devilishly warm.

Nedda's euphoria was short-lived. Before exiting the square, she was halted by Crooked Finger, Frump, and Limp. "Why do you have that smile on your face?" trembled Crooked Finger, her own righteousness seeming to overcome her. "You walk around like you are a queen. We saw it all. You're nothing but a whore."

"Poor Maurizio—such a good man, married to a tramp," followed Frump.

"You should be home with your daughter," said Limp.

The trio encircled Nedda, drawing closer like wolves. She feared what they might do next. "Please, leave me alone," she said. "I have done nothing to you."

"Your life is a scandal," Crooked Finger winced. "You're an embarrassment to us all and need to be punished." Crooked Finger pulled up her skirt, as if readying to kick the younger woman. The others did the same.

"Please," Nedda said, looking to the sky.

There was a splatter on Crooked Finger's head. She ran her hand through her hair quickly. When she looked at her fingers, she realized that she had been soiled by the droppings from a bird overhead. "Dear God!" she screamed. "The woman is a witch!"

"She has been sent by the devil!" followed Frump.

"Let's get home!" implored Limp.

"She is a sinner!" shrieked Crooked Finger. She wiped her hand against Nedda's dress. "And everyone will know it." She signaled to her cronies, and they scurried away.

Nedda's heartbeat calming from her scare, she could not help but smile about how the women who tormented her had been embarrassed, and had themselves felt fear. She was indifferent to the stain that Crooked Finger had put upon her—she knew that she would merely wash it out in the morning.

As Nedda walked home, reminiscing about her moment with the singer, she reached to open her collar. After some twists, the top button popped; the next two slid through with ease. In the darkness, the brush of cool air across her chest was invigorating.

# XXVIII.

## A Scary Attic

After Nedda had finished telling the story about the tenor, Maria was nibbling on her half of the boiled egg. "It sounds like men and women act funny when they are alone together," the little girl said.

"I guess you can say that." Nedda smiled as she stroked her daughter's hair.

"Here, mamma," Maria said, presenting her meager portion of the egg. "Have some of mine."

Nedda was tempted, for she too was starting to grow weary from hunger. But she could not stand to take food from her daughter. "No thank you, sweetheart—I really am full," she replied, sated with the memory of the concert in the square.

"Why did you kiss Marcello Di Bello?" Maria blurted out from across the table.

"Oh, I don't know. It was nothing."

"But weren't the ladies right? Isn't papà the only man you are supposed to kiss?"

Nedda looked at her mother. Angelina would not intervene—she kept to sewing her red stitches.

"There are different kinds of kisses," Nedda stuttered. "There are kisses for friends, kisses for daughters"—she leaned over and pecked her daughter's cheek—"and kisses for papà. The kiss that night was simply a kiss for a new friend."

"Do you and papà kiss a lot?" asked Maria, as she made her way through the egg.

Nedda smiled, hoping her daughter would not press further.

"When is the next time you and papà will kiss?"

"I don't know. Whenever we are together again." Seeing the disappointment in her daughter's eyes, she added, "Sometimes we kiss even when he is there and I am here, because we are together in our dreams."

"Mamma, I have a stomachache," Maria said, frowning. "I need to go outside—to the woods."

Nedda looked again to her mother for help. There was no plumbing for toilets in the town's houses; typically, a run to the woods had to do. With the German occupation, however, even that right was denied. No one stepped outside lest they meet the fate of Spezzano.

"You can't go outside," Nedda replied, nervously. "You need to hold it."

Angelina laid down her stitch-work and moved with purpose to the sill above the stove, where the three pots of water from the town square were lined. Two were filled completely, the other only halfway. They were the entire water supply inside the house, each drop a commodity to be guarded. But dignity too needed to be preserved.

Angelina grabbed all the cups that she could find and placed them on the table. She poured the half-filled pot into the cups, one by one, careful not to lose a drop. She then emptied the rest of the water from the pot onto the concrete floor, where it made a splashing sound. She reached overhead to a drawstring that pulled down a set of stairs to the house's small attic, where Maurizio's blacksmith tools were stored while he was away. "Come on," she said, extending her hand to Maria, "let's go upstairs."

Maria bit her fingernails and followed her grandmother's steady lead.

With her mother and child in the murky space above, Nedda could not resist opening the front shutters to see if there was any sign that the occupation was coming to an end. All she saw was Spezzano's corpse, staring back at her—his skin stretching as if to break, threatening to spew his insides onto the street.

"Mamma, I'm scared," cried Maria, descending the attic stairs with her grandmother behind. "It's so dark up there. I don't want to ever go up there again." She ran to her mother and hugged her around the hip. "I'm so scared."

Spooked by the persistent stare of the dead corpse, Nedda closed the shutter extra tightly. She took her daughter's hand. "Come, I will tell you a bedtime story."

"Which one?" Maria asked slowly. "The butterfly story?"

"No, something different," Nedda replied as she guided Maria into her bedroom. "The story of the bear and the boy."

"The bear sounds scary," Maria said, pouting as she hopped on the bed and under the sheets.

"He was," said Nedda, opening wide her mouth and hands, "with big teeth and sharp long nails."

"Mamma," Maria said, quivering. "The bear didn't eat anyone, did he?"

Nedda sat on the bed and placed her finger over her daughter's lips. "Quiet, and I'll tell you the story."

"Okay," Maria whispered.

"Not a word. Do you understand?"

Maria nodded obediently.

No sooner had Nedda uttered her last line about the bear and the boy, than Maria closed her eyes and fell asleep.

# XXIX.

## Spirits Humming

When morning came, the breakfast table was barren. It was Sunday, a time when the town should be filling its church. Angelina struggled out of her bed and onto her feet to cut a day-old *pagnotta* of bread. She took three slices and dipped them in one of the two remaining pots of water to soften them. "Good thing we have a lot of bread."

"*Achtung! Achtung!*" came the new daily call.

*Engine-wheel-engine, wheel-engine-wheel—on this the third day, the town was desperate for a meal.*

The soldiers fell in behind, their high kicks landing in unison.

"This is Padre Piore," preached the voice next to the driver of the lead war truck. "Everyone must remain calm and in your houses. There will be no masses today in Santa Maria Assunta." The ringing of the church bell from its tower was conspicuously absent.

Nedda rose from her bed, and shook Maria to wake her. She told her daughter to go to the kitchen, to be with her grandmother. Nedda threw on her thin robe. In the process, she knocked the juniper shoot off the edge of the table.

"I don't believe this," uttered Angelina in angry disbelief. She wanted to hide her contempt from Maria, but could not contain herself. "They know that we know we cannot leave the house to go to church. They are doing

182

this to humiliate Padre Piore—to torture us." Angelina quick-stepped to a drawer in her daughter's armoire, pulled out rosary beads, and began praying.

"What good have your little beads done you up to now?" shrieked Nedda. She approached the table, picked up a piece of hardened bread, and threw it down.

"Don't you dare!" Angelina shot back. "This is the day of the Lord."

"If it's the day of the Lord, why are we locked in here with no food and a dead man outside?" Nedda gasped. "I can't take it anymore." She looked up toward the odor of excrement wafting down from the attic. "I can't go on like this," she said, sobbing wildly. She bowed her head into her arms on the table, over the discarded bread.

Maria came to Nedda's side, and put her hands on her mother's shoulder, which bobbed up and down with her sobs. "Don't cry, mamma. Think of the butterfly song."

Nedda squeezed her daughter's hand, but kept her head down as she wept.

Maria sang the first line of the prelude to "Un bel dì, vedremo": "*Piangi? Perché?*" She stopped. "I'm sorry, mamma—that's all I remember of the song."

Nedda looked up with a smile, her face streaked with sorrow. "I don't know why I'm weeping, sweetheart." She reached out to hug her daughter as if it were her last. "I love you," she whispered, "my little butterfly."

In her chair, Angelina looked down on her rosary beads and also began lamenting, as much as her armor would permit.

Nedda pushed Maria back to admire her. She placed her hands proudly on Maria's shoulder. "Someday, you will sing that song on the stage at La Fenice in Venice, and the whole audience will applaud and yell for more."

"Like they did for Marcello Di Bello?" Maria asked.

"Like they did for Marcello Di Bello," Nedda answered. "But you know what? The prettiest song in the whole opera¾ there are no words."

"How can that be, mamma?"

"It's called 'The Humming Chorus.' It starts like this." Nedda began imitating the sound of strings being plucked *pizzicato*.

"What's that?"

"Picture a caterpillar, walking across the strings of a cello, nervous that it might never become a butterfly. Every time its little legs hit the strings, they make music." Nedda repeated the sound.

"So why is it called 'The Humming Chorus?'"

"Because the music is so beautiful, it makes the spirits come down and hum to the butterfly." Nedda emulated the peaceful section of the music, which was like the descent of the spirits. "It's like a lullaby that calms the nervous caterpillar."

"Do the spirits make the caterpillar into a butterfly?"

"In the end, all you hear is the humming."

"I want to sing that song at La Fenice one day!" exclaimed Maria.

"Of course." Nedda's tears of sorrow turned into tears of joy. A drop fell onto the bread she was holding. She ripped it to give half to her daughter. "Here—mamma's tears will make the bread taste better."

"I always thought the bread could use more salt," Angelina said, laughing through her own tears. She laid down her rosary beads and returned to her sewing.

"Now, aren't you going to tell me a nice story about Padre Piore, the same way you did about Pretore Clementino and Marcello Di Bello?" Maria said.

Nedda looked at her mother for guidance as to whether and how she should proceed. When Angelina offered neither a word nor gesture, Nedda began, fumblingly.

"Well, you see," she said. "It's like this." She glanced at her mother again, but Angelina would not budge. Nedda strained to smile. "Padre Piore is not very tall, but he has very big hands."

Angelina laughed to herself. She snapped her red thread, and replaced it with a spool of white.

# XXX.

Peppered Mussels,

## Making God Smile and Shout for More

Returning to her storytelling cadence, Nedda detailed for Maria the Sunday morning after the concert in Piazza Barrini. The townspeople—little rested and still picking the sand from their eyes—struggled to kneel in the pews of the church of Santa Maria Assunta. Padre Piore was in the midst of his mass, standing behind the altar with his back to the congregation—as was the rite at the time—so that he could give undivided attention to the crucifix. Shorter in stature than most of his congregants, he nevertheless stood tall in his sanctuary. His hands were large for such a small man—the right one slightly bigger than the left—and he used them to raise the chalice and Eucharist. He held the host between his long forefinger and sturdy thumb. Padre Piore's altar boys genuflected behind him. They picked up the wooden handles beside them and shook to jingle the attached altar bells, heralding the consecration.

The Altezzanas were in their usual spot in the front row. The signora wore her fancy hat; given her husband's donations to the church, no one dared ask her to remove the headpiece. Crooked Finger, Frump, and Limp were scattered with their families, anxious to huddle for their traditional gossip once mass was over. The rest of the faithful were in their usual places.

Nedda slipped in late with Maria, Angelina having deviated from her routine to go to church alone earlier that morning. The congregation's heads turned in unison. Crooked Finger, Frump, and Limp joined looks with one another, before setting their eyes back on Nedda. While studying Nedda, Crooked Finger whispered in her husband's ear, her low voice hissing. Frump, noticing that Maria was disheveled, straightened her own daughter's hair. Limp fought the ever-present aches in her legs to kneel at her highest.

Communion came, and the people queued in pairs to receive the Body of Christ. They knelt at the altar in turns, waiting for Padre Piore to make his way down the line. After taking the Eucharist, they returned to their seats with their best pious gazes, as the situation required.

As Nedda prepared to step with Maria to an open spot on the rail, Crooked Finger cut in front. "Crazy whore," she muttered over Maria's head. "You shouldn't even be allowed in our church. Your own mother is too embarrassed to be here with you."

Nedda stood with her hands firmly upon Maria's shoulders. She wanted to snap back at Crooked Finger, to publicly accuse her of her wicked hypocrisy, to pull the hair out of her wretched head until she cried like a baby—so that she might finally feel the pain that she had caused. But Nedda restrained herself, tightening her grip on Maria, allowing the handful of remaining communicants to go before her, so as not to cause a stir.

No one gave Nedda a nod of gratitude.

By the time Nedda took her place at the vacant railing, Padre Piore had run out of wafers. Embarrassed, he looked to Nedda for forgiveness, and asked her to wait. He then walked back to the altar where he placed his chalice down. He returned to Nedda and Maria. He placed both his hands on Nedda's head, closed his eyes, and spoke at length, with words that no one could fully hear. He finished by pressing his thumb against her forehead and making the sign of the cross. He did the same for Maria, even though she was not yet old enough to receive the sacrament.

The congregation was aghast at the extraordinary blessing given to Nedda and Maria. Judgment's foul breath filled the air.

"There is a reason why there are no more hosts for her—she's a sinner!"

called out a male voice from the pews. After some whispers and bobbling of heads, the voice continued, "She should not be blessed!"

On his way back to his chair along the side of the altar, Padre Piore turned to see who had spoken. He could not trace the voice. He turned again, and continued to his chair. He was about to sit, but then departed from tradition to walk behind the altar and face the congregants. He stared beyond them at the inscription carved in stone above the church's center doorway—Jesus's well-known plea to His Father for forgiveness toward his tormentors, for "they know not what they do." He read it calmly, but loud enough for everyone to hear: *"Padre perdona loro, perché non sanno quello che fanno."* He retreated to his chair and sat with his eyes closed. The only sound was that of the devout squirming in their wooden benches. The priest stood again, concluding the worship abruptly in Latin, without a recessional hymn: *"Ite missa est."*

Stunned and processing what had taken place, the churchgoers exited.

Outside, the church bell tower tolled, echoing off the town's thin rooftops. With the sun shining, the flock broke off into smaller gaggles just beyond the center doorway. While their idle chatter and rumor-mongering on other Sundays was dedicated to a variety of subjects, on this day of worship their subject was singular—the possessed and licentious Nedda Del Cielo, to whom Padre Piore had given a special blessing at communion. As they yapped, they felt the radiant warmth of the sun upon their faces.

Nedda was standing alone with Maria, waiting for Padre Piore so that she might unburden herself; she wanted to confess her moment with the tenor. But the priest was being smothered by the Altezzanas. "We know exactly what you were talking about in there," the signora preached from beneath her tall hat. "People should know better than to yell out loud like that during mass. No one except the priest should speak during such a sacred time. You said the right thing."

"I was just praying," replied the priest.

Close enough to hear, Nedda was shocked that the priest had not corrected the signora's interpretation of his message—that it was not the interruption of his service that needed pardon, but the judgment by her and others. Then again, Nedda thought to herself, maybe the priest did not want to engage in the same sin.

The signore stepped closer to the cleric. "We want to make our largest gift ever to the church. For a new set of steps leading to the church." He looked at his wife, who nodded at him to proceed. "We ask only that our name be carved on the top step."

"That's really not necessary. You have done so much already."

Maria tugged at Nedda. "I want to go home. Grandma said she would have lunch ready. She said it was going to be a surprise."

The signora glared at Nedda, imploring her to control her unruly child.

"We want to make this gift because these have been good times," explained the signore, still addressing Padre Piore. "And the old steps are cracking."

"Surely you are not serious about these being good times," responded the priest. "We're in the middle of a war."

"The war is not here; it doesn't affect us," interceded the signora on behalf of her tongue-tied husband. She pointed to him. "Except that he is in high demand. *Il Duce* wants the same High Sele Valley wood that the Romans used—he wants it for the handles on his guns."

"I thought your company made furniture," responded Padre Piore, his mouth agape. "Some of the most beautiful pieces I've ever seen."

The signora answered again for her husband, who hung his head low. "We do what *Il Duce*'s men ask, and they pay us well," she said, twisting as she spoke. "He'll have plenty of time to make his furniture once the war is over."

"Hopefully, the war will be over soon," said the signore, meekly.

The signora reached into her husband's pocket and pulled out a rolled band of lire. She deposited it into the priest's pocket. "The gift for the steps will come later, but this is for you. Every man has his needs—even a priest." She looked at the cleric's tattered shoes.

Nedda was disgusted by the Altezzanas' behavior—thinking that they could use their profits from war to buy God's mercy. She was glad to see that the priest was reaching for his pocket to return the ill-gotten gift.

But he did not. Instead, he patted down the band of lire, making it more secure. "Thank you," he said, smiling to the Altezzanas. "As always, you are too kind."

"C'mon, let's go," Nedda said, grabbing Maria by the hand and whisking her home. She decided that she did not need forgiveness, and would not ask for it from such a complicit priest.

The congregants took a break from their babble, turning their heads to enjoy the scene of Nedda pulling her child along angrily.

When Nedda and Maria burst through the door at home, they were greeted by the smile of Angelina, who stood waiting for them in the center of the kitchen. Steam billowed from her cast-iron pot on the wooden stove, filling the small space with the aroma of garlic, pepper, and fish. "Mamma, what did you cook?" Nedda asked, her indignation with the priest easing.

"Peppered mussels," Angelina responded.

"My favorite!" Maria yelled as she ran to embrace her grandmother.

"I know, my dear," Angelina said, looking down on the ebullient child. "You and your mother always talk about how much you enjoy eating them when you're at the beach in Salerno. I thought I would make them for you." She looked up at Nedda. "A little celebration after the concert. Last night must have been exciting. You came home late."

Nedda wanted to change the subject. "Where did you get the mussels? No one around here sells them. It's almost impossible to get seafood in Campania."

"I got them from Spezzano. They cost a little extra, but I thought you both deserved a treat." She headed to her bedroom. "It will be ready soon. Nedda, I need some money to pay Spezzano for the mussels. Can you get it for me? I'd like to go over and pay him before we eat."

Nedda went to her armoire and pulled open the top drawer. She stared at her tin and noticed how it was beginning to tarnish. Her mind was overtaken by a barrage of thoughts—the kiss, the Altezzanas, the priest, and the delight that the peppered mussels were giving Maria. She tried to escape the onslaught by pulling out the tin, only to see the brand name *Altezzana* emblazoned on the drawer's bottom slat. Feeling a pain shoot through her head, she asked herself whether the conspicuous display of her armoire, in her small house, was any more defensible than the signora's ostentatious donning of her hat.

Perhaps it was, she reasoned—after all, she showcased the piece in the confines of her home. But perhaps not—her intention was the same. She continued her self-inquisition: *Was the signore's donation of war profit to the church any worse than a husband, living separated from his family, sending money from America when it was still at war with Italy? And why shouldn't a priest take an endowment if it could help fix his torn shoes? We all make our bargains.* She pulled the lire from her tin and placed them on the armoire. "Mamma," she yelled, "I left some money. Take what you need. I'm leaving for a few minutes."

"Where are you going?" asked Angelina as she stepped back into the kitchen.

"To see Padre Piore," Nedda said—but cut herself off from saying anything more.

"If that's what you want to do," Angelina said, grinning. "But hurry back. We're all hungry and I can't wait to hear about the concert. They said that the tenor made every woman blush."

Nedda stared back at her mother, wondering what she had heard, and if in fact she knew about the kiss. "I'll be right back."

In the wake of Nedda's departure, Angelina's smile grew wider. She rubbed her granddaughter's head. "C'mon, help grandma finish cooking the peppered mussels."

Nedda marched to the rectory, determined to confess, but to do so in her own way—through a conversation rather than a screen. After all, the priest had shown that he was human, just like her. As she neared the padre's house, however, her feet got heavy. Her shoulders strained. She lifted her weight to the door and knocked as gently as she could.

The door opened stubbornly, getting stuck in its frame. It took two pulls from inside before someone appeared. "May I help you?" Crooked Finger asked harshly, wiping her hands in her apron.

"I'm here to see Padre Piore," said Nedda, startled that the padre's cook was none other than her chief accuser.

"He's not available. He's about to sit for lunch." Crooked Finger lowered her voice. "How dare you come here, you little disgrace. Why don't you just go back to the town you came from? You and your—"

"Who is it?" called Padre Piore, approaching Crooked Finger from his dining room.

"It's Signora Del Cielo," said Crooked Finger, with strained politeness. "Or should I say *Signorina?*" she added, dropping her voice for Nedda's ears only. "Since you act like you have no husband."

"What does she want?"

"She wants to see you, but I told her that she can't because you're having lunch," said Crooked Finger, beginning to close the door.

"Well, then—please ask her to come in," rebuked the little priest, clutching the door with his giant right hand, and making a smacking sound against the wood with his vocational gold ring. "Come in and wait here," said the padre.

Nedda could see the Altezzanas' money still bulging in the priest's pocket. "I just need to put something away," the priest told Nedda.

As Crooked Finger shuffled back to the kitchen muttering, Nedda took the priest's invitation to wait in the foyer. She could not resist scoping out each quarter. There was a kitchen down a hallway. The corridor itself seemed to her an extraneous space—something that she had never seen in a home. There was a sitting room to the right, also excessive; it was equipped with a phonograph, a luxury that she envied. The dining room to the left was set with food, and there was a shut door among the other doors in the impossibly long hallway; behind the door must have been the padre's bedroom. Indeed, despite the torn shoes that he wore in public, the priest appeared to Nedda to be well-off. She felt a growing boldness as she waited to confess her sin.

Padre Piore returned from the kitchen, his pocket empty of the band of lire. Seeing him in his collar, Nedda's newfound resolve began to wane. Though taller than the priest, she jittered in his presence. She moved sideways in the foyer for no reason, bumping into a small wooden table in the corner. With just a tap, the table rocked. "Oh, I'm sorry," she said, excitedly, catching a framed photo on the tabletop before it fell.

"No need to apologize. It was an accident. You scarcely touched it."

Nedda looked at the photo that she had straightened; it was of a young priest surrounded by a couple. "What a nice picture. Is this you?"

"With my parents on the day of my ordination," the priest said, glowing.

Nedda's spirit lifted. "I have a picture just like this of my husband and me on our wedding…" Her ascent in mood leveled as she looked into Padre Piore's eyes. She bent over to readjust the frame. "This picture must be very special to you."

"Yes, it is."

Nedda noticed that the legs of the wooden table were uneven, causing it to shift, looking like it would fall at any moment. "Father, do you need to put something under the table to keep it straight? It appears very shaky."

The padre pursed his lips. "Somehow, it always stays standing—just the way it is."

"If you say so," said Nedda, anxiously searching to fill the air with another thought. "I love your phonograph," she said, pointing to the sitting room. "Listening to the music must be wonderful."

"Not really," he said, laughing. "It doesn't work. It's just another memento from my parents. I figured if it didn't work, I would keep it as a reminder of them." He straightened. "So what can I do for you, Signora Del Cielo?"

"Call me Nedda, please," she stuttered. "I need to speak with you about something personal—a matter of faith." She looked anxiously from the foyer into the dining room. Crooked Finger was lingering over the padre's lunch, leaning toward Nedda's words.

"Oh, I see," Padre Piore replied. He turned toward his meal, rubbing his large palms against one another. "That will be all I need for the day, Signora. Thank you."

"But you have not even eaten," Crooked Finger protested as she walked toward him. "And who will clean up?"

"I'll be fine," said the priest. He walked around Crooked Finger to untie her apron strings for her.

"Padre," Crooked Finger smiled, nervously.

The priest removed her apron. "You can use the time to be with your family," he said. "Thank you." He pushed her politely out the door, locking it behind. He returned to Nedda in the foyer. "Would you like something to eat?" He gestured toward the dining room and his lone plate. "She's an excellent cook. She prepares my meal before mass and reheats it afterward. So devoted to her work. She always makes me too much. Please, have some."

"No, thank you."

"Well, let's go to the sitting room and hear what is on your mind."

"But I do not want to interrupt your meal. I can come back. Your food will get cold."

"Don't worry. Your need is now. Mine is not. I'll be fine." He stood and extended his right arm to his sitting room.

"Padre, I need to make confession," Nedda said from the edge of the sofa, facing the priest in his hard wood chair. His body barely filled the seat, but his right hand covered the armrest, as if it could lift the chair with him in it.

"Surely you know, Signora—"

"Call me Nedda, please," she interrupted politely.

"Surely you know that confessions are to be made in church in the confessional. I hear them three times a week at Santa Maria. Would you like the schedule?"

"I don't want to hide. I am here to face you—to face God—with my sins." She was comforted by a drawing on the table between her and the priest. It depicted children playing on a swing set. It was on top of a pile of other sketches. They must have been from the students at the school. Maybe one of the drawings was Maria's.

"Very well," retorted the priest, receding to listen. He loosened his white plastic collar and unbuttoned his shirt at the top, exposing the skin of his neck. "If you don't mind."

"No, of course not—it must be more comfortable without it." Embarrassed by what she might have suggested, Nedda tried to explain. "What I mean is that—"

"I know what you mean," the priest said, laughing. "Please, tell me what is on your mind."

Nedda gained her composure. "My husband, Maurizio, he has been in America for years—since the First World War," she explained. "He came back only briefly to marry me, and then went back to America, to a place called Newark, in New Jersey."

"How was the wedding?" the priest asked. "I bet you were quite the bride." He observed her angular features.

"1926. So many years ago. The wedding was brief. Nice, but brief. The whole thing was our parents' idea. He is ten years older than me. I was only eighteen. He was a successful man, and I was a pretty girl." She stopped herself. "At least that's what our parents said." She continued. "Right after we got married, he went back to live in Newark. So many years apart. I see him only sometimes." Her cheeks flushed. "During one of his short trips home, I became pregnant with my daughter, Maria. That was 1935."

"So many years without children?" the priest asked.

Nedda looked down. "Like I said, we were rarely together." When Padre Piore did not follow with another question, Nedda raised her head and proceeded. "After Maria, Maurizio went back to Newark. He's a good father. He sends envelopes filled with money—lots of money. I keep the money in a gold tin box, with a photo of him and me." She sighed. "But I don't even know him."

Padre Piore stayed quiet.

Nedda felt compelled to say more. "Some nights, as I sleep all alone, my head spins and spins, and I feel as if it is going to fly off my shoulders. My only peace is my daughter and my singing."

"Ah, you sing," the priest said, lighting up. "Your music is one of God's gifts."

"But I shared my music—God's gift—with another man," Nedda shot back. "I sang with him, and felt it in my heart—a jump." She placed her hand over her breast. "A jump in my heart that I never felt with Maurizio."

"I see."

"I drank from this stranger's cup of wine and…" She paused, and looked

194

down.

"Go ahead."

"And then I kissed him," she blurted out. "I kissed him, and it felt nice—nicer than it ever felt with my husband." Nedda put her head in her hands and started crying. "Oh Padre, I have sinned so."

The priest said nothing. Nedda feared that he had no sympathy for her plight. She kept her face in her hands, hiding, and bracing for a scolding. But he left her waiting. This must have been his way of having her begin her penance, she thought, in a humiliating silence. This was his show of power in his world. Pushed to the edge by his cold indifference, Nedda sat up and wiped her tears, intending to confront the priest.

He reached out with his giant right hand to offer her a handkerchief.

Her anger vanished. "Padre, how can I ever be forgiven for such a terrible sin?" she asked, with her breath lurching.

"Signora," the priest said, with his hand on her shoulder. "You will be judged not for yesterday's sin, but for how you celebrate God's love today and tomorrow." Feeling Nedda's ease, the priest removed his hand. "Your joyful journey to the light is what will keep you. My forgiveness will be of little help if you do not see the light." He smiled. "You will see the light only if you look for it with the innocent eyes of a child, without the prejudices and fears that our learned adulthood has given us."

"That's beautiful. See the light through the innocent eyes of a child," Nedda said wistfully. She looked over at the stack of drawings from the students. "Like the little ones who gave those to you?"

The priest picked up the papers and looked at them with pride. "These were not done by the students. They are mine."

"*Yours?*"

"They are drawings I did for the playground that I want to build for the children." He laid the papers back on the table. "And today someone gave me the money to do it."

"Really?" Nedda asked.

"Yes. Someone who wanted to remain anonymous."

Nedda was ashamed of how she had judged the padre's acceptance of money from the Altezzanas to buy new shoes. She felt that she needed forgiveness all the more. "How many prayers shall I say, Padre?"

"You said you like singing," said the priest, as if he did not hear Nedda's query. "What is your *favorite* song?"

"'Un bel dì, vedremo,'" she responded, puzzled. "From Puccini's *Madame Butterfly*. Why do you ask?"

"Go home and sing your song," he said. "Sing it for God, with all your heart. Sing it so loud that all the angels in heaven sing with you. Sing it so sweetly that God will smile and shout for more. That will be your prayer."

Nedda laughed.

"What is it?" the priest asked.

"The image of the Lord smiling. I've never seen it—never imagined it."

The priest laid his long finger gently on the left corner of Nedda's smile. "It's right here—this is Him smiling." With his smaller hand, he touched the other corner. "It's right now—this is Him shouting for more."

Overcome and overwhelmed, Nedda bowed.

The priest placed his right hand on Nedda's head, closed his eyes, and whispered incantations to himself. He lifted his hand. "I pray because I cannot sing. Go home and sing to the Lord. He's waiting for your music."

Nedda stood up to leave. "Thank you, Padre. For—"

The priest interrupted, and for the first time in his vocation addressed a penitent by name. "Nedda," he said, "make Him smile and shout for more. That will be your prayer."

# XXXI.

## An Unholy Communion

"Is Padre Piore God, mamma?" Maria asked as she gnawed on her wet bread.

"What do you mean, 'is he God'?"

"You described him the same way you describe God. It's the only time I hear your voice shake like that," Maria replied, struggling to swallow.

"Padre Piore is not God," Nedda said. "But he is holy. God speaks to him."

"When will God speak to us? When will we see him smile and shout for more?"

"Soon, I hope," Nedda said, staring at the back of her locked front door, knowing that the dead Spezzano lay on the other side. In her tortured thoughts, she saw the corpse rising, walking from home to home to devour those inside, his teeth covered with blood.

There was a knock on the door.

Nedda feared that her horrific image of Spezzano had in fact sprung to life. "Oh God," she said. "It's him!"

Maria screamed and ran to her mother. "Mamma, it's the Germans. They're coming to get us!"

With her daughter in her arms, Nedda moved over to her mother. The three of them huddled together, fortifying for what might come next. They waited for the intruder to knock again and say something. Maria's heart pounded in her little body; Nedda's nerves burned; Angelina's skin tightened.

The door shook again.

Nedda jumped.

"Stay here with her," Angelina instructed her daughter. "I'll go check who it is through the window."

"But mamma," Nedda pleaded.

Angelina placed her finger over her lips, instructing her daughter and granddaughter to stay quiet. She walked slowly and noiselessly to the shutters. When she reached the frame, she took a deep breath and whispered something to herself. She peered through a crack and studied the situation on the other side of the door. When the door trembled a third time, Angelina began sliding the latch on the shutter.

Nedda wanted to tell her mother to stop, but trusted that Angelina would remain unnoticed.

Angelina opened the shutters and her mouth, ready to say something to the person at the door.

"Mamma!" yelled Nedda.

Angelina turned quickly. She smiled at Nedda and Maria. "Our minds are playing tricks on us. It was only the wind." A wave of sun and fresh air came crashing through the window, carrying a butterfly upon it. The butterfly landed on the kitchen table.

"Look, mamma—a butterfly." Her dilated eyes growing as big as saucers, Maria got close and gawked. "How beautiful." The butterfly stayed still, allowing Maria to study it closely. "Look at all these colors and shapes. And its little legs. Is there something we can give it to eat?"

"There's nothing we can give the butterfly," said Angelina, keeping one eye on the opened shutters that allowed the mountain breeze to enter. "It has its own food."

The butterfly leapt and flew for the exit. Maria chased it. "Come back, pretty butterfly."

Nedda ran after Maria. "Where are you going? The Germans will see you." By the time Nedda caught up to Maria at the window, the butterfly was outside. "Oh, my God," said Nedda, looking into the Piazza. "Mamma, did you see this?"

"I didn't see anything except the wind blowing up against the door," Angelina responded as she rushed to join Nedda.

"Our minds were not playing tricks on us," Nedda said. "That sound must have been someone knocking."

Nedda saw townspeople entering Piazza Barrini, mutely. They were eating and drinking at a table that appeared to have been assembled hastily. The dead Spezzano was gone. There were no Germans in sight.

Nedda, Maria, and Angelina left their home and walked guardedly into the piazza, as if they were navigating a minefield. But everything appeared safe—eerily so. Unlike the normal Sunday coming together inside the church, there were no pews or prayers in the square—not even an icy glare toward Nedda. The congregants chewed their bread in the same hungry manner, with their eyes glazed over. Even the Altezzanas melded into the crowd, their usual front-row status unavailable. Crooked Finger was numb, her mouth and pointer in abeyance. Frump and Limp clung to their families, keeping to themselves, waiting for their turn to reach the table of unconsecrated bread and German white wine.

Away from the gathering, Nedda noticed a black tarpaulin draped over the obelisk of the unfinished monument. The tarpaulin was tied to a fatted lamb that acted as an anchor. The animal was kept in place by a generous serving of pulled grass. Open boxes of bread and wine protruded from the edges of the tarpaulin. It was plain that more food and drink was stacked on the monument's pedestal; the tarpaulin was to protect the reserves from being spoiled by the elements. The people paid little heed to the tarpaulin and lamb, for there was already plenty for them at the table.

As the wind picked up and the clouds moved in, the dirt of Lavenna swirled. The collective look of the crowd, however, remained vacant. Mouths moved not to the beat of hunger, but to the spell and pall of an uncertain liberation. As the people passed the bread and German wine to one another, they prayed to themselves that their ordeal was finally over. The lamb bleated in the wind.

A crackle sounded. "Mamma, it's the Germans!" Maria shouted, startled.

Angelina stooped to her granddaughter's shoulder, and pointed to the sky. Drops of rain began to fall. Though all were relieved, even the shower seemed like a cruel concession, for it upstaged any tears the town might shed in bearing witness to it all.

With thunder approaching, the freed stood frozen. The wind whistled louder and the rain began to pelt them. Though they were free to return home, the townspeople remained, separate and one, in the whistle and rain of the gathering storm.

# XXXII.

## Coffee with a Shot of Sambuca

In the Bennett kitchen, Guy and his sons sat hushed. Guy started to say something, but then stopped. Instead, he went to his liquor drawer across from Marie's island to grab a bottle of Sambuca, the sweet-potent Italian liqueur that usually serves as a nightcap. Guy poured the clear thick elixir into his cup of black coffee. "A little morning jolt never hurt anyone," he said.

Albert raised his cup. "Me too, Pop."

"Make that three," followed Edward.

Marie did not take Guy's offering. "Not now," she said, holding up her hand.

"C'mon, it'll make you relax," persisted Guy, holding the bottle in front of her.

"No," Marie bristled. She rose from her seat, reapplying pressure to her seared hand.

"That's it, Mom?" Edward asked, tentatively. "The Germans just left? What happened to the rest of the food and wine—all the stuff that was piled on the monument?"

"That's it," replied Marie, placing her hand under the cold running water from the kitchen sink. "At least that's all I remember."

"What do you mean that's all you remember?" Edward said. "I would think you would remember every detail of something like that."

201

"I told you—that's all I remember," said Marie, cringing at the water pouring over her hand.

"That's it," Guy said, after another shot of coffee with Sambuca. "No one got hurt, except for the grocery store guy who tried to run out for food. People get killed that way every day in New York City. That's the whole thing. I told you." He rotated his cup on the table.

"The killing of the grocery guy seems like it was a little worse than a New York City murder," Edward replied.

"Actually, a New York City murder is probably worse," Guy said as he stuck his finger into the sugared glaze that remained on the bottom of his coffee cup. "If you had gone to a Catholic university¾like me¾and studied St. Augustine and St. Aquinas, you would know that killing in war could be justified under the just war theory. A New York City murder has no justification. They're a bunch of animals."

"I'll let you slide on your not-so-subtle racist comments about Blacks in New York City. Regarding the Germans in World War II, you are assuming that the war is just," Edward retorted. "You can hardly say that the Germans going to war in World War II was just."

"I guess you never heard about the Versailles Treaty either," Guy said, licking his finger. "The way the Allies tore up Germany and humiliated it after World War I. That's why Germany went to war."

Edward was roused. "Dad," he said. "Mom described how the Germans in her town killed an innocent civilian. That is indefensible under the just war theory."

"As is a New York City murder."

"Stop it, you two," Marie interrupted. "There should be no war, and no theories to justify it."

"Ah, that would be one of Kant's categorical imperatives," declared Edward.

"What the hell are you talking about?" Albert jumped in.

"Immanuel Kant, one of the German philosophers I studied, along with Friedrich Nietzsche, at a school where we are taught that we don't always have to color within the lines. A Kantian categorical imperative would be that killing can never be justified, because it is murder."

"That just reinforces Dad's original point, idiot—that the killing of the grocery store guy in Mom's town was no different than a New York City murder."

Sensing that his wife was not amused with where the conversation was going, and feeling that he had won, Guy steered the discourse in a different direction. "The damn shame is that the United States deported Nedda after she was already here for years. They said she was never really a citizen because she came over here sick. Her husband—your grandfather—had a lawyer fight it for a little while, but then gave up. He just sent her back. That's it—end of story."

The cuckoo clock on the wall chirped prematurely. Guy went to it. "This cuckoo hasn't kept good time ever since we brought it home from Switzerland." He pulled the clock's chains and adjusted its hands to correct the time.

"Yeah Edward, that's it," Albert said, rallying behind his father again, taking another opportunity to chastise his brother. "Stop trying to dramatize. Mom can't make stuff up. What are you trying to do, write a book?"

"I would just like to know more about my mother and grandmother," Edward answered evenly. He wanted to say something more aggressive, but thought that might prevent his mother from speaking further.

"There's really nothing more to know," Marie said from the sink.

"So Grandma really loved to sing," said Edward, dropping back and trying a different approach.

"Her voice was so beautiful," Marie answered, turning off the water and cracking a quick smile. "In her letters, my cousin Luisa told me that she sang until the end—even after she was deported."

"So why did she love that song 'Un bel dì' somuch?" Edward asked.

"I told you, idiot," said Albert, emboldened now that his mother's pain appeared to have passed. "Grandma was sad at the long separation from Grandpa while he was in America. She was *Madame Butterfly*. Do we need to write it on the walls?" He looked to his father, who was downing his third shot of Sambuca-spiked coffee.

Edward roiled, annoyed by his brother's opportunism. "Grandma's separation from her husband may have been it, initially," he responded, "but I think it may have taken on new meaning after Grandma's encounter with the tenor. It sounds like they had a thing." He looked at his mother deferentially. "Only in the platonic sense, of course."

Marie had nothing else to say on the subject. "Albert, you need to get those opera tickets for you and your wife. It's important. Now, go to work and make some money to pay for them."

"Yeah, yeah. I'll get to it."

The doorbell rang.

Marie cleaned her hands on her apron as she went for the door. "I wonder who that can be."

"Maybe it's the Germans," quipped Albert, trying to get a rise out of his father.

"Or maybe it's the bar examiners, you callous twit, here to take back the law license that they should never have given you, you callous twit," Edward shot back, now that his mother could not hear him.

"I bet it's my daughter," Guy offered. "She's the brightest one out of the three of you, anyway. Nothing can keep her down. She keeps going no matter what—just like her mother."

"Maybe that's because she never realizes what's truly going on," Albert said, laughing.

"Dad's playing the Lisa Marie card again, isn't he?" Edward said, joining in rare support of his brother. "His way of saying that he is and always will be the most successful man in the house."

"Oh, you forgot," Albert continued, "our successes are not even ours. They're just an extension of his."

"You're right, Guy—it's Lisa Marie," Marie announced as she re-entered the kitchen with a skip in her step.

"Of course, I'm right," Guy said, smiling from ear to ear. "How's my Wall Street wizard?" He extended his hand without moving from his royal chair.

Filling her silk top healthily and brandishing a Fifth Avenue smile, Lisa Marie leaned over and kissed her father. "Good morning, Daddy," she said.

"Atta girl. Do you always show them those white teeth in the bright lights of the big city? You gotta show teeth. I always taught you—smile, and you will be successful."

"I give them teeth all right," Lisa Marie said, as she pinched at a lock of her jet-black hair, "while I buy low and sell high."

"Have you shown those teeth to a future husband yet?" Marie asked from the sink as she cleaned her pans. "You can't buy a family on the trading floor, you know."

"Mom, I'm only twenty-five. I'm taking my time."

"Let her have some fun," said Guy, stroking his daughter's silk sleeve. "Lisa Marie is going to wind up marrying a blue-blood and playing polo on the weekends. Her kids will have names like 'Slater' and 'Wellington.'"

"You never thought I could make it on my own, Daddy," Lisa Marie reminded her father. "When I went to college, you told me to just get Cs and come home and get married. I graduated *magna cum laude*, and I'm doing pretty well for myself."

"Goddamn, you're dynamite," Guy said. He looked at his sons. "Maybe you could teach these two cats about the business world. They don't know a dollar from a doughnut."

"I don't think a *magna cum laude* from that country-club college of hers qualifies her as any sort of teacher," Albert said. "She doesn't even have a graduate degree. Lisa Marie, did your membership at the country club include golf, or did the tuition cover only meals?"

"Hey, Lisa Marie has done well," Edward said. Just as she was about to thank him, however, he continued, "But in this market, it's kind of like throwing darts on the side of a barn, isn't it?"

"Or like rowing downstream," Albert added. "It's mindless. But this bull market can't last forever. It's already been about a year. When it's over, Lisa Marie and her friends will go back to selling insurance policies."

Having felt the sharpness of his edge, Lisa Marie squinted at Albert. "Not many people outside the market would know when the bull run began. Sounds like you've been watching closely, like you're jealous that you're not in it."

"Dad wouldn't let me in," Albert looked at his father. "But like I said, it's mindless anyway."

"I deal with guys every day who make so much money that they could break you. But then, they wouldn't have you to follow them around with your little pen and yellow pad." Lisa Marie reached over and poked Albert in the chest. "I hope the blisters on your fingers aren't too painful."

"Wow!" Edward yelled. "Forget the Law—I am going to Wall Street with Lisa Marie. You're right, Dad. She's on fire!"

"I don't know why you're coming after me," Albert said to Lisa Marie. "Edward said the same thing."

"It's the *way* you say it," his sister replied, lowering her voice. "There's more of a bite to it."

"So Mom is telling you to get married after she just finished telling me how I need to take my wife to the opera," Albert replied, in what appeared to be a non sequitur.

Edward perceived the statement to be an olive branch that his older brother was extending to Lisa Marie, who was only two years younger than Albert.

"It reminds me of how she wanted you to take piano lessons as a kid," Albert continued.

Edward mused that Albert was at once commiserating and needling—in his unique, subtle way. Everyone knew that Lisa Marie did not enjoy her days on the keys.

"I hated the piano." Lisa Marie closed her eyes. "I still hear that metronome ticking in my head." She opened her eyes wide and smiled. "I wanted to throw that thing through the window."

"I bet Mom would have loved to have had piano lessons as a little girl," Edward said, in defense of his mother.

"Oh, please." Albert placed his palm on his forehead as if he was checking for a fever. "No more stories about Mom's hometown this morning. We've had enough."

Marie put a cup of black coffee on the table in front of Lisa Marie, adding a spoonful of sugar. "Music is a gift, which you will appreciate one day." She ladled another scoop of sugar into her daughter's cup. "And so is family. You need to come home or get married." Her tone was soft but stern. "You're not a man."

"I know, Mom," Lisa Marie said, taking the spoon from her mother's hand so that she could stir her coffee herself. "Just let me see this through before I settle down. You have to know that you taught me good values." She paused. "Besides, I'm still having a lot of fun."

"It's not you that I am worried about, my dear girl," Marie responded, placing the lid on the sugar. "It's those men you are surrounded by in that city. It's not a good place for you." Marie hardened her brow. "And exactly what kind of 'fun' are you having?"

"Albert, I thought you would be at work by now, late on a Saturday morning," Lisa Marie said, in an obvious attempt to shift the focus away from herself. "You lawyers bill by the hour, don't you? Every minute counts." She looked at her beveled watch, strapped with white gold. "Tick, tick, tick..."

"New watch, huh?" Albert snickered. "Must be nice working from nine to four and going straight to the jewelry store before it closes. Mom just told us a story about what happened in her town during World War II. But being that there is no overseas market for the information, you probably wouldn't have been interested. So we're done."

"Mom went through some tough stuff," Edward whispered, looking at the Sambuca residue on the bottom of his coffee cup. He was trying to diffuse the tensions between his siblings. He was still hoping that his mother might open and finish what he felt was an incomplete story.

"Yeah, you know—like war and violence," Albert said, dropping his eyes and jaw, unable to keep himself from taking another jab at his successful sister. "Things that Wall Street cares about only if they affect interest rates or oil prices."

"You told them about the rape?" Lisa Marie asked, in a suddenly somber tone.

The table fell silent.

"What rape?" shouted Guy incredulously.

"Mom?" Lisa Marie said. "You never told Dad?"

"There was no rape," Guy insisted. He returned to the cuckoo clock, adjusting its big hand. "Damn clock," he said. He slid the weight up the pendulum to make it move faster. "The stories about the Germans are exaggerated. I don't believe that they killed six million Jews."

"Dad, you're the best businessman I know, but sometimes you say some really stupid things," Edward responded.

Guy did not respond. Instead, he continued to adjust the weight on the clock's pendulum.

"Mom, this is family," Albert said, parting ways with his father. "If something happened, tell us. That's what you always say."

"Mom, if you don't tell them, I will," Lisa Marie said, consolingly. "It's not just a woman's issue. I hate to say it, but Albert's right—this is family."

"I don't remember," gasped Marie as she planted her elbow on the table and buried her eyes in her seared hand. "It was a long time ago, and I have a headache." She took a deep breath and exhaled.

"Mom," Lisa Marie pleaded. "Of course you know. You told me. It's time you tell them."

"I don't want to—not now." Marie spoke from beneath the cover of her seared hand. "I honestly don't remember."

Lisa Marie reached into her purse. She pulled out the silver compact mirror that she inherited as an heirloom from her mother. The raised cherubim on the lid were polished to their original shine. She slid closer to her mother and stroked her shoulder. "Mom, look at me. At the mirror that you gave me."

Marie dropped her hand and opened her eyes, which were slow to readjust to the light.

"You always told me that whenever I was down, I should look in this mirror, the way Grandma did before she gave it to you, and the way you did before you gave it to me." Lisa Marie opened the mirror and sat it on the table. "Your greatest strength—is inside of you." She slid the compact across so that her mother could use it. "Tell them what happened."

Marie picked up the mirror reluctantly with her seared hand. She stared into it for a moment, without blinking or saying a word.

## XXXII.

Guy started to speak, but Lisa Marie kicked him under the table. Instead, he re-filled everyone's coffee cup with a dose of Sambuca.

# XXXIII.

## The Bear and the Boy

## And the Lamb

The wind was gusting, whistling through the thin alleys that separated the town's homes, and into Piazza Barrini. The townspeople lingered in the square, eating their bread. The black tarpaulin held, but only tenuously—the sound of the nailing rain distracted the lamb from eating its grass, and the animal was growing uneasy.

*Wind whistling and rain nailing—only one voice could be heard, that of the lamb wailing.*

Maria looked into her mother's eyes, but could not find any emotion. The same was true of her grandmother. Though the child had grown accustomed to seeing Nedda stare off at times, daydreaming, it was not something that she had ever encountered in Angelina, who was always ready to engage. Maria panned the entire square, searching for a sign—words, or a gesture from someone—that the situation was back to normal. Everything—and everyone—was solemn and gray. The children assumed their parents' pallid demeanor, daring not to question why. Maria scanned the skies for the butterfly that had preceded the storm, but could not find its colors. She began to feel a chill.

She then heard a roar approaching from the edge of town. As it drew closer, a tank's grind stirred the muted mass. The people turned to one another, but were unable to articulate a thought. They remained frozen, their feet stuck to the square. Maria could feel the cobblestones trembling as the tank's steel belts entered the piazza.

She watched as the tank passed. It went slowly, its brushed-on mix of brown and green paint looking like fur, reminding Maria of her mother's bedtime story about the bear. With its sharp teeth and claws, her mother had told her, the bear came down from the mountains looking for food. But it would not bother anyone as long as it was not provoked. The bear would eat the olives from the palm of the boy's small hand, smile, and go back to the mountains to be with his cubs. As the tank lumbered by, Maria saw it as the bear, its steel fur absorbing the pelting rain, the wind whistling at its back. Kindness would make the bear nice.

Indeed, just like mamma said, a boy sprinted from the huddle in Piazza Barrini to approach the bear. It was Nino Spezzano, the dead Spezzano's young son, wearing a cap. Maria thought that Nino had picked some olives from the tree, and was going to give them to the bear.

"*Bastardi*," Nino yelled, punching the bear's fur.

Maria watched. "What is Nino doing? He is supposed to be giving the bear olives, not getting it angry."

"*Bastardi*," Nino shouted again.

The tank stopped abruptly. As Nino stepped back, he fell to the ground. Maria's nerves frayed as the bear turned its head to face Nino.

The diminutive boy got back on his feet and stood his tallest beneath his cap. The barrel lowered to take aim.

"Nino," cried the boy's mother.

The boy looked at his mother, then back to the beast. He stepped closer.

Maria's thoughts raced. *Give the bear olives to make it happy.*

Instead, Nino spat into the gun's black hole.

The barrel clicked to load.

As everyone braced for the explosion, the boy's mother screamed, "Nino!" She ran toward her son.

Angelina quickly made the sign of the cross.

"Click, click, click," snarled the bear.

211

Nino's mother was an arm's length away from him. She lunged to grab him. The boy stepped closer to the beast, evading his mother's rescue. "Nino!" she screamed as she stumbled.

"Click, click," sputtered the beast. But there was no bite. The bear swiveled its head back. It resumed its crawl forward, and Maria was comforted by the thought that the bear was on its way back to its cubs—just the way the story ended before she fell asleep.

Nino Spezzano returned to the crowd a conqueror. The town let out a collective sigh of relief, the men whispering "bravo" from their dried throats, while the women gathered around the boy's mother to help her regain her composure.

But the whistling wind pushed back, more mightily than before. The tank released from its bottom a stream of alfalfa hay.

"That's so nice how the bear is leaving grass with purple flowers for the lamb, " mused Maria.

The lamb began to move away from the unfinished monument toward the more attractive feed, slowly pulling the tarpaulin with it. As the cover inched away, it scratched the cobblestones. Contrary to everyone's belief, there were no more boxes beneath the tarpaulin—at least not on the piazza. That was fine, Maria thought. The extra bread and wine must be on the pedestal that held the uninscribed obelisk.

As the lamb continued pulling, the tarpaulin began to rise up the obelisk on one side. There were no boxes on the pedestal either; instead, the gathered crowd saw three sets of human feet, tied with rope. The feet kicked against the knots.

With a fierce burst of wind, the lamb fled, taking the cover with it. Exposed were the judge, the tenor, and the priest—all three of them naked and strapped to the unfinished monument. The three town leaders were bound to one another, tied at the wrists, around the obelisk that had become a stake. Their only garment was a gag around their mouths, their only movement that of their leaping eyebrows.

The villagers rushed to save the trio, but braked when the withdrawing tank stopped in its tracks, still within view of the square. The top hatch flipped open.

Maria saw that the interior was ivory white, just like the sharp teeth of the bear.

A soldier emerged from the bear's open mouth. He pointed his rifle at the crowd.

The townspeople scurried to their homes, except for Nedda, who remained in the square with a blank expression. Angelina grabbed her and Maria, forcing them to join the hurried exodus. Amid the screaming of the fleeing mob and the scamper of her own feet, Maria looked over her shoulder at the bear, certain that it would go away without hurting anyone.

A gunshot pierced the bedlam. It tore through the heart of Pretore Clementino, extracting a grunt before he bowed his head. In equal intervals, the soldier cocked his rifle and shot two more times—first at Marcello Di Bello and then at Padre Piore.

Maria could not believe that the bear had attacked. That was not how the story was supposed to end. The streaming blood, bright red, kept Maria's eyes glued to the horror while she ran from it. She followed the flow down to the trio's feet, beneath which it pooled atop the monument's pedestal. The spectacle ended for Maria when her grandmother pulled her into the house, slamming and locking the door behind.

Nedda stood inside, face wan as she stared at the door.

Angelina pushed Maria into the bedroom.

Beginning to realize that the judge, the tenor, and the priest had been killed, and fearing that she, her mother, and her grandmother might be next, Maria began to cry.

Angelina embraced her granddaughter tightly. "It's okay, honey. We're safe inside. Everything will be all right."

"Are you sure?" Maria asked as she huffed.

"I'm sure," Angelina replied.

"I love you, Grandma."

"I love you too, my—" Angelina's solace was disrupted by the snapping of the front-door lock. She raced back to the kitchen. Maria trailed right behind, sobbing hysterically. "Grandma, what's happening? You said we were safe!"

Nedda had opened the door. She stepped outside and walked toward the piazza. "Nedda!" Angelina yelled.

It was too late. Nedda was already entering the square.

"Nedda!" Angelina shouted again, while the other townspeople peeped from behind their shutters.

"Mamma, don't go!" Maria screamed. "The bear is going to get you!" When Nedda kept walking, Maria moved to run after her.

Her grandmother pulled her back. "Stay here," she told Maria, her command quaking. Angelina knew that there was nothing more that she could do to help Nedda. She did not move from the doorway; though she dared not to step into the piazza, she could not shrink from watching over her daughter, even if it meant witnessing her murder. As Angelina suppressed her own tears, she placed her hands over Maria's eyes so that her young granddaughter would not be exposed to the impending carnage.

But Maria was able to peek through the daylight between two of Angelina's trembling fingers. She saw her mother pause at the unfinished monument. Nedda stood still, staring at the pool of blood gathering on the pedestal. The blood had changed from bright red to brown. It was starting to overflow, dripping onto the square's cobblestones. Nedda folded her hands.

*Mamma is saying a prayer that God will answer by bringing the judge, the tenor, and the priest back to life.*

The three heads remained bowed, their bodies draining.

Nedda slipped out of her shoes. Fighting the repelling rain, she climbed the pedestal and walked around its table, unfazed by the blood on her feet.

Maria was warmed by the way her mother touched each of the dead men with her smooth ivory hand—lovingly—just as she did with Maria herself every night at bedtime. She adjusted her head for a better view between her grandmother's fingers.

Having walked the pedestal full circle, Nedda ended where she began—before the judge. She crouched down to untie his feet. Although she pulled hard at the rope, she did not strain, working until the knot was undone. She did the same for the tenor and the priest.

Maria became concerned that after her mother untied their hands, they all would fall. *Someone should help mamma.*

As the rain continued to pour, Nedda had returned to the judge. She removed the white gag around his mouth, and then used it to wipe the area around his eyes. When she finished, she tossed the cloth onto the piazza's bricks.

The judge was not wearing his rimmed glasses. Maria surmised that someone had taken them, which must have made it harder for him to see before he died. She again fretted that once her mother unbound the judge from the other two, he would come crashing down into the blood. Why won't anyone help mamma?

Pushing her shoulder into the judge's chest to brace him, Nedda untied his left wrist, separating it from beneath the priest's right; she refastened the priest to the stake so that he would not swing in the rain and wind. She then unraveled the judge's right wrist from under the tenor's left, making sure to retie the tenor. Nedda gripped the judge beneath his armpits, and rotated him to keep his face pointed to the sky. She dragged the jurist slowly off the pedestal.

Mamma was so strong, Maria thought as she watched her mother take the judge down. Why couldn't papà be that strong and take the guns out of the hands of the mean German soldiers?

Nedda laid the pretore on the square. She picked up the still-twisted gag, folded it, and placed it under his head like a pillow.

Nedda headed next to the tenor, pausing momentarily to examine the judge's blood that was settling into the creases of her palms. She held her hands to the sky to cleanse them, but the blood would not wash away. She started to wipe her hands on her dress, but then pulled back. Instead, she grabbed the pedestal to scale it. The wind drove the rain against her. She pushed her way through the onslaught.

The tank remained at its distance—the soldier watching Nedda, his gun no longer pointed.

Nedda liberated the tenor's mouth. She passed her bloody palm over his blue lips, making them red again. Once more, Nedda pushed her shoulder into the dead, loosening the tenor's cuffs while managing to keep the priest upright. She hauled the tenor off the pedestal and rested him in the square, next to the judge.

Mamma was so smart, Maria marveled. She must have figured out how she was going to lay all three men in the square before she even started. *Why couldn't papà be that smart, and figure out how to convince everyone to stop fighting?*

Standing like Athena, Nedda gripped her cotton collar with each of her hands. She ripped her flower-patterned dress from top to bottom—the sound of the tearing louder than the wind's whistling. As she cast her dress aside, the only thing between her and the downpour was the thin veneer of her full slip. Her cheekbones were like shelves. Her clavicles glistened.

A collective gasp came through the cracks of the shutters.

Nedda knelt to the ground and picked up the tenor's gag; she placed it on his bleeding heart. A small red dot seeped through the surface of the cloth. When she lowered her head and puckered her lips, a droplet fell onto the red dot, causing it to burgeon. She kissed the tint and slowly pulled away. Raising her knee and planting her right foot into the piazza, she ascended.

*Pop. Pop-pop.*

Maria closed her eyes, and cried out loud. "What's happening?"

"Don't worry," Angelina said. "It's only the wind."

Maria opened her eyes. Through Angelina's hold, she saw that her grandmother was right. A strong wind had blown the tarpaulin against the church's front doors, making the popping sound. The black cover, pasted to the entrance, was still tied to the lamb. The young sheep was sniffing at the church's cracked front steps.

Nedda remounted the pedestal, against the rain. She removed the white restraint from the priest's mouth, tossed it, and leaned into a corpse for the third time. When Nedda reached around the stake to untie the holy man's wrists, she started by grasping his hands.

Maria could feel that the gold ring that the priest usually wore was gone. The Germans must have taken it, she mused angrily.

Nedda loosened the German rope, and pulled the priest down to the square, where she laid him next to the tenor. She placed the gag over his right hand; the cloth was not able to fully cover it. She touched the tip of the finger that had worn the ring, closed her eyes, and whispered.

Perhaps she was telling the priest not to worry, Maria thought—that she would find his ring. Mamma was such a caring person. *Why wasn't papà caring enough to come back and find them?*

The lamb wailed from the church steps.

Nedda picked up her torn dress from the square, and laid it over the trio. She then walked to her mother and child. She peeled Angelina's fingers from Maria's eyes, and gave her daughter a kiss. From between the chinks of their shutters, the townspeople watched in disbelief.

Once back inside, the air was still thick with captivity's stench. Nevertheless, Angelina closed the door tightly and slid its locks to keep out the whistle and rain, which she knew could intrude through the slightest breach.

Nedda was sitting at the kitchen table like a statue. She was unmovable, her body drenched, her slip dripping. Angelina threw the quilt that she had been stitching around her daughter.

Maria shook Nedda, trying to wake her from her daze. "Mamma, mamma!" Maria cried. "Mamma, are you all right? Say something, so I know."

Nedda began to smile. Her lips moved, but her words were incomprehensible.

"That must be the butterfly song," Maria said. She reassured herself. "That's the butterfly song, mamma. You're telling us that everything is going to be all right, just like the pretty lady did in the opera."

Angelina went to the wood armoire to get a brush; she returned to straighten her daughter's hair while Maria stood by Nedda's side.

"Mamma's okay," Maria said again. "She sang the butterfly song. And now you're taking out the knots."

"Your mother is very strong," explained Angelina, stroking her daughter's hair. After three long passes, Angelina returned the brush to the armoire.

The whistle and rain eased.

Angelina went back to the kitchen table, where her daughter was draped

217

loosely in the quilted patchwork of white, red, and black, not fully ensconced in it. Angelina pulled at the corners of her creation to better cover Nedda's legs, and lifted Maria into Nedda's lap to warm her. Throughout, Nedda remained completely still.

Rather than prodding her daughter to speak, Angelina assumed her own seat. Noticing that her spools had been toppled on the table, she stood them upright, one by one. "Everything is going to be just fine," she said. "Just fine." Her hands trembling, she pushed the spools closer to each other, until they touched to form a triad.

# XXXIV.

"        "
·······

**M**arie paused in her story.

Albert stared out the window, twisting his wedding ring back and forth on his finger. He took it off and squeezed it in his fist. He punched the corner of the table three times before putting his ring back on his finger. He continued his twisting while staring through the glass pane.

Edward bit his nails. Discovering that they had already been cut short, he searched his hands for something else to correct. He found a hangnail and pulled it, painfully. He was disappointed—angry—that he had left Lavenna so proud of himself, yet had missed so much. He searched his hand for another hangnail, but could not find one. Instead, he zeroed in on a cuticle and bit it, drawing blood. He sucked his finger to stop the flow.

Guy was restless in his seat. He threw back a shot from his cup of espresso, even though there was nothing left—not even the sweet residue.

Lisa Marie scratched her wrist and forearm around her designer bracelet. She undid the clasp from the bracelet, and put it in her pocket.

The cuckoo emerged from the clock, its call loud in the silence.

Edward looked at Albert, and nodded toward Guy as if to ask his brother whether his father would say anything.

Albert shrugged his shoulders.

Guy looked at his watch, and saw that his prized clock was still behind.

He got up to fix it.

Lisa Marie covered her mother's seared hand with her own. When Marie tried to pull away, Lisa Marie squeezed Marie's hand so that her mother could not escape. She locked her mother's eyes with her own, and nodded.

Marie nodded back, and picked up where she had left off.

# XXXV.

## Behind a Closed Door

Angelina pulled back from her spools of thread, and settled into her seat at the kitchen table. She exhaled, relieved that the commotion was over and her daughter was still alive.

The front door was kicked in. In a blur, the high black boots of two enemy soldiers stomped into the house. The soldiers' eyes were hidden behind the obscurity of military sunglasses, even though it was raining.

Angelina shot to her feet.

Maria looked to her mother, who was unmoved. She hopped off Nedda's lap, and scampered to Angelina to bury her face in her grandmother's stomach.

The lead and taller of the two soldiers swept his arm across the table to clear it. Angelina's spools of thread, however, were beyond his reach.

When Angelina went for her spools, the younger soldier beat her to them. He buried them in his right hand, and stared down upon her through his dark lenses.

Her face to the table, Angelina begged, "They are my sewing threads—please."

The soldier paused. He squeezed the spools in his raised right hand so that Angelina could hear the grinding of the wood. He extended his palm beneath Angelina's eyes, and offered back her threads.

"Thank you," Angelina said meekly. When she reached for the soldier's palm, he closed it swiftly like a trap. He cocked back his arm, and threw the spools out the front door.

Angelina tried to see where they had landed, so that she might scoop them up later. But their colors were quickly lost in the rain and carnage.

The two soldiers stood over Nedda. Their faces contorting with anger, they yelled at her incomprehensibly in German.

Nedda mouthed "The Humming Chorus," summoning the image of a caterpillar walking across the strings of a cello, nervous that it might not become a butterfly.

The soldiers looked at each other quizzically, not knowing what to make of this woman who defied them. The leader barked an order, to which the younger man responded by nodding his head. They continued yelling at Nedda, their collective screech echoing. They stripped her of her quilt, and let out a churlish laugh.

After a pause, Nedda stood up and walked to her daughter. She placed her hand on Maria's shoulders while the little girl's face remained hidden in her grandmother's belly. She continued humming with a clarity that silenced the savage chaos.

Mamma must be trying to tell me that papà is on his way just like the man in the opera, Maria thought to herself. *Yes, papà would come back and find us—would save us from the mean men.*

Before Nedda could complete her final note, the soldiers removed her hand from her daughter. The superior whisked Nedda into her bedroom, slamming the door behind him. The subordinate filled the frame, standing guard.

Maria looked up at her grandmother, crying. "What are they doing to mamma?" she asked, eyes streaming.

Angelina had no answer. Instead, she pulled her granddaughter back to her stomach to avert the child's eyes and ears as a shriek joined the thunder from the reawakened storm. In the darkness of her grandmother's embrace, Maria sobbed wildly.

Through the open front door, the wind whistled and the rain fell like nails.

# XXXVI.

## Ode to an Uncle

The Bennetts sat motionless in their luxuriant kitchen, robbed of their words.

"War is a horror," Marie said with a stern formality.

"What did your mother ever say to you afterward?" asked Albert.

"Nothing."

"So then you really don't know what happened to her that day?" offered Guy.

"Your father didn't hear me, did he?" an annoyed Marie asked, addressing only Lisa Marie.

"It's okay, Mom," Lisa Marie whispered.

"All that Dad is saying," Albert replied on his father's behalf, "is that you're only assuming that your mother was raped. You really don't know for sure that such a horrible thing ever happened." He sensed that he had his father's approval and support. "We can only hope it didn't happen."

"You guys don't get it," Lisa Marie shot back, looking at both Albert and Guy. "Is this how you live—by creating alternative realities and not letting anyone or anything take you out of them?" She rolled up her sleeves and took the washcloth from her mother. She rubbed the table clean of the stains from the men's coffee.

"They wonder why I don't talk about it," Marie said.

"Marie, I was only trying to say that maybe your mother didn't suffer as

223

much as you think she did," Guy said, reaching for his wife's hand. "Why torture yourself when you don't know?"

"How do you know it didn't happen?" she responded, pulling away. "Were you there?"

"It's just that, in all the stories about the war, I've never heard anything about atrocities committed by the Germans against the Italians."

"We were not Italians. We were living in a place forsaken by both Italy and God."

"What are you talking about?" asked Guy, put back by the depth of his wife's feelings.

"Let me make it simple. Do you think I made up the whole story about how they killed the judge, the tenor, and the priest, and how my mother took them off the monument herself?"

Edward sat quietly. He pondered how he could be sensitive to his mother while eliciting more from her. "Mom," he said, "your mother's bravery is beyond words. Her comforting you even when she was surrounded by the soldiers is unimaginable."

"If in fact Grandma wasn't in some altered state of shock, and really did not know what was happening," Albert rejoined, not wanting his younger brother to have the last word. "What Grandma went through would be enough to give anyone a nervous breakdown. Particularly when, as we now know, Grandma was suffering from schizophrenia. Like Dad said before, that is why she was sent back. That day—that moment—in Piazza Barrini might have been when she broke. From that moment on, she might not have even known where she was."

"My mother knew where she was that day," Marie insisted. "That's not what broke her."

Albert cleared his throat. "It had to have been the separation from Grandpa. The helplessness of him being here while all this was happening. Hence the humming from *Madame Butterfly*. She was sure Grandpa would return and everything would be all right. The tragedy is that once they were finally together in America, it was too late. The damage had been done."

"She was singing 'The Humming Chorus,' you bloviating meathead," said

Edward with his chin elevated. "She was afraid she might not escape. It was serenity in the turmoil."

Albert raised his voice. "It was I who made the connection between the separation and longing of Puccini's *Madame Butterfly* in Japan and Mom's in Italy."

"You were pontificating," said Edward, delivering a comeuppance that he knew would rattle his brother. "It was meaningless."

"So meaningless, little brother, that you decided to steal it and take credit for it."

"I can't believe you guys are trying to interpret the work of some Italian guy portraying a Japanese woman and applying it to Mom," said Lisa Marie. "Sounds to me like you are being chauvinist pigs."

"Stop," Marie shouted at everyone. She looked at the men in particular. "None of you know what's meaningful. None of you know cruelty until you see it yourself. I'm sorry to disappoint you, but life isn't always explainable. It doesn't play by the laws you learn in school and argue about in court. It was war, and war is a horror." She looked around, her family cowed. "There's no meaning in war. No final act. When you live through it, there's no curtain that comes down." She closed her eyes. "It's a horror that lasts forever."

"I don't think we should talk about this anymore, guys," Lisa Marie said, solemnly. "Mom is upset." She went to her father's clock and adjusted it.

Marie bowed her head.

Guy shuffled over to his wife, and put his arm around her shoulder. "It's okay, honey."

Marie grabbed her husband's hand, keeping her face down. "He'll be fine. I pray every day. Antonio, please."

"It's all right, Mom," said Lisa Marie, drawing closer to her mother. "Grandpa is happy in Heaven with Grandma." She stroked her mother's hair. "I'm sure that Saint Anthony is already watching over both of them."

"Yeah, Ma," Albert added. "They're both saints themselves. Right next to Saint Anthony."

"Real inspirations for all of us," Edward capped the family ode. "The same way that you are."

"Those are beautiful thoughts, kids," Guy whispered. "But I don't think it's Grandpa your mother is referring to." He took a deep breath. "And I don't think it's Saint Anthony she's praying to."

"Well, we know that you're Mom's only husband," Albert joked.

"And you always bragged that you were her only boyfriend," Edward added.

"Your mom has a brother," Guy said.

The room went silent.

"*What?*" Lisa Marie said, looking at her mother. "You told me about the rape, but never said anything about a brother."

"His name is Antonio." Guy slid his thumb slowly over his upper lip. "Tell them. They should know."

"I can't," Marie stuttered. "You tell them."

"I don't get it," Albert gasped. "This is too much. It's too much for you to have held back and us not to know."

"I knew it," Edward interrupted, disregarding his mother's deterioration. "I knew there was something strange when I was back in Lavenna. When we went through the photo album, a picture of a young guy slipped out. I remember it was cracked. Everyone clammed up, and Giovanni insisted it was a picture of someone outside the family who got mixed in with the other pictures by mistake. That must've been mom's brother." He snapped his fingers. "And that was the name on the birth certificate. The priest thought it was a godparent. It was mom's brother!"

Guy raised his hand toward Edward to quiet him.

Marie's tears, long dammed, flowed.

Guy lowered his voice. "We never wanted to tell you kids about your Uncle Antonio. She goes to see him on Saturdays."

"Where?" asked Lisa Marie, clinging to her mother's side. She began to cry. "Where does Mom go to see her brother?"

Guy looked at Marie.

"It's okay, tell them," she replied.

"Your uncle lives in a hospital."

"What do you mean he lives in a hospital?" Albert asked.

"Actually, it is an asylum," Guy looked down. "He has schizophrenia." He paused. "Just like your grandmother. But they couldn't deport him because, in those days, he was an American citizen, as the son of your grandfather. Your grandmother was not an American." Guy tapped the table. "Your mother never wanted to say anything to you children. It was her problem and she didn't want to scare or burden you."

Marie continued crying quietly.

"How would we have been scared?" asked Edward.

"Who knows?" replied Guy. "She thought you might have been afraid of having children of your own because they might become sick like him."

"You all are fine," Marie mustered the strength to explain. "If it wasn't for your Uncle Antonio, you might not be here."

"Your Uncle Antonio loves your mother dearly," Guy emphasized.

"More than anyone knows," Marie continued, regaining her composure. "He saved me from the Germans," she said, banging her knuckles against the table. "And it cost him. What they did to him was a horror."

"What?" Albert's brow jumped.

"You got me," Guy said. "She never told me anything about her brother saving her from the Germans."

"You never asked," Marie shot back. She turned to Albert. "My brother was an Italian soldier during the war. When Italy switched sides to be with the Americans, my brother stayed with the Germans to make sure that they would not hurt us. He had learned German in school. He was so smart. But the German soldiers were angry at the Italians. That's why they did what they did to my town. They took out their revenge while the Americans were coming after them. Antonio couldn't stop them. He was so innocent and brave. They were so cruel and conniving."

"I'll be damned!" Edward slapped the table. "The German holster I found in your house. It was probably your brother's."

"He became a German soldier. Or at least he pretended to be." Marie glared at Guy. "He tried to make them fight what you call a 'just war.' It didn't matter. It got him into more trouble."

"Did they take him as a prisoner?" Edward asked.

"Worse. They put him in the prison that he's in now. They were animals." Her voice cracked as she drowned in her sorrow. She put her face in her hands. "Antonio, *povero fratello mio,* I'm so sorry."

The cuckoo clock sounded, finally with the correct time.

"Tell us, Mom," Albert urged. "Tell us what he did for you. Tell us what they did to him."

"They were animals," Marie repeated.

As the family huddled around their matron, one of Lisa Marie's tears fell upon her mother's burnt hand.

Marie spread the tear over her burn. She pressed a vein, and began her ode to the uncle that her children had never known.

# XXXVII.

## Black Boots,

## A Monumental Stone

Maria continued to sob onto her grandmother's stomach, waiting for the darkness to end. The onslaught of the rain against the house was unceasing.

Finally, the door to Nedda's room opened. Instinctively, Maria turned—but out of fear, she glued her eyes to the floor. She saw only four black boots, polished perfectly, one pair larger than the other. The man in the larger black boots—the ones that had emerged from her mother's room—uttered something to Angelina in German, which Maria could not understand. The black boots shone, and did not move.

Angelina pleaded in Italian, though she knew her words meant nothing. "Please, she's just a little girl," she cried, pounding her chest. "If you must, take me instead."

Maria saw the larger boots come closer, their fresh leather crackling. She snuck a look up the pressed pants, at the soldier's trim waist, where he tightened his belt and secured his pistol in his holster. He took a large sniff of the air above Maria's head. "Hmmm," he growled.

"Don't look," Angelina whispered to Maria. "Everything will be all right." But her grip on Maria's shoulders trembled.

A third soldier stepped hurriedly through the front door. The storm's waters rolled off his broad shoulders. "Lieutenant," he said in a perfect German cadence, "what are you doing in here?" He continued, respectfully. "This is my house, my family." He stood next to Angelina, behind Maria. "This is my grandmother and my sister."

"Antonio," whispered Angelina. "You are alive."

It was Antonio Del Cielo, Maria's older brother. His face was unblemished, and his eyes were hazel; his sockets rose before dipping at the ends, making them appear as winged seeds, suspended in mid-air as they floated down from the canopies of his plush eyebrows. His black hair was combed back, undulating in robust waves. Though not tall by any measure, his height was greater than his father's. He was not the great tenor, but the young women of the town nonetheless admired him for his looks and mind, and for the soft touch with which he entertained children in the square with stories and games.

"I…" He paused to correct himself. "*We* are with you, loyal to the German army and the Führer."

"Yes," the lieutenant replied slowly. "It was smart for you to break ranks with your fellow Italians, the traitors who betrayed us." He stroked Maria's face. "Your knowledge of the area has helped us evade the Americans and the British." He looked around.

"Yes, it has," Antonio responded. "And you promised me that you would do nothing to hurt this village or my family. You already killed Mr. Spezzano, and what you did to the others…" He tightened his fist to restrain himself, and spoke through his brandished and gritted teeth. "We had a deal. Leave my family alone."

"The problem is," the lieutenant's junior cackled, "we have gotten word that your father is an American—that makes all of you American." He laughed. "Including your mother, the piazza stripper." He tipped his head toward the bedroom where Nedda lay quietly. "Your little sister," he hissed as he wrested Maria from Angelina, "is even prettier than your mother. I bet she will taste even sweeter to the lieutenant."

"Antonio," Angelina pleaded. "Help us! They already took your mother."

Antonio stood firm, without blinking.

"Antonio." Nedda's voice cracked from the bedroom. "Is that you, my son?"

Antonio leapt at the junior soldier and grabbed him by the collar. "You bastards, what have you done to her?" His body swelled with fury. "After all that I have done for you!" He thrust the German against the wall. "Keep your filthy hands off my sister."

"Lieutenant," the frazzled soldier said, looking to his commander. "This man has just committed an act of violence against the German Army. On the Führer's orders, he must be executed."

"Now, now," the lieutenant replied coolly, separating them. "Mr. Del Chellow is right," he said. "This has all been a mistake, for which we apologize." He adjusted the arms of his sunglasses, which he kept strapped tightly over his ears despite the absence of the sun. "He has been very loyal to us and the Führer, and it is time that the people of his town know about it." He grabbed Antonio by the arm. "I will bring him back into the square so that we can tell his friends what a good German soldier he has been." He nodded toward his subordinate, then to the empty pail next to the kitchen table. "You go fill that. You know what I want."

The lieutenant led Antonio into Piazza Barrini, to stand before the corpses of the judge, the tenor, and the priest.

Angelina and Maria ran to the door to see what was going to happen to Antonio. Angelina tried to curl her granddaughter into her, to shield her once again from impending horror. Maria would not turn her back on her brother. She stood with her eyes wide open.

"I am going to give a message to your townspeople, which you are going to translate for me into Italian," the lieutenant told Antonio. "Schreiber," the lieutenant yelled toward another soldier from the platoon, who was standing by the tank. "Come here. I need you to make sure that what I say is translated properly by Del Chellow."

"But Schreiber speaks both Italian and German, like me. Why don't you just have him talk directly to the people?"

"It's better if the words come from your mouth," the lieutenant said, leering. With an armed Schreiber at Antonio's side, the lieutenant began. "My Italian friends," he exclaimed. "I have an announcement to make. Please, come to your windows."

His throat dry, Antonio translated the lieutenant's words.

Schreiber looked to the lieutenant and shook his head, confirming that Antonio had conveyed the message.

The small shutters surrounding the square began to edge open.

"There is nothing for you to fear," the lieutenant shouted through the rain. "Our time here has ended. We leave in peace."

Antonio translated again.

More shutters creaked ajar.

"Before leaving, we wanted to share with you our gratitude to Antonio Del Chellow," the lieutenant continued. "When many of your compatriots were cowards and sided with the Americans and the English, this young man remained true to us and the Führer."

Antonio looked askance at the lieutenant.

"Tell them what I said, Del Chellow," ordered the lieutenant.

Antonio averted his eyes, looking over the homes. He bore the pain of his eyes being pelted by the storm. He spoke as ordered.

Hearing Antonio describe his allegiance to their captors, the townspeople mustered the courage to open their doorways and stand in them.

The lieutenant smirked down at the dead judge, tenor, and priest; he kicked the priest in the rib. "In fact, our stay in this fine town would not have been possible," he said, "without the help of Antonio Del Chellow. He was invaluable in helping us find this place."

"You are telling them a lie," Antonio countered. "You are not telling them everything."

"Everything that I have asked you to say is true," responded the lieutenant angrily. He placed his hand over his pistol holster, prompting Schreiber to cock his rifle. "Speak so that things do not get worse for your people. We will go house to house." He scowled at Antonio's sister and grandmother. "Starting with yours."

All the doors slammed shut—except for Antonio's own, in which Angelina and Marie stood in brave vigil.

"You scared everyone," the lieutenant smiled. "Now you will have to speak louder so that they can hear you."

Antonio stared at his grandmother and sister beneath their lintel. He began speaking with a volume greater than he was accustomed to.

"They can't hear you," bellowed the lieutenant, looking over at Schreiber to ensure that his last words were conveyed by Antonio to the people.

Antonio spoke slowly, his throat dry. With each pause, Schreiber prodded him with the tip of his rifle. Antonio conveyed the lieutenant's dark tribute to him.

The lieutenant's junior, the smaller set of black boots, entered the square with a pail overflowing with stones. He laid the pail directly in front of Antonio, on the other side of the corpses. When the top stone fell out of the pail, the soldier picked it up, and put it back in its place.

A *Kübelwagen* pulled up to the lieutenant on cue. He and his junior boarded, as Schreiber marched back to his tank. "*Addio!*" the lieutenant yelled, waving to the people. With a churlish laugh, the military vehicle sped away.

The house doors flipped like dominoes, and the natives entered the square. Encircling Antonio, their jaws were locked, their fists closed. With the blood of the judge, tenor, and priest settled into the square's cracks, the town was thirsty for something other than the falling rain. The circle closed tighter.

Antonio stood in his place, without wavering. Remorsefully, he uttered, "I would never do anything to hurt any of you. I thought I was protecting you."

"Grandma, Grandma." Maria tugged at Angelina in their doorway. "Let's go—we have to help Antonio. They are going to hurt Antonio."

Angelina pulled her granddaughter close, not allowing her to go anywhere.

Arrigo D'Abruzzi approached Antonio, and stepped on his toes. A full head above Antonio, D'Abruzzi stared down, breathing heavily. When Antonio tried to speak, D'Abruzzi squeezed his ear to silence him. With

Antonio standing straight, D'Abruzzi circled him like the lead wolf of a pack. Seeing the gun in Antonio's holster, D'Abruzzi pulled it out and threw it onto the square.

Antonio had no reaction, indifferent to the loss.

As the rain soaked through his shirt, exposing the spirals of thick hair on his chest, D'Abruzzi came face-to-face with Antonio again. *"Leccaculo,"* he rasped.

Antonio looked up into D'Abruzzi's bushy nostrils, and restrained himself from speaking.

D'Abruzzi reached for Antonio's neck. His hands landed on Antonio's throat with no resistance; the farmer nearly fell forward from the overexertion. He held on to Antonio's neck, which had not budged, and pulled himself back up to regain his footing. He looked to the rest of the crowd for a reaction.

The mob's silence was its verdict.

D'Abruzzi moved his grip to the collar of Antonio's German uniform. He ripped Antonio's shirt open, causing its buttons to pop and fly. He picked up the rope the Germans had used to bind the judge, the tenor, and the priest. "Someone else take off his pants," he said simply as he walked toward the pail of stones. He grabbed the top stone and tossed it in the air, catching it in his palm.

"Shall we tie him to the obelisk?" asked one of the townsmen.

"That would be disrespectful to them," replied D'Abruzzi, looking down at the corpses of the judge, tenor, and priest. He pointed to the corner of the piazza. "Let's take him to the olive tree."

Without hesitation, other men answered the call. They jeered Antonio as they stripped him down to his white cotton boxers. They proceeded with the efficiency of a work crew, carrying him to the olive tree, and finding the right place for him on the twisted trunk.

"He has nothing to say," laughed one of the men as he tied Antonio's feet. "Not even he, with his clever tongue, can talk his way out of this one," added another, bloody rope in his mouth, as he stretched Antonio's arms behind his back and around the girth of the tree.

"The Lord will judge you," Crooked Finger said shrilly.

"And see inside your dark heart," followed Frump.

"You have violated the commandments," finished Limp, dragging her lame leg closer for a better view of Antonio's suffering.

Still holding the first stone, D'Abruzzi reached down with his left hand to empty the pail onto the square. He held the empty pail over his head, and called for the young son of the dead Spezzano. The mob made way for the boy, who was pushed along by his mother. D'Abruzzi handed the boy the pail. "Fill this again. We'll need more."

The boy hesitated, and looked to his mother, who turned away. He swiveled back to D'Abruzzi, who pointed to a pile of stones just beyond the square. "There are plenty remaining from the building of the obelisk."

As the boy scampered away with his pail, the people were not willing to wait; they vied for the weapons already before them. With the wind whistling, they began to pillory Antonio Del Cielo.

"Traitor," shouted D'Abruzzi as he cast the first stone at the head of the damned, cracking his nose. Antonio's head slumped to one side as his blood began to pour down his chest.

The others paused to enjoy the sight and sound of Antonio's agony.

"Thief," shouted Signore Altezzana, his hurled mass crushing Antonio's groin.

"What they are saying is not true," Antonio groaned. "What they are doing I do not deserve. Why?"

The boy Spezzano returned with his pail, overflowing with stones from the monument.

"Wait!" Crooked Finger yelled out. She escorted Signora Spezzano to her son. She took a stone from the boy's pail, and handed it to the widow. "It's your turn."

Signora Spezzano's hands dropped when she received the stone from the unfinished monument; she studied it with her grief-ringed eyes. "This is from the obelisk?" she asked her son.

"Yes, mamma," the boy answered.

She turned toward Antonio. "And I am to throw it at him, while he is tied to the sacred olive tree?"

"It is God's will!" shouted Limp. "He is a Judas. It would be better for him if he had not been born!"

Signora Spezzano remained reluctant.

"Your son will never see his father again," lashed Crooked Finger.

The signora drew back her thin arm, behind her ear. She stopped, her palm quaking, the stone seeming to be too heavy to hurl.

"Do it for your son," Frump implored her.

Closing her eyes, Signora Spezzano thrust her arm forward and cast her stone.

It hit Antonio squarely on the heart.

The others came unleashed, throwing wildly and repeatedly.

His body being pummeled and awash in blood, Antonio marshaled the energy for one last yell. *"Vater, vergib ihnen; denn sie wissen nicht, was sie tun!"*

"What is he saying?" asked one of Antonio's persecutors. "He mocks us by speaking in German."

"Maybe he is calling his *crucco* friends for help," shouted another.

"No one can save him now!" growled D'Abruzzi.

The lamb, having descended from the church steps and now by the obelisk, wailed again.

D'Abruzzi looked with displeasure toward the animal. He stuffed a steel handle into the back pocket of Spezzano's son, and an order into his ear. The boy darted to the lamb, pulled out the instrument that D'Abruzzi had given him, and flipped it open. It was a knife. With a swift stroke, he slit the lamb's throat. The lamb did not cry, but instead twitched before going lifeless. Its blood decanted into the square.

Maria freed herself from Angelina's hold, and ran into the house. She pounded on her mother's bedroom door. "Mamma, come, come." When there was no answer, she pounded harder. "Antonio needs your help, mamma. They are going to kill him." The door remained a wall. Maria slumped down against the separation from her mother and wept.

The doorknob turned. As if summoned from the dead, Nedda rose from her bedroom tomb. She wrapped her bed's white sheet around herself, and

236

lifted Maria off the floor, onto her feet. "Take me to your brother."

Maria led Nedda into the square. Seeing her son being assaulted, Nedda took the lead, wading through the dead and the ravenous throng until she reached the olive tree. She lifted Maria in her arms, and whispered as she turned to face the attack. "Be strong for your brother."

Maria scrunched herself into a fetal position.

The stoning slowed.

"The little girl is innocent," called out a faceless voice.

"The ass licker is probably already dead anyway. Look at him."

Antonio's face hung; his eyes were closed.

"Even if he isn't already dead," said Crooked Finger, letting go of her rock but keeping her finger pointed, "he will have to live with his mother, alone. They don't belong."

One by one, the people dropped their stones and returned to their homes.

Nedda lowered her daughter to the ground, where the little girl watched her mother untie Antonio from the tree. Nedda worked slowly, Maria thought, so that she would not disturb Antonio or cause him any more pain. With the last knot untied, Antonio fell into his mother's arms.

Maria breathed a sigh of relief.

She then saw Nedda recline to sit upon a bend in the tree. She cradled Antonio in her lap. With the sheet over Nedda's body flowing toward the roots of the displaced tree, her mother's head held high, Maria recognized a shape that she had learned in school—that of a triangle with three equal sides. Within the perfect triangle, Antonio was turned toward his mother's womb. Maria was amazed at how her mother did not seem worried for her naked and bloodied son, or angry at the mean people who had hurt him. With the rain glazing her face, mamma looked so sweet.

Angelina tapped Maria's shoulder. "Your mother and brother need to be alone. Let's go back to the house."

"Okay, Grandma," Maria responded, placing her small hand inside Angelina's.

As the two passed the slaughtered lamb, Maria pulled away to pay her respects. She was saddened by the blood on the small creature's soft white fur. Her grandmother keeping her distance, Maria picked up the knife that the boy Spezzano had left behind. She cut the cord that attached the lamb to the tarpaulin, as if relieving it of being choked by the weight of the black tarp.

Angelina looked at Maria tenderly, extending her hand for her granddaughter to come.

Instead of going to her grandmother, Maria proceeded to the tarp. She sliced a large square from the covering. Casting the knife aside, she picked up the cut-out and draped it over her extended arms. She bent over and scooped up the lamb. She walked to the obelisk, and managed her way onto the pedestal. Sitting down to face her mother and brother, Maria emulated Nedda's sweet expression. The lamb cuddled in her arms, facing her mother with the covered bodies of the judge, tenor, and priest between them, Maria had formed a perfect triangle of her own.

She sang "The Humming Chorus," inspiring her mother to do the same.

# XXXVIII.

## The Bride's Mother Hidden,

## A Night at the Opera

"And then what?" Albert asked. "What happened to Antonio?" He amended his words. "What became of Uncle Antonio?"

"My mother held him until he woke up," said Marie, biting her lip. "I stayed with the lamb, while my grandmother prayed from the door."

"So when he woke up, he had schizophrenia?" Lisa Marie stuttered. "Like—multiple personalities?" She shook her head. "Never mind. I don't need to know."

"It's okay," Marie said, placing her hand over her daughter's. Though Marie had felt a pressure upon her shoulders when she thought of Antonio, her daughter's cold hand, in need of warming, loosened the yoke. "You can ask about Antonio. He's your uncle."

Guy interrupted, speaking slowly with his eyes glazed. "Everybody thinks schizophrenia gives you multiple personalities—turns you into some kind of Dr. Jekyll and Mr. Hyde. But it cuts you off from reality. It rejects you and in return you are forced to detach." He snapped out of his momentary daze. He breathed in, and pushed his hand through his hair. "It happens over time."

"So it sort of puts you in your own world," volunteered Albert.

"It puts you in many worlds," said Marie, arching her eyebrows more. "It makes you hallucinate, hear voices." She took a deep breath. "It robs you of your ability to have emotions. It steals your happiness. He was..." She paused, taking another breath. "He is *always* afraid."

"So is it genetic?" asked Edward. "Did Uncle Antonio inherit it from Grandma?"

"They say there is a gene that causes it," explained Guy. "The real risk of passing it on is between parent and child. So you kids are fine," he assured. "Your mother and I have done a lot of research and spoken to a lot of people."

"I think the German doctor that we first saw years ago, Dr. Schmidt, had it right," said Marie, looking at her husband, who had always comforted his wife about her brother, despite never knowing what happened to him that day in the piazza. "It can be in the genes, but it's brought out by a traumatic event. For both my mother and my brother, it was that damn war." She squinted with disdain. "The Germans lied about my brother. He would never do anything to hurt our town. It was a lie."

"I can't believe you would even go see a German doctor about your brother," Albert said in disbelief. "After what the Germans did to your town?"

"Albert, the doctor was trying to help my brother, and he told it like it was," Marie said, emphatically. "Besides, forget about what the Germans did to my town. How about what my town did to my brother?"

"How did the town treat you after the..." Edward felt a strange taste from the words that were about to come from his mouth. "After the stoning?"

"We stayed inside most of the time," Marie said. "Who wanted the stares and sneers?"

"Wow, Mom," replied Lisa Marie. "I've never heard you use the word 'sneer.'"

"I know it well—in both languages."

Edward moved the conversation on. "What happened next?"

"My grandmother died the next year and my mother and brother became more and more withdrawn. When the war was over, we left for America in the middle of the night, so that no one would notice. We ran away from our neighbors." Marie placed her hand over her mouth and tapped the kitchen table repeatedly. "We escaped from our own home," she said, as her tapping sped. "Once we got to America, they both went downhill. After my mother was deported, Antonio fell apart completely. None of the medications worked anymore, and he had to live permanently in the psychiatric hospital. Greylock Park—just thinking about the place makes me sick."

"So that's why Grandma is not in your wedding pictures?" asked Edward, trying to rewind the story. "She was already deported?"

"No, she was here. She stayed home that day. The way she was, she couldn't come to our wedding." Marie curled her burnt hand into a fist, and pounded it on the table, knowing the pain she would feel upon impact. "She was locked in her room so that she would be safe."

"I had a nurse keep an eye on the place," added Guy softly.

"So behind that beautiful picture of you and Dad on your wedding day," Lisa Marie said in disbelief, "was the mother of the bride, locked in her room." She folded her arms and sat upright.

"She always went to her room," Guy said. "I remember the first time I came to the house for a date with your mother. I looked through the window and saw this shock of white hair. She glanced at me and shot into her room, like a ghost."

"And you thought it was something about the way you looked," joked Marie. "Like I said, the disease makes you anxious—always scared. Yet, my mother and my brother had been so brave."

"This is terrible, Mom," Lisa Marie said. "Why didn't you all just go back to Lavenna with Grandma?" She lowered her voice. "Instead of sending her back alone?"

"What would we go back to?" Marie said, her face dropping. "My father wanted us to be Americans. When he finally got us here, we weren't about to turn around."

"It was a different time," Guy added. "People like Mom's father made major sacrifices." Guy's face widened with a smile. "I will never forget when I brought the little guy to our new house while I was building it," he said, referring affectionately to his father-in-law. "He was beaming. '*Caro Gaetano, va bene,*' he said." Guy looked at his wife. "He always called me

'*Caro Gaetano.*' That day, he knew his sacrifice had paid for a better life."

"A better *material* life," Lisa Marie snapped. "Tell that to Grandma."

"Do you ever remember a special time that you shared with your mother and brother before everything fell apart?" Edward asked. "Some special moment?"

"The night we went to the opera," Marie said without hesitation.

"Wow," Albert said quietly, getting up from his chair. He went to the sink to get a drink of water.

"My mother got the tickets with the money she saved in her gold tin box. She, Antonio, and I went to the opera."

"What about Grandpa?" Edward asked.

"He was busy working," Marie said, scrambling for an answer. "Besides, he never had a great love for opera."

"Tell us about the night at the opera, Mom," urged Lisa Marie.

"Well, of course my mother saved her money to see *Madame Butterfly*. She scrimped enough to buy a new dress on sale. It was a simple green dress with a yellow collar—but to her, it was as if she were queen that night. She and I put makeup on each other and then I helped Antonio knot his tie."

"Tell us about the opera, Mom," said Edward anxiously. "Did your mother cry when she heard that song?"

"I don't remember anything specific about the performance that night, except that it was beautiful. And I don't read minds. It was *Madame Butterfly*. If you want to know about it, go see it yourself." She paused to ponder, her eyes widening. "I was such a daughter that night, such a little sister."

The phone rang. Edward jumped out of his seat to yank the receiver into his ear. After finding out who was calling, he covered the mouthpiece. "Mom, it's that woman, Sylvia. The one who volunteers with you at Whitebridge General."

"That's not exactly true," Guy uttered as Marie rose to her feet. "Sylvia is the nurse at Greylock. She takes care of your Uncle Antonio."

Edward winced at Guy, with his palms open and upward.

Guy responded. "She did everything she could to keep you guys from finding out. So the part about Sylvia was a white lie."

The family listened attentively to Marie's phone call. Her spaced responses were simple. "Okay."

"They're probably calling to talk to her about your uncle's meds," Guy said softly. "They changed them Wednesday, and yesterday he was doing better."

"We'll be right there," Marie said, finally. "Thank you."

"What is it, Marie?" Guy asked.

Marie responded, "Sylvia said Antonio took a bad turn."

"But they just told you yesterday that he was doing fine," Guy replied. "What changed in one day?"

Marie glared at Guy, unflinchingly. "We need to go." She looked to her children. "You stay here. We'll be back."

"Fat chance," said Albert, standing up. "We should be there as a family."

"I'm going to put on my sneakers," Edward said.

Lisa Marie pushed back her chair to join the exodus.

In the panic and hurry, the Bennetts slammed shut the doors. After the rattling subsided, there was an uncharacteristic stillness and quiet at the table. The empty coffee cups lingered.

The corrected cuckoo clock sounded noon, and the automated stereo system clicked on as programmed. The sound of mad violins filled the air.

# Part Three

## *FLIGHT*

# XXXIX.

## A Hidden Canvas

Outside the house, all of the Bennetts crammed into Guy's luxury sedan.

"You get in the middle," Albert said, smiling at Lisa Marie gleefully, animated by the prospect of being in the scrum with his family.

"You guys always make me sit in the middle," Lisa Marie said, elbowing Edward in the ribs.

"He's my older brother," Edward said, grinning. "I need to listen to him."

"That's a first," Lisa Marie replied, rolling her eyes. Her brothers threw their arms around her.

Without looking behind, Guy reversed the car out of the driveway.

"Put the radio on," said Marie, calmly. "Let's hear the news."

Incredulous of his wife's cool, Guy clicked the radio dial.

"I wonder if there will be traffic," mused Marie.

"We'll get there in no time," responded Guy, pressing down on the accelerator.

Marie stroked her husband's arm in appreciation.

After a few more turns and straightaways, the Bennetts approached the guard station at Greylock Park Hospital. Guy clicked a button on his door just once to lower his window.

A young guard greeted them with a smile. "Mr. and Mrs. Bennett—I didn't know it was you," he said, humbly and apologetically. "It must be the new car. It sure is nice," he marveled. The guard detected that Guy and Marie were not as chatty as usual. He looked in the back seat.

"They are our kids, Freddie," said Marie.

"I see," answered the guard, lowering himself to look through Guy's open window into the back seat. "They haven't been here before."

"They came to see their uncle." Marie smiled.

"That's very nice." Freddie tipped his cap. "I wanted to thank you, Mrs. Bennett, for the clothing you sent my wife. They're perfect sizes for my kids."

"It was my pleasure, Freddie," nodded Marie with in-kind humility. "I hope they enjoy them." She tried to be polite. "If you can, Freddie—we need to get to my brother."

"Yes, m'am." Freddie stood up straight. "You go right ahead. I'll call ahead to tell them that you're here."

The Bennetts entered Greylock Park, where they were met by a sign that read SPEED LIMIT 13.

"That's an odd number," Edward said.

"I think it's their way of getting your attention, to tell you how important it is to obey the rules while you're here," responded Guy, doing his best not to drive too far over the limit.

Edward beheld the stone buildings all around—each cut with the same squares of leaden glass. On the horizon was the grand façade of the main building—its marble columns tall, its front doors tiny. The grass was uneven and brown. There was an amphitheater, but its rows were empty and crumbling. The trees that lined the way were wilted and in need of pruning, the drive pocked with potholes. This was where Mom traveled every week while her children were playing, Edward thought. This was the place Uncle Antonio called home.

The car hit a pothole. "Before we come here again, I have to send my men over to fill in some asphalt," Guy said.

As soon as the Bennetts walked through the door, a sturdy Black female nurse with gray hair and a fresh smile greeted them. "Hello, Maria," she said with a Jamaican accent, referring to Marie by her birth name. She extended her arms for a hug. "And this must be Albert the hot-shot lawyer, Lisa Marie the Wall Street whiz, and Edward who is going to save the world."

"That's right, Sylvia," Guy said, turning to the kids. "Sylvia's good. She knows everything."

"How's Antonio, Sylvia?" Marie interrupted.

"Well, Maria..." Sylvia said, looking down. "Not so good today." She grabbed Marie's hand as if she herself were a family member. "C'mon, let's go see Brother Antonio."

Escorted by Sylvia, the Bennetts walked Greylock's tormented halls. A bent man in a bathrobe crossed their path, talking to himself while swatting the empty air. Down one of the side halls, an orderly restrained a woman who was pulling the hair of a fellow patient. Along another side hall, a young boy was kept from opening a window for fresh air, bribed by a nurse with jello and a plastic spoon. Amid the stench, Edward reflected, Greylock was a chatter of voices speaking to others who were not there.

Sylvia turned the corner into the infirmary and stepped up to Antonio's bed. The frame was a thin hollow aluminum; the sheets were discolored. All that filled the bed was a shrunken man with dulling eyes. "Maria," the near-corpse puffed.

"He recognizes me today," said Marie with a cautious spike of excitement.

"That's right, Sister Maria," said Sylvia, adjusting Antonio's bed to upright. "He has been asking for you all day. *Dov' è Maria? Dov' è Maria?*" she repeated in her Jamaican accent.

"See that, guys?" smiled Guy. "I told you Sylvia was good. She has given your uncle so much care over the years that she even learned some Italian."

"Yeah, she speaks Italian better than you do," Albert jibed his father, drawing a much needed laugh from everyone.

Marie gathered her children together and presented to Antonio his nephews and niece, speaking in a whisper. "*Antonio, questi sono miei figli. I tuoi nipoti.*"

A smile crawled up Antonio's face. He propped himself up in bed, and waved, encouraging Albert, Lisa Marie, and Edward to draw nearer. He studied them momentarily, his lungs filling with air. "*Nipoti*," he beamed.

"*Bravi.*"

The children looked at one another, Edward trying to ascertain from his siblings whether he should be expressing glee or sorrow.

"He knows who we are," spouted Albert.

"I think we made a connection," said Edward, his mouth gaping.

"Uncle Antonio?" asked Lisa Marie. She moved closer to touch his chest. "How are you...?"

Antonio reclined to his pillow, and started gasping in German. "*Vater, vergib ihnen; denn sie wissen nicht, was sie tun.*"

The children jumped back instantly, startled by the German.

"It's okay," Marie reassured them. "He says that a lot."

"It sounded like what you described him saying while he was being stoned," said Edward, squinting.

"It is," replied Marie curtly.

"Probably a flashback to something that was happening in combat," Albert offered.

Marie plumped her brother's white pillow to comfort him.

"I doubt he saw any real combat," said Guy.

"Father, forgive them, for they know not what they do," said Marie as she kissed her brother on the forehead.

"I didn't mean to offend your brother," Guy apologized.

"You didn't," Marie said, smiling. "I was just repeating what Antonio was saying—'Father, forgive them for they know not what they do.'"

"*That's* what he said while he was being stoned?" asked Edward rhetorically.

The others stood quietly, admiring Marie and her brother.

Antonio snapped back, sitting up again. He looked at Guy. "*Sigarette?*" he asked.

"*No sigarette*, Antonio," said Sylvia, scoldingly.

"*No sigarette,*" repeated Guy, moving his raised forefinger from side to side.

"For some reason, the cigarettes make him feel better," said Marie in her brother's defense. "But they gave him the emphysema that put him in the infirmary."

"They say the cigarettes help people with schiz…" Guy said, before changing course. "Cigarettes are a way for people like Antonio to self-medicate."

"*Maria, dov'è mamma?*" asked Antonio, his voice trailing as he looked at Marie longingly.

Marie smiled sadly at the kids. "He wants to know where mamma is. I have to tell him that she is with papà, not coming back, but doing well." She turned to Antonio. "*Con papà.*" She shook her head. "*Non ci vengono qua oggi. Ma, stanno bene.*"

"*Va bene,*" he rasped. "*Va bene,*" he repeated, trying to draw moisture into his parched mouth.

Shifting his weight, Edward inadvertently kicked a wooden frame, causing it to slide out from beneath Antonio's bed. When he stooped to return it to its place, he noticed that it was a canvas. "Hey, there's a painting under here." He looked up at his brother. "Albert, give me a hand."

They lifted the canvas together. It was an oil of a butterfly. Its forewings were emerald green in the main, its hindwings butter yellow. All of the wings were trimmed by a shadow of black that took a turn at the top corner of the green forewings to cut diagonally to the head. The yellow wings were adorned with lunules.

Guy found a chair in the corner of the room. He slid it across the concrete floor, to the foot of the bed. He had his boys mount the canvas upon the chair.

Stepping back from Antonio's bedside, Marie studied the painting on its makeshift easel. "Sylvia, what is this?" Her mind raced. "Who did…? How…?"

"Brother Antonio is quite the artist."

"But Sylvia, how?" Marie asked in wonderment, as she tried to process the butterfly's array, within its presiding glow of green and yellow.

"After your visits, he would always ask for his paints. '*Dammi miei colori,*' he would say. 'Bring me my colors.'"

"What paints, what colors?" Marie replied, her heart thumping. "He was

251

never a painter."

"He taught himself in here. He made me promise to keep it our little secret," Sylvia giggled. "He said that it was the butterfly that you saw in your house one day when you were a little girl, the way you described it to him."

"But how do you know that?" asked a still incredulous Marie. "You don't speak Italian, and Antonio doesn't speak English."

"Let's just say we learned how to understand one another."

Antonio lay in bed, expressionless.

"It's absolutely gorgeous," said an enamored Marie. She stroked the emerald greens. "I wish mamma could have seen this. She would have been so proud." She looked at her children. "You see, your uncle has all this emotion bottled up inside of him." She bit her lip. "This must be how he lets it out."

"Amazing," Edward said as he admired the painting, choking back his tears.

Albert glided his pinkie finger along the black diagonal line across the green forewing, saying nothing.

"I love these little arches on the bottom wings," said Lisa Marie as she gaped at the lunules that floated near the margins of the yellow.

"Through these openings we can see Mom's entire story," expounded Edward touching the lunules for himself. "I want to walk through these arches." He gripped the frame. "This is ours for posterity."

Albert pulled his brother by the shirt. "The painting is Mom's—not yours."

An annoyed Edward let go of the frame.

"Sylvia, when were you going to tell me?" Marie asked.

"He said I couldn't peep a word until he was done. As he was coughing this morning, he told me it was time. That's when I called you."

A tear streamed down Marie's cheek.

"We should get him more paints," Guy's voice jumped. "He obviously has a talent." He began to map out a space. "We will make a little studio for him..."

"*Ti piace, sorella?*" Antonio said weakly, turning to Maria.

"He wants to know if I like the painting," Marie began to break down. She scurried back to her brother's side, nodding and smiling as she sniffed back her tears. *"Mi piace moltissimo!"*

Antonio moistened his mouth with a smile of his own. *"Mamma ha detto che ti sarebbe piaciuto molto. Ha scelto i colori, lo sai."* He folded his hands upon his chest. *"Dille quanto ti piace."*

Marie turned to her children. "He said that mamma told him that I would love the painting. He said she picked the colors. He wants me to tell her that I love it." She stroked Antonio's thin gray hair. *"Ma forse sarebbe meglio se tu le dicessi."* She repeated herself in English, this time in a whisper: "You should tell her yourself."

*"Va bene."* Antonio closed his eyes to sleep. The bouncing sound of his life support system evened; its green line flattened. His heart had stopped.

Knowing that this moment was long in coming, Marie was not taken aback by her brother's passing. She leaned over and kissed Antonio on the forehead. *"Grazie, fratello."*

Uncle Antonio has shed his worldly cocoon, Edward thought.

Marie pulled Antonio's blanket over him. *"Dormi bene,"* she said, pausing. "Sleep well." After hugs from everyone, she walked to be in front of her brother's gift. Her arms were hanging down to her waist, moored by her clasped hands. Her family gathered around her.

Albert looked to his siblings. "Even though we never knew him, he'll always be a part of us."

Marie touched the frame of her brother's work with the tip of her finger.

"It's beautiful," said Guy as he put his arm around his wife.

Over and beyond the painting, Marie was struck by the sunlight bouncing off a mirror. In the mirror's reflection, she saw that her brother's smile remained, wider than before.

Miles and worlds away in the Bennett kitchen, "Un bel dì, vedremo" from *Madame Butterfly* played to an empty house.

# XL.

## A Difficult Return

The Bennetts pushed their way through the chaos of Capodichino Airport in Naples, Italy. Albert tried to help his father decipher the signs while the others trailed behind. Edward was last among the clan, yawning, not having slept a wink during the overnight plane ride.

"Looks like they haven't done much with this place since the Americans used it in World War II," Albert commented insolently.

"Tell me about it," replied Guy. "It's a goddamn cattle call."

"Why aren't you five paces ahead of us the way you usually are?" asked Lisa Marie of her mother.

Marie did not answer.

Lisa Marie grabbed one of the bags that her mother was lugging. "Mom, you're carrying too much. Let me."

Even after being relieved of the extra weight, Marie's pace remained the same.

"You don't look good, Mom," said Lisa Marie. "Are you sure you want to do this?"

"I told her that we should have buried Uncle Antonio back home, next to his father," Guy shouted, trying to be heard over the noise of the terminal. "She wanted to bring him to Lavenna." He looked into his wife's eyes. "I just don't know that it's worth it. Like Albert said, since the Americans left after the war—"

XL.

"My brother needs to be with our mother," Marie said, recoiling.

"Edward!" a voice called out.

"Giovanni?" Edward replied groggily.

Giovanni embraced Edward like an old pal. "You look tired, cousin."

"I couldn't sleep much on the plane. I was thinking about a lot of stuff. Seeing you again, the family, you know…"

Giovanni interrupted Edward by feeling his biceps. *"Bravissimo!* You are even stronger than before. I am only thirty-five, but you make me feel like an old man."

"Mom, meet your cousin, Giovanni," Edward gestured to Marie.

Giovanni hopped over to Marie, and placed his hand on her shoulders. "You are just as pretty as papà always said you were." He bit his lower lip. "We are so sorry about the death of Antonio."

She nodded her head in gratitude.

Giovanni turned to Marie's brood. *"Bellisima!"* he exclaimed.

An awkward silence followed.

A passenger rushing the other way bumped into Marie.

Giovanni caught her before she fell. *"Stai attento!"* he scolded the passerby. He lifted Marie back to upright. "Everyone is in such a hurry."

*"Grazie,* Giovanni," said Marie softly.

*"Di niente,* Maria," he replied, bowing his head.

Guy stepped up. "Thanks, Giovanni—that happened so fast that I didn't even see it."

"You must be Gaetano. We have heard so much about you."

Guy hurried to speak in his parents' native tongue—the language he had first known. *"Ma, io parl' Italiano,"* he uttered in dialect, brandishing his million-dollar smile.

"You might be better off keeping it in English," Albert said, cutting in. "Hello, Giovanni. I'm Albert. Thank you for coming to meet us." When Giovanni tried to speak, Albert spoke over him. "My wife Elizabeth could not make it, but sends everyone her best."

Giovanni paused to process what Albert was saying. "'Thank you' is not necessary. You are family and I…I understand about your wife. These things

255

can get complicated." He tilted his head to one side, and smiled. "I am so happy to meet my cousins after so many years." He glanced at Marie. "I wish it were under different circumstances."

Marie raised her eyebrows in agreement.

"And *la Principessa*," Giovanni bellowed, moving on to Lisa Marie. He viewed her from top to bottom. "The men of Lavenna will be watching you." With his forefinger, he touched the corner of his eye. "And the women of Lavenna will be watching their men."

Everyone laughed, Albert throwing his arms around his father and brother.

Marie cut into the merriment. "We're not going to be staying long, Giovanni." She spoke slowly. "We'll have the funeral and, of course, spend some time with your parents. But then we have to get back to Rome, and home tomorrow."

Giovanni held Marie by the shoulders again, and looked at her squarely. "It took this many years. Won't you stay at least for a few days?"

Marie wriggled out of Giovanni's grasp. "Not this time. We have to get back. There's a lot going on at home." She pulled at Guy's elbow. "We need to get back."

Giovanni looked at Guy.

"I would stay a month," protested Guy. He turned to his wife. "But she wants to get back home."

"To my *house*," Marie clarified.

"I understand." Giovanni addressed all of the Bennetts. "Let's go. The hearse will be by door five."

"How the heck does he know the hearse is at door five?" Albert asked Edward.

"Beats me."

When the family stepped outside the airport doors, two drivers, dressed smartly in suit and black cap, waited on an island; one held a placard with the name "Bennett" written on it. "There's the hearse and limo," Guy said, walking quickly toward his name. "C'mon, Giovanni. Let's get everyone in the limo."

"But what about your car?" Albert asked Giovanni as his Italian cousin opened the front passenger side door.

"I didn't bring one," Giovanni answered before entering. "Your father had the limousine pick me up at my house." He smiled. "It got a lot of attention when it pulled into town. It's so big that it barely fit in the street."

The doors of the limousine slammed smoothly into their rubber-padded jambs, sealing the Bennetts off from all noise. As the luxury car pulled away, everyone sunk into the plush black leather seats. The bustle of the airport diminished in the rearview mirror; the mood became sedated.

Though Marie was a naturally curious person¾always filling the air with her questions¾she was uncharacteristically mute during the trip through the hills. From her window, she stared long into the valleys. She could recall only warplanes overhead and artillery shells in the distance. It would take time for her to see the richness of the native colors, the vividness of a world forgotten by the amnesia of war—it was too much to absorb in one trip. For now, she told herself, she needed to put her brother to rest alongside their mother.

Fighting his drowsiness, Edward nodded off. In his sleep, he dreamt of his lover that night among the ruins of Lavenna. The stranger was again walking away, into the darkness. He called for her again, as he had done that blissful evening. This time, she began to turn back toward him, the unknown plateau in the distance behind her.

"Yo," Albert said, poking his brother.

"Why did you do that, you pain in the ass?" Edward shot back.

"You need to stay awake. It's only a short ride."

"Easy for you to say. You slept like a baby on the plane."

"I go plenty of days on no sleep."

"Really?" Edward answered. "I guess that's the deal you made when you went to a big law firm—great salary, but a lot of all-nighters."

"No. It's the deal I made when I married Elizabeth. A lot of lonely time in bed, staring at the ceiling."

Edward felt bad for his brother. He realized that traveling without Elizabeth was affording Albert a sense of family that he did not otherwise enjoy—and that made him want to relish every minute, even if it was for a funeral. Edward placed his hand on Albert's knee. "You're right. I'll stay awake."

As they approached Lavenna, Giovanni addressed the Bennetts from his place up front, pointing through the windshield. "Maria, you probably don't recognize the town, but that is Lavenna." He thrust his finger toward some jagged edges, and the broken foundations spilled along the hillside. "That is where most of the houses were. The earthquake took everything." He paused. "But we are rebuilding it." His voice rose as he lifted his head. "Since Edward's visit, much has been done. Everyone agrees that the reconstruction has brought the town together like never before."

Marie's head spun. Her stomach churned, and her body trembled at the thought of how anything kind or communal could be said about a town that had been so cruel to her family. She began losing her breath. She held up her hand. "Giovanni, please stop. I mean—have the driver stop. I don't feel well."

"Marie, are you all right?" asked Guy, his hand on the back of his wife's neck. "You're soaked with sweat."

"I'm okay," Marie said, swallowing hard to hold down her stomach.

When the limousine pulled off the road, the hearse followed. Marie bolted from the door.

"You guys stay here," Guy said. "I'll take care of Mom."

Marie raced to the hill's edge, hand over mouth. She bent over and coughed into the valley.

"Let it out," whispered Guy, stroking Marie's back.

Marie gagged.

"Let it out," Guy repeated.

Marie kept trying to purge herself, pulling back with hard swallows. But nothing came. She stood up, brushing away Guy's hand. "I'm okay."

"It's all right, sweetheart," Guy said, his face taut with compassion. "You're probably just a little carsick. It was a long ride—a lot of turns." He resisted the impulse to touch his wife, knowing that she would be more comfortable if he didn't. "The mountain air should make you feel better."

But there was no mountain air to inhale. Though it was still morning, the day was already heating like an oven.

Marie took a deep breath. "You're right. I'm never good on long rides." She looked at her watch. "We should get to the cemetery. The priest is probably waiting."

Giovanni held open the door of the limousine for Guy and Marie to reenter. "Everything okay, Maria?"

"I'm fine," she said, ducking her head to get inside.

"Do you want the driver to take us past your old house, or do you want to go straight to the cemetery?"

Seated, Marie looked again at her watch. "Let's go straight to the cemetery. We're late. We shouldn't make the priest wait."

Edward glanced at his mother's watch, which had stopped ticking hours before. "Mom, how do you know we're late? Your watch is not even—"

Albert grabbed his younger brother by the arm to restrain him. "Mom's right. The priest is probably waiting."

# XLI.

## The Entrance to a Cemetery,

## An Unsettled Place of Rest

The driver adjusted his black cap so that it was secure on his head. "Hold on, guys," Giovanni grinned. "The road is going to get a little rocky as we climb the hill."

As if on cue, the car hit a pothole, jolting the passengers.

"I hope that we didn't get a flat," Guy looked at Giovanni.

"We're fine," Giovanni replied. "But it's going to get worse before it gets better."

The bumps began hitting in rapid fire.

"We should've worn helmets," Albert shouted through the rattling.

"Or maybe they should have padded the ceiling of the car," joked Edward, looking to his mother to see if she would laugh. When she remained unaffected, he leaned forward, sticking his head between Giovanni and the driver. "Are we almost there?"

"Just a bit more," Giovanni answered. "You will know when you see the arch. That will be the entrance to the cemetery."

Edward sat back and relaxed despite the roughness of the ride, delighted by the notion that the family would parade through a classic remnant. For sure, the monument would not be as grand as the Arch of Constantine, but it would nonetheless pay tribute to his family's passage to America. Edward—unlike his pals Prigler and Coyne—would take a real-life triumphal march, with greater virtue and rectitude than the Romans ever had.

"We're here," Giovanni exclaimed.

The limousine stopped.

Edward burst out the side door. He looked around. "I don't think so. Where's the arch?"

Giovanni came around, and put his arm across his cousin's shoulder. He pointed to a set of stones. "It's right there."

Though the configuration was an arch, all of the stones were on the ground, flat rather than rising. There was an opening or gap at the rear, where the keystone would normally be placed. To Edward, it appeared like the arms of someone dead, lying face-down, his or her hands reaching for one another but not touching. Disappointed that the family had not been welcomed by a classic Roman arch, Edward protested. "But Giovanni, that's not an arch."

Giovanni looked askance.

Edward continued. "You know—block upon block, meeting miraculously at the apex, forming a crown." Judging by Giovanni's silence, Edward thought he had an audience, as he always did with his newfound cousin. "There's no crown. This is a horseshoe with a hole in the back."

"It used to be the type of arch you probably expected to see," Giovanni responded politely. "We rebuilt it this way after the earthquake."

"But if it's not standing, and with the hole," Edward persisted, "it's just not an arch. I would've rebuilt it the way it was before."

Giovanni pulled his arm off Edward's shoulder. For the first time, he was terse with his American cousin. "As I said, it used to be a standing arch. We rebuilt it this way so that a future earthquake could not knock it down." Giovanni shook his head, incredulous that Edward had not picked up on his cue. "We all will pass from this life, *cugino*. Everyone will be leveled no matter how high they once stood. Even you, my friend," he said with a biting tone.

Edward bowed his head in embarrassment.

Giovanni would not let up. "Unlike you, *we* have seen death. *Death* commands humility."

"C'mon, you two," said Marie, who had been observing the rift. "Let's get going. They're waiting for us." She nodded to the hearse behind. "Go get the coffin."

Edward wanted to say something to Giovanni, but was afraid of making the situation worse. Instead, he lifted his head to look timidly beyond the arch, where he saw an older couple standing in the distance—the man in his Sunday suit with hat in hand, the woman beside him in a simple black dress. The woman held a rose, and a veil covered her face. Edward pointed toward them in an effort to escape the disturbingly awkward episode. "We should get going. People are waiting."

Marie grabbed Lisa Marie as if her daughter was a little girl. "Come meet my cousin Vito and his wife Luisa." She turned to the men. "Be careful with my brother." She focused on Albert and Edward. "Your uncle."

Edward stepped carefully toward his cousin. "Hey, Giovanni. Sorry about what I said back there. I don't know what got into me."

Giovanni grunted.

"Must be the lack of sleep," Edward offered as a defense.

"I understand," said Giovanni, looking away rather than into Edward's eyes.

Edward felt terrible about the pain that he had caused. His mouth was filled with a foul and bitter taste.

Giovanni looked back into Edward's eyes. "You heard what your mother said. Let's go get your uncle."

As the men filed in behind the hearse, the driver opened the rear doors. He gave instructions to Giovanni in Italian.

Giovanni translated. "He said that it usually takes six men to carry the coffin. He said that the limo driver will help, but that will only be five. He apologizes that he himself cannot lend a hand, but he has to drive back to Rome."

"No problem. We can handle it," Guy said, buttoning his jacket.

Giovanni continued. "The driver said that there should be three pallbearers on one side, and only two on the other. He needs the strongest of you to carry the back corner on the side where there are only two."

"That would be Edward," answered Guy without hesitation. "Albert, you take the back left. Edward will take the back right. I'll take the front right."

Edward looked at Albert, fearing that Guy had offended his older brother.

"I guess Dad thinks your left hand is stronger than my right," Albert groused. "Go for it, Hercules."

Marie and her daughter walked arm-in-arm toward Vito and Luisa. As they got closer, Marie saw a trace of the boyish glint in her cousin's eyes, pinched at the corners and topped by gray brows. His head twitched slightly. One ear was clipped with a hearing aid. "Look at my cousin Vito," Marie said proudly. "He always had such dignity. Such a gentleman—just like his father."

"Mom, no offense," Lisa Marie responded in a whisper, still far enough away that no one but her mother could hear her, even if they understood English. "But if they were such good people, why didn't they do anything to help your family when the town attacked Uncle Antonio? I've never heard you mention them once."

"That's because they left town before the Germans got there. Vito's father knew it wasn't safe to stay. He pleaded with my mother to come with him. Mamma had taken such good care of his wife before she died of cancer."

"So Grandpa's brother wanted all of you to go with them," Lisa Marie clarified.

"Of course," Marie corrected herself. "But we didn't go. My mother was afraid that if we went, people would talk—you know, make a big scandal out of it." Marie was warmed by the sight of Vito. "Vito's father was so handsome. I think he was falling for my mother. But he would never have acted on it."

"Who wouldn't want her?" Lisa Marie asked as she guided her mother over the littered path. "Grandma was gorgeous."

"Maria," said Vito, his deep basso voice cracking. A tear crept into the corner of his eye. He gave her a kiss on both cheeks, and hugged her modestly. "*Cara Maria*," he exhaled. He turned and pointed to the priest, who stood in the sun's glare, wiping the sweat from his brow. Vito tried to speak, but instead pointed again. Then he walked away to summon the priest for the funeral.

Luisa lifted her veil to greet Marie and her daughter. She embraced each of them with a kiss on both cheeks. She then presented the rose she was holding to Marie. "For you." Luisa placed the veil back over her face and took Marie by the hand. *"Andiamo da tua madre."*

Marie looked behind, to see that the men had finally finessed Antonio's coffin out of the hearse.

The pallbearers moved quietly and in unison.

"This coffin has such beautiful natural grains," commented Giovanni.

"You think this is nice, you should've seen the one that I wanted," said Guy, losing some of his breath but wanting to complete his thought. "It was mahogany with a gloss finish. Marie thought the mahogany was too much."

"So what is this coffin made of?" Edward asked.

"White poplar."

As they approached the arch, Giovanni's reprimand clamored in Edward's head: death commands humility. He noticed that fronting the arch was a row of stout weeds of the same height, brandishing thorns. Edward bit the nail of his middle finger on his free right hand. Anxious that he had made his fingernail into a serrated edge, he closed his eyes to gather himself while he walked.

When he opened his eyes, there was a trash can just beyond the entrance of the arch, wasps hovering around it. As one of the toxic hornets darted toward Edward, his hand shot out on its own, catching it. With the same lack of premeditation, he began to squeeze. When the treacherous captive remained resilient, Edward lanced his serrated nail into it, grinding his teeth during the impaling. But before he could finish, the demon stung him, sinking its venom into Edward's palm. Edward pushed his nail harder, deeper, until all that he could feel was liquid spewing on his hand. *Blood!* He did not know what had come over him—what had caused him to react so aggressively. He wiped his hand against his pants, ridding himself of the wasp's residue. He called out to the others, to check whether he was in a delirium, or the victim of the southern Italian sun. "Who put that trash can there?"

No one responded.

Suddenly, Edward and the other pallbearers were in a shadow. Everything appeared blurred. All that he could see before him were the weeds and the trash can. A chill ran up his spine, and he became disoriented. A fleck of something fell into his hair; he pulled it out to find that it was chipped stone. Looking up, he saw that the arch was upright, towering over him in classic style, bereft of any opening. The chip had fallen from the keystone, the surface of which was different than the others, etched and scraped over like a palimpsest.

Imprisoned in the arch's shadow, Edward called out to the other pallbearers. But they were gone, as was the coffin. He was in frightening isolation. He wanted to run, but was deterred by the wasps above the waste bin, now an opaque swarm encircling the arch. Immobile, he heard a harsh grinding overhead. Edward craned his neck to see that the keystone was slipping from its place. Desperate, he cried for help.

Whether it was a genuine response to his plea, or just a cruel joke of his consciousness, his Uncle Antonio appeared in front of the waste bin, eclipsing it, dressed in the same hospital garb in which Edward had last seen him. "*Nipote*," he gasped.

The keystone halted.

"*Zio*," Edward answered in kind, relieved that his uncle had saved him. "*Grazie.*"

Antonio would not move or utter a word. He gazed at Edward wanly.

"What is it, Uncle Antonio?" asked Edward with a nervous smile.

Antonio walked slowly toward Edward. Everything was muted, except for the sound of the burnt grass crackling beneath his steps; bands of once-green blades were crushed by the phantom's soles. He stopped at Edward's side, and placed his hand over his nephew's ear.

Edward dared not turn.

Antonio whispered. But with the blood rushing through Edward's head, his uncle's words were unintelligible.

"I don't understand..." Edward began.

Antonio whispered again. This time, the message was clear. The hairs on Edward's neck stood on end.

Antonio walked away and turned around to face Edward, reassuming the position that supplanted the view of the hornet-spewing bin.

Edward could hear the keystone slipping again, preparing to begin its murderous drop. Antonio moved his index finger back and forth, like an inverted pendulum, warning his nephew that he should not try to escape. Edward bent over in a fetal position so that he might somehow survive. He begged his uncle for mercy, but was struck dumb; he stuttered profusely. Amidst Edward's babble, a tremendous weight crashed upon his back. He was shocked by the suffocating feeling of being buried alive.

But the weight remained upon his back without breaking it, the corners of the mass settling into Edward's hands like pegs into their rightful holes. Feeling compelled to hold the mass—fearful of letting go of it—he braced and straightened, lifting with all his might. He tilted his head back slightly—enough to see that he was not yet being crushed by the arch, but that he had been strapped to the white poplar coffin; off to Edward's side, on the ground, was the entirety of its lid. With Uncle Antonio looking on, Edward realized that the coffin was his own, not yet filled—protection from a dark infinity if only he could carry it. Edward heard the keystone grate louder and longer, foretelling its imminent fall. He squeezed hard.

Edward looked to his uncle for relief. This time, Antonio repeated the words he had uttered at his stoning. *"Vater, vergib ihnen; denn sie wissen nicht, was sie tun!"*

Human forms emerged from the graveyard, their hue a sharp sepia—as if walking out of an old photo album that had never been opened nor exposed to the light. Dressed in dated clothing, they were the prisoners of his mother's suppressed past. They strode through the ring of hornets and past Uncle Antonio, indifferent to him, toward Edward.

A little boy ran into the fold from the side, appearing in black and white, offering a pail. He was wearing a cap.

The menacing horde reached into the bucket and pulled out stones caked with dirt. "No one can save him now!" shouted the lead man among them.

Edward fretted that if the falling arch would not get him, the stones of his persecutors certainly would. He hardened himself for the violence endured by his uncle decades before.

None came.

Instead, he heard a thumping, repeated like a hail storm. He peeked to the side to see that the villagers, one by one, were dropping their stones into his coffin, singing dirges as they processed by. With each offering, the coffin's corner sunk deeper into his right palm. When the pain in the center of his hand became too much—feeling as though it was about to be penetrated—Edward relieved it by allowing the sharp edges to slide to his fingers. The box tilting to the side of his weakened hand, one of the villagers' stones spilled onto the burnt grass, giving off a dusty mist. He heard the keystone grind again—but this time swiftly, like a match being lit. The other stones rushed out of the coffin, causing the white poplar to rotate clockwise, leaving Edward partially exposed. Once he saw that the arch's abutments were collapsing, he knew that the immense crown was descending upon him, fated to smash his bones into a pearled ash.

Edward wept.

"Open your eyes, Hercules," Albert admonished his brother. "Quit squealing and keep moving."

Snapping out of his altered state, Edward felt no stone-filled coffin on his back—saw no arch crumbling above him. He and the others were again carrying the coffin together, Uncle Antonio contained inside. Looking up, he saw a cloud cover, which must have been what precipitated the darkness that preceded his mad interlude. When he opened his hand, there was a tear in his palm. He noticed blood, both on his hand and beneath his serrated nail. *I must have gouged myself while killing the wasp!*

"Keep it up, boys," Guy yelled encouragingly. "We're almost there."

Edward trained his view back on the graveyard's arch. It no longer appeared like the arms of someone dead, but instead those of someone living, lying prostrate in submission. The grass was singed only at the top rather than all the way; the blades were untrammeled. The sentinel weeds stood down. There was no trash can, and no wasps obstructed the opening. It must all of have been a dream—the perilous venom and weight of the coffin figments of his imagination. Though the injury to his palm was real, it was made by his own hand.

Edward sucked his hand to remove the blood. The stain spread, and the pain smarted. He heard a buzzing.

A wasp zipped across his purview and stopped at his focal point. The buzzing became a hissing; it unnerved him. The wasp pivoted, and flew away.

Edward became anxious to cleanse his wound. He crouched while maintaining his hold on the coffin, placing his hand upon the stone at the entrance. Even though the sunbaked rock was bound to exacerbate the stinging, he believed that he needed the discomfort as an antidotal penance. He placed his hand over the rock's surface, prepared to bear the consequence. To his surprise, his palm cooled. His skin tickled. When he lifted his hand, the blood was gone. Edward saw a clump of moss on the rock, which he had not noticed before his contrition; he was astonished that it had grown without the benefit of shade. As his discomfort eased, he was exhilarated. Edward rubbed his hand in the moss, eager for more of the sensation.

"Edward!" Albert scolded his younger brother again. "You're going to make us drop Uncle Antonio."

Edward popped up, his head feeling clear, his step fortified. His weariness from the long journey was gone.

When Marie reached her mother's grave, she meditated on the gray tombstone, carved with Nedda's name and a prayer. She moved her lips as she read the supplication; when she finished, she touched the inscription to feel how deeply it had been carved. "The words are so moving," Marie said, glowing.

"Vito's father made it," Luisa explained.

"Mamma," Marie whispered. She looked to the gray sky. "Dear God," she cried. She wiped her eye and spoke softly to Luisa. "*Grazie di tutto.*" She sniffed the rose Luisa had given her.

"*Tua madre era speciale,*" replied Luisa.

The women already shared an intimacy and understanding others could not have achieved with years of conversation.

Luisa stepped back to her place, leaving room for the approaching men. As they closed in on the open grave, Guy gave the orders. "Let's put Antonio down for the blessing—nice and easy." The men complied, lowering the coffin onto a plush patch of grass.

Vito returned with the priest. It was Don Raimondo, the young cleric who had greeted Edward during his first visit to Lavenna. Don Raimondo spoke to Edward in perfect English, and Edward reciprocated, excitedly, with his rudimentary Italian.

While Don Raimondo searched for the correct page in his Bible, Marie noticed dirt on Vito's pant cuff—making her realize that her cousin had lent his aged back to the digging of Antonio's grave. She pointed to the fresh soil on Vito's pants, and smiled her appreciation. "*Grazie,*" she said, squeezing Vito's hand.

"Ah," the priest said, looking up. His face free of lines, Marie thought he was young enough to be her son. With all the austerity he could muster, Don Raimondo read dutifully the reverence that marked the passing of every soul from this world to the next. All bowed, perspiring as they struggled with thoughts of loss, guilt, and mortality.

Although the sun was still hidden behind the clouds, the heat became too much for the priest. He took a break from his verses to pat-dry his head with an ivory white handkerchief.

Edward did not mind the temperature, as he was still reveling in the fact that there was no arch falling upon him, no villagers stoning him.

The priest resumed the ceremony, dipping his gold-plated instrument into a pail of holy water. He cast the purifying liquid onto everyone.

Marie's stiff upper lip caught one of the thrown droplets. She licked it dry, tasting for the first time since childhood the fresh mountain water that was the town's cherished gift before the long drought that came after the war. Her mind reverted to a time when she and Antonio splashed one another playfully in the Sele River, away from everyone and everything. Antonio would always let his little sister get him more wet, scooping back only a handful—just enough to get her excited. Then the sensation passed. Antonio was in his poplar box, where he splashed no more.

On cue from the priest, the men began to lower Antonio's coffin with rope. Sharp rock at the bottom of the hole made the bed uneven. The coffin groaned from the repeated efforts to lay it flat. "C'mon boys," Guy rallied his crew. "Almost there."

Seeing that Antonio was struggling in death as he had in life, Marie whispered, "Leave it. That's fine. The important thing is that he is next to his mother."

"Are you sure?" Guy huffed.

Marie nodded that she was certain. Antonio would have to remain as he was—unsettled and on edge.

The priest offered his condolences. "May God have mercy on Antonio's soul." He closed his book, caressing its leather cover. He made the sign of the cross before he set off for the village.

After Guy emptied a shovel of dirt into his brother-in-law's grave, he hurried to catch up to the priest. He tagged Don Raimondo just as the priest was about to descend the hill. "Padre," panted Guy. He sucked for air, reaching into his deep custom-tailored pant pocket. He handed the pastor a wad of crisp American dollars. "*Grazie para...*" He fumbled. "*Grazie di tutto.*"

The priest studied the money without counting it. "No, thank you." He made the sign of the cross in front of Guy's head, causing Guy to bow. He then gave a blessing in English, for Guy's benefit. "Naked I entered my mother's womb, and naked I shall return. The Lord giveth and the Lord taketh away."

"Thank you, Padre," Guy said, genuflecting.

As he parted, Don Raimondo waved over his shoulder to Edward.

Guy returned to his wife and children, where Marie kneeled at her brother's grave. She closed her eyes and her lips began to move, speaking words that only she could hear. She looked down into the dark hole and dropped into the plot the rose that Luisa had given her. She stood and dusted her skirt.

Lisa Marie was sobbing, her makeup running. Albert and Edward stood solemnly. Vito, Luisa, and Giovanni remained in the background.

"I wish we had more time with him," cried Lisa Marie, wiping her eyes. "I wanted to talk with him."

Marie reached out to her family. She looked to Vito, Luisa, and Giovanni, and waved them over. "*Anche voi, venite qua.*" Her demeanor was straight, yet comforting—indicating that if she was okay, everything was good. "Your uncle is finally at peace," she said.

Guy tried to elevate everyone's spirits. "Hey Giovanni, can you take us back to Marie's house?"

"Of course," replied the teacher. "It's just down the hill."

"You take the kids, Giovanni," said Marie. "I want to stay behind with Antonio."

"Marie and I will meet you in the square," interceded Guy.

"What square?" asked an annoyed Marie, raising her hand, pressing her fingers against her thumb, shaking them Neapolitan-style.

"Maria," Giovanni smiled. "Gaetano is correct. I told you that we have been rebuilding the town. We started with the square—Piazza Barrini—where you and Dad used to play."

"Whatever," Marie answered curtly. "We'll meet you there."

"We go," Giovanni said, smiling to his parents and Marie's children.

Reaching the edge of the cemetery, looking down upon the town, Edward realized he was on the obscure heights he had observed from afar while on his back that night with Bowed Lace, consummating in his mother's ruins. Unbeknownst to Edward in the wake of his ecstasy, the mysterious plateau was the place of the dead, ennobled by the fallen arch. Respectful of the plot, but grateful he was leaving it behind, Edward descended.

Marie walked back to the grave to behold her brother, beneath the rose.

271

Guy put his arm around his wife's shoulder.

Marie stared at the coffin, the corners of her eyes dripping, her lips motionless.

"Let's go," said Guy.

"But I don't want to leave him."

"He wants you to go on—to be with your family while he rests."

When Guy pulled his wife, she did not resist. He squeezed her hand affectionately.

Marie stopped at the precipice. She scowled at the fallen town below, and the dicey trail that led to it.

Guy took two steps down on his own, and then turned and extended his hand. "C'mon, Maria," he said with an Italian accent, inviting his bride to cross the threshold with him. "Your brother will watch over us."

# XLII.

## Discerning the Butterfly

I n Guy's sure hold, Marie made her way carefully down the slope. Though she was anxious to see the town, she was preoccupied with her footing. With each step, she dug in harder, and concentrated more. She was not going to allow herself to fall.

Guy continued to press ahead, pulling his wife along. "Are you all right, honey?"

Marie gritted her teeth. "I'm fine."

"We're almost there," Guy said, excitedly. "I think I can see the square."

When the couple reached Piazza Barrini, Marie stopped at the olive tree at the center. Its curved trunk was unmistakable. The villagers had brought it back to its original place, Marie realized, after they uprooted it to make way for the hideous obelisk.

Guy kept going, anxious to move forward.

Marie touched a bud from one of the tree's branches, skeptical of whether it could bear any olives. She snapped the bud off its stem, and tried to open it to see what was inside. Overanxious, she fumbled it onto the square, onto the new bricks that had been laid.

"I think this is the old church," exclaimed Guy from atop the steps that led to an austere façade.

"Yes, it is," Marie replied evenly. She cast her eyes upon the tall front. Beside it, the fallen bell tower and the severed clapper remained. "Totally destroyed," she sighed.

"C'mon, let's go inside," Guy said, waving for his wife to follow him through the threshold.

Marie proceeded reluctantly, touching the frame of the door to test its sturdiness. Assured yet still cautious, she entered.

"What a shame," Guy said as he picked up a piece of the rubble.

Once inside, Marie surveyed the collapsed altar and two confessionals. Upon noticing the baptismal font, she went directly to it. Arriving, she saw that the font had a puddle of water at its center. She went to dip her fingers into the font, but then pulled back. Her jaw tensed, and she looked to the crumbled altar. She stared.

"I bet the place was beautiful," said Guy, reaching for where the sidewalls once rose.

"Not all of it," said Marie softly, pointing up. "The ceiling."

"What about it?"

"It was a fresco of Heaven and Hell."

"I bet the heaven was beautiful."

"I remember only the Hell."

"Where did you used to sit?" Guy asked, trying to divert his wife's attention away from her memory of the ceiling.

"The back row."

"Why the back row?"

Marie raised her brow. "My grandmother used to say that we did not deserve to sit any closer to God."

The carved inscription above the interior of the main doorway caught Guy's eye. "*Padre.*" He squinted, but could not see what followed. "I think I know what's there." Roused as if in a hunt, he placed a large rock beneath the doorway and stood on top of it. With his bare hand, he brushed away the dust and debris from the buried text. He read slowly: "*Padre Perdona Loro Perché Non Sanno Quello Che Fanno.*" As he leaned further, he almost fell off the rock. He braced himself on the doorway's frame. "Father forgive them because they know not what they do." He admired the words. "Padre Piore said that in mass to the people when they were harassing you; your brother said that while they were trying to take his life."

"I guess you really were listening."

"I always do," Guy said, rubbing his hands to clean them.

Marie stepped closer to her husband. "Thank you," she said.

"For what?" he said, coming down. "All I did was wipe off some dust."

"You know what I mean," said Marie, having difficulty finding the right words for her emotions. "I couldn't have done this without you." As she fell into Guy's embrace, she noticed in the rubble a broken bough resting precariously upon a pile of fallen slabs. *Perhaps it was from the olive tree.* In the branches, she could have sworn that she saw her mother, brother, and grandmother reaching—arms upraised while singing from the same Sunday hymnal, imploring her to join in their fleeting moment of grace.

Guy eased his wife away so that he could catch her eye. "We did this for the family. We all needed to visit the place where you were born."

Marie rested her head back upon her husband's shoulder, to see that her mother, brother, and grandmother were gone, and only the broken bough remained. The severed limb oscillated upon the fulcrum of the fallen slabs, yet Marie did not detect a breeze that would have caused the movement. She was unsure whether the branches were about to fall or were waving. When the bough stilled, Marie smiled and waved back. As she did so, she began to cry.

Guy moved on from the embrace, extending his arm outside the doorway. He pulled Marie forward. "Let's go back to the piazza. We rushed through it."

Marie quickly dried her eyes so that Guy would not notice, and looked down to navigate the remains.

Guy yanked his wife's arm, lifting her from her apprehension. He led her through the church's façade. In the square stood the Bennett children, with Giovanni, Vito, and Luisa. The townspeople surrounded them.

"What's going on?" Marie asked, losing her breath.

"I was kind of surprised myself," replied Guy, as he nodded at Giovanni. "I guess they came to see how your story had a happy ending."

Marie bristled. She wanted to free herself of Guy's swelled leading hand, but could not. She needed his strength while she processed the incursion. Almost everyone from the ordeal was present, including Arrigo D'Abruzzi, Signora Altezzana, and the grown son of the murdered Spezzano—now a mirror image of his slain father. Marie recognized them all immediately. Their hair was merely grayer, their skin more creased, and their backs bent. There were no balloons or music, no cries of homecoming joy. Although the piazza had begun to be repaired, it was yet unfinished. The olive tree at its center bore no fruit. For Marie, the silence was eerily reminiscent of the end of the war and the horror that came after—the pall that would prevent this place from ever coming back again.

A hooded crow flew by, cawing sharply as it passed.

Marie was ashen. Her thoughts swirled in anger and fear. She did not understand how anyone or anything could recreate her real-life nightmare. "*Padre perdona loro,*" she whispered to herself.

Guy was oblivious to Marie's tumult, thinking that he was doing her good. "What's that, Marie?" He was ebullient. "Are you surprised by everyone being here? Giovanni suggested it, and I thought it was a great idea."

Marie's mouth moved as if she had been hypnotized. "*Perché non sanno quello che fanno.*"

Guy plowed forward. "C'mon—everyone's waiting for you." Guy tried to pull Marie, but she would not budge. "Geez, what did you do, put lead in your shoes?" he kidded nervously, sensing that something was awry.

Signora Altezzana stepped forward from the pack, wearing a dress and hat that were obviously left over from her more glorious days, relics of lost nobility. She walked the distance from the crowd to Marie, her gait frail but dignified. Her husband was no longer at her side. Her once high hat was rumpled, but the *contessa*'s pride was still palpable. When she reached Marie, she stopped and marveled. She grasped Marie's cold hand, and admired the American's gold necklace and custom cloth. She caressed Marie's smooth sleeve with a smile. The First Lady of Lavenna removed her hat from her head and laid it on Marie's. She took a step back, studied her placement of the hat, and adjusted it to make it right. "*Ecco,*" she exclaimed.

"Mom hates hats," Albert muttered in his father's ear.

"Don't worry," Guy responded with a smile. "She'll keep it on. I think she looks great in it."

The signora grabbed Marie by the hand to tow her toward the waiting crowd.

Marie dug in, staring at the assembly. She let go of Guy's hand.

Altezzana was stopped in her tracks by Marie's resistance. She looked back at Marie, and waited.

Marie scanned the crowd. It was apparent that generations of families had assembled for her. But these were the same people who had run her family out of town. She struggled over what she could possibly say to them. She looked over at Guy and her children. They were all smiling, anxious for her to proceed. Turning to the gathered mass, she inspected it once again. In the middle of them all, Marie spotted a lone adolescent boy, who reminded her of Antonio. She nodded her head slightly at Altezzana, indicating that she was ready to walk.

The signora escorted Marie to Arrigo D'Abruzzi. His once-bulging muscles had dropped, as had his height. His brow was gray, yet still furry. A young goat stood at his side, without the restraint of one of D'Abbruzi's leather leashes.

Marie stood her ground before D'Abruzzi, without saying a word.

D'Abruzzi could not look up. He stared down at the cracked leather of his shoes. *"Buon giorno, Signora."*

Remembering the brand that D'Abruzzi seared on his livestock to make them his property, Marie peeled back the kid's ear. There was no charred mark. The goat rotated its head, wallowing in Marie's touch with a contented sigh. She tickled it under its chin.

The laughter of Marie and the kid drew a smile from D'Abruzzi, who now raised his eyes toward her, slowly. Still finding no words, his lips quivering and curling inward, he bobbed his head with half a smile.

Marie straightened her look, causing D'Abruzzi to do the same. *"Buon giorno,"* she said before moving on.

Next was Spezzano, who was now older than his father had been when the Germans bludgeoned him in the square. His slim waist was tied with what had been his father's apron, stained with the marks of his trade—the dye of vegetables, the brush of crates, and the blood of meat. His wife and three children were at his side. The youngest was a small boy, who perfectly resembled his father as Marie had last seen him.

Before Spezzano could say anything, the little boy stepped forward. He spoke in the English that he was learning in school. "My papà say you live here when you were young.".

Marie kneeled to address the boy. "That's right. I did live here."

"He say you very nice little girl when you live here."

Marie smiled.

"Why you leave here if this your home?"

The boy's simple question had no answer, Marie realized, other than cruelty and the need to escape it. Marie looked at Spezzano, who shrugged. His shoulders seemed narrow like those of a child—as if his development had been arrested.

His wife put her arm around him, feeling his pain while looking to Marie to ease it—to forgive, or at least forget, that he had gathered the stones that dreadful day. The young matron was desperate for her husband to have peace, but would not beg Marie, lest she worsen his burden.

Marie heard the silent plea from Spezzano's wife. "Why did I leave here?" she said, addressing the boy again. "My papà was waiting for me in America. So I went there to be with him."

"I like America," the boy chirped.

Marie stood. "Maybe you will come see me in America one day. But first, you need to become big and strong like your papà. He works hard for you." She glanced at Spezzano's wife, who gave a look of profound gratitude—one that Marie knew only another wife could appreciate.

A commotion rippled through the crowd. The rows of people behind the boy began to part. An elderly woman emerged, led by a teenage girl. The woman yapped at everyone, determined to get to the front.

Marie did not recognize who was shoving toward her. Even when the shriveled figure arrived, Marie was at a loss as to her identity or purpose. She had a toothless mouth that rendered her words largely inaudible. Her eyes were glazed and dull, and her ability to see was questionable. Her right hand was ensconced in that of the young girl who had ushered her. Trailing behind and joining was an old man, who was younger than the hag.

"*Siamo qui, bisnonna,*" the little girl said, telling her great grandmother that they had arrived. The girl's long black hair was tied with an amber ribbon.

"*Grazie cara.*" The woman smiled. She removed her right hand from her great-granddaughter's tender grasp, and extended it toward Marie's face to feel it.

As the woman's hand approached, Marie recognized it instantly as belonging to Crooked Finger, the tormenter of her mother. By some stroke of fate, Crooked Finger had gone blind. The finger approached Marie's brow.

Marie froze.

The finger slid across Marie's forehead, down the ridge of her nose, and along her high cheekbones. It paused, and then moved around to Marie's chin, where it rested. "*Si, questa è Maria Del Cielo!*" the old woman exclaimed.

Marie let out a deep breath.

Crooked Finger then turned her malformed digit on herself, stabbing at her chest with it. "*Perdonami per quello che ho fatto a tua madre.*" Crooked Finger thrust her bent finger into her chest again, and spoke in monotone, as if she were praying. "*Perdonami per quello che ho fatto a tuo fratello.*"

Edward pulled on his cousin's sleeve. "What did she just say to Mom?"

"Amazing, after all these years," Giovanni reflected before answering. "She said that 'I'm sorry for what I did to your mother. I am sorry for what I did to your brother.'"

Crooked Finger poked her own chest a third time. "*Perdonami per quello che ho fatto a te.*"

Marie chose to stay silent.

"*Vieni qua,*" the old woman ordered, beckoning Marie over. She turned around, and extended her hand for her great-granddaughter to lead her. "*Andiamo.*" She tilted her head toward the old man who was part of the trio, commanding that he too come along.

"*A dove?*" asked the great-granddaughter, sweetly.

*"All'ullivo."*

Marie followed until Crooked Finger stopped at the olive tree. Marie studied the bark to see if she could see any of her brother's blood from that forbidding day. She quickly realized the folly of her search, how Antonio's blood, spilled so many years ago, was nowhere to be found in the new layers.

Crooked Finger lowered herself and felt the surfaces of the piazza's bricks, searching for something. She smiled, suggesting that she had arrived at her destination. *"L'ultima pietra è fracassata,"* she said, pointing to the last stone that had been laid in the square. It was fractured. She stood up, and pushed the man beside her toward a pile of unused bricks, left behind by the masons who rebuilt the piazza.

Hearing Crooked Finger's cadence, and noticing for the first time the prosecutorial ascot that the man wore, Marie surmised that he must be Crooked Finger's son—the prosecutor who had brought the case against her mother.

The son protested, reaching for his tunic, which was yellowed. *"Mamma!"*

Crooked Finger directed her son to remove the broken brick and bring her a new one. *"Alza questa e portamene un'altra."*

The audience watched in suspense.

When she did not hear any movement from her son, Crooked Finger punctuated her command for immediate action. *"Ora!"*

In order to break the cracked stone, Crooked Finger's son scrambled for a tool that, by chance, may have been left by the laborers. All that he could find were empty pails and cement trowels. On his knees, he tried chipping away with a trowel, but to no avail. In his impatient and embarrassed scramble, he noticed two feet planted in front of him. He stopped to look up. It was D'Abruzzi, with a sledgehammer.

D'Abruzzi motioned for the prosecutor to step aside. He rolled up his sleeves and, with all the potency remaining in his aged frame, raised the sledge overhead. He paused and looked at Marie. She averted her eyes. He moaned, and then brought down the long-handled hammer. In one stroke, the stone was shattered. Debris from the impact landed in the prosecutor's eye.

The prosecutor wiped his face clean. He removed the shrapnel, cupping it in his hands. Not knowing where to put the fragments, he unloaded them at the foot of the olive tree, among its roots. He made a sweeping gesture with his hand—to everyone, but no one in particular—suggesting that he would clean the mess later. He scurried to fetch a new brick for his mother. Exhaling loudly, he laid the replacement in her hand. *"Eccolo, mamma,"* he said.

Crooked Finger said nothing. She gave the brick to Marie, telling her to place the last stone. *"Tu devi mettere sopra l'ultima pietra."*

The cloud cover thickened, and a slight breeze blew.

Receiving the brick, Marie was taken off guard by its weight. She grabbed it with both hands so that it would not slip away. She held it, taking note of the smooth surface, and the irregular edges. She thought how she would be repairing the piazza: where her mother had sat under the stars to listen to the tenor's music, and laid the judge, tenor, and priest to rest—at the threshold of where her mother had cradled Antonio, and she the lamb.

Marie gave the stone back to Crooked Finger's son. "No."

Crooked Finger called out, *"Solo tu puoi farlo."*

Marie turned to Guy, who repeated Crooked Finger's last words—"Only you can do it."

Marie looked at her own family—Guy, Albert, Edward, and Lisa Marie. She locked on Lisa Marie.

Lisa Marie took the brick from Crooked Finger's son, and gave it to her mother.

Without Lisa Marie saying a word, Marie replied "I know." She crouched, and with one hand tried to place the brick in the empty spot. It would not fit. She rotated the brick to find a different angle, but the brick and space still would not conform.

Rain began to fall. Marie raced to beat its onslaught. She had spent decades trying to forget the torrent of the massacre. She did not want to experience any of that horrific storm again.

The townspeople looked to the sky. *"Vai!"* the Spezzano boy cried out, wishing the weather away.

Marie grabbed one of the trowels left by the masons, and got down on her hands and knees to shave the brick's edges. As the rain picked up, she continued to whittle away. After several rapid strikes, she missed. She threw down the trowel, and looked long into the void that she was trying to fill.

D'Abruzzi stepped forward, ready to pick up the trowel and finish the job. Hearing his steps, Crooked Finger held him back.

With both hands wrapped around the brick, Marie raised it over her head, and began sobbing. She closed her eyes and slammed her arms down, causing the hat that Signora Altezzana had crowned her with to fly off her head, and her gold bracelet to snap open.

"*È finito!*" Crooked Finger announced.

Fatigued, chest heaving, Marie kissed the stone, which was snugly fit among the others. Not able to take her eyes off the brick, she extended her arm for Guy to join her. With her sinewy reach, she came upon a child's leg.

Spezzano's son was standing with a pail, covered by a cloth. "You need this," he shouted, as he presented the pail.

Marie did not understand. She thought her decades-old nightmare was over. The boy could not possibly be giving her a pail of stones—the same way his father did on the day of Antonio's stoning!

The boy gave the bucket to Lisa Marie to hold. He got down on his knees. He looked at Marie, and then ran his finger through a gap between the newly laid brick and the rest of the square. He opened his palms so that they faced one another, and then brought his hands together. "We need to make one." The boy looked up to Lisa Marie.

Lisa Marie pulled the cloth off the pail, and reached to grab what was inside. She raised her fist and opened it. From between her fingers, sand cascaded.

Marie paused to admire the young boy's crystal-blue eyes. She placed her palms together, mimicking him. "Yes, we do need to make one." She signaled for Lisa Marie to give her the pail, which she poured around the brick. Marie and the boy worked the crevices, their clothing soaking from the rain. The separation was being eliminated.

The brick firmly in place, Marie raised herself up. Sand stuck to her soaked body.

Crooked Finger stared, her toothless mouth agape. Despite the rain, she remained unflinching.

Marie's heart raced. She wanted to say something that eloquently captured her anger, sorrow, and joy. She took a breath, but the words did not come. She reached for air again, looking into Crooked Finger's cavernous blind eyes. "*Signora, l'ultima pietra è posata,*" Marie said, pointing to the final stone. She mustered the strength to convey her fatigue. "*E io sono esausta.*"

"*Ma si vede che tu sei contenta,*" Crooked Finger replied with a smile.

Giovanni poked Edward in the rib with his elbow. "She said that even though your mother is tired, she can see that she is happy."

Before Marie could reply, a teenage boy shouted from the crowd. "*La strega cieca ci vede. È un miracolo!*"

Everyone laughed, including Crooked Finger.

"And he played on her words 'I can see,'" Giovanni struggled through his own mirth, "to say that the blind witch can see again. It's a miracle!"

Vito took a step forward, stood still, and removed his hat. His solemnity in the rain caused the merriment to ebb. All eyes upon him, his voice thundered, celebrating the return of one of Lavenna's children. "*È tornata una figlia da Lavenna. È un miracolo!*"

Guy placed his hand on Vito's shoulder so that he, Guy, could finish the ode with Marie's favorite aria. "*È un bel dì!*"

The crowd erupted. "*È un bel dì!*" they shouted in unison.

Guy grabbed Marie and hugged her as he never had before. He whispered in her ear "This is a beautiful day."

As a fiddle played and voices sang, Giovanni pinched at Edward's arm. "You remember this guy?" he asked, pointing to the older man next to him.

Edward knew that the man was Stubble, but wanted to play a joke by pretending not to recognize him. He spoke the lines that he had rehearsed back at home, in anticipation of this reunion. "Help me," Edward pled in Italian. "You were a bricklayer?"

Stubble planted his walking stick in the square. He spat in the rain as he spoke. "*Facevo il fabbro. Come tuo nonno!*"

"He was a blacksmith like your grandfather," Giovanni said. "You don't remember him? He brought you to us that day. Say you remember him even if you don't. He has been waiting to see you."

"Of course I remember him," Edward answered coyly. He reached into his back pocket and pulled out a silver horseshoe. "*Un regalo per te.*"

Stubble beheld the present like a child on his birthday, his eyes wide open. "*Grazie,*" he said as he stroked the shiny surface of the horseshoe with his forefinger. "*Grazie.*" He rubbed it against his pant leg to make it immaculate. He shuffled off to show his family his piece of America.

"You made him very happy," Giovanni said.

"It was nothing. If it weren't for him, we might not be here."

"You know what, my American cousin," Giovanni nodded his head several times. "Maybe you can come back someday, and help us rebuild the arch the way you like it—tall and strong."

Edward looked toward the hill wistfully. "I think that arch is better just the way it is."

"*Va bene,*" replied Giovanni with subtle jubilation.

Wanting to share the excitement of the day with his mother, Edward rotated to search for her. When he spotted her, he waved, but was obstructed by the crowd growing around her. He started to walk toward her, only to be stopped by a hand on his back. "Yes, Giovanni?" He turned to face his cousin again.

It was not Giovanni. Instead, it was Bowed Lace. She stood squarely with Edward. Her wet clothing clung to her, accentuating her bounty.

"Philomena," she said, introducing herself.

"Edoardo," Edward replied, his body brewing.

"*Lo so,*" Philomena whispered, nodding.

Edward looked for his mother, but could not see her because she was surrounded by admirers.

He turned back to Philomena, and drove his eyes into hers. He reached for her face slowly and held it. Her cheeks were warm, despite the cool rain pouring down. The touch of her hands over his propelled him toward her unpainted lips. As she closed her eyes, he kissed her. Tasting peppermint on her tongue, he tightened his hold on her cheeks so that he might extract more.

Philomena pulled Edward's arm away, and unwrapped his hand. She pointed to the cut in his palm. *"Che cos'e?"*

Edward looked at the wound which was smeared with spores from his rubbing of the moss. *"Niente."*

Before Edward could brush away the moss, Philomena seized Edward's hand and kissed it.

Edward grabbed Philomena by the hips to pull her closer. Her hair matted from the shower, it framed her face so that it shone without distraction. He locked his lips to hers, enjoying a stimulation that numbed him.

The rain had stopped.

Sensing from the brightening of his eyelids that the sun was emerging, Edward pulled back to look. The bold light had created a shimmering mirage, making it difficult to identify the faces in the crowd. After searching earnestly, he finally found his mother, away from the crowd, observing him and Philomena from afar.

Marie wiped the last grains of sand from her face, before nodding and smiling gently.

Drenched from the rain, Edward took a step away from Philomena, still holding her hand. He smiled back at Marie, reminiscing about his journey. He reflected that while there was virtue in his pursuit of knowledge about his mother—be it in uncovering her past or interpreting her arias—the true prize would be in his aspiring to become what she had always been. The real riches, it dawned on him, were in throwing off one's skin, in daring to beat one's wings without understanding how to remain airborne, and in giving off that dazzling ray of light without knowing each color in its column—inspiring others to chase the mystery, knowing that it defies capture.

Edward looked to the olive tree, where he saw a butterfly resting on a branch. It was identical to what his Uncle Antonio had painted on the canvas: emerald green and butter-yellow wings lined in black—the green slashed, the yellow featuring the lunule arches.

The butterfly took off into the sky.

Edward followed it with his eyes as best he could. It appeared to reach the sun in an instant. Holding its wings in abeyance, it became a Chi Rho. The brightness was blinding, compelling Edward to look away. He closed his eyes so that he might correct his vision. It was impossible for a butterfly to be motionless while flying, he thought.

When he opened his eyes, he saw the butterfly wave its wings a single time, slowly, before melding with the sun's corona. A burst of air swept across the piazza—so strong that it blew away the debris left by the prosecutor among the roots of the sacred tree.

As a lamb nibbled at an olive flower that had blossomed from a branch of the desiccated tree, Edward knew that something extraordinary had happened. He stroked Philomena's hair with his hand, leaving behind a spore of moss; the fluorescent green bead adorned her.

Savoring the wonder, Edward watched contentedly as the people of Lavenna patted themselves down and gaped at their clothing in disbelief. He did not question how it came to be that everyone was dry again.

# Commentary

## Taking Flight: The Ego, Repression, and Forgetting in Iron Butterfly

Given a college prompt to use psychoanalysis to interpret a piece of art, I decided upon *Iron Butterfly*, a work by an unknown author who put to words, under the auspices of a novel, his real-life struggle to know his mother and be the first in his family to discover her Italian history. While other students in my class chose well-known pieces of literature—criticisms and analyses of which number in the thousands—I selected what was at the time an unpublished manuscript of loosely bound pages that I had kept stored deep in the bottom of my desk, figuring that I would be the first to tell its untold tale. The following is what I submitted:

The Bennett family has lived the American Dream. Guy, a boastfully proud first-generation Italian-American turned titan of industry, has afforded his family all the luxuries that his forefathers in the "old country" could only imagine. Constantly yet quietly by his side is his wife, Marie, whose childhood in Campania, Italy has remained a mystery to even her husband and children. Her youngest son, Edward, seeks to uncover the truths of his mother's beginnings despite her warnings—unspecified intimations that dark stories should remain untold within the family's new prosperous American narrative. Yet, Edward is compelled to defy his mother's request to let the past remain in the past, demonstrating an unyielding attraction to what turns out to be her horrifyingly traumatic childhood. Given the psychological dynamics that pervade this plot, psychoanalysis can shed light on the two motivating behaviors of this narrative: first, the reason why the protagonist is compelled to immerse himself within Marie's past trauma; and second, the reasons why Marie is incapable of telling even her loved ones her innermost secrets.

The narrative begins as Edward rushes home after missing his mother's strict curfew, walking in to find Marie broken down in tears for what Edward views as a meaningless infraction. Confused and frustrated as to why his mother is so upset, he begins asking his father Guy why his mother is so protective. Rather than taking seriously Edward's inquiries about his mother's beginnings and her sensitive nature, Guy is more preoccupied with assembling his prosciutto and mozzarella sandwich, intermittently interjecting trivializing remarks such as "if there was something interesting about your mother's past we would all know it," and how nothing bad could have happened in Italy given that it is the "greatest civilization man has ever known." Edward finds Guy to be "trapped in his own version of history," making his oblivious and uninformed assessment of his wife's past unpalatable; just like the sandwich Guys assembles with gourmet Italian meats and cheeses, Guy's constructed view of the Bennett family's Italian heritage highlights only the superficial. He fails to show any interest in Marie's Italian childhood that Edward is now beginning to realize is not so transparent. Edward is even admonished to stop pressing the question since his father views him strictly as "an American kid." Obsessed with his desire for the family to integrate into American society, Guy demands that Edward focus only on his belonging in the United States, as opposed to chasing any romanticized notions of life on the other side.

What propels this narrative is Edward's Oedipal complex. Occupying the filial space within Freud's triadic structure, Edward covets that which his father possesses, yet will not share with him: his ability, as male in a patriarchal family, to own and control Marie's narrative by willfully resisting inquiries about it, while also determining to what extent his family belongs to one culture as opposed to another. Edward's unyielding curiosity about his mother is thus fueled by his desire to occupy the father's position—to be able to possess the right to tell his mother's otherwise untold past. If Guy is originally the powerful builder of highways and skyscrapers, yet also the ignorant steward of Bennett family history, Edward desires to overthrow his father in his life's occupation and hold the power to construct his family's saga.

Driven by these Oedipal urges, Edward fashions himself as a crusader. He desires to possess this aspect of his mother by traveling to and conquering the abandoned landscape of her hometown, and in turn, learning the secrets of her identity. It is early in the Roman Forum, moments before heading south to his mother's town, that Edward becomes infatuated with the Arch of Constantine and the triumph that he discerns within the monument. Gazing in wonderment before the ruins, he imagines himself like "the victorious general, processing through the Forum with his face painted red—the immortal man—with Cleopatra in chains." Here, Edward discovers his Lacanian ideal "I." For the first time, he witnesses and identifies with the glorified image of himself: the family member who will travel to Lavenna and vanquish his mother's mystery. Just as he learns that the arch was built with excavated *spolia* scavenged from across the Roman Empire, Edward, now captured by this primordial narcissism, desires to uncover the fragmented and scattered *spolia* of his mother's past, forging them into a monument to her legacy and, in turn, to his own.

Yet, Edward is ridiculed by his friend, Prigler, for only skimming the truth rather than peeling away at it, like the layers of an onion. Not to be shaken from his self-aggrandizing convictions, Edward chooses to fixate on a copy of Carlo Levi's "Christ Stopped at Eboli" that slips from his friend's bag—the story whose title gives tribute to the belief that even Christ was unable to save the abandoned region of his mother's home. Edward's Lacanian *imago* thereby intensifies as the protagonist develops a savior complex. He becomes even more animated by the idea that if Christ could not redeem his mother's town, it is up to him to travel south, harrow this Italian underworld, and save his mother from her phantoms.

Upon his arrival in Lavenna, Edward discovers that he does not know even the most basic facts about his mother. Finding himself alone within the dark squalor of this abandoned town—ravaged by war, frozen in time, and physically severed after an earthquake—Edward explores the space that manifests his mother's fractured and troubled unconscious. Seeing that this town has never been rebuilt, Edward at first comments how his father's construction company could quickly resurrect his mother's shattered home. Rather than being an honest appraisal of his father's ability, however, this comment is only another symptom of how his journey is compelled by his desire to outdo Guy; he believes that only his truth-seeking can fully repair Lavenna's infrastructure and, in turn, heal the ruptures of his mother's unconscious. But when locals attempt to help Edward find out about his mother, bombarding him with questions regarding Marie, a precocious Italian boy in his broken English asks, "You even know you mamma?" Here, Edward realizes that what he is attempting to uncover is not just a trivial fact about his mother's past, but Marie's essence. Guilt pervades this scene as Edward believes Marie to be the person with whom he is closest, while he now understands that he barely knows who she really is.

Nonetheless, at the end of this first trip, Edward believes that he has unearthed his mother's secret. After hastily examining the birth records and finding out that Marie's mother was deported back to Italy, Edward falsely believes that he "had captured his family's fallen town for posterity," and thus, triumphantly reproduced all the pieces of his mother's childhood. Ready to return to America from his mother's unconscious past, he revels in his belief that he has become his ideal vision of himself: an immortal Roman Emperor whose conquest of this Italian village will earn him the praise of his family and give him a sense of not only belonging to this forgotten culture, but being its foreign ruler. During his excavation of his mother's psyche, however, perhaps out of his own Guy-like willingness to ignore the most inconvenient parts of Marie's past, Edward fails to notice the two most important pieces of *spolia* that are profoundly repressed within this spatial unconscious: the German Nazi holster buried deep beneath the dirt, and the cracked picture of an unknown man that falls from the back pages of an otherwise happy family album.

During the last hours within his mother's unconscious, the possession of which he initially sought to wrest from Guy's dominating control, he even becomes infatuated with a young villager who later seduces him into his first sexual experience. In this moment of intense stimulation and fulfillment with a sexualized representation of Marie as a youth, the protagonist admits that he has sex with her "(A)nd he did not even know her name." Edward's carnal victory, emblematic of his belief that he has intimately possessed his mother's past and fulfilled his Oedipal rebellion, is one of the protagonist's ephemeral moments of pleasure that comes with meaningless reward.

After returning to America, Marie admonishes her son for disobeying her order to not travel to Lavenna, and for failing to respect the complete pain of her past. Here, she demonstrates a paradox: she wants her secret to remain hidden, but desperately needs for it to be discovered. After hearing the child next door crying because her father recently ran away, coupled with news reports covering the bombing of innocent villages in the Middle East, Marie's ability to exist within this paradox breaks down. What she has attempted to repress has escaped her and manifested itself before her eyes, and she is psychologically compelled by these recent calamities to make her secret known.

As Guy prepares to listen to his wife's story, he distracts himself by playing with his prized but flawed cuckoo clock, attempting to rewind and control its time. This is the patriarch's final effort to determine his wife's past—his unconscious acknowledgment that Marie's story may break free of his executive grip. He struggles with his dawning realization, one that he will never consciously admit to, that hers may be a story whose possession can no longer be vied for by father and son as its repercussions escape the very narrative of possession. In reality, what she is about to tell is not something positive that anyone would or could possess. It is an absence within Marie's self-conception which must be filled by putting this past to words. As a result, Marie's need to tell her story is intended to fill in the hole that exists beneath the protective shell that she has created around her being. Her mistake has been that by repressing her past, she has forced herself to remember it by leaving this conflict unresolved within her unconscious. She must find a way to purge herself of this desolation.

The story's psychoanalytic gravity shifts from Edward's desire to possess his mother's narrative toward Marie's own difficulties in owning and relating to her chaotic childhood. In beginning her story, Marie at first tells only insignificant facts, claiming that what she has previously shared is all she remembers, but then pushing further into her past for more information. These inevitable gaps within her story convey how the very structure of language is in conflict with this undefinable childhood; even as she attempts to give substance to this nebulous past through words, some aspects of her history initially defy representation. At first, the Nazis invaded Lavenna but hurt nobody; in a later iteration, these soldiers killed only the grocer once he missed the German curfew; and in the next installment, she reveals how a black tarp, anchored by a fattened lamb, covered the piazza's obelisk, which is an unfinished monument to Benito Mussolini. Soon, the dark shroud at first covering a hidden part of her past is slowly pulled off by this therapeutically salvific lamb. The tarp, now removed like a stage curtain, reveals her repressed memory of how the Nazis had tied to the obelisk the naked town tenor, judge, and priest—Marie's childhood personifications of cosmic beauty, justice, and faith— and brutally put them to death in a place she called home. A world without these virtues is unworthy of creation or re-creation—this is why Marie has abandoned this past Italian life, which in her initial view, should have never been.

With the tarp pulled, Marie pauses. Edward realizes that her past has multiple layers— just like the onion that Prigler warned him about in the Forum, needing to be peeled away to the point of tears. The metaphor that Edward would not let stand in his way in his campaign to uncover his mother's past is now given meaning by Marie's attempts to mine deeper and conquer the truths of her suffering.

But as Marie prepares to retell the story of her mother's rape, language completely breaks down. The matriarch, in so thoroughly repressing this memory, allows it to remain trapped in *the Real*—that external dimension of unchangeable truth beyond the senses—to the point where her storytelling is incapable of portraying the trauma's epicenter. Whereas Marie has full vision of the public massacring of the three martyrs, she unconsciously positions herself in a space that prohibits her from witnessing what was most likely her mother's sexual assault. All that Marie is able to recount is that "the superior [Nazi] whisked Nedda into her bedroom, slamming the door behind him. The subordinate filled the frame, standing guard," while her grandmother covered the little girl's ears to prevent her from hearing her mother's cries. Marie physically and mentally blocks herself off from this act of cruelty, denying herself full access to her mother's agony. She has unconsciously constructed psychological boundaries around this reality—whether through her grandmother's muffling embrace, the Nazi standing guard, or even the door that cuts her off from her mother so that what happened behind it remains unknown. To survive this violence, Marie must make herself mentally unavailable. The narrative shifts from Edward's initial inability to know Marie to Marie's inability to know Nedda, underscoring the transgenerational wall between mother and child. She does not permit herself to fully experience her mother's boundless pain, and with these barriers around her memory, Marie claims that she cannot recall for certain if her mother was raped or not. As to avoid the same schizophrenia-inducing effects that her mother suffered from this event, Marie must submit to the indecipherable horrors of the Real as "life isn't always explainable."

Refusing to concede the rape, and thereby protecting herself, Marie is prepared to confront the ultimate verse of her trauma. As Guy's "cuckoo clock sounded, finally with the correct time," Marie shares the story of her otherwise unknown brother, Antonio, who aided the Germans when given the promise that they would spare his townspeople. She describes for her family how when the citizens of Lavenna saw that the Nazis did not keep their promise, they viewed Antonio as a traitor. In their public rage, the townspeople took Antonio to the sacred olive tree that had been transplanted from the center of the town square to make way for the obelisk. This is the same tree that Edward is told on his first trip to Lavenna holds a Messianic promise: as the people of Lavenna wait for Christ's Second

Coming, they believe that his new cross would be made from this tree's wood. Marie's recounting makes it clear that this promise has already been fulfilled, but gone unnoticed. Stoned alive by his own people while crucified to this tree, Antonio cries out: *"Vater, Vater, ihnen den sie wissen nicht was sie tun."* We even see the boy Spezzano slit the fattened lamb's throat. Marie thus unconsciously fashions Antonio's stoning as the sacrifice that affords her new life in America for which she feels unworthy. Out of this guilt, she, along with her now schizophrenic brother and mother, become sheared off or *spezzati*—not surprising as the persecutor boy's last name translates to the Italian plural verb for fundamentally snapping in half. This communal act of Marie's family being physically and mentally divided is engraved into the very language of the plot. Even as Antonio is put to this figurative death, and where Marie is physically held back and feels guilty for not saving her brother, this Christ figure cries out from the deepest parts of Marie's unconscious to forgive.

For forty years, unable to understand Antonio's plea in a foreign language, and unwilling to come to terms with the fact that she was the only member of her family to physically survive the ordeal, Marie has not forgiven herself for breaking her own promise just as the Nazis did: to help and protect her family. Rather than outwardly blaming herself for not preventing these crimes—as this would alienate her from her loved ones—she is forced to project her guilt upon the townspeople and her entire Italian identity. Her psychic split that explains her unwillingness to embrace her Italian culture is therefore exacerbated. To remain connected to her family, she must see herself and her loved ones strictly as the exiled victims of their culture, her co-citizens the perpetrators that cast them out of this now-lost Eden of childhood innocence. Feeling herself stranded in this state of homelessness—shunned by her village, her culture, and history—she does whatever it takes to protect her suburban family. They are the only thing that has not abandoned her.

After unburdening herself of this repressed story, Marie uneasily returns to Lavenna to bury the recently deceased Antonio next to their mother. If Marie is to forget, her family must do the same in order to move on with their lives. It is for this reason that the family's shared effort of burying Antonio is so apt for demonstrating this communal act of forgetting—just as tombstones are constructed not as a reminder of loss, but rather, as ways of coming to terms and forgetting about the irretrievable loss of life, Marie through her storytelling must allow her family to forget about her past only by remembering and subsequently burying all that is dead within her.

As Edward prepares to be one of the pallbearers for an uncle whose existence he never knew, and therefore, aid in this act of forgetting, he is still trapped in this conception of himself as conqueror. He sees an arch of stones formed around the cemetery—one that, rather than being erected tall like Constantine's, is laid flat and impotent, its structure resembling "the arms of someone dead." Even as his Italian cousin explains how after the earthquake the villagers constructed this unrisen arch so that they could live outside of the grasp of inevitable loss, Edward is frustrated that this monument does not conform to his desire for eternal glory in uncovering the entirety of his mother's past.

Once he and the other pallbearers lift his uncle's casket to bury Marie's formerly encrypted past, Edward finds himself abandoned in a space that straddles reality and his own psychic participation within his mother's unconscious. Unsure whether he is in a "delirium or, the victim of the Italian sun," Edward is forced to carry his uncle's casket alone, condemned to bury this part of his mother's trauma. His inherently illusory ego implodes. The arch is emblematic of his self-constructed and glorious self-image—at first lying on the ground, now towering above him, its cornerstone collapsing as its mass violently hurls toward his head. This crashing down, beyond demonstrating the nothingness of the *imago*, also serves as a form of self-imposed stoning so that he can commiserate with the trauma of his uncle. Edward feels the perpetrator's guilt for invading the most intimate core of his mother's past without any sincere concern for who or what resided there—like the Nazis who had ravaged his mother's home. Edward, who initially perceived himself as his mother's Christ figure, at once feels the venom of guilt in the stigmata of his palm left by the wasp's sting—itself an underscoring of his delusions of grandeur— and is overjoyed to see his uncle appear.

Rather than saving him from this disaster, Antonio only cries out the same foreign-language plea he had screamed aloud while being stoned alive.It is a latent demand that Edward forgive himself for his own shortcomings. No longer worshipping an apotheosized image of Constantine, or his comfortable Sunday School faith, Edward is now forced to kneel before a crazed figure adorned in rags of hospital garbs. In order to forgive, Edward must subscribe to a religion of the mad—one whose inherent Messianic Promise is not found in dutiful prayer or conquest recited for the sake of blissful immortality, but in submitting to one's essential mortality as to escape present consciousness and return to the dust. As a manifestation of his Freudian Death Drive, Edward too must go to the grave and hope for nothing beyond its headstone, for that would be better than the alternative.

Opening his eyes for the first time to his own finitude, Edward becomes implicated within this tragedy and burdened by a sense of transgenerational guilt. He shamefully realizes that he has lived his life as a lie, ignorant of his uncle's plight that made possible his privileged life. Not only burdened with helping his mother excuse herself for repressing her brother's memory, Edward must forgive himself for never having said thank you to his uncle. Inheriting this sense of unresolved guilt from his mother—who has repressed her brother's memory due to her own inability to pardon herself and her town—Edward feels responsible for Antonio's stoning, for which he was not physically present.

Only if Edward comes to terms with his mother's past can Marie hope to do the same as he becomes the heir of her unresolved psychic conflict. He is forced to mend his and his mother's torn realities by a process of what Nicolas Abraham, in his critique and expansion of Freud, describes as "placing the effects of the phantom in the social realm." For this reason, it is of therapeutic necessity that, during this vision, Edward allows the sepia hued "prisoners of his mother's suppressed past" to rise from Lavenna's horizon and roam freely around the city's landscape even if they threaten to harm him. Edward charges himself with visibly confronting these demons so as to fully exorcise them from his mother's unconscious and cleanse his family's shared wound. As these mental prisoners gather rocks, instead of using them to stone the protagonist, they only drop them in the casket that was thrust upon his back, making the weight of Edward's guilt unbearable. As he is about to break under this self-imposed guilt, carrying the sins of this town's past, the narrator writes that "Edward wept." For the first time in his charmed life, Edward, in attempting to help his mother forget, is forced to remember this pain vividly, himself an accomplice in the violence visited upon his family. In attempting to save his mother, he is awakened not only to his own mortal shortcomings and the inherent nothingness of his ego, but also to the fragility of his family's otherwise fairytale-like narrative.

With Edward's remembrance physically integrating him into his mother's psychic core, Antonio's body and memory can finally be buried in Lavenna. Prepared to confront the life from which she fled, Marie hypnotically mutters under her breathe her brother's final message. Here, Marie initially demonstrates symptoms of her own Death Drive. Just as Edward is forced to repeat this trauma within his own vision, Marie obsessively repeats her brother's final words, demonstrating her desperate yearning to personally disintegrate as the means to escape her presently fractured worldview. However, upon further analysis it seems that she now understands the content of Antonio's plea and that this repetition is regenerative, translating what once emerged from the indecipherable German into her own native tongue: *"Padre perdona loro perché non sanno quello che fanno."*

After finally giving a voice to her otherwise silenced past, Marie is determined yet reluctant to reassume a place in her town, even if the reunion is of Guy's doing. For the first time in decades, and after Edward partially resolves his own guilt in his vision, Marie sees her persecutors in the same piazza where her family's agony took place, making her past fully public within the social realm. It is in bringing these phantoms into the realm of the visible that the city is now being repaired by its erstwhile villains. Marie's willingness to absolve both herself and her persecutors of their guilt thus allows the town to be not only recreated, but created anew. Her mother's chief tormentor, now blind, demands that Marie place the last stone, explaining to her that only she can take this final step toward forgetting the broken past and building a new life over its ruins. After she slams the stone into its incongruous opening, Edward sees the butterfly that he had been seeking throughout the novel. Rather than trying to capture it, however, he allows the creature to take flight to the sun's corona where it suspends itself and flaps its wings once, causing a gust of wind. Coming to terms with his own guilt, Edward realizes that the power of Marie's story is in renouncing his claim to this shared yet lost life—embracing yet submitting to the mysteries which will always remain outside of his reach. It is for this reason that after the pouring rain fills the piazza during this psychological rebirth, Edward does not question why everyone is suddenly dry again.

In the final analysis, *Iron Butterfly* seems to be the saga of a protagonist who believes that he must cure his mother of her own trauma, but is actually the story of how this same protagonist is curing himself of his own psychic imbalances. Originally compelled by his desire to possess his mother's true beginning and fulfill his ideal conception of himself, rather than conquering her story, he allows it to conquer him. The author, in molding Edward after himself, unconsciously acknowledges that his mother's story may always remain hidden in *the Real*, and thus, her very identity may remain unknown to him. His writing is an interpretation of his own emptiness and his longing to fully know and relate to his mother, who is so loving in her embrace, yet remains a stranger to him. It is a final and earnest attempt for a son to impossibly give birth to his mother. As he fears that she may never reveal her past, language is his only recourse to fill this empty space within him. His words create *ex nihilo* this irretrievable piece of his mother's past life, allowing him to still meaningfully identify with her.

With many of the chapters featuring the Italian aria "Un bel di, vedremo" —an allusion to the hope that one beautiful day we shall all see—this story of loss promises yet stands defiantly on the edge of quasi-religious revelation. Just as the villagers jokingly remark how the sour blind woman seems to miraculously regain her sight in the final chapter, the writing is a testament to the author's own religiously imbued hope to gain for the first time his own life sight in a world where he sees himself only as blind—not of the external world, but rather, of an internal sacristy that contains all that lies deeply within his mother, and in turn, himself. In many ways, this book is the author's personal eschatology, which makes these desolate relics of his mother's past the complete object of worship, blurring the lines between the sacred and the profane. He waits patiently not for a kingdom to come, but rather, for a vision of one that is already irrevocably passed.

If one day his mother tells him the real story, the writer's effort would allow him to healthily move from a purely imagined account of past trauma to what could be the real horrors that overshadow these fictitious disasters. The author stands within a fundamental paradox of his own creativity, just as Marie originally both desires her secret to remain untold, while desperately needing for it to be discovered by her family. As he waits patiently for this real-life unveiling, he desires both to dwell within this forgotten past through his own fiction, and to be spared its horrors through his mother's promised account. He is not dissimilar to that abandoned town in Campania that looms eternally enduring, waiting to one day be saved from the past, yet stubbornly defying the possibility of its own deliverance.

I would be remiss if before finishing my analysis I did not disclose that Anselmi, besides being this little-known author, is also my father. But being that I find this psychoanalysis now complete, I deem this fact of little importance.

N.A.A., Box 1294, Williamstown, MA

# Acknowledgements

I would like to thank the many individuals and places that inspired this book, including my greater family and the infrequently visited region of Campania, Italy. I owe a particular debt of gratitude to the following people: my editors, Andrew Durkin and Shawn Reilly Simmons, who kept my writing tethered; the entire team at Level Best Books, who have created a community of great authors; my childhood friend with whom I rode the school bus, Gabriel Valjan, who led me to Level Best; my daughter, Gabrielle, whose voice and concern for others are comforting reminders that we are never alone; my son, Luke, whose mettle and public spirit serve as a role model for a father; my son, Nicholas, whose creative energy in life and in editing this book have encouraged me to break down my walls and venture far afield; my wife, Sole, whose love, intelligence, passion and grace keep it all together...

And to my mother. The probability that her full story will never be told is of no literary consequence, for that which we already feel in her presence cannot be reduced to words, but instead is under lock and key in the world of the Real.

# About the Author

Andrew Eustace Anselmi was born in Livingston, New Jersey, in 1965 to a household rooted in Italian-American ways. He has worked as an attorney in private practice for thirty years, during which time he has received extensive praise for his work in complex litigation and recognized for his charitable works. In 2017, Pope Francis bestowed upon him the title of *Knight of the Order of St. Gregory the Great.*

Drawing upon his career and experiences as a husband, son, and father, he has become a novelist. He seeks to have his readers travel with him the yet undiscovered terrain of the twentieth century American Dream, and the untold costs of an otherwise glorified voyage. His *Mezzogiorno Trilogy* tracks a fictional Italian-American family, the Bennetts, through the cultural conflicts and hedonism of the 1980s and 90s. The center point of the series is *The Autumn Crush,* his debut novel that will be republished by Level Best as the second installment. It is a murder mystery for which young Edward Bennett takes up the legal defense for his business titan father, recounting the first-generation family's odyssey to attain wealth, social distinction, and political power in a dizzying American present, while at once masking and celebrating Old World traditions. *Iron Butterfly* is a prequel that is a mystery of a different kind, weaving together a delicate past and present by exploring the functions of storytelling in crafting family identity. This time, however, Anselmi brings this dynamic into bold relief by having Edward break the fifty-year silence of his mother to reveal the suppressed details of her childhood in wartime Italy. This novel also includes a psychoanalytic commentary by a third party whose identity will surprise the reader. *Sarapiquí* will be the last in the trilogy, depicting the existential struggles of a disillusioned Edward who, after his father's trial in *The Autumn Crush*, accepts an invitation for exile in the jungles of Costa Rica.

Andrew currently lives in Chester, New Jersey with his wife Soledad. They are the proud and loving parents of Gabrielle, Luke and Nicholas.

# Also by Andrew Eustace Anselmi

**Praise for THE AUTUMN CRUSH - to be re-released in 2022**

"For his debut, Anselmi has written an ambitious and downright old-fashioned novel."
—*Kirkus Reviews*

"An epic story of pursuing the great American Dream... Rich character development and lots of surprises kept me flipping the pages as fast as my eyes could read them."
—*Luxury Reading*

"In a dramatic novel exploring the cost of assimilation ... Anselmi explores grand themes of family, loyalty, wealth, and devotion in a promising plot that reveals the hardships and triumphs of twentieth-century immigrants."
—*Clarion Review*

"Anselmi's ongoing commentary on racism ... may make readers cringe, but it's a realistic reflection of multicultural America."
—*BlueInk Reviews*

CPSIA information can be obtained
at www.ICGtesting.com
Printed in the USA
LVHW032206210521
688193LV00005B/231